TROUBLE IN THE GREEN LANDS

Trouble in the Green Lands

Copyright © 2021 by J. Houser.

This book is a work of fiction. Names, characters, businesses, organizations, places, events and incidents either are the product of the author's imagination or are used fictitiously. Any resemblance to actual persons, living or dead, events, or locales is entirely coincidental.

For more information, visit: JHouserWrites.com

Cover design by Jervy Bonifacio

Edited by Nia Quinn

ISBN:

978-1-7370621-3-4 (ebook)

978-1-7370621-4-1 (paperback)

978-1-7370621-5-8 (hardback)

First Edition: December 2021

10 9 8 7 6 5 4 3 2

Note from the Author

Thanks so much for joining me on the next part of Saff's journey, meeting new characters along the way!

I want to offer another huge thank you to the beta readers, critique partners, and editors that have helped me get this story out there.

*

Sign up for my newsletter to get news on upcoming publications, promotions, and bonus content at JHouserWrites.com

<u>Content Warning</u>

As someone that personally struggles with darker themes in literature, I wanted to address some topics that come up in this book a little more intensely than in the first.

I love a good adventure and romance, but I also aim to bring up meaningful topics in a fantasy setting that could spark conversation and help readers feel less alone in their struggles.

That said, there are topics that some may find more difficult to read about, e.g. mental health, self-harm, assault, discrimination, etc.

I aim to tactfully include sensitive topics, and have had positive feedback from beta readers and editors about the way they're approached here. My intention is never to glorify or justify harmful behavior, even if a fictional character doesn't get it quite right. If you find yourself struggling with any of these issues in real life, please know you're not alone, not past hope, and not beyond help from professionals, friends, and family.

~J. Houser

TROUBLE IN THE GREEN LANDS

J. HOUSER

Pronunciation Guide:

People

Elonta: ee-LAWN-tuh

Guillen: GUY-en

Kaylah: KAY-luh

Lyza: LIZ-uh

Murial: MYUR-ee-ul

Nuren: NYUR-en

Saffrona: suh-FRONE-uh

    (Saff: saff)

Thod: thawed

Places & Things

Fortinda: for-TIN-da

Guenjalis: gwen-YAWL-iss

Unitas: OO-knee-tas

The Outer Rim
Grand Sea
Seeder Territory
South Fortinda
Neutral Woods
Ivy Kingdom
Ivy Palace
The Green Lands

Prologue

THE GREEN LANDS WERE DIVIDED into two peoples—the Seeders and the Ivies. They once lived and associated with each other, free to share the land, nurturing growth and community. But something changed over two centuries ago; a rising regime put an end to that. Where there was once community and cooperation, there was now conflict and contempt.

Seeder communities embraced the differences amongst their people. They found joy in simple comforts, honest work, and most of all, nurturing families and being wise stewards of nature. Each village would elect leadership to coordinate with neighboring communities, but any sort of formalities and laws were minimal. A code of ethics was deeply ingrained into Seeder society; it was rare to have a truly bad seed.

The Ivies turned to centralized leadership; they rallied around those who flattered them most. Pride swept through their kind like a whisper in the dark. A monarchy was established in the far mountains; the subjects withdrew from shared communities to start anew in their own kingdom. They were not without their own talents and skills, but their disdain for Seeders—and all that they stood for—

grew. The Ivies claimed their lands had been usurped, those very communities they had deserted in favor of relocating to start a new nation. Their leadership demanded the best, and would settle for no less than unwavering respect. It needn't be earned when it could be taken.

***

The Green Lands stretched from the majestic Ivy palace in the mountains to the humble, bustling streets of the Seeder lands, with a great divide between. The Ivy side of the Green Lands was much more barren and desolate, a wasteland. The Seeder side was lush, green, well cared for. In the middle were the Neutral Woods.

At the edge of the Seeder side of the woods was a tall thicket, the Outer Wall, a heavily patrolled line of defense. Just miles further in was the Inner Wall, a thicket three times as tall, and the final line of defense against invasion and attack.

***

Ben donned a crisp uniform, walking down a quiet path through his home village to report for duty. Most people were still sound asleep; few lightkeepers glowed behind the windowpanes he passed. Happy cottages lined the dirt lane, the gardens on each property loosely resembling a vibrant jungle. The air, as always, was fresh and invigorating. He confidently squared his shoulders as he approached his new assignment.

Walking further from the center of the village, he became more aware of the thump and crunch of his footsteps on gravel, dirt, and twigs, all the while taking in the beauty of the sun rising behind the Inner Wall in the distance. Approaching the temple depositories, he nodded at the few women he passed, as was polite. They would acknowledge with a nod and a quick flash of neon-green eyes; he in turn extended his purple hair tips. Such was protocol in the border zones, as proof of identity that you were, indeed, a Seeder. Of course, some males could flash green eyes too, but that was hardly polite, as it was an ability only a mated male could possess.

He stopped to admire one attractive short blonde in particular as she fulfilled her duties at the temple depository. She stood at the carved jade well, her hands grasping an emerging root system. Closing her eyes, she breathed deeply, her chest rising. Her hands glowed a soft yellow, transferring energy to the roots—the roots that led to the border walls. The walls were that much stronger, more capable of protecting their people from harm, thanks to her contribution.

When she opened her eyes, Heather must have noticed Ben's gaze fixed on her—she blushed. She quickly finished, then walked toward her admirer, meeting him near the Inner Wall security point. She flashed green eyes; he responded with a wink.

He started the conversation with a smile. "Excuse me, ma'am. I must say that your eyes are *absolutely* stunning."

"Oh please, that's what all the guys say," she replied in her usual slightly nasal voice.

They shared a laugh, and he offered his arms for a hug. She accepted, squeezing him tight.

"You know, I think I might just marry you someday," he whispered into her ear.

"I might be okay with that. I'll pencil you in," she whispered back, still in his embrace.

Ben released her, they gave each other a knowing smile, and she snuck a quick kiss.

"I want to hear all about your day when you get back," she said, before leaving to return to the village.

He watched her walk away with a grin on his face. She was the most beautiful girl he knew—heart, body, soul. Someday, she'd be the mother of his children. Remembering their short exchange wasn't the reason he was there, and fully aware he had an audience, Ben shook his head and forced himself to focus on his responsibilities.

"Hey now, don't let a pretty face like that distract you from your important new duties," his colleague teased, standing by the large stone doorway at the security point.

"I don't understand why *any* girl would go for this loser. She falls for him just because he spends a year on human detail?" another poked fun at him.

Ben went along with the razzing from his friends, tucking his hands in his pockets and cocking his head to the side. "I don't know, guys, I got a girl *and* a promotion, and you've got what? Your sarcasm?"

"Ooooh, ouch!" one replied, while the other just laughed.

The friends playfully swung and blocked their blunted arm blades before letting him pass through.

Much more alert to his surroundings, he made his way through the forested safety zone to the Outer Wall. The giant Inner Wall cut off any residual sound from the villages. Out here eerie silence persisted, only punctuated by the soft buzzing of a passing dragonfly, a chatterbird scolding him from an apple tree that he snagged a ripe snack from, and the rustle of his own shoes marching forward. Once closer to the Outer Wall, he tucked the apple in his pocket and found a familiar clearing in the trees—a good launching point. He shifted his Seeder energy to his calves, communing with the wind around him. Taking a couple of steps, he launched himself up and forward, somersaulting and balancing in the breeze as he shot toward the wall. Gaining speed, he angled up toward the top of the thicket. With another somersault to slow his descent and get sound footing, he landed on the large platform at the top of the thicket wall.

Taking a left on the narrow walkway, he headed for his commander's platform station. "Reporting for duty," he announced on his approach.

"Ben, right?"

"Yes, sir."

"Murialson?"

"That's the one."

"You know your way around by now?" the commander asked. "Go relieve Caleb."

"Yes, sir."

Ben found Caleb, a soldier nine years his senior, who was more than happy to see him, ready to head home for some well-deserved sleep.

"Any news?" Ben asked.

"It doesn't look good," Caleb reported. "Several more vines have made their way across the Neutral Woods." He shook his head, his frown conveying the severity of the problem. "I don't know how they're doing it. But these are just like the others. Fast-growing, thick, nearly impenetrable."

Why do we even call them that—'Neutral Woods'? Sure, they'd been named that after the old treaties were formed, around the time of the Great Division. But the Ivies had never respected those boundaries, constantly crossing them to ensure no Seeders could leave the confines of their own borders.

He stared at the massive bundle of vines below, which was easily six feet wide. A crew of a dozen men and women were hacking and sawing away at them, with minimal success. "You've got to give it to the leeches. These bastards know how to get creative," Ben said.

"Yeah." Caleb rubbed his chin and winced. "I might admire it more if I wasn't so worried about how we're going to stop it."

The news of this never-before-seen tactic still hadn't been widely shared throughout the Seeder nation. But that wouldn't last forever. And neither would their border walls if they couldn't find a solution. Ben's gut twisted with dread.

There was trouble brewing in the Green Lands.

Chapter 1

SAFF WOKE TO THE SUN peeking through the open screened bedroom window. Cherry blossoms just outside perfumed the room. The pendulum clock in the corner quietly ticked away. Sometimes when she was exhausted, the clock woke her a little later, but after three years in the Green Lands, her body had become used to the energy shifts in the seasons, and even in the days. The sun was up, and so was she. But she stayed in her cozy, warm bed for a while longer, soaking up the peace and serenity of the morning.

She glanced at the intricate cream tatted curtains above the bed—a gift from one of many aunts. A wood dresser dominated the far wall, handcrafted by Devin's grandfather. She smiled, basking in the love and community embodied by each item in their cottage, most of which were gifts from their wedding.

One item hanging on the wall in the bedroom hadn't been gifted for their wedding—a painting Devin had insisted they keep. It was no Monet, but it was something he treasured—a seaside landscape she'd once painted for him in the human world, complete with creases from being folded in his pocket as he'd caught a breeze home.

Her gaze rested on Devin peacefully sleeping next to her. It wasn't possible to be happier. After the chaos and rush of the time they'd shared in the human world, they'd taken things slower when he got back. He'd ended up staying in the human world to help protect his last two sisters, returning just shy of a year after Saff had left. That year had given her ample time to meet people, take courses, grow closer to her Seeder family, and really find herself. Despite her love of the Green Lands, there hadn't been a day that went by that she hadn't thought of Devin, worried about him, and waited for him.

But he'd come back to her. They'd taken their time touring Seeder territory together and getting to know each other on a whole new level. Marriages in Seeder culture were serious and permanent. Not that divorces never happened, but the Seeder mating bond was for life. They'd known in high school they wanted to be together, but had agreed to take their time to ensure they weren't rushing into anything. Their wedding, just a few months prior—in the early spring—had been as simple as Seeder ceremonies got, and absolutely perfect.

Devin stirred in bed, opening his eyes with a gentle moan. Saff beamed and snuck a kiss.

Sliding his arms around her, he pulled her close. "Mmm, my favorite person."

"Yeah?" She studied his face.

He nodded.

"Ditto."

He raised his eyebrows. "You're your favorite person, too?"

She rolled her eyes, grinning and wrapping a leg around him. "Maybe I am now, after a ridiculous joke like that."

He frowned. "I thought it was a good joke. And if it didn't earn me a laugh, I know another way to get one." His smirk was mischievous.

Saff glared playfully as he inched his fingers to her sides, beginning his attack. She squirmed and giggled at his tickling. With the boost of energy that had accompanied her rooting in the Green

Lands, and with three years of training under her belt, she could easily win this skirmish. But this time, she let him win. Devin pinned her down, getting lost in her eyes, sneaking a peck on the lips.

"I love you," she said.

"Ditto."

She bit her lip. "You love you, too?"

He busted out laughing, rolling off and snuggling up to her. "Touché." He ever so gently moved the sleeve of her nightgown to expose her shoulder, placing a sweet kiss there. "How much time do we have?"

"Hmm. I don't know." She reached her hand up and ran her fingers through his bedhead of sandy blond hair. "I was thinking about baking some muffins before work."

He wore a crooked, dimpled smile. "Liar. When was the last time you baked anything?"

She adopted a far-off look, as if calculating the days. "Baked? Or burned?"

Devin leaned forward, giving Saff a sweet, lingering kiss, the kind that always took her breath away. The clock chimed.

Lifting her head slightly, she pulled her strawberry blond hair to the side. She fixed her gaze on his dark brown eyes, now flickering with a hint of green. A neon, glowing green that he'd only had since their wedding. The warmth in her own blue eyes told her they were also shifting. The clock chimed once more. "I guess we have *that* much time."

"Mmm. You don't say. I can work with that."

***

Saff stood at the front of her log-hut classroom, a board of slate mounted behind her scribbled with chalk bullet points for the day's lesson. "Who can tell me why you have to be extra careful when playing sports with the humans?" she asked her classroom of two dozen eight-year-old boys.

A dark-haired boy named Dennis shot his hand up. "Because you can accidentally cut someone with your blades, or hurt them with your strength."

"Yes." She lifted her chin. "Any other reasons?"

Skyler, one of the shyer ones, raised his hand. "Because a human or Ivy might notice that you're too strong, or that you've transformed."

"Good job." She smiled, sitting on the edge of her wooden desk. "We have to be safe, and we have to be careful about detection over there. And," she held up a finger, "it's really not fair to use your powers when matching up against a human. We want good sportsmanship in either world."

"Not like Christopher in afternoon sparring yesterday," another boy chided.

Christopher glared at the other boy while several of their peers snickered. Movement at the open door caught Saff's attention. Devin stood there, lunch basket in hand. Saff glanced at the clock; he was ten minutes early.

"Hey! Your husband's here!" One of her boys had apparently also noticed. "That means lunch!"

"Nope." She slightly narrowed her eyes at Devin and he flashed a guilty frown. "Speaking of entertainment and games today, guys," she continued. "Let's revisit our discussion from earlier this morning—board games. I wouldn't want you to give away your lack of knowledge about something like that."

Devin let out a short laugh, then tried to disguise it as a cough. They shared a grin, knowing that was one of the things he hadn't been as well-versed on when he'd been trying to blend in as a human, back when he'd been one of her protectors.

"Someone asks you what your favorite board or card game is," she said. "I want to hear what you'd say if you forgot the names of the ones we've talked about."

"I think they're boring. I prefer video games!" one boy said.

"Very good. And believable. Any other ideas?"

"I can't pick a favorite. What's yours?" another boy offered.

She beamed. While she disliked lies, these would be the kind of lies that saved lives. "Brilliant deflection. Best when said with full confidence."

Devin winked at her.

Her stomach growled, and she decided to give in. "Alright. While at lunch, I want you to discuss what you've learned about games from your moms and aunts and uncles, okay? Board, card, video—all of them."

They all sat on the edge of their seats, barely listening anymore. "Dismissed."

Devin backed away as the room erupted into a storm of little boys snatching their lunch satchels and bolting out the door.

Saff sighed and sauntered up to Devin, taking his free hand. "You are such a troublemaker. You know that?"

He squeezed her hand and pulled her outside. "I thought you liked that about me."

She chuckled as they walked across the grass to their usual path. One of Devin's sisters caught their attention from a nearby sparring field and waved. They returned the wave.

"Roasting me like that, though, ouch!" Devin continued.

Saff grinned. "Serves you right for barging into my classroom."

"Fair enough."

"Want to know what we're going to discuss next week in our unit on foods?" she asked as they turned onto a gravel path, waving at her brother Kyle.

"I'm scared to ask now." Devin arched an eyebrow, his tone playful.

She considered the other deficiencies in his Seeder network training before his assignment in the human world. "Road-trip snacks and elephant ears."

He let out a breathy laugh. "Alright. I need to see the list of all my shortcomings and deep, dark secrets that you're sharing with these boys. I thought I was a decent covert ops agent."

Releasing his hand, Saff wrapped her arm around his waist. "You were fantastic, love."

Ten minutes later, they sat on their favorite park bench, unpacking their lunch. Just yards away rested a peaceful little pond surrounded by cattails. Bright red-and-white butterflies danced from flower to flower. They made Saff think of her Seeder mom, Murial. She and Murial had spent countless outings painting nature scenes together, and Murial would always happily point out which plants and wildlife were unique to the Green Lands. These particular butterflies were also found in the human world, though the flowers they hovered between were a Green Lands exclusive.

Devin handed Saff a cloth napkin.

"So how has your day been?" she asked.

He shrugged. "Good. Like most days."

Devin worked mostly with the teens and preteens, with particular focus on covert operations—the kind he'd been part of, working protection detail for Saff and his sisters when they were in high school.

She took a sip of juice and smiled. "I'm glad you're back. And thanks for the letters."

He grinned. "Happy to do it."

His teaching position afforded him the special privilege of occasionally being chosen to deliver deep-cover boys to their fathers. Seeder families trained up their boys at an early age, selecting the most promising one of each family to leave as young as possible. Devin described escorting the boys as one of the most touching things he'd ever experienced, a great honor to be a part of. The journey was so difficult for each little boy, but the payoff was equally rewarding. Seeder fathers and husbands had been in the human world for years—working on their covers, keeping their distance while coordinating their daughters, and missing their wives and the sons they'd yet to meet.

That meeting—the first time a Seeder father got to meet one of his children, and they knew him for who he really was—was tender.

From that point on, he placed them under the care of someone trusted, and continued their training in secret.

"They looked like they're doing alright?" Saff frowned, thinking of her human parents, Pam and George.

"Yeah. They're doing great."

It was a complicated subject, that Devin was physically able to go between the worlds more easily, more often. But he only did it for work and for the week each spring he joined Saff for her visit. She'd accepted the limitation as best she could. Whenever possible, if the boy he was dropping off was within a reasonable distance of her parents' current location, he'd take a letter from Saff to swap with her parents. She appreciated that extra line of connection, as rare as it was.

Three years prior, it had been a rude awakening to learn of her true nature and the dangers and limitations that came with being a Seeder. But to be a botanical being, having powers and abilities no human could fathom, enriched her life beyond compare and validated her decision to leave behind the world she was raised in.

While she never lacked for company, having twenty-three siblings, and having gained twenty-three siblings-in-law when she and Devin had married, she'd still exerted the effort to make the grueling journey back the last three springs to see her human host parents. She cherished the short amount of time she could spend with them. And with only a few years left where she would be able to make that journey, she vowed to not waste a moment, and never miss the opportunity when it arose. Seeder women generally only had ten years between their initial rooting and becoming fully-rooted, making them incapable of leaving the Green Lands.

"And thanks for Zach's letter." She smiled again, thinking of her human best friend. She'd only been able to coordinate seeing him once since she'd left, but he sometimes sent letters to her parents to pass along.

Devin popped a raspberry in his mouth. "No prob. How's he doing?"

"He's good. Questioning his major. Dating a new girl."

Devin grabbed a handful of grape tomatoes. "Hmm. Indecisive. Not the same girl as this spring?"

"Nope." She picked out a couple of tomatoes for herself. "But he sounds happy."

Devin wore a warm smile. "Good."

She pulled a fork and a glass jar of carrot slaw from the basket. While happily munching in silence, she mentally planned the rest of her day. Just one more hour with the little boys, then she had three hours at the healing station of their learning institution.

After they finished up their food, Saff leaned against Devin as he wrapped his arms around her. He planted a kiss on her cheek. "So… Are you nervous? Or excited? About next week."

She blushed. "Yes."

She'd accepted a new position at the school. She would miss working with the boys, and also helping at the healing station, but she was moving on to something she wanted even more.

"You'll be amazing." He nuzzled her neck.

She beamed, sneaking a kiss. "We don't make a horrible team."

He narrowed his eyes, stealing a peck on the lips in return. "Not at all."

She blew out a puff of air. "We'd better head back. Last time I took a longer lunch than my class, it was a madhouse when I got there."

He chuckled as they stood up. "Isn't it a fun glimpse into my childhood?"

They started to walk the weeping-willow-lined trail back to the school, hand in hand. Devin swung the woven basket in his free hand.

"Heather and Ben are still coming over for dinner tonight, right?" Saff said.

"Yes, ma'am. But Ben and I might be a little late."

She scrunched her eyebrows.

Devin shrugged. "I don't know. He asked me to drop by his station after work."

"Okay… Well, I guess I'll see you then. Love you."

Just short of being in sight of the school, he stopped her, giving her a hug. "I love you, too."

***

Saff made it home to their cottage first, as expected. The tiny little thing was the perfect size for a married couple like Saff and Devin, too young to have a clutch yet, or for those who'd decided not to. It was as quaint as any of the cottages in this part of the village. The thatched roof sat atop a sturdy frame of raw wood with a charming pattern to it. Before opening the front door, she snapped off a handful of fresh pea pods from the front garden box.

Once inside, she set out a few juicy peaches on the round wooden dining table, then surveyed the living area to make sure it was all tidy. Their small kitchen and dining area connected to the living room. A wood-and-cotton sofa accompanied matching chairs. On the wall hung several pictures. Saff walked up to them, smiling wide. This wall of pictures was something she treasured as much as her own wedding ring or jade necklace—photos from her childhood and from visits to the human world. She lifted a hand, rubbing the bend from one photo. She'd always loved that one—Devin, Zach, Ben, and Heather on a roller coaster in the human world after she'd left. Devin wore a goofy expression for the camera, just for Saff. He'd said it was fun, but hadn't really seemed that impressed—he could fly, after all, so a little roller coaster plunge hadn't been that remarkable. Cotton candy and elephant ears had been the highlight of that day for him. Next to that photo, a small glow-in-the-dark star clung to the wall, a little piece of her first home.

A knock sounded on the door and Saff opened it, happy to see her sister-in-law, Heather.

After a big hug and swapping a jar of honey from Heather for a basket of peaches, they settled down for a chat.

"So, have you guys been looking for a place of your own?" Saff asked.

Heather sighed with a frown. "I wish. I'm afraid we might have to push back the wedding."

Saff matched her frown. "Why?"

Heather shrugged. "He's going to be so busy with his promotion. I don't know… Maybe I'm just overthinking things."

Saff gave her a reassuring smile. "We might have simpler ceremonies than some humans, but we sure have a lot more family to coordinate, don't we?"

Heather laughed. "Yep!"

"Either way, it'll be perfect." Saff mused about her wedding day. Her heart had swelled, not only at marrying Devin, but at all the family support they'd enjoyed. The exact same family members would be attending Heather and Ben's wedding, seeing as Heather was Devin's sister, and Ben, Saff's brother.

Saff had returned to the Green Lands filled with both curiosity and fear of the drastic changes that faced her upon leaving the human world. But this huge family, all of these built-in friendships, had made all the difference in the world. The energy of the realm was almost addictive, but more than anything, the people here made it home. Giving up the internet and a lot of modern comforts had been a token sacrifice for the free time and community she'd gained here.

"Did you hear Tabatha went out with Greg again?" Heather grinned.

"What?! I just talked to her a couple days ago. She didn't tell me that."

"Yeah." Heather fidgeted with a loose thread on her shirt. "I think she doesn't want people judging her and assuming he's the reason she's changing positions."

"Hmm…" Tabatha had recently stopped taking optional courses provided by the community, instead moving to full-time work at a local grain mill. The mill where this guy, Greg, worked. It was hard for Saff to keep up with all of her family, but Tabatha wasn't only her sister, she had also been one of her best friends back in the human world. "Well, I'll try my best to not draw that conclusion." Saff snickered. "Are *you* still going to join me for more classes?"

Heather wrinkled her nose. "I don't know."

Saff frowned again. They'd taken a lot of classes together, having returned from the human world within a few months of each other. There were mandatory classes upon Seeder girls' returns—courses on mastering their powers, basic history and cultural lessons. But several more courses were offered as optional. Having been a nearly straight-A student in human high school, and being enthralled with her home realm, Saff was trying to take them all.

"I get it. Not everyone's thrilled with the idea of school when it's not mandatory."

Heather fidgeted with her engagement ring. "Well… Maybe it's hypocritical of me to mention Tabatha … but if Ben's going to be so busy with work soon…"

Saff raised her eyebrows.

"Well," Heather continued with rosy cheeks. "I've applied to work at a healing station just inside the Inner Wall."

"Gotcha. And I really don't judge you for it. Devin and I both love our work, and it's an awesome perk to work so close to each other. Ben's a great soldier. You're a great healer. It makes sense." Both of Heather's human parents were nurses.

Heather smiled. Saff swallowed hard, trying to stay positive. Ben really *was* a great soldier. He'd saved her life back in her human high school. But it still gave her a lot to worry about, having him positioned at the Outer Wall. That wall hadn't come close to falling from Ivy attacks in decades. But that didn't mean casualties didn't happen. Their border walls were charged by a massive root system running the length of the entire Seeder territory. Any regular thicket would be relatively useless as a defense, but this one was not only massive, it harnessed the energy given by Seeder women, making it near impervious, and every village contributed. The energy imparted to the thicket made it fire- and cut-resistant. Resistant, not proof.

The Ivy Kingdom only seemed to care about one thing—Seeder annihilation. Seeders still had to patrol the border walls to stop Ivies from converging on a single point to weaken it and break through. If it wasn't the Ivy assassins sent after her kind in the human world, it was their soldiers constantly patrolling Seeder borders.

After another half hour of chatting, Devin and Ben arrived. Ben settled down on an armchair and wrapped his arms tight around Heather as she sat on his lap. Devin claimed a spot next to Saff on the sofa.

"So, what made you two late?" Saff asked.

Devin and Ben passed a look between one another, frowning. "Well, um…" Devin started.

"I'm sure we'll figure it out," Ben chimed in. "Just the leeches, as usual. But their approach is … not usual." He cleared his throat, shifting in his seat. "Don't worry about it. The elders are saying they don't remember hearing about this tactic, but they're searching the archives."

Anxiety settled into the pit of Saff's stomach. She loved her life here. Nearly every part of it. The uncertainty of a new kind of attack reminded her of something she'd struggled to put behind her—the fact that they never figured out how the attacks on her and her family in the human world were connected to Ivy royalty. Attacks that had left ten Ivies dead at her childhood home. Attacks that had something to do with an Ivy royal named Nuren.

Chapter 2

SAMANTHA GREW UP WITH A cousin her same age next door. They were like two peas in a pod. That is, until Samantha's cousin, Lyza, turned seventeen. Lyza became distant, too busy to spend time with Samantha; and then she left. Lyza, as it turns out, wasn't human.

As much as she missed her best friend, Samantha looked forward to the few moments she would spend with her cousin during spring break each year. The last year Lyza would ever be able to visit her in the human world, she asked Samantha for a favor. Samantha happily accepted the request. She was unmarried, but willing to take on the challenge of adopting a little girl. Lyza's little girl. Or at least one of them. The day after Samantha received her cousin's daughter, the sweet baby molted her birth wisps, transforming into a tiny little human. Promising to do everything in her power to make this child happy and safe, she gave her a human name for the time she would be hers. She would be known as Rachel.

***

Rachel lay in bed, snuggling the teddy bear she figured she was probably too old for, but she didn't really care. She stared at her bedside table, eyes fixed on a folded letter.

She knew, statistically, that she was loved. Being confident about that, however, wasn't always easy. Rachel grew up with three father figures in her life. She was aware from a young age that she was adopted. As it was a partially open adoption, her birth father—father-figure number one—would sometimes send her letters. Usually on birthdays, but sometimes for holidays, or at random. This letter was from father-figure number one, Garrett. He'd sent her a letter to wish her a good school year. It wasn't that her mom wasn't enough, or that Garrett wasn't caring in his letters, but Rachel always asked herself why he even tried to maintain a relationship with her after all these years, if he had been willing to give her up when she was a baby.

Rachel sighed, squeezing the bear tighter. That wasn't fair. Parents gave up their kids for a large variety of reasons, and she knew it was usually in the best interest of the children.

She frowned a little, thinking of father-figure number two, Brad. Brad had given this stuffed animal to her when he adopted her. He'd come into her life when she was five years old. He was kind and loving to both Rachel and her mom. They were husband, wife, and daughter—the whole package. But then Brad only stayed for two years. Like many children, Rachel was assured his decision to leave had nothing to do with her, but it didn't make it any easier. He never even said goodbye. He never once visited or reached out after leaving. It had been devastating for both Rachel and her mom.

But her mom had learned to love again. Less than a year later, a new man came into their lives—Rob. He took to Rachel quickly and treated her like his own. And he treated her mom right. Despite the pain of previous rejection, Rachel was grateful to have a good man in their lives. But she'd never been able to call her mom's new husband 'Dad.' It hurt too much to use that title again. And the older she became, the more she appreciated her mom and stepdad for not pushing that on her.

The shower turning off downstairs announced she had to stop dawdling. Rob was up, and that meant Rachel needed to get ready for school. She groaned, throwing off the covers. After a quick shower of her own, she blow-dried her hair and put on a full face of makeup. She pulled out her favorite pair of jeans and a cute button-up shirt. Smirking, she left one more button open than she normally would have.

Downstairs, she poured a bowl of sweetened puffed rice cereal. After eating in solitude and leaving the bowl in the sink, she grabbed her backpack, slinging it over her shoulder. Her mom, a curly-haired brunette of medium build, came down the hallway, offering a bright smile and a hug.

"Are you ready for today?" Her mom squeezed tighter.

Rachel smiled. "You're not getting too sentimental, are you?"

Her mom pulled back, holding Rachel's shoulders. "It comes with old age." She winked.

Rachel rolled her eyes. "Not old. *Aged.*"

Chuckling, her mom reached over and buttoned up a couple of Rachel's buttons. "Aged sounds so much worse. Unless you're wine or cheese, and I am neither."

Rachel shrugged. "I tried." She gave her mom another quick hug before heading out the front door, undoing the buttons her mom had just done up.

****

"Dang! Why do you look so sexy now that you're a senior?" David greeted Rachel from his shiny red car, picking her up for school. She often felt a little plain with her brown hair and brown eyes, but he never failed to remind her exactly how much he liked everything about her.

"You don't say." She grinned, throwing her backpack in the back seat and getting in. "That much difference between the summer-me of yesterday and the senior-me of today, huh?"

"You've definitely matured." He looked her over from top to bottom. "Yep, I'd definitely say you've matured." He wiggled his eyebrows.

Rachel squinted. He was tall, in great shape, and had dark brown hair and stunning green eyes. "Hmm…" She shook her head. "Nope, don't think I see it in you. That's too bad."

His jaw dropped. "You did not just say that."

She winked at him, and he stretched over the center console to greet her with a kiss. And it was *not* a little peck on the cheek.

"Ahem." Someone clearing their throat broke them from their mini make-out session.

David wore an awkward smile. "Hi, Mr. Samuels."

Rachel sheepishly wiped off her lips. "Have a good day at work, Rob."

"I intend to, thanks. One small problem—Romeo here is blocking my car." Rob furrowed his brow, holding a coffee cup with his company's logo on it. He had a kind face, but knew how to show when he meant business. Right now, he was somewhere in the middle, though his trimmed beard had a way of pushing it more toward the intimidating side.

"Sorry, sir," David said. "I'll make sure to pull forward more next time."

"I'd appreciate that. And perhaps you can save some of that energy and concentration for school and driving, instead of expending it all on my girl."

Rachel pressed her lips together, turning beet red. "K, bye, Rob!" She gave David a look begging him to floor it. Not that she disliked Rob; he really was a nice stepdad. And he obviously cared for her well-being. And Rob generally liked David, but … getting handsy with his stepdaughter was not on his list of approved activities.

David and Rachel had been an item for two years now. He enjoyed basketball and his time with the guys, but he always carved out time for what mattered to her. He came to most of her volleyball games and made a point of having special date nights.

After a short drive to school and the nightmare of finding parking, they walked hand in hand to the benches near the front entrance. Sliding onto a metal bench, they waited for their friends.

They didn't have to wait long; her best friend Meg strolled up with her boyfriend, Eric.

Rachel had met Meg the summer after her dad had left them. Meg had moved in down the street and they became instant friends. They always had each other's backs, no matter what. They'd enjoyed countless slumber parties and hiking adventures over the years. Rachel's mom had tried to teach her how to wear makeup when she'd wanted to learn, but Meg had been the real teacher—she could nail a winged eyeliner better than a winged bird could fly.

Unlike Rachel, Meg never struggled with self-confidence. Rachel was cute, but Meg was a bombshell, and had the kindest heart of anyone Rachel knew. But there wasn't any jealousy or rivalry between them. If anything, they were practically sisters. Meg was the one who had helped Rachel build up the courage to ask David on a date in the first place; Rachel had been drooling over him for weeks.

Meg's messy bun of jet-black hair bounced as she and Eric approached Rachel and David. She was wearing bright-red lipstick and an adorable top she'd bought when she and Rachel last went shopping. Her jeans hugged her curves in the right places, and Eric smiled with his arm around her.

Eric was a newer addition to their posse; he and Meg had just started dating over the summer. But he fit in well. He and Meg made a great pair; just like her, he was easy on the eyes and had a huge heart. He dressed sharp for the first day of school—he'd have fit right in on the cover of a magazine, or in a country club. Paired with his outfit, his blond hair and strong jawline made it easy for people to misjudge him as a stuck-up preppy kid. But the way he'd met Meg in the first place—at an animal shelter—was so sickeningly sweet, and so absolutely them.

Meg held two coffee cups and Eric had another in his hand. Rachel moved onto David's lap to make more room on the bench, but their friends stayed standing.

"I bring *good* beverage for *good* luck," Meg announced while handing one of her cups to Rachel.

Rachel savored the warmth in her hands, taking a swig. The piping hot liquid had a hint of hazelnut and French vanilla. "Mmm. Have I told you how much I love that you're a barista? Crappy hours, great perks."

"I can't help but notice you forgot one for yours truly," David said, eyebrows raised. "You know, they *do* make drink holders for four cups, right?"

"Yeah. I mean, I considered it. But," Meg pointed to Eric, "boyfriend," she then pointed to Rachel, "best friend." She shrugged. "And you're just ... David."

"You wound me," he replied wryly.

"It is okay. I shall share my spoils with you," Rachel said, taking another sip before handing it to him.

"So, Meg, how was your fun adventure this summer?" David asked before taking a drink.

"Paris is *not* overrated. Nor are the hot French guys." She winked at Rachel.

"Hey! Right here," Eric complained lightheartedly.

"I kid. I only have eyes for you!" Meg nudged him. "I mean, you're lucky we met *before* my trip, 'cause…"

Eric challenged her with a smirk, clearly knowing she was joking just to get a rise out of him. "If you need some time alone with your fantasies, I can head inside now." He pointed to the front doors of their high school.

She chuckled and gently rubbed noses with him.

Rachel extricated her drink from David's hands, taking another swig. She lifted the mostly full cup of coffee over her head, looking to see the bottom where Meg made a habit of writing her a little message each time she brought her a drink from work.

"Seriously?" David snatched it from her hands.

"Hey! I was looking at my love note," Rachel protested with a slight pout. "It's like a fortune cookie—it may be vital for a good start to my day."

"Yeah, well, fortune cookies don't give you second-degree burns. I like your face the way it is," he chided. "And mine as well, thank you very much."

She rolled her eyes. "I was being careful."

He gave her a disapproving look.

"Fine, whatever. Maybe you need the caffeine more than me if you're going to be grumpy." She got off of his lap, moving back onto the bench next to him.

Meg and Eric glanced at each other with wide eyes. "Yeah, we're going to head inside. We'll see you guys later." Eric wrapped his arm around her again, and they left.

Rachel let out a sigh, taking her coffee back. "Wait to read the bottom until the scalding hot liquid is all gone—noted."

"Thank you."

She sipped her coffee with a scowl.

David's lips formed a mischievous grin. "I know how we can make that coffee better."

She waited a moment, then took the olive branch. "How's that?"

"It's a little black for my liking, maybe it needs some more sugar." He winked.

She laughed. "You think you can sweeten things up for me, do you?"

"It's my forte." He leaned in for a kiss.

Rachel recoiled after a small peck. "Ouch!"

"What?" He scanned her face with concern.

"My boyfriend warned me about being burned, and you're pretty hot." She smirked.

Rolling his eyes, David stood, offering his hand. "Let's get to class, dork."

Chapter 3

SAFF SAT ON THE GROUND, weeding in their garden, lost in thought. She'd recently started working as a welcoming apprentice. Once Seeder girls returned to their homeland, they still had so much to learn. They received minimal training in the human world to keep them safe and get them home to the Green Lands, but their education was far from over once they rooted in their ancestral lands.

Saff had an undeniable natural aptitude and strength when it came to harnessing Seeder energy. Devin had told her it was because she was stubborn and determined, and just naturally gifted. But Saff sometimes wondered if it was something else. There had to be an explanation for her ability to harness nearly as much energy as a fully-rooted matriarch. Before the Great Poisoning, Seeder women had actually been more powerful, but the lingering Ivy poison in their soil must have affected them, even if it didn't kill them like it did their young daughters before their powers came in. Saff must be immune—no one could offer a different explanation for why she could harness more energy than other girls her age.

She dug deep into the soil, trying to get to the bottom of the bindweed root system attempting to choke out their beets. This had been a recent discovery for Saff, that she might be immune to the poison that had forced her to grow up in the human world. She hadn't met anyone else immune, not that they made it a practice of testing those waters. Seeder girls were swept away to the human world the same morning they sprouted. Taking a risk to see if one was immune wasn't something any caring parent would do—it meant certain death if they weren't. From unfortunate and rare experiences, Seeders knew their lands were still poisoned; daughters who weren't taken away at the seedling reveals always died. *Always.* Saff couldn't imagine her Seeder parents gambling the lives of their twelve daughters to discover one of them held an immunity no one else had heard of.

Either way, the reason for Saff's extra capacity to wield energy didn't matter—she was still embarrassed by the attention. It had taken her some time to accept the offer to apprentice in a welcoming position, but she found it immensely rewarding. Girls were often confused, unsure, and even overwhelmed when they first returned.

It gave Saff a deep sense of fulfillment, being able to guide girls just like her in the wonder of their abilities. Equally rewarding was helping in the more emotional aspects of their transition to a new way of life.

As she finished weeding a row in the garden, a pair of hands slid onto her shoulders. "Mmm, that feels nice." She moaned as the hands worked on her knots. "But we need to be careful, my husband will be home any time now."

Her masseuse crouched down and whispered in her ear, "Mi amor, take me now before we're caught!"

She giggled like a giddy schoolgirl. "Hey, you, how was your visit?"

Devin ruffled his hair, sitting down next to her. "It was … a visit."

"Hmm… That good, huh?"

"Not as good as this part of my day." He smiled warmly, giving her a peck on the cheek.

She let out a frustrated sigh, surveying the garden. The row of beets she'd just finished with had been planted wonky from the start. "You know, for being *green* folk, in the *Green* Lands, I really don't have much of a *green* thumb."

He scrunched his face, shaking his head. "Yeah, I guess there's a reason we take our parents up on their offers for Sunday dinners."

"Rude!" she protested, her jaw dropping.

"I'm kidding, you know that." He held out his hand for the trowel she'd been using. "I've always said we're better together, right?" He nudged her arm.

After some time working in the garden together, they stood and put the hand tools away for the day. Devin reached over and wiped at a smudge of dirt on Saff's forehead.

"Dirty work," she commented, dusting herself off.

"I like you when you're dirty." He puckered his lips.

"That's a shame, I was going to hit the shower." She raised her eyebrows and flashed neon-green eyes before heading into their cottage.

"Well, I mean, I like dirty. Or showers. Or being dirty in showers." He followed after her. "I'm not picky."

***

"So, tell me about the meeting," Saff said while brushing out her wet hair. "What's the bad news? I saw Ben's face earlier. It can't be good."

"Yeah, it's not great." Devin frowned. "There's been another surge. They breached the Outer Wall again last night."

Saff stopped, swallowing hard. "That's … *really* not good." She hoped she was overreacting, but that hadn't happened even in her parents' lifetimes. "We still don't know how they're doing it?"

"There's … a theory." He shook his head in despair. "It's probably unrelated. We're just kinda grasping at straws at this point. But, if it's what the neighboring council suspects…" His voice trailed off. "It's unimaginable," he whispered.

She put the brush down and wrapped her arms around him. "We'll figure it out."

"Yeah." He failed at sounding as though he believed her assertion. "Either way, I'm taking my class to the Inner Wall tomorrow; they're going to get a hands-on lesson in defense."

Saff nodded, sick to her stomach. Word had crossed the entire nation, from village to village on the borders, and even in the back territories. *No one* could explain what the Ivies were doing, or how they were accomplishing it. Elders had been consulted, as had old archives. But Saff had known from the start that the archives would be useless, or at least she'd feared they would be.

Devin had been right all those years ago when he'd first explained the threat to her. Ivies were clever liars, thieves, and murderers. Something they'd stolen in their exodus during the 'years of parting' and in raids during the following years of escalated fighting, were books packed with knowledge of their history. Barely any books remained in Seeder possession about the Ivies. Elders swore up and down that the Ivies had taken even more than that.

Very few Seeders were assigned to spy duty, which involved quick flybys to check on the state of the Ivy Kingdom. But they still did it from time to time. This new form of attack at first sounded like something the elders had called the 'Mother Vines,' and they'd wondered if the Mother Vines had mutated. But this was different, something altogether new. Something that crossed the Neutral Woods and led right to the Ivy palace.

Chapter 4

RACHEL AND MEG LOVED DOUBLE dates with their men, but the guys didn't much care for the idea. Eric and David got along fine, but they didn't exactly have a blossoming bromance. The four of them would hang out on occasion; usually a movie or game night a couple of times a month.

Three weeks into school, they gathered for a movie night at Rachel's place. They'd planned to stream a much-anticipated new release and Rachel's place was always the go-to location. Her mom and stepdad weren't helicopter parents, but they understood how teenagers worked. Their door was always open, and Rob's income as a regional sales director gave them a nice house with an amazing theater room.

Meg was cuddled up next to Eric on the love seat, chatting away. Rachel and David arrived with fresh popcorn and licorice. After setting the popcorn down on the coffee table, Rachel crawled into his lap on the leather sofa.

"You know, I think I'm going to try out for the hockey team this year," David said while yanking off a piece of licorice with his teeth.

Meg lifted one eyebrow in disbelief. "We don't have a hockey team."

"What?" David furrowed his brow. "But I love hockey."

Rachel shook her head in confusion. "Do you even know how to play hockey?"

He grinned. "I think I'm pretty good at the tonsil variety."

She let out an exasperated sigh.

"Dude, get a room," Eric said. He was never afraid of sharing his opinions, especially when annoyed.

"That's what I keep suggesting." David shrugged.

Rachel punched him hard in the arm. "That's not funny!"

"TMI." Eric rolled his eyes.

Meg covered her ears with her hands. "Nah-nah-nah-nah. I'm not hearing this."

"Can we just get the movie started?" Eric asked, clearly irritated.

"We're actually waiting for someone else," Rachel announced with a forced smile.

Meg and Eric were visibly surprised, but David looked rather put out, having already heard the news.

"Jeff is coming over to watch," Rachel said.

Meg frowned, reaching for a drink on a side table. "The junior that comes over for piano lessons with your mom?"

"That's the one," David said, gnawing off another piece of licorice.

"Why?" Meg asked.

Rachel sighed again. "My parents think it would be good for him. I guess he's had a hard time adjusting after moving here over the summer."

"Yeah, that's 'cause he's awkward," Eric added, adjusting in his seat before taking Meg's hand again.

"And he's already over here all the time," David complained. "I swear he's been over here every other day since school started, doing one thing or another."

Rachel glared at David. "Don't be a jerk. He needs money to save up for college. Rob's happy to give him some yardwork to do." She stood, grabbing the bowl of popcorn, then sat on the opposite end of the couch. "Speaking of not being rude, I don't want to make him feel like a fifth wheel." She munched on popcorn, making it clear with her gaze that the distance between herself and David was intentional.

He tilted his head to the side. "I don't see why this charity case means *I* have to suffer."

Rachel scowled. "Don't be a dick. Go take a cold shower or something."

He winked. "I'll take *any* temperature of shower, if you'll join me."

Rachel's face didn't budge. She could admit she was flattered by how much he flirted. But sometimes, he took things too far, and she didn't always speak up.

"David," Meg said in warning.

David sighed. "Fine. I can play nice." He placed a hand over his heart. "I will be on *my* side of the couch. Contemplating a sad, lonely existence." He melodramatically sniffled while wiping away a fake tear.

Rachel grinned. "You're so giving." Sarcasm was one of their love languages.

The doorbell rang and Rachel stood to go get it. Leaning down as she passed David, she whispered in his ear, "If you can behave, I can make it up to you."

"I will be an A-plus student," he hollered down the hall as she walked away.

Jeff joined them and quietly watched the movie from the comfort of a recliner. Rachel and Meg tried their best to make him feel included in the conversation after the movie, but he ended up leaving before everyone else; it was still awkward. The poor guy was an underclassman, had just moved to a new area, and was … not ugly, but also not the kind of guy girls were swooning over. Rachel couldn't help but feel bad for him. He was physically fit, but his hair was a bit unruly, and his parents obviously couldn't afford as nice of clothing as hers could. And like Eric had said, he was just … awkward. He'd sometimes make odd references, or would be confused by normal ones. And he had very little filter. While she wouldn't have chosen to do it on her own, Rachel had agreed to her parents' request to try and incorporate him into their group activities until he found his place in school.

***

Not long after Jeff had left, Rachel ended up sending everyone else home, too. Meg had wanted to hang out longer, and David would have been more than happy to spend some time alone with Rachel making out, but Rachel had started to feel under the weather.

Nauseous and tired, Rachel took some antacids and went to bed early. But she was restless the entire night—tossing and turning, overheating, then shivering. Eventually she found sleep, only to be woken by a text from David. She cancelled their plans for the day.

Too drained to get out of bed, she pulled the covers over her head to block out the sunlight shining through her window. The next thing to wake her was a knock on her bedroom door.

"Come in," she muttered, forcing herself to raise her voice.

The door clicked open. "You okay?" her mom asked.

Rachel pulled back the covers and scratched her arm where it tingled—between her wrist and elbow. "Just feeling like crap."

Her mom surveyed her with slightly narrowed eyes. "Yeah? What's wrong?"

It was probably just a twenty-four-hour flu, but Rachel shared her symptoms.

Nodding, her mom stayed silent for a moment. "Well, rest up. We'll see how you feel in a little while? Want me to bring you something to eat?"

Rachel declined breakfast but guzzled the water her mom brought her. The water at least seemed to help.

A couple of hours later, her mom came back to check on her. "Alright, you and me. Movie and chicken noodle soup." She wore a forced smile.

After significant coaxing, Rachel finally rolled out of bed, throwing her hair into a messy bun and planting herself on the couch of the theater room. The soup was perfectly salty, with the right mix of egg noodles, chicken, and vegetables. It was one of her mom's few signature dishes, and it always helped in one way or another.

As they slurped down their soup, they watched an old DVD of *The Inn of the Sixth Happiness*. That had always been one of the classics they watched together when one of them was sick. Sometimes it was *Dancing in the Rain* or *The Sound of Music*—Rachel's mom loved the older stuff.

Without fail, Rachel cried when the older lady died in the movie. While trying to inconspicuously wipe away tears, she noticed her mom watching her.

"What?" Rachel chuckled. "You always cry in this one, too."

"Yeah," her mom whispered, frowning and turning to look at the screen.

For the rest of the movie, Rachel kept feeling her mom's eyes on her, but every time she looked, her mom would get up to grab something else to drink or snack on, or turn to watch the screen again.

By the time the end credits were rolling, Rachel was ready for a nap. If anything, she was feeling worse. Her mom grabbed her a blanket as Rachel lay down on the couch.

"Are you getting sick, too?" Rachel asked, her brow furrowed. Her mom's agitation was plastered on her face and spelled out in every action. She often doted on Rachel when she was sick, but not normally to this extent.

"No, I'm fine." Her hesitant smile and tone were far from matching her words. "And you'll feel better in no time." She kissed Rachel on the forehead and turned off the lights, heading out of the room.

Hours later, Rachel joined her mom for dinner and then in the living room once Rob got home from work.

"We need to tell you something, sweetheart," her mom said, sitting next to Rob on the sofa.

Rachel glanced between the two. Rob showed a hint of a frown, her mom a much more grim expression. Samantha gripped Rob's hand tightly.

"What's wrong?" Rachel's heart rate skyrocketed. "Did someone die?"

Her mom took a deep breath. "No, sweetie. It's just—" She pursed her lips, fighting back tears.

Rachel looked to Rob.

"There's no easy way to say this," he began. "You know you're adopted."

"Yeah…"

"Here's a letter from your biological father. It'll explain what's going on. We can help fill in any of the gaps."

Rachel hesitantly stood and took the envelope from her mom's hand. It was odd to get another letter so soon after the surprise back-to-school one.

This new letter was nothing like the others she'd gotten from her biological father over the years. While the penmanship was recognizable as his, this one *had* to have been written by a madman. It told her she wasn't human, of all things. It warned she was in danger. And worst of all, it said she'd be leaving behind the world as she knew it. She read the letter twice to try and grasp what he was getting at.

Rachel lowered the letter, gazing into her parents' eyes. "This has to be a really bad joke. You've read this?"

They nodded. Samantha found her voice. "It's not a joke. I grew up with your mom. I know what you are." She grimaced, fighting back more tears. "I, uh… Your arms hurt, don't they?"

Nodding, Rachel gently rubbed them. Where they'd been itching earlier in the day, they now ached a bit.

"Yeah, your blades," her mom said. "And your eyes … during the movie. We have something for you that you'll need to wear at all times. It'll help you feel better, stay safe, and give us more time together."

Rachel shook her head in disbelief. "No. What are you talking about? I've never even met this man. *This* is my home."

"You know we love you," Rob said. "But it's time for you to go live with your people."

Rachel's eyes filled with tears, and she appealed to her mom. "You both think I should go?"

A tear rolled down Samantha's cheek. "Yes."

And just like that, Rachel knew her life would never be the same. She sniffled, looking down at her fidgeting hands.

Rob stood and approached Rachel with a small white box, handing it to her. "This is from your biological dad. It should make you feel better."

Opening the box, Rachel eyed the contents—a necklace, a long chain with a green stone pendant.

"You need to wear it with the carving next to your skin," Samantha added.

Rachel lifted the necklace from the box, running her thumb over the sun symbol carved into the rock. Rob continued to explain what it could do for her. The charm would temper the change she was going through, letting it remain undetected and allowing them more time together.

She slipped on the necklace, tucking the pendant under her shirt, and all of the aches and pains and nausea Rachel had been dealing with shrank away within a matter of minutes. It didn't, however, do anything for her struggle to grasp her new reality.

Samantha cleared her throat, wiping away tears and putting on a brave face. "Your blooming will probably take three or four months to progress, and then you'll have another three to four months to train with your powers. For Seeders, it's customary to wait longer to break the news to you girls, but we agreed," she looked at

Rob, squeezing his hand before turning to face Rachel again, "that this would be better for you. Knowing earlier will give you a better chance to prepare for training. And you'll be able to enjoy the time you have left here."

Rachel nodded, her mind lost in a sea of confusion and hurt and shock.

"There's a lot you can still enjoy over the next few months," Rob encouraged. "Especially before your formal training starts. You'll be doing that with Jeff—he's one of your brothers."

Rachel blinked, shocked at the additional revelation. The letter had said she had a ton of siblings. "Okay," she said in a daze. "Can I go lie down?"

Samantha frowned. "Yeah, sweetheart. If you want to. We can talk about the rest later."

After ambling upstairs to her bedroom, Rachel set the letter from Garrett down on her bedside table. Before plopping down in bed, she stared at herself in the mirror. She was … a Seeder. She wasn't from this world.

She removed her necklace for just a moment. Her shock grew as a flicker of bright green rose in her own eyes. Eyes that had only ever been brown before. She lifted a hand to the mirror. The more freaked out she became, the brighter the green glowed.

Swallowing hard, Rachel forced herself to look away, put the necklace back on, and lay back down in bed.

***

Rachel was already standing in front of her house the next Monday morning when David rolled up, not blocking the driveway. She wore a blank expression, the events of the weekend weighing on her mind as she got into the car.

"Everything okay?" David asked with a concerned frown.

"Yeah, just tired," she lied.

"You sure you're feeling better? You sounded pretty sick."

"Yeah. I just want to get to school, okay?"

He reached over for her hand, giving it a squeeze. "Let me know if you need anything."

She forced a small smile. "Thanks."

Their car ride to school was quieter than usual. David made sure she knew he had missed seeing her all weekend.

After going their separate ways at school, Rachel continued to be in poor spirits all day, processing her news and barely even responding to any texts between classes.

As she meandered back to their parking spot at the end of the day, she was greeted by a smiling David. Sitting on the hood of his car, he opened his arms as she approached, and she melted into his comforting embrace.

Moving her hair to the side, his finger brushed across the chain clasp of her new necklace. David planted a soft kiss on her neck. "Still not feeling great?"

She didn't respond, just shaking her head slightly.

"Would it cheer you up if I took you out to dinner, or something else fun?" he offered.

She shook her head again.

He held her at arm's length, then kissed her sweetly on the forehead. "I hate seeing you like this. Do you want to talk?"

"I'll be fine," she responded unconvincingly.

"It's not guilt weighing you down, is it?" he asked with raised eyebrows.

She scrunched her forehead in confusion. "No."

"You don't usually wear necklaces."

She took a step back, eyeing him with suspicion. "Why should that matter?" Supposedly, the enemy looking for her kind didn't know about the jade charm helping her stay safe and feel better. But the mention of it put her on edge.

"I'm just wondering if there's a handsome gifter I should be jealous of." He winked.

Her muscles relaxed. "You know I wouldn't do that to you."

Looking her in the eyes, he frowned again. "I know, sorry. I'm just trying to cheer you up. Let's get you home, okay?"

The ride was just as silent and depressing on the way back from school as it had been on the way there in the morning. Rachel gave David a small peck on the lips before going inside.

It took a couple of days for her mood to improve as she tried to reconcile the lost future she'd always envisioned, and the nebulous one now in front of her, if she met the unfathomable expectation to leave her human life behind.

***

Rachel imagined some host parents had a harder time than others in letting go of their Seeder charges. Not that it wasn't hard for them, but Rachel's mom and stepdad were adamant about her returning to the Green Lands, like the expectation of attending a parents' alma mater—Rachel was informed of her impending plans, not really having much say in the matter. At least that was how it felt when she'd dared to bring up the topic again.

Though they were more focused on Eric, being the newest addition to her circle, Rachel's parents reminded her that no one was above suspicion of being an Ivy, not even David. They discussed having her break up with David sooner rather than later so she wouldn't get distracted, and just in case he wasn't what he seemed to be. Rachel wouldn't have it, and luckily Rob ended up agreeing that she should be allowed to still spend time with him until she had to leave, as long as she was careful, and David didn't get in the way of her training goals.

Just as they had done their best to allow Rachel a normal, happy human life, they wanted these last few months to be something she could look back on with fond memories. She had been warned to always be alert, always remember her jade charm, and always have something on her for self-defense, especially until her powers came in. She would need to let her parents know where she was at all times. Realizing the severity of the situation, she agreed to follow all of their rules to the letter. She desperately wanted to share her struggle with Meg and David, even Eric. But she wrestled through it in silence.

Jeff was fine, but they didn't have an instant bond by any means. It was more of a casual mentor-mentee relationship than a joyful sibling reunion. He was around often to 'take piano lessons' and 'help around the house for college money.' She'd greet him as they passed, and regularly texted him her whereabouts. For the first few months, there were opportunities to learn about her people and how their powers worked. She just didn't have her powers to perform her unique abilities yet.

It was helpful they'd made an attempt to integrate Jeff into her circle of friends *before* the change had started—it had made it a smoother introduction. He found his place with them; not that they were exactly thick as thieves, but the group didn't grunt and groan anymore when he would butt in on movie and game nights, or join them for outings.

Rachel took every opportunity to savor her time left in the human world. She played on the school volleyball team and went to homecoming and winter formal. Every available moment was spent with David or Meg. The clock was ticking, and Rachel's focus would soon be divided between maintaining a normal life and training for her new one. She was fairly apt at observing, concealing the truth, being discreet. She was even happy most of the time. Until she had to lie to David about submitting college applications.

"It's okay, we don't have to talk about it," he said, when the spark of joy left her eyes at his mention of plans after graduation. "If we don't go to the same college, we can still make things work. We'll cross that bridge when we come to it."

In a lot of ways, she wished that 'bridge' would burn to the ground.

Chapter 5

DURING WINTER BREAK, THEY TESTED to see how Rachel's blooming was coming along—taking off the charm, waiting a few hours to see if she would feel ill, checking to see if she could control any Seeder energy. Eventually, the time came when the charm had fulfilled its purpose and she was ready to move on to the next step.

Jeff had already helped her prepare for energy control by going through visualizations, so it was exciting to finally be able to put it into practice with her full powers. In awe at the amazing new energy coursing through her body, Rachel warmed up to her expected future. They worked on concealing her change and separating emotions from energy, before heading back to school after Winter Break. Even though she was fairly confident in her ability to do it right, she planned to keep a bit of distance from David for a few days. At least until she felt absolutely sure she could continue their relationship without giving herself away. As much as she trusted David and her friends, Rachel wasn't too keen on the idea of humans discovering she was different.

Perhaps it was a little paranoid of her, but every time she imagined letting her identity slip, she thought of the old *E.T.* movie where the government kidnapped and studied the friendly little alien—it sent a shiver down her spine.

***

Rachel and David sat next to each other on a bench in the school's enclosed courtyard, waiting for Meg and Eric before classes. She held his hand, but turned down other affection. Meg and Eric approached right on schedule.

"Give this girl a hot beverage, stat!" David called to Meg. "She's icing me out over here."

Rachel shook her head, smiling. Meg handed her a latte, pulling one out of a drink carrier for herself and another for Eric, and even handed one to David.

David's eyes lit up. "For moi? You are too kind."

Meg smirked. "Consider it a belated Christmas gift. Don't get your hopes up."

"I shall savor every last drop of it and take a picture of this momentous occasion, to remember it always." David laughed and took a selfie with his cup of coffee.

"Speaking of selfies…" Rachel said, tapping Meg's shoe with her own. "How is it possible you go on an amazing Caribbean cruise for Christmas and lose every single picture of it?" She raised her eyebrows. "I need to live my life vicariously through you, you know. My mom and Rob don't ever take me on lavish vacations like your parents do."

"You think *you're* the one that's upset? That was a brand-new phone, too!" Meg whined.

"So, what happened?" David inquired.

"Let's just say butterfingers and breathtaking views from the railings don't go together." Meg frowned. "I would like to ask for a moment of silence for my phone, please."

They all lowered their heads respectfully before laughing.

"Yeah, this *new* new phone is going to be synced up." Eric smiled, squeezing her hand. "So next time a body of water claims your phone, you don't lose everything."

"My hero." Meg sighed dramatically before planting a kiss on him.

"You don't even really look all that tan," Rachel noted. "Didn't you take time to enjoy that cute new bikini you showed me?"

"Girl, you know I'm not going to be the broad who looks twenty years older than I really am, with wrinkly, leathery skin." Meg puckered her lips with attitude. "I know how to SPF."

"What is this about a new bikini? Now I don't get to see pictures of the bikini? I want to see the bikini," Eric added with puppy eyes before growing a mischievous grin.

Meg blushed and whispered something into his ear. He whispered back, pulling her in tight and starting to lip wrestle.

"Oh brother." David rolled his eyes. "Can we change the topic?"

Rachel smiled at Meg and Eric. She was really going to miss this dynamic, these friends, more than any other friends. Swallowing hard, she tried to remind herself of all the positive things her parents and Jeff had been telling her. Things about heritage, about discovering her true nature. She'd be learning to heal and even fly!

David slid an arm around Rachel and she smiled again, trying to focus on the here and now. She glanced over at his coffee cup. "French vanilla. Mmm."

David raised an eyebrow. "Wanna try it?" He offered his cup, and she took a sip. Rachel reciprocated the offer with her drink. David read the side. "Hmm. Chai latte? Not feeling it, but thanks." He pulled Rachel in closer, nuzzling her neck.

She grinned until she felt the telltale signs of her emotions and Seeder energy mingling. She leaned away from David. "Not today."

He gave her pouty lips. "Are you mad at me?"

She huffed. "We're capable of keeping our hands and lips off of each other for more than two minutes, right?"

David shrugged. "Capable? Yes. But it's not nearly as fun."

Rachel rolled her eyes as the bell rang.

***

Despite her best efforts over the next couple of weeks, Rachel's emotions were taking a turn for the worse. Spending more time in training was stressful; trying to keep up her grades, and not making any noticeable changes in her daily pattern—it was all weighing her down.

And things were coming along slower than she had anticipated with her abilities. Slower than *any of them* had anticipated. While the first few days after her powers came in had been invigorating, that boost of energy had seemingly died off, and it became exponentially harder for Rachel to complete the tasks and exercises asked of her. It wasn't as though she couldn't keep her Seeder energy in check— she was even comfortable being around David more—but it was like she couldn't tap into the energy like Jeff expected of her, not to the level she needed.

Rachel and Jeff practiced in the basement family room with the furniture lined up against the walls. Jeff set up a target for practice with darts.

"Alright, like we've done before, channel your energy down to your hand," Jeff instructed.

Rachel followed the ample coaching he'd already given. The warmth of Seeder energy resided in her heart, and she envisioned moving it through her arm, down to her hand. Her hand glowed, but no excess energy pooled into a ball of light as she'd expected it to. She'd slept well. She'd even had a special coffee from Meg earlier. She was plenty energized…

"Come on," he said. "I know you're capable of more."

Rachel took a deep breath, focusing harder. Eventually, a tiny little ball of light formed above her palm.

Jeff looked thoroughly unimpressed. "That's really all you've got today?"

Rachel reabsorbed her energy, crossing her arms. She glared at his condescension. "Maybe I'm just too worn-out from yesterday's practice."

He shook his head. "I told you: it doesn't work that way. It might take a few hours if you're depleted, but you should be up to full-charge by now. Unless you've been doing practices in your own time?" He raised an eyebrow.

She stared at him, perturbed. He'd grown up with his powers, in their home realm. He didn't know how this felt for her.

"Yeah. Maybe I've been practicing too much," she lied.

"Doing what?" His head tilted to the side in challenge.

Her jaw clenched as she tried to remain calm. "That's the best you're getting out of me today. Maybe we should do something that doesn't demand so much energy."

Jeff sighed. "We can only *talk* about your abilities for so long. Theory only gets us so far. I need you to step it up."

Rachel's gaze dropped, and she swept her bare foot over the soft carpet. One of the most annoying things about Jeff was his inability to pick up on social cues. She'd come to realize some of his 'weirdness' stemmed from not being human and not blending in perfectly, but at times like this... He genuinely didn't seem to recognize when he ought not to be so blunt with her. He wasn't trying to be mean, so she couldn't fault him for it.

"Then let's... I don't know. Maybe go out back and work on practicing communing with the wind?"

Jeff shrugged. "Fine. Won't do you much good down the road if you can't focus enough to extend your blades and learn to catch a breeze. But I guess it's ... *something*..."

Rachel followed after him, wiping at a runaway tear. She'd asked him already about where she landed on the spectrum of Seeder girls with regards to powers. As he had explained it, there wasn't really a 'spectrum of powers' amongst Seeders. Some specialized more in one power than another, or had a *slight* difference in harnessing energy. But it wasn't that Rachel was low on energy or bad at energy-harnessing like she'd thought, that she had been born that way. To Jeff, she was a lazy disappointment. To herself, she was … just a disappointment.

***

Rachel's parents and Jeff had promised her the training wouldn't be too exhausting, and that she'd be able to have a seminormal extracurricular life, to keep up appearances and enjoy what time she had left in the human world. But the practices were more draining than she'd expected, and they were starting to ask for more and more time. Rachel demanded a free afternoon the next day after school to hang out at Meg's house. She *desperately* needed this break.

After ambling to Meg's place, two houses down the street, Rachel rang the doorbell. Meg greeted her with a huge smile. "Come on in!"

They walked upstairs from the split entryway and headed to the kitchen to raid for snacks. Meg's tutor, Michael, popped his head in to wish Meg a good night. Meg was dyslexic and her parents had paid for tutors for as long as Rachel could remember.

Rachel leaned back against the kitchen counter as Meg stuck her head in the fridge, and then freezer.

"We've got like five kinds of ice cream in the downstairs freezer, but it looks like just mint chocolate chip up here," Meg reported.

Rachel shrugged. "Meh. Whatever."

Meg closed the freezer door and gave Rachel a calculating look. "Hmm. I'll be right back."

Meg's mom came into the kitchen before she returned.

"Hi, Ginger." Rachel smiled. Meg's parents were always welcoming, which made sense with how Meg had turned out. And they were pretty cool, wanting to be called by their first names.

Ginger's full lips turned up in greeting as she filled a glass of water from the fridge door. "Hey, Rach! Glad to see you again. I forgot Meg said you were coming over." Ginger was trim, tall, and her wavy red hair was true to her name.

Meg walked back in, clutching a container of ice cream. She stopped when she spotted her mom, giving her a humorous 'caught-in-the-act' side-glance.

"Hey!" Ginger protested. "That's *my* special ice cream. There's a reason I hide that!"

Meg laughed. "Yeah, but Rachel is having a 'meh' kind of day. It's an *emergency*."

Rachel grinned at the comedic duo.

"Yeah, whatever." Ginger rolled her eyes. "Since it's for Rachel." She winked.

Meg set it on the counter. "Yup, we know who your favorite is." She playfully narrowed her eyes at her mom.

Ginger smirked. "You girls have fun." She pulled the scoop from a drawer, handing it to Meg. "Don't forget to write it on the shopping list!"

They scooped some ice cream and took the bowls to Meg's room to hang out.

Meg sat on her bed, while Rachel claimed the purple reading-nook chair in the corner.

"So, what's up?" Meg asked.

Rachel looked down, poking at the raspberry-and-cheesecake ice cream with her spoon. "Things are just weird lately at home."

Meg frowned. "Like parental-problem weird?"

"No." Rachel shook her head. "No big problems there. I guess maybe it's not really home stuff. I've just been off, is all."

Meg lifted an eyebrow. "Off?"

Rachel took a deep breath. "You know what? It's nothing. I didn't come over to be a downer." She forced a smile.

Meg pursed her lips, clearly unconvinced. "Whatever it is, just remember things get better, okay?" She gave a reassuring smile.

Wanting to move on, Rachel nodded. "So... This year's prom theme, am I right?"

Meg pointed her spoon at Rachel. "Seriously. *So* cliché."

They chatted for over an hour before someone knocked on the bedroom door.

"It's unlocked," Meg called out.

Her dad opened the door. "He's here."

"Oh." Meg scrunched her eyebrows, grabbing her phone.

"Hi, Rachel." Meg's dad nodded.

"Hi, Nathan." She smiled and waved before he took off. Nathan had dark hair like Meg and was a bit shorter and quieter than his wife.

"Well, crap," Meg said. "I had my phone on silent. Eric's here."

Rachel picked up her empty ice cream bowl. "Let's go say hi."

As they walked down the stairs to the living room, Rachel smirked to herself. She followed the Seeder family network and her parents' rules, but they could sometimes be a smidge overreaching. Jeff had sounded a bit paranoid when he'd described the kinds of activities he thought Rachel should report. Something like this—Eric showing up at his own girlfriend's house earlier than expected, coincidentally while Rachel was there—was something Jeff would probably want to hear about. Rachel shook her head. Eric was a solid guy, and had shown no increase in attention toward her at all.

She followed Meg into the living room. Eric got up from the couch and Meg launched herself into his arms.

"I'm sorry. I didn't see any of your texts," Meg said, standing tall for a smooch.

"No worries. I just got off early and wanted to see you." He squeezed her tight, rocking them both side to side.

"Problem is, I'm still hanging out with Rachel." Meg pouted. "Girl time and all."

Rachel didn't want to intrude on their time. "Honestly, I should be getting home, anyway."

Meg frowned. "You're sure? Eric wouldn't mind hanging out in the car for a couple of hours while we keep chatting." She winked.

He leaned forward, tickling her sides while she giggled. "A couple hours, huh?"

Rachel shook her head while she grinned. "I'm good. Thanks for the hangout."

"Okay." Meg walked up to Rachel and gave her a hug, then held her at arm's length. "Remember: the glass isn't just half full, it's three quarters full. And you get to be the one that fills it up." She smiled.

Rachel strolled home, musing on her best friend's cheesy and well-intentioned advice. She wanted to think that way. And it would have been easier to do so had things not gotten so complicated.

Taking a deep breath, she prepared to text Jeff to let him know she was free for training. She was going to try to be more positive.

Chapter 6

SAFF RETURNED HOME FROM A long day of working as a welcoming apprentice. There was an influx of new girls returning. They were being rushed home as soon as their powers were sufficiently up to snuff to make the journey. Their energy was in high demand back home, their safety still more guaranteed in the Green Lands. Their hastened return also freed up brothers and fathers needing to take on other tasks.

Saff gazed out of the window at her sad patch of a garden, now wilted and neglected. She didn't have the energy to put into it today. The last time she'd felt this drained was right after her bloom in high school. Plopping down at the kitchen table, she laid her head down to rest for just a moment.

The front door squeaked open, and she moved her head to the side to see Devin coming in.

"You've never looked more beautiful." He smiled at her limp frame.

"Lies," she mumbled, forcing herself to sit up in the chair.

He walked over to greet her, pulling her up into a tight embrace as though he would never let her go.

"Any updates?" she asked, wary.

His chest shuddered with a heavy exhale. "We think there's been another one."

She stepped back and cupped a hand over her mouth. "No," she whispered. There were rumors and all sorts of speculation surrounding the new tactic being used by the Ivies to breach Seeder border walls. But official, reliable communication between Seeder communities traveled slowly. Scouting groups had taken to the Neutral Woods in an attempt to find answers. Most of those groups never came back, or returned with heavy casualties and no helpful information.

"Yeah," Devin whispered in defeat. "I'm going to go get cleaned up."

Devin took off his shirt, heading into the bathroom. He slammed the door behind him, causing Saff to jump. The door only slightly muffled his swearing. A jarring thud was promptly followed by the crash of glass. Saff ran to the bathroom and opened the door. Devin sat crumpled on the floor, surrounded by glass shards from the full-length mirror. His hands were balled up in fists pressed against his forehead, one of them bleeding.

Ripping a pair of towels off of the rack, she laid them over the glass so she could walk across safely. She crouched in front of him and grabbed the bleeding hand, picking a few small pieces of glass out of it and holding it between her hands to heal. She looked into his eyes with compassion.

He shook his head and pulled his hand back. "You shouldn't be wasting energy on an idiot like me. I can heal the human way."

She grabbed it again. "I get some say in this. I take care of my family."

He looked down, frowning. "Thanks."

"Are you going to be okay?" she asked.

"Yeah, it feels better."

She bit her lip, knowing how much of a toll this new surge in the war was taking on him, on all of them. Instead of full-time teaching and supplemental border duty, he was working full-time on border duty, and also almost full-time at the school. "No, I mean are *you* going to be okay?"

He took in a deep breath while squeezing her hand. "It's divide and conquer, Saff. If we pull more from the wall for protection detail, the wall will fall. But our girls in the human world are more vulnerable now than ever. We never saw this coming. Never. And we're stretched too thin to mount an offensive to stop it. How are we supposed to end this?" He shook his head. "Damn leeches. Damn every last one of them."

She glanced down at the stone floor. "I'm going to swing by the temple."

He looked up. "Saff…"

Her gaze stopped his protest. They both knew she was tired. She had been making *several* times more energy deposits a week than would normally be necessary. All of the women were. It was taking everything they had. She was worn down, but it was needed. Without the extra energy deposits, these enormous mystery vines were ripping up their border thickets like a can opener to a tin of tuna.

"I love you," he said. "There and back as quick as you can. Stay as far away from the wall as possible. They're sending out more and more soldiers on foot. The woods are crawling with them at night."

She nodded, and he released her hand. "I'll be careful," she reassured him with a weak smile.

He surveyed the mess of broken mirror around him. "I'll clean this up."

***

Saff left their cottage, hands washed free from blood and now hugging herself. She pondered their dilemma as her feet shuffled down the dirt lane toward the moss-covered temple. They still didn't understand how the Ivies were commanding vines strong enough to pierce the Seeders' borders. And their attacks on foot at the walls had become much more aggressive. This didn't feel like the two-hundred-year war she'd read about in her courses. There was something more to it. Sightings and attacks by Ivy assassins in the human world were also skyrocketing. The numbers didn't add up.

It felt like her high school days all over again—the nightmare she'd lived through, that her whole family and Devin's had been through, just to keep her and the other girls safe. Something hadn't made sense about the enemy tactics then, either. By the time both of their families had returned, they hadn't learned anything new. And she hadn't dwelt on it. She'd just been elated to have everyone home, safe and sound.

Until now.

Approaching the nearest temple depository, Saff frowned at the line of women waiting for their turn at the well. It was sickening. It was somber. She wished she could do more.

Saff watched on as other women took turns, giving a part of themselves to help bolster the border walls. Her heart dropped when she recognized one of them—the mother of one of Devin's former students. The boy had died a month ago on duty during a breach. He was only fourteen.

Pursing her lips, Saff fought tears. Things had changed so quickly. She looked away, studying the temple walls. Beautiful carvings decorated the stone, framing the entrances to several inner rooms most people never entered. She'd once painted some of this artwork, back when she'd had more time and energy.

People really only ever came to the temples for the energy wells anymore. She gritted her teeth in anger. It was one more thing the Ivy Kingdom had stripped from them. Seeders used to have a much richer culture, including nature-based worship. But their entire society had become overshadowed by human customs. She still loved humans and their world, but it hadn't been this way until Seeder families were forced to raise their daughters in the human world. An Ivy biological attack, dubbed 'The Great Poisoning,' had torn their society to shreds.

She had to admit that Devin was right to describe the Seeders as 'pacifists to a fault,' as he'd once said. Ivies had stirred up problems, ransacked Seeder temples, and then attacked in open war. In the midst of brutal battles, Seeders had channeled everything they had to create their border walls, giving them hope. But with their lands protected, they'd taken a breath instead of pushing back. And then the poison had somehow been snuck in and released. Seeders had never been sure if that had somehow been part of Ivy strategy, that the Seeders would box themselves in—their main protection becoming their prison. Her heart ached—what would the history books say of this current attack another hundred years down the road? If they made it that long.

Looking down at her wedding ring, Saff allowed a small smile to surface. Devin had brought back a traditional human engagement ring for her, though she'd given him a traditional Seeder one, an intricately carved wooden ring she'd bartered for, made by a local craftsman. And their ceremony had been as traditional as any Seeder wedding. She wanted to spend the rest of her life with him, and they'd discussed having kids when the time arrived. She suddenly frowned again. Plans for their first-year wedding anniversary were on hold. Sometimes she feared, when he was on wall duty, that Devin might not even make it to that anniversary.

And the yearly sprout reveal… What would that look like this year? How many Seeders would actually choose to bring new life into this mess? Taking a matriarch's focus away from defense, instead raising little boys. Sending away a soldier to defend his own girls in the human world. Her chest hurt thinking of it. *If the Ivies keep this up long enough, maybe we'll just die out because everyone chooses to not have kids anymore.* Her stomach knotted. *As if we could last long enough for that strategy to come to fruition.*

Once Saff's turn came up, she approached the well to deposit as much energy as she felt her body could spare. Like all the other times before, a warmth flowed from her heart down through her arms. With glowing hands grasping an emerging root system, she pushed her energy into it, coaxing as much out of her reserve as she could. She left once dizzy, and headed straight home, speaking to no one.

Something has to change.

Chapter 7

ONE SATURDAY AFTERNOON, RACHEL SAT on her bed, sinking into a deep depression. She'd walked out on a training session with Jeff that morning. She couldn't handle his condescension that day. Then again, it wasn't really *him* that was the problem.

Rachel was the failure. She should have been a lot further along in her training than she was. She was useless, weak, unworthy. In her isolation, she stewed in her disgrace, disappointed in herself more than her parents and the Seeders claimed to be, but she couldn't shake the self-criticism.

Her eyes glazed over with tears as she rolled a sewing needle back and forth on her palm.

The doubt had become crippling. The training futile. The expectations unrealistic.

She grasped the needle between her thumb and pointer finger, and sank it into her forearm, pushing past the stinging pain. She pulled it out; a drop of blood pooled at the puncture site. Putting her middle finger on the wound, Rachel healed it. It was practice, that was all. She just needed to practice her healing. This much she could do.

But then she plunged the needle in again, pulling it out, then quickly healing her arm with a touch.

And again.

And again.

She found the self-torture cathartic. She stared at her arm, repeating the process time and time again, her mind playing her worst failures on a loop. Birth parents she'd never met, who were likely disappointed in her progress. A dad who'd left her as a five-year-old little girl because she wasn't enough. Her grades dropping. No time to play volleyball or even attend David's basketball games. Her inability to do even the *simplest* of things in Seeder training. The knowledge that she was going to have to leave behind and hurt the people she loved.

Despite her healing, smashed droplets of blood coated her finger and the injury site.

She dug in once more for good measure, twisting it and starting to pull it out slowly.

"What are you doing!" Meg gasped from the now-open door.

Rachel yanked the needle out, wide-eyed and panicked at seeing her best friend in the doorway. She breathed hard as a drop of blood rolled down her arm and fell on the white comforter. Releasing the needle, Rachel applied pressure to the wound.

"Nothing. Just…" She swallowed the lump in her throat as the floodgates released tears.

Meg set down the drink she'd brought and rushed to her friend's side, hugging Rachel until she stopped shaking and whimpering.

"You can't do this to yourself," Meg whispered. She pushed Rachel's bangs to the side. "Let's get you cleaned up."

They got up from the bed and headed to the bathroom. Rachel turned on the faucet, washing off the blood. The wound had stopped bleeding due to the pressure she'd applied; it looked much worse than it really was from the blood buildup. She left it unhealed since she'd been caught in the act.

"Where are your bandages?" Meg asked.

Rachel examined her arm again. "It's really not all that bad, look." She held up her arm.

Meg locked eyes with her, sporting an indiscernible expression. Likely a mix of concern, frustration, and fear. "It's not the size of the wound that concerns me, Rachel. It's the fact you were doing that to yourself in the first place. Where are your bandages?"

Rachel frowned in shame. "The hallway closet on the left. There's a first aid kit."

Meg left the room, returning with a small bandage, handing it over. She disappeared again while Rachel put it on herself.

Meg reappeared with the drink she had brought. Instead of handing it to Rachel, Meg took off the lid and poured it down the sink, setting the cup on the counter upside down. She pointed to the permanent marker on the bottom of the cup, a love note of sorts, like she always did for her friend. This time it had a picture of a sun with a smiley face on it. "I love you, and this is not okay." Meg hugged Rachel from behind. "Let's get out of here and talk," she suggested.

"What if I wanted to drink that?" Rachel asked with an ironic frown while looking at the dregs of caffeine lingering in the sink.

"I think you need something a little different to drink. Come on. I'm driving."

***

"When you said we were getting a different kind of drink, I kind of thought you meant the hard kind," Rachel confessed, holding a triple-chocolate milkshake. She pressed a fingernail into the styrofoam cup, drawing an indented line.

Meg winced. "I think you've done enough harm today."

"Yeah." Rachel looked down at the restaurant table between them.

"Have you ever even had alcohol?" Meg asked.

Rachel rocked her head side to side. "Two Christmases ago David and I tried a wine cooler."

"That boy." Meg rolled her eyes. "Sometimes I wonder about him."

They sat in silence, the slurping of their straws and the music overhead filling the blank spaces.

"Do you want to talk about what just happened?" Meg asked cautiously.

Rachel closed her eyes and swallowed before shaking her head.

"Okay. But you need to talk to someone. I'm seriously worried about you."

Rachel nodded, unable to make eye contact.

Meg narrowed her eyes. "Have you ever done something like that before?"

Biting the insides of her cheeks, Rachel shook her head again.

"Is it something about David? Or your parents? Is there something I can help with?"

Rachel rubbed her forehead. "No. I'm just," she searched for the right words, "a screwup."

"No!" Meg scolded. "You're better and stronger than you're giving yourself credit for. I understand if you don't want to talk about what's going on with you lately, but the Rachel I know can overcome anything she sets her mind to."

Rachel gave her a weak smile.

"And I'm not taking you home until you promise me you won't do that kind of thing to yourself again."

Rachel fidgeted with her hands, nodding again.

Meg stared at her unblinkingly.

"I promise."

***

Later that night, Meg drove Rachel home and left her with a long hug. "Twenty-four seven, any time, day or night, I don't care when. I'm a call or text away. Okay?"

"Thank you."

Rachel went straight to bed, drained from repeated healing and the emotional buildup. She cried herself to sleep, desperately wishing she knew what to do.

After a solid night's sleep, Rachel woke up in a much healthier headspace. She told Jeff she needed to take the day off to rest up. He protested, but she insisted she would work twice as hard the next week.

And she did. She was really starting to feel a lot better. As early as Monday morning, her spirits were up and her Seeder energy even felt like it was stronger, almost like when it first came in. She hadn't realized how much her emotions must have been hampering her efforts. She thanked Meg profusely for taking care of her and for a life-saving pep talk.

***

"I'm glad to see you smiling," David said on Thursday morning. He pulled Rachel in for a hug and cheered her up with a little more PDA than most would prefer to see.

"Hey, now, break it up. Break it up," Eric chimed as he and Meg walked up.

Rachel bit her lip and gave Meg a warm knowing smile of gratitude.

"Even one for David this time," Meg announced while handing out their ritual drinks.

"Ooh, what did I do to get in your good graces?" he asked with a grin.

"Oh, nothing," she replied with a disingenuous smile. "In my goodness, I try to make the little people and knuckleheads feel worthwhile sometimes."

That garnered a look between Rachel and Eric. Meg and David would sometimes throw quips at each other, but it didn't usually rise to this level of veiled hostility.

As they headed off to class, Rachel asked David what the awkward interaction had been about.

"I don't know," he replied with a shrug. "She's probably just PMSing."

Rachel scowled at him. "Sometimes, you have the sensitivity of a jackhammer."

***

Meg came over for an hour after school, before Rachel would have to kick her out to train.

"How are you doing?" Meg asked, taking a seat on the family room sofa.

"I'm better," Rachel said, joining her. "A bit tired today, but this week has been a lot better than last week."

Meg beamed. "I love it."

"So, did something happen between you and David?" Rachel lifted an eyebrow. "You seemed a little … off … this morning."

Meg gingerly set her purse on the coffee table. "How are the two of you doing? Are you guys good?"

"Yeah… Why?" Rachel asked.

Meg shrugged. "I don't know. I just wonder sometimes if you're too serious with him, not getting to know other guys."

Rachel furrowed her brow. "Isn't the point of dating to be with someone you like? Not just date around because you can? He can be an idiot sometimes, but you know how much he means to me."

Meg huffed. "Maybe I'm overthinking things. Maybe part of me wondered if you were in such a bad place last weekend because you guys … did something you regretted."

Rachel's eyes grew wide. "Oh… I see. No. He knows I'm not there yet. He may be an annoyingly horny flirt sometimes, but he's never really pushed me. I promise, he's a good guy."

Meg nodded, not appearing convinced, pressing her lips together.

"Plus. You know I'd tell you." The two had made a pact years ago, that they'd let the other know if they'd ever gone all the way with a boyfriend. Not in a silly, gossipy kind of way. But just to help each other out, perhaps motivated by a touch of curiosity.

"Okay," Meg said.

"Though I do wonder…" Rachel smirked. "Are you and Eric taking things to the next level?" She hummed playfully. "You're not usually a scarf kind of girl. Are we hiding something behind that?" she teased while moving her hand to pull on Meg's scarf.

Meg slapped her hand away; Rachel practically jumped back in surprise.

"Sorry!" Meg said reflexively, her eyes wide.

"What's that about?" Rachel asked, fully confused at Meg's dramatic reaction.

"Sorry. Just drop it." Meg begged with her eyes.

Rachel sat perplexed, searching her friend's face for answers.

"I mean it, Rachel. It's nothing. Please, just don't say anything. Not to Eric, or anyone, okay?" Meg pleaded.

Rachel frowned. "Now you're worrying me."

"I should go." Meg gathered her purse and keys. "Promise me you won't say anything."

"Yeah… Sure…" Rachel agreed hesitantly, still stunned. Of course, she didn't even know what she was promising not to talk about. Was Meg … cheating on Eric? No, Meg wasn't like that. She really seemed to be falling for him. And Eric seemed like a genuinely nice guy; he wouldn't do anything to Meg. Nor would her parents. The mystery started to eat at Rachel. She thought about the Seeder and Ivy dilemma—things were rarely as simple as they seemed.

Right after Meg left, Rachel shot her a text.

<I'm here for you, too. Remember these phones go both ways. Love you. <3 >

She then sent Jeff a text.

<Ready to start early if you want. Head over when you're ready.>

Chapter 8

RACHEL'S ENERGY WAS WANING AGAIN. She started to feel easily worn out. Too ashamed to bring it up to anyone, she wondered if Seeders struggled with a chemical depression of sorts, like humans. Something as simple as an off conversation or two affecting her mood, to the point that she was useless in training, didn't seem right.

Rachel's gaze acknowledged Meg's silent plea the next morning at school as Meg wore another scarf around her neck. It was just one more thing eating at Rachel. Keeping secrets. Having secrets kept from her. Eric and David both seemed oblivious to either girl's struggle.

***

As he would sometimes do, David came to the rescue of Rachel's mental health by whisking her away on a romantic date Saturday night. She'd been better at keeping up appearances with her parents, not wanting to disappoint them further, but David had commented more than once on her downcast mood. He knew she needed cheering up, and they were approaching the anniversary of their first date—this time would be extra special.

He said it would be a surprise, but she demanded to know where they were going, as it was her parents' rule (especially given her vulnerable position as a Seeder, not that he needed to know that part). He finally agreed to give up the secret location if he could tell only Rob—that way it would still be a fun surprise for Rachel. They agreed on the compromise.

"You're really not going to give me *any* hints about what we're doing? Or where we're going?" she asked as they drove out of town.

"Nope." He enjoyed torturing her too much.

"Not even a teeny, tiny one?" She smiled at his hand resting on her knee, right above the hem of her little black dress.

Smiling, he shook his head. "If you must know—I plan to take you far from town and have my way with you." He threw her a smoldering look.

She glared at him.

"In any consensual way you will allow me to."

She let out a heavy sigh, her reply dripping with sarcasm. "That is just … *the* most romantic thing any girl has ever heard."

"Okay, fine. But that's what you get for trying to force my hand on the surprise." He crept his hand from her knee up her thigh before she intercepted it, moving it back down.

"Down, boy. I haven't been lying about taking self-defense classes after school." Most of all, she and David disagreed on how far they were willing to allow themselves to go. Rachel wanted to wait until she turned eighteen, or until after graduation. David was always chomping at the bit.

"I like you feisty." He removed his hand from her leg altogether, placing it on the steering wheel. "But seriously, I always want you to feel safe around me, okay? I respect you enough to wait."

"Thank you."

They turned off of the main road and drove through a wooded area, finally stopping at a cabin in the middle of nowhere.

He parked the car and turned to her. "Surprise. Romantic getaway. And I promise you'll be back by curfew."

She lifted her eyebrows, her heart beating faster. "I have a hard time imagining my parents being okay with this."

He frowned. "I know something's been bothering you, but it's not something I've done, is it? I just … sometimes feel like you're taking it out on me. And I'm just trying to help, and enjoy our time together."

She matched his frown. He was right. He hadn't done anything out of the ordinary; it was all her subpar acting job and heightened suspicion of everyone around her. David had planned plenty of sweet and elaborate dates over their time together; his parents had always given him a healthy allowance.

"Cross my heart. I'll be good, and you'll see I didn't even plan this alone," he reassured her. "Plus, here—let me ping our location, as promised. They can send the cavalry if I'm lying." He sent a ping on his phone and showed her.

She considered it and decided to enjoy the gesture. He had never forced anything before, and she had more self-defense training under her belt by now. It was probably just hormonal nerves driving her crazy.

"Okay. Don't betray my trust," she warned as they got out of the car.

***

David led Rachel into the snug, romantic cabin, turning on the lights as he entered. It was clean and cozy, adorned with rustic and tasteful Americana-style decor. Just being away from the buzz of the suburbs and the demands at her house helped to melt away some of Rachel's nerves.

He gave her the short grand tour. "This here, of course, is the living room, opening to the kitchen and dining room. To the right is the bathroom, to the left the bedroom."

She glanced at him suspiciously when he mentioned the bedroom. He matched it by raising his hands, signifying he'd be a gentleman.

"Oh yeah, and out those sliding glass doors is the deck." He pointed past the dining room table.

She lifted her chin to look out. "Is that a hot tub?"

"Yes, ma'am." He grinned. "To soak away your worries."

She looked down at her dress, then crossed her arms. "Well, I'm not going in with these clothes, and I'm not going in without them, either."

"Everything has been prepared ahead of time. I've been planning this for a while." He gave her an innocent smile. "Go check out the bedroom. I won't move a muscle."

She scrunched her nose in curiosity and headed down the hallway, glancing behind her to see that he had crossed his arms and was leaning against the wall, watching her.

A towel and a small bag sat on the end of the bed.

She unzipped the bag. *Meg.* She must have smuggled the swimsuit from Rachel's room on a recent visit. *Thanks a lot for picking the skimpiest one… Let's make this as hard as possible for me.* She smirked.

Rachel sometimes questioned how much she could trust herself with David, despite her goal of wanting to wait. They had grown close; not many couples in high school made it as long as they had. She had even let her persistent frustrations in the Seeder energy department allow her to consider giving up on training altogether and taking root in the human world. She was perfectly happy with David, Meg, her mom, and Rob. No one could physically *force* her to catch a breeze and rift to the Green Lands.

After her mom and Rob had gone over the Seeder version of the birds and the bees, Rachel felt confident that intimacy with a human could still be safe. And it was only Seeders that mated for life with each other. She was trying to decide if she would cave and go further with David, knowing she was going to have to leave him. Or if it would be better to avoid it altogether, saving that experience for a Seeder someday, in her unknown future.

But maybe tonight would be the night. For them, and for her, to make up her mind on what her final decision would be, which world she'd claim. She'd never told David she loved him. She felt like it would flow naturally when the time was right, and was kind of also waiting for him to say it first.

Leaving the bedroom and bikini behind, she sauntered up to him in the hallway. She leaned up against him, teasing him with a couple of kisses.

"Is that a yes for the hot tub?" he asked with a smile.

Her cheeks warmed. "That's a maybe."

He invited her into the dining room and pulled out a packed meal that had been brought there ahead of time, complete with chocolate-dipped strawberries. He was pulling out all the stops. They enjoyed reminiscing over the times they'd shared together, laughing, poking fun, smiling.

After dessert, he excused himself to go to the bathroom, where he changed into navy-blue swim trunks. He emerged with a towel over his shoulder and a lighter.

"You're free to do what you want. I'm going to be out there." He winked.

By the time she came out of the bedroom in her black-and-white polka-dot suit, he was soaking in the jetted tub with his eyes closed; candles were lit around the place, and the scent of pine from the woods filled the air. She stepped inside and tried to not move her hands or arms to cover more skin.

David opened his eyes with a giant smile, and held out his arms. Rachel studied the tub, considering her options as hot bubbles collided with her calves.

"I promise I can be a perfect gentleman."

"Hmmm…" She narrowed her eyes. "I think *this* side of the hot tub looks pretty comfy."

"You look stunning," he said in a measured tone. "Which means nothing compared to your mind, which I admire so much."

She blushed again, sitting down in the tub. Amidst his sometimes-crude hints and declarations, he could be sweet.

"I wanted to make this something special; you deserve it for putting up with me for so long."

She smiled.

He tilted his head slightly. "And, I wanted to bring you here to tell you two important things."

Her heartbeat quickened as the tension rose.

"I love you, Rachel." He searched her eyes. His face had a vulnerability to it she hadn't seen in him before.

Her heart was likely to pound out of her chest, as the butterflies in her stomach viciously multiplied.

She gazed into his handsome green eyes. "I love you, too, David."

Rachel scooted across the hot tub onto his lap, caressing his lips with her own. Even though they were both still clothed, she was acutely aware of how much of their skin was touching.

Her frustration grew at their special moment having to be weighed down by her caution to keep her energy under control. David would *definitely* notice if her brown eyes and hair changed to neon-green eyes and glowing yellow hair. But as it had been lately, her Seeder energy was pretty sparse and hidden anyway. Rachel considered giving in and not even trying to conceal it—it may not surface at all. And if it did, she could probably reel it back in before he noticed. Or perhaps it was time to tell him? All of her thoughts were playing ping-pong, distracting her from what she really wanted.

Luckily, he was leading things, as she was only partially in the moment with her thoughts. He kissed her more passionately, moving her hands down to his sides, then rested one of his arms on the middle of her back. The other slid up to the nape of her neck. His lips changed course to her neck as well.

Before she realized what was happening, her arms were tight against her body, his hand over her mouth. Her eyes shot open, now emanating a bright green glow, filled with terror. Adding to David's strong arms and hands restraining her, his *vines* were pulling tighter and tighter, keeping her from being able to move her arms or even extend her Seeder blades.

"I promise I won't hurt you. You have to believe me. I won't hurt you. I promise. I won't do anything to you," he rattled off, his voice and eyes almost as frightened as hers.

She struggled with everything she had to get loose, thrashing and even landing a kick in his swim trunks that made him curse and bend over. It loosened his grip enough for her to get off of his lap and let out a small scream before he wrapped a vine around her head, covering her mouth.

"Rachel, I'm not going to hurt you!"

Her whole body was heaving with rapid breathing and exertion in the struggle.

He spoke in a soothing voice. "I need you to stop. I'm not letting you go until you calm down. I could have hurt you by now—you know that. But I haven't. And I'm not going to. I just need you to calm down."

Determined not to let this be how she lost to an Ivy assassin, she continued trying to free herself. The water sloshed around unforgivingly.

"Please," he pleaded, looking as though he might cry. "I love you. I just want to talk to you. We can sort this out. Please stop struggling."

She sat still, catching her breath, realizing she wasn't going to be able to get out of his grip. Her rage turned to despair as she began to cry. He leaned over to wipe away a tear, and she jerked her head away.

"Rachel. Please. This is the only way I could bring this up."

Her eyes faded to their natural brown as her breathing slowly returned to normal.

"Before I release you, I need you to promise you won't run or scream. Just remember that I haven't hurt you, and I love you. And we're out in the middle of nowhere. I just want to talk. Okay?"

Her eyes were hot with rage, but she nodded in agreement.

He released her mouth; she didn't say anything. He loosened his grip on her arms and she stayed still.

"We can talk about this calmly," he said.

Her voice shook through clenched teeth. "I hate you."

He frowned. "You don't mean that."

"I hate you!" she yelled and lunged at him, punching him in the chest with what little strength she had left until he wrapped his arms around her, pulling her in tight. She sobbed in his arms. "Why did you have to ruin everything?"

"It'll be okay," he whispered reassuringly.

She pushed off of him and he let her go. "You don't get to do that! You don't get to talk like that after what you just did." Neither of them moved for a moment. "I'm going inside and you're taking me home."

Rachel grabbed her towel, wrapping it around herself. She marched inside and slammed the bedroom door behind her, locking it.

Sitting down on the end of the bed, she again sobbed. This couldn't be happening. Two and a half years together, and he was one of the enemy. An Ivy. A leech. The race that hunted down her kind. Her boyfriend was an assassin, and she was stupid enough to have never noticed.

She looked at her dress, neatly folded on the bed. Next to it sat her clutch purse, the smaller purse she'd picked out to match her date outfit. The one that was too small for the Taser she'd promised her parents she'd carry for protection. *You're the smartest girl ever. Sacrificing safety in the name of fashion. Great job.* Grabbing the purse, she yanked out her phone, wanting nothing more than to talk to her mom. To even talk to Meg and confess everything. One of them would show up and take her away.

No service… *Brilliant.* She dropped it on the bed in defeat.

Rubbing her arms, she acknowledged the truth. He hadn't really hurt her. He could have. He hadn't sharpened any of his leaves. At most, she might find some bruising from their tussle. But he could have easily killed her.

She frowned. Just before it had all happened … he'd said there were two things he needed to tell her. The first was welcome; the second, not so much. Rachel pinched the bridge of her nose. At least he'd been honest about it. Either way, they were going to have to find a way to end it, and keep this all a secret. She couldn't endanger her family. And she couldn't imagine killing David, or having Jeff kill him. Even if he was an Ivy.

Rachel closed her eyes, deciding how to handle this. She had to ask herself if she'd really meant what she'd said. Did she genuinely love him? Moments like this made her wonder if they were only still together because she was afraid of being alone after having a boyfriend for so long. She wanted to think she was strong. *But my training proves just the opposite.*

Maybe it wasn't love. But just thinking that hurt, like she was betraying him, them, their two-plus years together. Either way, the fact remained: the Ivy Kingdom only sent *assassins* to the human world. She'd have to find a way to convince David to let her live.

Chapter 9

RACHEL SAT ON THE EDGE of the cabin bed, putting her hair up in a ponytail, then changed back into her dress. She threw her bikini in the trash can with a scowl. She'd never wear that thing again. Not after what had just happened.

When she came out, David was sitting on the couch in the living room, still in his swim trunks, wrapped in a towel.

"Let's go," she ordered.

"Not until we talk."

She glanced at the clock on the wall. "They're expecting me soon. Take me home."

He looked down, biting his lip. "I begged your parents for an extra hour for your surprise."

She shook her head, glaring. "The one time in my life I wish they were more strict."

"Come sit down. Let's talk." He gestured to the open spot next to him.

Rachel sat as far away as possible on the couch. "Okay. Talk."

"You have to believe me that I *do* love you." He pleaded with his eyes.

She crossed her arms. "Get to the point."

"Rachel, that *is* the point! I came here to tell you that, and come clean with you."

"What do you want from me?"

"I just want us to be happy." He raised his eyebrows.

She glowered. "How could I be happy with an asshole leech?!"

"Hey, watch your language." He scowled.

"That's what you are, David."

He looked away with a frown. "It's not like I'm going around calling you a weed."

She busted out laughing. "That's what you got from that? That I called you a leech?" Jeff had told her the term 'leech' was fairly synonymous with 'Ivy,' but that it had a more negative connotation. The same went for 'weed' in regards to Seeders.

David looked back at her, scratching his arm. "Yeah, well, I probably earned the other part."

"Probably?"

He pursed his lips. "Pretty certain."

"Who kidnaps their girlfriend and takes her to a cabin like an axe murderer, and then lures her into a hot tub before attacking and restraining her?" She threw daggers with her eyes.

"Okay, definitely." He picked at his fingernails. "I maybe should have done things differently. I just … got caught up in the moment."

"Why? Why now? How did you even know?"

"I realized last week." He winced. "Your eyes gave you away."

She frowned; more evidence she was a failure.

"I wanted to come clean because I know that means we don't have much time together here. How long until you leave?"

She shook her head. *At this rate, never.* "I don't have to answer all your questions."

"Fine. I … just didn't want things to end. We could be together, on the other side."

Flabbergasted, Rachel furrowed her brow. "So, you are insane, then? How would that ever work? Our people hate each other."

"You can't judge a whole race by the same standards. You didn't get to choose what you are or that you came to the human world, and neither did I."

Her mouth hung open at the audacious comparison. "You have got to be kidding me. *My* people come here to try not to be murdered. *Your* people come here to do the murdering. It's not the same!"

He nodded ever so slightly. "But we're not all like that, you have to believe me. There's a growing faction amongst our people that want things to go back to the old ways. There's a rebellion. We could find a place, make things work."

She narrowed her eyes in disbelief. "Really? Who are these good guys? Anyone I know? Eric? One of your basketball friends?"

He crossed his arms. "I'm not going to betray my network, just like I won't ask you to betray yours."

"Who all knows about me, then?"

"No one. I'm the only one that really knows what you are."

She tilted her head to the side. "What about the ping you sent of our location? How can I believe you don't have others on the way?"

A flash of guilt crossed his face. "That was a fake. I needed you to trust me."

She scoffed. "Yeah. Trust."

He looked down into his lap. "I'm sorry."

Sitting in silence, she fidgeted with her hands. "That's the first time you even apologized for this."

"I'm sorry. I can be a jerk sometimes."

She rolled her eyes. "Let's say I believe you that none of your people know—how highly do they suspect me?"

David shrugged. "We suspect everyone."

That wasn't nearly good enough of an answer. "Have you identified any more of my people here? Is someone I know in danger?"

He shook his head. "No. Not that I know of. But I don't know how much they trust me. I should have moved on to a new girlfriend a long time ago. I convinced my general that I've stayed with you to get close to Meg."

Rachel gave him a death stare. Meg had been acting weird… What if… "If you hurt her, I will kill you myself."

His eyes grew wide. "I wouldn't! I don't even know that she is— it's just my story." He sighed. "Can you please try to see this from my perspective? I didn't have to expose myself. I could have hurt you, or I could have let you go on your way. I'm risking a lot by hoping you really *do* love me, and you'll keep my secret as much as I keep yours."

"I hear what you're saying, but have you really thought it through, David? What happens when we break up? What stops you from killing me when you decide you're tired of me, or the other way around?"

David looked at Rachel sheepishly, not having an answer.

She scowled. "Right. I didn't think so. You threw everything away by being selfish."

"Do you want to break up with me? Do you want to kill me? Nothing has changed—I've always been me."

His face was vulnerable, but the facts remained. "Listen to the words that are coming out of my mouth. You. Are. An. Assassin. You were *literally* sent to this world to kill me and my family. And you want me to get weak in the knees at that? I don't have bloody Stockholm syndrome!"

He furrowed his brow, raising his voice. "Well, I can't undo this now, can I?"

She rubbed her temples. "I don't even know if I'm going back to the Green Lands. What if I forfeit my powers and stay here? Will your people leave me alone? Or now that I've been identified, will I always be a target?"

"Really?" His voice was soft. "But you have so much potential."

She scoffed. If only he knew how much she was struggling. If she was even a half-decent Seeder, she could have put up a much better fight just now. "Hypothetically."

"Well, we don't really care about humans. We just let them be. And that's what you'd become." He frowned. "But that's why I've stayed with you all this time. You're special. Something about you helped me to become better and really want to do things differently."

Rachel swallowed a lump in her throat, her eyes threatening to mist. That wasn't fair. He wasn't allowed to compliment her after betraying her. He was supposed to be a villain she could properly hate.

"Special. Yeah. So special," she whispered.

He reached his hand out toward hers; she pulled away.

"No matter what you decide, I'm making a promise to you, right now," he said. "Your secret is safe with me. And I only want the best for you. Even if it means not being with me, I want to see you fulfill your full potential back home."

She looked at him in disbelief. "I'd be your enemy. You want me to believe you're okay with that?" Jeff had taught her the number one rule in Seeder-Ivy relations: Ivies don't want Seeder girls to return home. Convince them to stay and become human, or kill them—*anything* that weakens Seeder border walls.

"Like I said, there's a rebellion. Change is coming. But yes. I want you to be happy, no matter what you choose."

She bent over, cradling her face with her hands. "When am I going to wake up from this nightmare?"

"Will you tell me how long you have left?" he asked again.

"I don't know. Let's just say a couple of months."

"Okay. How about this—we can agree to keep each other's identities safe until you leave. No matter what we decide with our relationship. But I don't want to waste a minute while we're both on this side of things. Don't think of me as an Ivy. Think of me as … a foreign exchange student. And either way, if you decide you don't want to see me anymore, we have to be careful. Weird behavior from either of us could blow both our covers."

Sitting up, she studied his face. The face she had come to know and love, the one she looked forward to seeing every day. All of the fond memories welled up in her eyes. "Yeah, we can see how things go. You can trust me, as long as you promise I'm safe."

"You will be." He spoke softly, confidently. "Think of me as one of your brothers right now—I'm on your protection detail, too." He wrinkled his nose, shaking his head. "Wait, no. Don't think of me as your brother… That's all kinds of wrong. But you know what I mean."

She sniffled and chuckled. "Yeah. Not my brother."

"Do you have any more questions for me before we go? Obviously, we can talk more later."

She chewed on her lip and thought about it. She hated herself for what she wanted to ask. No, she couldn't do it. You can't ask for a hug from the person that hurt you. That's like asking to cuddle with a cobra while the venom takes hold. David had given up his right to any affection.

But no one else could do what he did for her. And no one else would know the agony she was in. She couldn't tell Meg about this, or her mom, Rob, or Jeff. "Would you hold me for a little while?"

He smiled. "Always."

She crawled onto his lap, and he enveloped her in his arms.

The next thing Rachel knew, she woke up to a kiss on the forehead. Taking a moment to get her bearings, she was taken aback by the wood-paneled walls. She was still in the cabin and must have nodded off. Looking up at David with suspicion, she moved to the other side of the couch. "What time is it?"

"We'll be late. But I'll call Rob and text him a picture of our flat tire as soon as we get to the car. It'll buy us enough time to get you home." He stood. "I made sure to have backup plans for my backup plans."

Looking at the floor, she remembered their conversation and agreement. "Yeah, you're an Ivy. Always planning and plotting."

"That's not fair," he said softly, but defensively.

"Maybe not," she admitted. "Sorry."

"I'm going to get changed, okay?" He left for the bathroom after she nodded.

***

David turned off the lights before locking up the cabin. He opened the car door for Rachel and they drove off. The wedge between them was palpable, the silence deafening.

Finally cutting through the stillness, the ping of her cell phone announced they'd gotten back in tower range. She opened it to a text from Meg.

<I won't pry, but I hope it was as special as David told me it would be. Happy Anniversary, I'm excited for you guys! :) >

The final approach to Rachel's house made the tension peak.

"So." He shifted the car into park. "Maybe we can talk more tomorrow after you've rested and had a chance to think about things?"

"Maybe." She looked down at her hands. As if finding out she was a Seeder, and a weak one at that, hadn't been enough, now her boyfriend had turned out to be one of the enemy. *You really know how to screw things up, don't you?*

"Okay," he whispered. "Let me know? Just remember—I'm going to keep you safe. And I hope I can trust you, too."

She nodded and got out of the car. Entering the house, Rachel put on her best possible smile to let her mom and Rob know she was back.

"How did the surprise party go?" her mom asked with a bright smile.

"No booze, right?" Rob asked with raised eyebrows. "David promised it would all be on the up-and-up."

Party? *The lying bastard.* She hated doing this to them, of all people. "It was great. You know me—no drinks or drugs. Do a lie detector or a drug test if you want," she said convincingly with a casual shrug.

They each gave her a hug, and she excused herself to go to sleep.

As Rachel sat on her bed in her fleece pajamas, she looked around the room. She wanted to scream. She wanted to throw things, smash anything she could. She wanted to punch the wall. Her skin was crawling with pent-up aggression, but she was impotent. She was trapped in her own head as much as she had been in David's vines just earlier that night.

Lying down, she stared at the corkboard on her wall, wondering what the pushpins would feel like compared to a sewing needle. She fought the urge, her promise to Meg the only thing that held her back.

Chapter 10

THE NEXT DAY, RACHEL TURNED down David's offer to talk. It was too soon; she needed more time to think things through. She worked with Jeff all day in the basement family room, and despite her energy abilities being low, she wasn't pulling any punches with hand-to-hand defense training. He seemed to at least approve of her efforts in that regard, but it still wasn't enough.

"Rachel, I have to be honest. I'm worried about you," he said at the end of practice.

She frowned. He'd never said, in so many words, that he was outright disappointed in her abilities, but she'd known it was coming.

"I need you to give everything you have. I don't understand why you're holding back."

She resented that; she wasn't intentionally holding anything back. She was giving a good, honest effort. "I'm not. I'm trying my best!" She tried to ignore the sting of tears in her eyes.

He was never one to coddle. "I know you don't want to hear this, but I don't think you'll make it back in time if we keep going at this pace. And I haven't wanted to worry you, but things are getting really bad back home. They need as many of us to return as possible, and as soon as possible. The Ivies are actively pursuing war; they need both of us."

She couldn't look him in the eye. "I promise I'm trying. I really am. I'm just not good at this."

He took a deep breath. "I'm sure you can get it down; you just have to figure out what's holding you back. I know a girl that had only a month to get home from the time she bloomed, and she mastered it. You can too, with the time you have left."

Jeff had obviously meant it as a pep talk, but being compared to someone more talented didn't exactly boost Rachel's morale.

He continued, "And … we never do this, but you could say we're short-staffed. I can't afford to dedicate all my time to training just you. So, we're going to introduce you to one of our sisters that's also learning."

Rachel looked at the ground, considering his words. "Okay. We'll see how that goes." That might be exactly what she needed—more support from someone like her.

But it wasn't. The next couple of days, Rachel trained after school with Jeff and her new sister, Emma. Emma had bloomed after Rachel, but was *much* further along in training. She attended a different local high school; she and Rachel had never met before that day. It took everything Rachel had to not just sit it out while Jeff focused on Emma. Rachel was wasting his time.

Tuesday night, she overheard her mom and Rob having a conversation about her.

"But would it really be all that bad if she stayed here with us?" Rob asked Samantha. "I know how much it hurts you to see her struggling so much. She was so much happier before this."

"You know I'd love it if she stayed, but I can't do that to my cousin. I can't take her daughter from her like that."

"I get that you made a promise. But Rachel's an adult in their world. She should have some say in her decision. She deserves to pick what would make her happy."

After a long pause, her mom added, "I love her. But I love my cousin, too. And they need *every* female Seeder back right now. Lives are on the line, Rob. I can't be selfish."

It gutted Rachel to be talked about in that way. To cause contention in their marriage. To know that people in her home realm could die if she didn't suck it up and return to contribute. And to not even know anymore *what* would make her happy.

***

Wednesday morning, David pulled up to Rachel's house as usual, picking her up for school. He didn't lean over for a smooch. They still had a long way to go, figuring out where they stood with everything.

"How are you doing?" she asked.

"I'm fantastic," he drawled, staring straight forward.

Okay, so we're starting off in a bad mood. Grumpy and won't make eye contact... "Sounds like it. Why won't you even look at me?"

He turned his head to face her, revealing a nasty black eye.

Her eyes grew wide. "What the heck happened?"

"Basketball," he muttered, turning off the radio. "Some morons don't know where their elbows belong."

Rachel frowned. While she felt bad for him, she still wasn't completely sold that he could be trusted. "Basketball? Not assassin network problems? Nothing about me?"

He sighed forcefully, clearly frustrated. "You know the world doesn't revolve around you, right? Why would this have anything to do with you?"

She scowled. "I think I grasp the concept of it not revolving around me. Never said it did. But you'll have to forgive me if I get worried when my boyfriend hangs out with a rough crowd. I need to make sure our secret is safe."

David rolled his eyes. "Your secret is safe. I'll say it again: basketball, elbow."

She frowned. "Does it hurt?"

He narrowed his eyes. "What do you think, Rachel?"

Crossing her arms, she pursed her lips. "I think you're taking it out on me, and I did nothing wrong."

Gripping his hands tightly on the steering wheel, he closed his eyes. "You're right. Sorry."

"Do you still want to meet up today after school?" She'd decided it would be good to go over her thoughts about where they stood, now that she'd had a little time to process. She'd told Jeff she needed the night off. He was going to be working on catching a breeze with Emma anyway, and Rachel was nowhere near that level.

David reached over, squeezing her hand. "Of course."

After driving to school, they waited at their usual bench for Meg and Eric. Rachel was happy to see Meg was no longer wearing a scarf, and she was even smiling.

"Oooh. Ouch!" Meg wore a pained expression on their approach. "Nice shiner!" She put a hand to her head, closing her eyes as if divining something. "Hmm, let me guess. Biker bar?" She opened her eyes, grinning. "No. Defending some dame's honor?"

Eric joined in the fun as David glared. "No." He pointed at David. "Saving a cat?"

"I've got it! Saving a cat from a biker?" Meg added.

Eric snickered. "Even better, saving a biker from a cat."

"You're truly a pair of asshats," David replied wryly.

Rachel tried with every ounce of her being to not join in on the razzing. Their jokes were much more fun than the boring truth. But he was still in such a sour mood. And he had to be going through a lot, keeping secrets from other Ivies, from everyone close to him. Rachel frowned. "Be nice, guys."

"Okay, fine." Eric cleared his throat. "But some guys wear makeup. Do you think your foundation would match?" He turned to Meg, smiling triumphantly.

Meg did a poor job of stifling a laugh, pushing Eric along to go inside. She winked at Rachel before turning around.

Rachel rubbed David's back. His face was red with anger. She glanced around, making sure no one was within earshot. "I could try to heal it."

He glared again. "Really? And how would I explain to everyone that it magically disappeared? I'll just heal normally like a stupid human."

She pulled her arm back. "Is that really what you think of humans?"

He rubbed his temples. "Sometimes you are so dense. Humans are fine. Seeders are fine. Ivies are fine. We're all fine."

Rachel stood up, scowling. "I get that you're hurt. And I don't know how much of it is your face, and how much of this is your stupid pride. But you're being a real jerk. Maybe we shouldn't waste our time talking tonight."

David frowned, grabbing her hand. "Please. Just…" He sighed. "We're all allowed a bad day now and then, right?"

Rachel took a deep breath, looking at the hurt in his eyes. If only Meg and Eric had known who he really was—a trained assassin—they wouldn't have done that. "Fine."

***

David started up the car after school. "Thanks for meeting with me."

"Sure." Rachel wrung her hands. No one had come for her or her family—David was keeping his word. And now that school was over for the day, she had time to ask her questions—she'd prepared a list after a warning Jeff had recently shared. "Where are we going?"

"Somewhere we can talk and not be disturbed."

She raised her eyebrows. "Can you be more specific? The last time I went somewhere with you matching that description, it didn't end well."

He sighed. "Fair enough. But your family isn't going to be very happy with you being alone with me anywhere, are they? How about I take you there, and if you don't feel safe, we can go somewhere else. You can tell them whatever you want to tell them."

She rolled her eyes. "Thanks. No pressure, right? *I* get to choose the lies I tell my mom and Rob? Like you made me lie to them Saturday night?"

He cocked his head to the side. "C'mon. Don't be like that. We both have to lie all the time. That's just part of the package of being green folk in the human world. You know that. You lie constantly. You lied to me about plans after graduation, didn't you?"

Twisting her lips, she fiddled with the zipper on her backpack. "Fine. Whatever."

They drove through a residential area and parked on the street.

"This is my place; we can talk in privacy." He gestured to an apartment building.

She furrowed her brow. "What do you mean, 'your place'? I know it's been a long time since I've come over, but this is not your house."

"That couple moved. I've been living on my own for a little while. It wasn't hard, with us always spending time at your place."

"That couple? Obviously not your parents, right? Who were they to you?"

With a hesitant pause, he tapped his fingers on the steering wheel. "No talk about our networks, right?"

She let out a heavy sigh. "Fine."

They entered the studio apartment, and she looked around. Did this place represent the 'real' David? It was tidy and minimalistic, which made sense with him being there on a military mission. He hung back after shutting the door, letting her peruse the room. There was a small bathroom and a tiny kitchenette. Next to the bed were a closet, laundry hamper, and dresser. Rachel noticed a framed picture on the dresser and picked it up—a photo of them where they both wore mile-wide smiles at homecoming. Knives twisted in her stomach. They'd shared a lot of happy memories. Even if he *was* being honest about loving her, how many of those memories were tainted by who he was before he came to that conclusion? Before he'd discovered her real identity?

Was it really possible he loved the human Rachel, *and* the Seeder Rachel?

David stepped up behind her, wrapping his arms around her waist. "That's my favorite picture of us," he whispered.

She set it down and removed his hands, walking across the room. The only furniture for sitting was the bed, and she knew good and well she was not going anywhere near that. Instead, she sat on the floor, against the wall on the other side of the room. He took the cue to sit on his bed so they could talk.

"How much do you know about what's going on in the Green Lands right now?" she asked.

"I know things aren't good," he said.

She shared what she'd concluded over their time apart. "If there was ever a time to be careful about our choices, with the state of our people, it would be right now. I think maybe … if things were calmer, we'd have more of a chance of working things out."

"But that's the thing. I mentioned the rebellion, right? If there was ever a time our people could come together for change, it's right now. It's more of an opportunity than you realize."

She hesitantly rocked her head back and forth. "Then tell me more about this rebellion. What's the purpose? How is it going? How does it work? What part would you and I play?"

Pulling his legs up, David sat cross-legged on the bed. "Right now, we're working on building up our numbers to petition the Ivy government. People are tired of the feud. And … I'm sure we could find a way to include you and keep you safe." He shrugged. "And I don't see why you wouldn't still be able to be with your Seeder family over there."

She loved the sound of it. Jeff had confessed he'd been keeping details of the raging war a secret, that he hadn't wanted to dissuade her from returning to the Green Lands out of fear. But it actually made Rachel want to go more, once she'd heard how much they needed her, as did this—she wanted to help, she wanted to be part of the solution. But… "That sounds too good to be true."

David raised his eyebrows in acknowledgement. "Sometimes *any* hope in a war seems too good to be true."

"Maybe so, but I don't understand it. How does your people fighting against one another have anything to do with them also fighting us? Why would they spend their time attacking my people when they already have trouble to deal with?"

His voice carried hope. "The faction is growing rapidly in strength, as a *result* of the recent aggression. We want it to end."

Nodding thoughtfully, she considered something else Jeff had warned her to keep her ears open for. "Do you know any Ivy royalty?"

David chuckled, shifting positions on the bed. "That's cute. No. Regular soldiers might be a dime a dozen, but trained assassins are, what? A quarter a dozen? I'm not important enough to meet or report to the royal family."

She tucked her knees under her chin. "Who is Nuren?"

David's brow furrowed as he tilted his head. "How would you even know that name? I'm surprised you'd learn that kind of thing when you have all of your powers to learn, still."

Rachel shrugged. "Who is that? We think he has something to do with recent war tactics."

David took a deep breath, lightly scratching his comforter. "We said no talk about networks, but since I don't actually deal with Nuren, I'll throw you a bone." He arched an eyebrow. "Nuren is a member of the royal family and a consultant to the queen and king."

"Do you know where he is?"

David shook his head. "No. And like I said, it's not like I'm chummy with the royal family. You know Nuren just as well as I do."

The reality of how big this all was sank in a bit. Her emotions, hopes, and concerns ricocheted around in her heart. She felt like a coward for being on the fence, for being so wishy-washy. "I'm not sure if I'm even going back. I've seriously thought at times about staying here."

"But why?" David asked with a frown. "Why would you want to stay here?"

Rachel huffed. Was he ignorant, or just selfish? "You and I have very different options. Your people can practically come and go whenever they want. Mine can't do that. We're a lot more limited in how often and when we can go between the worlds. Especially us women. It's not that big of a choice for you, but it is for me."

He bit his lip. "You're right. That sucks. I'm sorry."

"Plus." She frowned in disgust. She couldn't just *hope* things into existence. "I don't think I could go back even if I wanted to."

He was visibly confused. "What do you mean?"

Finally, she had someone she could say it to out loud. "I'm pretty sure I'm the biggest disappointment in the history of my people. I'm doing horrible in training."

He cocked his head to the side. "I'm sure it's not all that bad."

"Yeah." She fidgeted with her hands. "You should have heard what my mom and Rob were saying the other day. And…" She almost slipped on Jeff's identity. "My brother, too. None of them think I can do it. It's so frustrating. I just want to give up."

David scowled. "Well, screw them. You can do it if you put your mind to it, I know you can."

His words of encouragement gave her the slightest reason to smile. "Thanks. I mean it. That means a lot to me."

"Is there any way I can help?" he asked.

"I don't know. I think some of it is just stress."

He pursed his lips with obvious guilt. "So, I guess I'm not helping with that."

She quietly chuckled. "I don't even know how you could help. It's not like you guys fly or manipulate energy the same way we do, right? Or heal? Honestly, I really don't feel like I know all of the differences between us; I just know to watch out for your vines."

"I could teach you about us. About my people. *Anything* you want to know."

His support and willingness to help was uplifting. Ever so slowly, the wall between them was crumbling.

Rachel found herself forming a genuine smile. "Yeah, tell me about your people."

"Can I come sit next to you?" he asked.

Chapter 11

FOR THE NEXT COUPLE OF hours, David sat on the floor by Rachel and told his people's history from their perspective, including the Great Division that led to the Ivies moving across the Green Lands. Of course, a major difference in their beliefs was that the Seeders were the conceited race, thinking themselves morally superior, as well as physically more able.

"You guys have healing, and blades, and darts, and flying, and *way* more energy. You're the real deal. We're taught as kids that your people were starting to oppress ours because we don't have as many bells and whistles."

"No, we're not like that at all!" Rachel defended.

He raised his eyebrows. "Okay, first of all… We're talking mostly about people from well over two centuries ago who thought this way. Second of all, you're not the most qualified to vouch for your people or the state of things. You've never even been over there."

She sighed in frustration. He was right. "What all can you guys do? Obviously, the vines."

"Yeah, that's obviously our main thing. Good for," he cleared his throat, "restraining." He avoided her gaze. "And when they're flexed, the leaves become sharp. We can't heal like you guys can. Our healing is more accelerated than humans, of course, but we can't actively control our energy to speed it up the way you do."

She felt a little better, knowing his black eye would fade sooner rather than later, even without her help.

"And of course, rifts to go between the worlds. Yours do it in the air, ours through the trees. I'm terrified of heights, so I can't even imagine how your people get used to that."

"C'mon, doesn't everyone want to fly?" She smiled.

He shook his head vigorously. "No, thank you."

She laughed. "How does that work, with the rifts?"

"Maybe I could show you some day." He smiled sweetly. "I really love being able to share this side of my life with you. Isn't this nice? Maybe someday you'll learn to forgive me." He offered his hand.

She accepted, slipping her hand into his.

He gave a reassuring squeeze. "I meant it when I said I love you. And I'm going to keep you safe." He opened his mouth, pausing as though hesitant. "Can I kiss you?"

She stroked the back of his hand. "Yeah."

He leaned toward her, his lips pressing against hers. The kiss was sweet and gentle. He was the same David she'd known this whole time. And maybe … maybe even something more, now that they had this intimate secret between them.

"Can I see your vines?" she asked, gazing into his stunning green eyes.

He extended a short tendril from his wrist, and she ran her fingers over it. It was a sinewy, strong green cord. The short length he was demonstrating had a pair of small leaves on it. She rubbed them between her fingers. His leaves were soft and papery, not that different from how a normal leaf would feel.

"They get sharp when you flex?"

"Yeah, here, don't want to cut you." He moved her hand away and then the leaves became rigid.

She carefully felt the side of a leaf. It was as stiff as metal, as sharp as a razorblade. She ran her finger over it. "Ouch. You weren't kidding!" She pinched another finger against the cut to heal it.

He shook his head. "To live in a world where you don't have to suffer through paper cuts." He laughed, and she smiled.

"So, is there anything else about your people?" she asked. "Oh yeah, don't forget the poison."

He nodded guiltily. "Yeah, that about sums it up. But if we're looking for a silver lining, we probably never would have met if it weren't for that poison."

She scoffed. "Right. I can see it now, at our wedding reception. 'These two love birds were brought together thanks to his kind attempting genocide against hers.' And then everyone lets out a big 'Aww' in unison."

He sighed heavily. "You're being a little 'glass is half empty.' I'm just trying to stay positive, okay?"

"How does that even work, David? Relationships between our people?" She ran her fingers across the soft cream carpet they were sitting on.

"Ideally, like this." He winked.

"No. I mean … like, physically…" Her cheeks warmed. "My kind mate for life. So … there's something different there. It's not like we teach about mixing green folk races."

"Why do you want to know?" He wiggled his eyebrows suggestively.

"Stop it." She elbowed him in the ribs.

"Ouch! Okay, fine. I mean, we're not all that different. In the basics, we're all human. That's why we blend in so well here. Green folk have additional unique traits, so we may not be able to have kids together, but I don't see why we couldn't still have completely fulfilling lives and relationships."

"That's a nice perspective. I'd love for that to be true." She moved in closer, leaning her head against his chest. "Do you think there are ways for our abilities to be used together?"

"Hmm, that's a good question. I'm sure books on that haven't been around for a long time. But we draw our abilities from the same place, so maybe? Let's see."

He pricked his finger with one of his leaves, and she moved her hand up to heal it. It healed even quicker than she'd expected.

"That's cool; it really did work," she whispered. "I learned I can heal humans, too. But yours was so fast…"

He planted a kiss on her head. "We're not all that different. We could complement each other well."

Rachel smiled.

"I'd love to learn more about your people," he said. "You haven't been back there, but I'm guessing you've learned a lot."

She hesitated. "I… I want to believe that this is the real you…" Her mind recalled the lessons Jeff had been giving her about their people, their conflicts with the Ivies. She sat up straighter to get a good view of David's face. Feeling stupid for not having led with this question, she dared to ask, "Have you ever killed a Seeder?"

"No!" he replied emphatically and without hesitation. "I promise. I'd been prepared to…" He looked down. "It's actually pretty rare for an assassin to return successfully, having taken out a Seeder here. It gains you a lot of honor, career choices, and money back home."

That was nauseating to hear. But she also realized how much more he was giving up by not turning her in. By not hurting her. By not *killing* her.

"I'd say I'm sorry you're losing your prize, but…" she said lightheartedly.

He smiled warmly. "The better prize is that you're giving me a chance."

"How did it happen that you became an assassin?"

David puffed up his cheeks, then blew the air out. "Pretty much every male Ivy is trained to be a soldier. Those who can prove their worth and ability to blend in over here are picked for extra training." He softly glided a hand across her calf. "It used to be a point of personal pride for me, that I was chosen for an assassin network."

It made her even more sick to her stomach. Her own brothers were soldiers, but not assassins…

David studied her face. "It's easy to paint the enemy as monsters or savages. But then I met you. Guess I'm not a very successful assassin."

Rachel grinned. "I'm still kinda grateful for that."

He held her hand again. "So, tell me something fun about your people that I don't already know."

"Um…" She searched his eyes, still nervous to divulge anything. "What do you already know about? Other than what we've already discussed?"

David shrugged. "How about the necklace you were wearing a while back? Do you guys use any other tools like that?"

"Wait, what?" She slowly leaned away. "I thought you guys didn't know about those. And you told me you just barely found out I was a Seeder because of my eyes."

He smiled. "Your eyes gave you away, but I remember when you started to wear a necklace, after you were sick." He took a deep breath. "What the necklace does is actually newer intel."

Frowning, she toyed with her necklace. How had the Ivies gotten that intel? How could it be anything other than torturing it out of someone?

"Hey." He met her gaze. "No pressure. I just think it's cool to learn more about each other." He pulled her in tight.

They sat on the floor for some time. She loved being in his arms.

"So, where do we go from here?" David asked.

That was the pressing question that made Rachel's heart sink. "I really don't know. I'm still not sure if I'll make it back. How long are you supposed to be here?"

"No idea; we don't always know ahead of time. Sometimes it's till we graduate, or our cover is blown, or we … complete a mission… It also depends on how things go back home. I imagine I'll be here until graduation. But I'd leave early, in a heartbeat, to follow you over there."

She glanced down at their hands, which fit perfectly together. "But let's say I don't make it over?"

He kissed her forehead. "I don't see why we can't plan for both options. Put your heart into your training to see if you can go back. But let's also enjoy every minute we have together, knowing we may only have a couple of months left."

She agreed to his proposal. Ultimately, even before his big reveal, that had been her plan—learn how to go home to the Green Lands, enjoy the last of her time with David, break up when she had to leave. His being an Ivy added stress in some ways, but in the end, the gut-wrenching decision of having to break up with him was now possibly off the table.

***

Rachel could breathe a sigh of relief. David's reveal as an Ivy was something new and exciting in some ways. He was showing a more vulnerable, sensitive side than she had ever seen in him. Their relationship grew stronger. Between practices and carving out some time for them and for Meg, Rachel was doing much better than she had in a while. Emotionally, things were finally on the mend.

Jeff was also really encouraging at her practices. When she was finally able to sustain a decent hover, she let David know. He beamed and took her out for ice cream to celebrate. They didn't talk too much about any green folk things, needing to be discreet, and promising to enjoy their time together in the human world. But they'd share a knowing wink now and then, and he'd text her words of encouragement.

Things had been going great for a solid month. Maybe, just maybe, she could pull this off.

***

Without warning, Rachel grew weak again. She was physically drained of energy, and it felt at times like there were barely any wisps of Seeder energy residing in her heart.

Nothing had been bothering her. She did everything she could to not start on a downslide. David was a huge support through it all. It was hard for her on nights he was unavailable because he had to keep up appearances with the other Ivies. Spring break was even more difficult because Meg's parents took her out of town to go visit extended family. Meg still wouldn't talk about acting weird earlier in the year, but she seemed to be more her normal self.

Rachel accompanied Jeff and Emma in training, watching Emma practice catching a breeze in preparation for her return to the Green Lands the next week. It was majestic, and beautiful, and inspiring. And also overwhelming to imagine Rachel could even come close to that by her rooting deadline. The next day, she met yet another sister who needed help training. Rachel wondered how few brothers she must have in the area if Jeff needed to divide his attention so much between them.

One particularly hard night, Rob invited Rachel into his home office. His beard was neatly trimmed, his hair parted and combed to the side. "I just wanted to chat before I leave." He traveled a lot for work. "I've noticed you're having a hard time. And I know I told your mom it would be good for you to keep dating David, but now I'm wondering if he's too much of a distraction."

"No! I'm not breaking up with him." She frowned. "He's really helpful, getting me through … whatever this is … that I'm having a hard time with in training."

Rob furrowed his brow. "You haven't told him anything, have you?"

"Of course not! David just helps me feel better. I promise, seeing him isn't distracting or harming my training, okay?"

He hesitantly nodded. "Alright. We just want what's best for you."

"I appreciate that." She hated lying to Rob. Though … technically, her stupid eyes were the ones that had given away her secret; she hadn't initially done any blabbing…

***

One Friday night, Rachel was lying in David's arms, back at his place, crying.

"I'm never going to get this down." She whimpered.

He held her tight, showering her with encouraging words and comforting kisses. "You will. I know you will."

After a few more minutes without talking, he spoke up. "I have an idea." He rubbed her arm. "How about you turn in early tonight? Don't expend any of your energy tonight or tomorrow. I have a theory. I'll pick you up at two."

***

Two in the afternoon rolled around the next day and Rachel met David out at his car. "What's this theory of yours?" She was desperate; she needed something to get her over this hurdle. He'd hinted at it being something their powers could possibly do together.

"Mmm, a surprise," he answered cheerfully. "I promise you'll like this one." He smiled. "We're going on a field trip."

They drove out of the city and toward the woods.

"While I like surprises, I'm not too fond of ever seeing that cabin again," she warned with a side glance. The grapefruit-scented air freshener in his car drove the memory home; that had been the smell in his car the night of their hot tub fiasco.

David shook his head. "No, we're putting that behind us. And we won't be going out that far."

They turned down a small dirt road and parked just out of sight of the highway.

Rachel raised her eyebrows quizzically.

He asked with a grin, "How would you like to see the Green Lands for yourself?"

96

Chapter 12

RACHEL'S EYES GREW WIDE. "What do you mean, see the Green Lands?"

David grabbed her hands in excitement. "I told you once that I could show you how we travel through rifts. But I think this could be more than a show-and-tell. I think I might be able to take you with me."

She searched his face. "How? How would that work?"

He squeezed her hands. "It's just a theory. But I was thinking about how you were able to heal my cut. That we could combine my method with a boost from your energy. I'm pretty sure the rift could let us both through."

Her jaw dropped. "You really think it would work? Is it dangerous?"

"I don't see how it could be. I've never heard of anyone getting hurt by a rift. Green folk use them all the time. We'd just use your energy to make it open more, for two of us to go through."

"What if we get stuck over there?" she asked. He sounded and appeared completely sincere, and even if he was, and it worked, she wasn't ready to say goodbye to her parents and Meg yet.

He shook his head. "Oh, no. That's never the problem. We draw strength from the realm on that side. It's at least twice as easy to get back."

She considered his proposal. He hadn't done anything to betray her trust, not even a hint of deception since that night at the cabin. "Where would we be arriving on the other side?"

He lifted his eyebrows. "Neutral territory. We'll be far from any dangerous action or prying eyes. When I was a kid, my sister and I stumbled upon the place—it's an old deserted area."

She smiled at his mention of having a sister. Like with his network, he hadn't discussed any family. It was endearing; she envisioned little David playing with a kid sister. "How about I watch you go through the first time, and then we try together the second time?"

"Sorry." He shook his head. "Even with your help, I wouldn't be able to make it through twice in one day. It's not that easy. That's one of the limitations of our powers."

Rachel took a deep breath, knowing she should be more patient. She studied his face, both nervous and excited. "Let's do it. What do I need to do?"

Their portal tree was selected, a nice healthy pine with a trunk a smidge wider than his hand from wrist to fingertip. With her permission, he held one of her hands, wrapping a short length of vine around her wrist to keep them together. Using his free wrist, he extended another short vine and ran it down the spine of the tree—it cracked under the pressure. A mesmerizing, shifting glow surrounded the crack.

"I think this is where I need you to focus your energy on my hand and vine. I'll go first and bring you through."

She closed her eyes and opened the energy pooled in her heart, willing it to head to her fingertips. He started to pull her through the rift. It felt like a warm hug, as easy to pass through as walking through a light breeze.

"Dammit! Ouch." She grimaced, clutching her wrist where his now rigid and sharp leaves were digging in.

"I'm so sorry! I didn't know that would happen. Are you alright?" He released her and tried to get a good look at the cuts as she healed her wrist.

"It's okay. No big deal." She smiled, showing him it was all better. There was barely any blood. She didn't have anything to clean it up with, so she cringed a bit while wiping it on her jeans, reminding herself to clean them properly when she got home.

He pulled her wrist up and kissed it. "I'm really sorry. I don't think there's a danger of that happening on the return."

"It's fine. Really."

With her injury tended to, she could seize the moment and survey the area. The air was somehow more refreshing, the energy that flowed through her invigorating. The woods even seemed greener. The forest floor was covered in pine needles and cones, leaves from other trees, mushrooms, and a scattering of vibrant wildflowers. While it was probably similar to some forests in the human world, this place felt … different.

"This is amazing!"

He smiled and pulled her in close. "You're here. It's where you belong. I'm ecstatic we could share this, just you and me."

He met her contented smile with a gentle caress of the lips. She pulled him in closer, holding the nape of his neck, daring herself to be more carefree than she had ever been with him since her bloom.

Taking a moment to catch her breath, she leaned back to search his eyes.

He bit his lip. "You're amazing. I could lose myself in those eyes."

She felt the signature warmth accompanying her Seeder change—glowing green eyes. He'd said exactly what she was hoping to hear, confirming that Seeders and Ivies really did stand a chance of working things out. "I love you," she confessed.

He pulled her back in, their lips and hearts becoming one in this special moment.

Neither Jeff nor David had exaggerated the invigorating feeling of being in this realm. It made perfect sense why the Ivies preferred their home realm over the human world. Rachel sensed the energy building in her heart: The energy of the Green Lands. The rush of being in an entirely different realm. Something made possible thanks to David.

Her heart beating a mile a minute, Rachel pulled back and gazed into his bright green eyes. "I think I'm ready," she whispered. "If you want to."

Grinning and still catching his breath, David slid his hands down to the button on her jeans. "Really?"

She smiled, wanting nothing more in this magical place, in this magical moment. "Yeah."

He looked her squarely in the eyes, his expression dropping. "No. Not yet." He removed his hands from her waistband.

Her brow furrowed in confusion.

"I don't want to take advantage of you. I don't want you to ever worry if that's why I brought you here," he said.

"You're not the one asking." She gently took his hands, moving them back to her jeans.

Without hesitation, he removed his hands again, tucking them into his pockets. "No. And after all this time, it's killing me. But I can wait longer." He tenderly kissed her forehead. "This is your first time feeling the energy here—I don't want it messing with your head and leaving you with any regrets." He then kissed her hand. "I have something else in mind. Follow me."

He motioned with a nod of the head in the direction they were going to walk. After several minutes of exploring, weaving through a sea of trees, passing a lovely spotted frog and a half dozen blue-and-yellow butterflies, they found a rundown log cabin.

"I hope not all cabins are tainted for you. This is an old abandoned one I found. We can sit down and relax. I think you'd benefit from energy-bathing. Or at least that's what I'm calling it." He smiled. "Like sunbathing, but relaxing and soaking up the energy here before heading back."

"Let's give it a go."

The cabin door barely opened, the wood swollen from years of neglect. David pulled dust covers off of a wooden table, chairs, and a couch. They sat, wrapped up in each other, and just took it all in. It gave Rachel a couple of carefree hours to think, ponder, and heal.

"Do you know where you'll be leaving the human world from?" he asked after a while.

Rachel drew a deep breath. "I'm not sure. I don't think I actually find out until it's time."

He offered a sweet smile. "It would be awesome to see you off."

She frowned. "You know that couldn't work. They don't exactly allow many humans into our circle. And definitely not Ivies." Shifting, she lay down with her head in his lap.

He studied her face. "I know. Maybe I could sneak there and hide or something."

She smiled softly. "I'd rather keep you out of harm's way." She gazed into his mesmerizing green eyes. "You're not lying about being part of this rebellion?"

He shook his head. "I wouldn't lie about that. I was initiated a few months ago. I'm trying to think of the right way to get you involved, assuming you really want to."

"Of course I want to!"

He grinned. "I knew you'd be up for it. I *definitely* look forward to you meeting people in the movement. I just need to make sure we do it in a safe way. That we have all our bases covered."

Rachel closed her eyes, breathing in the energy, the hope, the peace. "I could get used to this feeling," she mused.

He lovingly tickled her face with his fingertips. "Ditto." He blew out a long exhale. "But we should get you back. Without cell service over here, I don't want anyone to get worried."

Sighing, Rachel sat up. He was right.

They threw the dust covers back on the furniture and fought to close the door tight.

"So, you just pick any tree, right?" she asked.

"Not quite *any* tree—there's an ideal size, and some other details. But most of these would do. Would you like the honor of picking one?"

She tapped a pointer finger against her lips and glanced around. Squinting, she walked up to one. "Maybe this one, let me see." She grabbed his hand and backed him up against the tree, playfully stealing kisses.

Pulling back, she bit her lip. "Nope, not this one." Looking around, she spotted another target, leading him by the hand, and again pressed herself against him, gently nibbling on his earlobe and caressing his neck with her lips.

He chuckled. "Okay, down, girl."

She grinned mischievously. "Alright, fine. I think this one will do."

Sizing up the tree, he extended a vine to make the rift. Without any extra effort, they both walked through, David again going first and holding Rachel's hand. His leaves barely broke her skin on the return; it was a quick heal. She didn't draw any attention to it so he wouldn't feel bad.

The difference between the realms was palpable. The air was cooler, more stale on this side. But it was still home. Before getting in the car, Rachel stopped and studied the tree they had chosen to take them to the Green Lands earlier. The area around where the rift had opened was discolored, the bark peeling. Yellow needles were falling to the ground.

She frowned. "Does this always happen?"

"Yeah. That's just a byproduct. We can always plant more trees."

***

David had been right about what Rachel needed—it was perfect. Perhaps taking a quick trip to the Green Lands now and then for a refresher was what she could use to get her through training. Of course, she had to dial things down so Jeff and the others didn't notice she went from ten to a hundred overnight.

On a beautiful star-filled night, Rachel and David talked about their future, how their plans might unfold. She was going to try and master flying to return on her own, and then find a way to meet up in the Green Lands when he returned. He couldn't safely make it past the Seeder border walls to sneak in and visit, but she'd be capable of flying over the walls to rendezvous in the Neutral Woods. And if for some reason she couldn't quite get back to the Green Lands by catching a breeze, he'd be able to help her get there in time to root. He'd then guide her to Seeder territory. And unlike Seeders normally did, he could help her come back to the human world and visit her mom and Rob, and Meg, as often as she wanted. There weren't a whole lot of negatives.

Other than the lies. How would she explain it to her family? 'Oh, no big deal. I'm not up to snuff with flying, but I'm also not worried because I'm finding alternate transportation. What's that? Oh yeah, dating the enemy. No biggie.' That was the sole concern right now, so she was putting her all into breeze-catching practice to avoid the topic at all costs.

"And no one on your side suspects me yet?" she asked as they cuddled under the moonlight in her backyard. "What would happen to you if they found out you're helping me?"

"We've done a good job. I haven't spotted any hint of suspicion. And don't worry about me. I know what I'm doing. I can take care of myself." He kissed her on the head. "And you, too."

"You're sure I can't meet someone else from the rebellion? We'd be on the same side, right?"

He shook his head. "No, we can't risk that yet. I've only got one guy on this side with me for sure."

Rachel sighed wistfully. "My brother doesn't seem to think there even is a rebellion."

David sat up, visibly frustrated and concerned. "You've talked to him about it? That's not very smart! Where do you think he'll assume you're getting that information from?"

"I'm being smart about it. I'm not stupid." She scowled. "All I did was ask him if he thought anyone from your side would feel like we do, and want to help."

His muscles relaxed.

"Why can't you just meet with him?" she asked. "If my people knew about the cause, couldn't we work together?"

"Frankly," he spoke softly, "I'm not high enough in the network to make the introduction. And I'm guessing your brother isn't either. Things will work out; we just have to be careful as we approach your departure. And be patient, and ready when everything falls into place. Okay?"

She nodded, and he went back to holding her.

A star fell from the sky and Rachel made a silent wish. If things could just slow down, smooth out, go undetected—she could be perfectly happy and up to the challenge.

***

The countdown to rooting day continued. They estimated two and a half to three weeks. Prom was in two weeks. Rachel's mom asked her to sit down for a chat in the living room. Her short curly brown hair framed a concerned face.

"You know we're proud of you and love you, right?"

Rachel glanced at the family pictures on the wall. "Of course, Mom."

"You've made a lot of progress. Do you feel like you're going to be able to do it?" she asked, clearly worried.

"It's okay. I know I've been a little hot and cold. But I'll have it down. I'm not worried, and I don't want you guys to be either, okay?"

"Alright. If you're sure about it." Her mom frowned, evidently not sharing her daughter's cavalier attitude. "We've talked about pulling you from school for extra practice. Is that something you want to risk doing?"

"I'm fine with that, but can we wait until after prom? I really still want to go to prom before I leave, and then I'll give one hundred percent of my time to flight practice." Realizing she was being too casual, she tried to frown convincingly. "I really want to go to prom with David. And then I'll break up with him, and dedicate every last second I have to training."

Chapter 13

THE NEXT MORNING, RACHEL AND David were canoodling on their usual bench in front of the high school, waiting for Meg and Eric. She was ecstatic to share with David that they were definitely going to be able to attend prom together. They were midsmooch when Rachel spotted Meg approaching. Meg handed Rachel her signature drink and then handed one to David.

Rachel took a sip. "Where's Eric?"

Meg averted her gaze, but not before Rachel caught the turmoil in her eyes.

"He's not coming." She wouldn't make eye contact.

Rachel's face twisted with curiosity. "Is he sick?"

Meg pressed her lips together. "I'm going to go. We can talk later." She walked away at a brisk pace.

Rachel turned to David, who also wore a look of confusion.

"Go check on her," he said.

Meg ducked into a small bathroom. By the time Rachel went in, Meg was sitting on the tile floor, back to the wall, bawling into her knees.

Rachel crouched down next to her. "Hey, what's wrong?" She tried to move Meg's hair away from her face. "Are you and Eric fighting?"

Meg let out a whimper.

"Did you guys … break up?"

Meg's shoulders shook as she sobbed, nodding, still staring into her lap.

Rachel sat on the cold tile floor next to her and shooed away a pair of girls that opened the bathroom door.

"Do you want to talk about it?"

Meg shook her head.

The first bell rang. Meg lifted her head, leaning it against the wall. She sniffled, wiping off her face with the back of her hands. "You should go to class."

"To hell with class, I'm staying here with you," Rachel said, standing and grabbing some tissues for her.

Meg dabbed her face, still sniffling.

Rachel frowned. "What happened? Did he do something? I've never even seen you guys fight."

"I don't want to talk about it," Meg squeaked.

"Okay. No pressure." Rachel leaned shoulder to shoulder with her friend, just being there for her.

She was a little worried her mom and Rob might get a truancy call for her skipping first period. But why did it even matter? Twelve years in the public education system and her Seeder nature was stealing the validation of walking at graduation. She couldn't care less about her attendance record at this point.

Right now, Meg was the priority. It already killed Rachel that she had to lie to her best friend, and that she'd be abandoning her. Rachel had felt more optimistic lately, now that she knew she could return more often with David's help. But leaving Meg right now, with a broken heart, wasn't going to make any of this easier.

***

107

David asked about Meg at lunch. "So, what's that about? What happened?"

Rachel scowled at him, remembering his 'cover story' amongst the assassins, that he was still dating Rachel to get close to Meg. "Is that a recon question?"

He rolled his eyes. "I can't ask about a friend's well-being?"

"Yes. You can ask her directly. I'm not your spy."

He narrowed his eyes. "Why are you pissed at me? I didn't do anything. Grow up." He stood up from their table, taking his food and leaving her alone.

She was angry on her friend's behalf. And she knew it wasn't David's fault, and felt a little guilty about questioning his motives. Near the end of lunch, Rachel spotted Eric walking in a nearby hallway and chased him down.

"What happened?" she barked. "What did you do?"

Eric's face spelled contempt. "You're kidding me, right? She's the one that broke up with me and wouldn't even tell me why!"

***

Rachel was able to smooth things over with David pretty quickly. She tried to coax information out of Meg about the breakup, but Meg refused to talk about it. They had planned to double to prom; Meg now told her to go without her, that she wanted to stay home instead. It ate Rachel up. She felt like Meg and Eric had enjoyed a really healthy, happy relationship. And to end it so abruptly, and right before prom…

Rachel was starting to wonder more if maybe, perhaps … Meg was a Seeder, too? Breaking up abruptly before leaving was what Rachel was going to have to do, before she'd found out David's true identity. As much as she wanted to broach the topic, she knew it wasn't wise. If Meg was really a Seeder, she could look her up soon enough over in the Green Lands. If she wasn't, Rachel might give away too much by asking. She did love the idea, though, that Meg might even secretly be one of her sisters. Neither of the sisters she'd met thus far even went to their high school.

For now, Rachel planned to be there for Meg, and enjoy as much time as they could together, until Rachel had to leave. She hoped to visit often once things calmed down in the Green Lands and she and David could spend time together. Ivy rifting was so much more accessible compared to the grueling journey and limited capabilities of Seeders to go between the worlds. And by his description of things, the rebellion was growing rapidly; she was holding out hope that there could someday be peace.

With how busy things had been, Rachel hadn't gotten around to prom dress shopping yet. She'd kept putting it off, despite Meg's frequent prodding before her breakup with Eric. But it turned out to not be all horrible; Rachel was able to spend one-on-one time together with her mom, something she hadn't really been able to find time to do lately. Everything about Rachel's future was up in the air. She wasn't sure if she would ever marry, and if she did, if it would be her biological Seeder mom, or Samantha, that she would wedding dress shop with. But this felt like that special kind of moment, something equally sentimental.

Rob told her to spare no expense, his going-away gift to Rachel. She still felt guilty about spending too much, so she picked one that was midpriced. She settled on a wine-red dress with a rhinestone empire waist. It had thick straps and perfectly matching heels. Wanting to at least share something of prom with Meg, Rachel texted, offering to pay for Meg to get dolled up with her at the salon, just for fun. Meg declined.

***

An hour before David was set to pick her up, Rachel sat on her bed, a bundle of nerves. Her mom peeked in after softly knocking on the door.

"How are you doing? Need help zipping up?"

Rachel pulled her hair to the side. "Yeah. Thanks." She wrung her hands while her mom came around and zipped up the dress, then sat beside her.

"What's going through your mind?" her mom asked.

Rachel took a deep breath. *Too much.* "Just prom, and, you know, leaving…" Her room was untouched, as the cover story for her impending disappearance wouldn't require her parents to move.

Her mom frowned. "If you can't make it, or choose not to in the end … we wouldn't be disappointed."

Rachel bit her lip, catching an unexpected stray tear with her hand. "The moment this all started … it just felt like you guys wanted to ship me off."

Her mom threw her arms around Rachel. "No! Never. I'm sorry if it came across that way. I just…" She pulled back, wiping away a few tears of her own. "We wanted to be encouraging. We felt like you should embrace your heritage. And I promised your mother we'd get you back to your biological family." She wiped up a couple of Rachel's tears as well. "Who was right about waterproof mascara, huh?"

Rachel laughed and sniffled.

Her mom sighed. "I'm sure it's that much harder, saying goodbye to your friends and David. And it's probably the last thing you want to hear, but I know you'll make a lot of new friends over there."

Rachel frowned. As if giving up her human life wasn't bad enough, there had to be the lies. She didn't have the tiniest of hopes her family would understand her relationship with an Ivy. "Thanks. I'm nervous, but I've made my decision. Things will work out."

Her mom smiled. "They will. I'm sure of it. You've got a lot going for you." She grabbed Rachel's hand. "No matter what … you will always have a place in our home and hearts. Okay?"

Rachel's heart swelled as she realized how much she'd really miss her mom. The two of them had started this journey together, and had gotten through it all. "Thanks. I love you."

"Love you, too." Her mom got up to leave, stopping with her hand on the doorknob. "I understand David means a lot to you and it's prom night. But I'm assuming you guys aren't going to… 'Cause of the whole energy and emotion thing, right?"

Rachel buried her face in her hands. "Seriously?"

"Hey, I wouldn't be a half-decent parent if I didn't check. You've worked hard. Things are different now."

Rachel looked up, smiling. "We'll be fine. Thanks for watching out for me."

***

Rachel was pacing around with nerves, waiting for David to arrive. Par for the course, she had been taking a dip on the energy roller coaster lately—she needed this kind of pick-me-up.

He arrived, looking sharp in a tux, wearing the biggest smile she'd ever seen on him. He brought her a wrist corsage with a yellow rose, ivy used as the greenery. He winked and whispered how it represented them as a couple—the ivy being an obvious nod to him, the yellow rose representing her hair when she transformed.

David even rented a limo, sparing no expense, just like he'd gone all-out for their anniversary-gone-wrong. In part, she guessed it was his way of trying to make up for the botched event. They made sure the divider was up so they could talk in private and … get a little frisky without peeping eyes. But not so heated as to mess up her hair. They hadn't discussed it, but Rachel wondered if they'd revisit the topic of sex later that night. She wasn't nervous about that part of their relationship anymore.

"What restaurant are we going to?" she asked as they headed to the city limits.

"We're going to make a stop before dinner, if that's okay. I think you could use a little something magical to give you energy to dance the night away." He winked.

She didn't protest his idea. Rachel had considered asking him if he thought a second visit would do her some good, give her that burst of energy to really put her all into the last days of training before heading out. She genuinely didn't think she would be able to make the flight without it in her current state.

"I've already paid the driver to drop us off and come back a half hour later, so we won't be too late to everything else tonight." He smiled.

He always had a plan.

Her mind wandered to worries on the long drive. "What are we going to do if I realize last minute I can't make the flight?"

He squeezed her hand reassuringly. "First of all, you'll make it just fine. But if, for some reason, you realize you're not ready, then hold off. I think it would be a good idea to have a letter ready. That way I can get you home in time before you root here, and they won't be worried about you. That way you can let them know you found a way to the Green Lands and you'll be in touch."

"Yeah, that's a good idea." She rubbed one of her temples. "I don't know why I didn't think of that. My brain is all muddled."

He frowned. "You've got a lot on your mind. And I know with us officially 'breaking up' tomorrow, even if it's only for show—I'm going to be sad I can't be there with you." He gave her a half-smile. "Just remember I'm a text away. I'll be waiting to hear from you."

"Thank you." She glanced down at her fresh manicure. "What are we going to do to meet up on the other side?"

"Ah, yes." He smiled wide. "Part of the surprise tonight… I have a map over there. I'm going to show you where we have our meetups and I can briefly go over my plans to get in touch, assuming you catch a breeze home."

Things were starting to line up like they ought to. Except for Meg. "Do you think Meg could keep it a secret if I told her about being a Seeder? I've kinda been thinking about it lately." Leaving Meg with a broken heart, and so emotionally distant, was still killing Rachel.

"You really haven't told her, huh?"

Rachel shook her head. "I've been following the rules. Well," she grinned, "minus the 'dating an assassin' part."

He shared her smile.

"But no. Meg doesn't know yet. Whether or not you can help me visit more than the once-a-year that Seeders normally can, I feel like she deserves to know."

Looking down pensively, David shrugged. "I don't see why not. If you think she can keep a secret."

Rachel's tension about leaving eased. "Yeah. I think I will. Maybe the night before I leave."

He kissed her on the forehead as the limo pulled to a stop. They got out and waved the limo on.

"He has *seriously* got to be wondering what the heck we're doing out here," she said.

"I don't know about that. I'd think it's obvious I want a romantic stroll with the most beautiful girl in school." He pulled her in close, nuzzling her neck.

She giggled, until she realized he was giving her a hickey. "Seriously, David? Before prom?" She punched him lightly in the shoulder and moved her hand up to heal it.

He flashed an apologetic pouty face. "Sorry." He chuckled. "I'll admit I'm spoiled having a girl who can clean that sort of thing up so quickly."

She rolled her eyes. "I'm already drained, remember? And you need my help to get us both through, right?"

He sighed. "Yes. I'm sorry. That really was stupid. Speaking of, I know it hurt you last time. I hope it doesn't this time, but are you going to be okay if it does?"

She nodded confidently. "I can handle it. Especially once I get to the other side."

They picked a tree and followed the same procedure as the first time; he wrapped a vine around her wrist that didn't have the corsage.

"Dang it! Yeah, that definitely hurt worse this time!" She was bleeding a decent amount, with deeper gashes than on the previous visit.

"Shoot! Well, we'll figure it out eventually. Sorry." He pulled out a tissue. "I brought this just in case." He wiped up the blood before she healed it.

She calmed again with the pain now gone. "No harm, no foul." She inhaled deeply, the wonderful charm of this realm rushing into every cell of her body. With the time difference, it was already much darker in the Green Lands than back home in the human world. A few fireflies danced in the sky nearby.

Holding her hands, David looked lovingly into her eyes. "I can never thank you enough for giving me a chance, knowing who I am. I know not everyone would do that."

She smiled. "You're worth it. I love you."

He gave her a peck on the lips and then reached into his pocket. "Now, to add to the surprise, I want you to see what I've done with the dusty old place on a recent visit." He held up a blindfold.

She raised her eyebrows in curiosity.

He tilted his head. "All your training leaves me with some free time. I wanted to plan something as special as you are."

She bit her lip, and he covered her eyes, guiding her through the woods by the hand. Pine cones crunched under her feet along the way. He let her hand go for a moment while he yanked the tight wooden door open, then brought her inside. David moved one of his hands to her waist, standing close behind her. He gently kissed her neck.

And then it happened again. David's hand over her mouth, his other arm restraining her. But this time there were *several* vines wrapping her arms and legs. David released her from his grip and stepped away, but the vines only tightened.

"What the hell are you doing!" she screamed, struggling against the restraints, still unable to see anything. "David, please! Don't do this!"

"Get her out of here. But don't hurt her more than you have to," David's voice ordered coolly.

"Yes, Your Highness," came a female voice she didn't recognize.

New vines wrapped around Rachel's throat, the leaves sinking into her flesh. Searing pain emanated from the leaves as she fought for air. Weakness and nausea crippled her. She would have fallen to the floor had the vines around her not intentionally guided her down. With her sight still obscured by the blindfold, her mind joined in the darkness, her body unconscious on the floor.

Chapter 14

SAFF TRIED NOT TO CRY as she walked home from work. She was beyond worn down. They'd announced just before classes ended for the day that her village had lost several people to the war the night before. She recognized two of the names this time. While grateful neither victim belonged to her immediate family, it gutted her nonetheless. She wished there was more she could do. All the Ivies ever did was murder—here at Seeder borders, and back in the human world, as she'd so personally experienced, thanks to their assassin networks.

She kicked a stone in the lane, barely missing someone. "Sorry." She frowned. This path hadn't always been this busy, but *all* lanes in her village were busy at this point. Before this newest surge in the war, the western villages had done their part in keeping the border safe through their own temple wells, depositing energy. They'd also sent regular volunteers over for patrol duty. But more and more help was needed, and the burden of keeping their lands safe weighed too heavily on the border villages, like Saff's home, South Fortinda. Full-time troops from the inner villages were now stationed in the border communities. While they were needed assistance, it strained resources. Fields where Seeder boys used to play were now filled with soldiers' tents. Housing was full. Food supplies taxed. The walls that had protected them for the last century were failing, no longer enough.

Saff entered their cottage only to find a letter on the kitchen table. It was a note from Devin asking her to meet him at her parents' house. She hadn't been able to spend much time visiting family lately anyway, so she was more than willing to walk over, though afraid of what might be prompting the visit.

Her fear of impending bad news was quickly realized after she entered the house. The kitchen had food laid out everywhere, cooking being one of her Seeder mother, Murial's, coping mechanisms. The major players in their family Seeder network gathered around the table. Her Seeder father, Thod—who was looking increasingly gaunt from the stress; Devin's dad, Simon; her brother, Ben; and a couple of other brothers. Their expressions were grim. Devin sat with them, glancing over his shoulder when the door opened.

"What happened?" she demanded. "What's wrong?!"

Devin jumped up from his seat and hugged her. "The family's okay."

She was still braced for more bad news when he had her sit down.

"They got another one, Saff."

She twisted her face, trying to hold back tears. "How is this happening? How can we be letting down our girls so much?"

This was the sixth known kidnapping of a bloomed Seeder from the human world in the last year. Six wasn't really a huge number—that many female Seeders or more died in the human world in car accidents each year. But these weren't accidents. No bodies had been found, so they weren't typical assassinations, either. A disturbing trend had been recognized. With each girl's disappearance, the Ivy attack grew stronger. These menacing gigantic vines were crossing the Neutral Woods and ripping through the Seeders' protective walls, forcing more hand-to-hand combat. Saff's heart ached for the girl and her family, and the hopelessness of knowing things were only going to get worse.

Devin swallowed hard. It was obvious by his expression he wasn't done delivering the intel. "She's one of ours. She's from home." He frowned, defeated.

"What do you mean? From our village? Or do you mean my hometown back on the human side?"

He wouldn't look her in the eyes. "Yes. Both."

She bit the insides of her cheeks, wringing her hands, trying in vain to hold back the tears.

While rubbing her back, he glanced at the men seated at the table. "We're going to take care of it. Her dad is investigating now, and … my dad and I are going to see what we can do on that side of things."

She sniffled. "I'm coming with you."

Devin shook his head, and Simon spoke up behind her. "We'll be okay. We don't need you to come."

"I'm going, Simon!" she snapped. Her outburst triggered looks of shock from everyone in the room. She had a great relationship with her in-laws and had never once raised her voice at either of them.

Devin pressed his lips together, surveying the room. "Let's go for a walk." He took her hand, leading her outside.

Just a couple of houses down the dirt lane, he dared to try to talk her out of her decision.

"I don't even know that *our* going will make a difference. It's not worth the risk to have you gone. You're needed here. And you know you don't have it in you to make it all the way there and back."

She dropped his hand and crossed her arms. "I don't need your permission."

He huffed. "No, but I think as your husband you'd at least care what I have to say."

"Don't talk to me like that; I'm not a child," she snapped back.

"Then don't act like one, Saff," he scolded. "I knew you'd do this."

She stopped walking and turned to face him, desperation taking over. "I *need* to do something different. I can only do so much here, and I'm losing it! Maybe I just need to give that poor girl's mom a hug. Just go for a day or two. Let my parents know I'm okay—they have to be worried that I haven't contacted them; it's so late in the season." Her voice betrayed her. "Please, just let me join you. I can't live like this, without hope. I want to try."

He drew a deep breath, moving a hand up to gently caress her cheek. "I'll talk to my dad. But you're going to have to rest up for an entire day, at minimum, to regain your strength. And then two days max over there. We can't be selfish with how much you're needed here."

She nodded. "Yes, I can do that."

***

The next day, Ben dropped by their cottage while Devin was at work.

"The door's open."

He entered and glanced at Saff in disapproval. "I don't think doing chores is considered 'resting up' in the strictest of meanings."

She kept drying dishes. "I'm not at work and I'm not at the temple. But you can't keep me from doing everything. I feel calmer with a clean house."

He hummed playfully. "Then by all means, want to go clean up my place, too?"

She threw a dish towel at him, and he caught it.

They sat on the couch to chat.

"Are you here to talk me out of going?" she asked, tucking her legs up underneath her.

He laughed. "You? I thought we learned a long time ago that you never listen to what I say."

She pursed her lips, remembering when he was her trainer just a few short years ago and she'd defied his orders time and time again.

He sighed. "Actually, Heather's kind of jealous you're going."

Saff raised her eyebrows. "Get me her parents' phone number. I'll call them when I'm over there; I'll let them know she's okay."

"While I'm sure she'll appreciate that, it's not what I meant. You know we got you home by the skin of our teeth, right? Back when our people had to start sending our daughters over to survive, we realized right away that we needed to find a way to temper the changes."

"The jade charms." She reached up, feeling her own.

He nodded. "Yeah, the charms. Not only is the change more violent over there, they just didn't have the same amount of time to learn everything, with the accelerated rooting. The fact that you learned so quickly and made it home in time—I really don't think you give yourself enough credit for the power you possess."

She blushed. "I wish I could say it made more of a difference now, with everything going on."

He pointed at her. "You make a difference. Stop selling yourself short."

"Thanks." She rested a hand on his shoulder. "You always were my favorite brother that left his toothpaste in the bathroom sink." She smiled.

"Yeah, well, you're still my favorite sister that made me want to strangle her every other week as a teenager." He jutted out his chin sarcastically.

She laughed.

"What I wanted to tell you is that I think you have a lot of opportunity to do some good over there. Even if it's Devin and Simon doing the tracking and investigating, you could do even more good by giving some personal lessons to Rachel's sisters. Make sure to set it up as soon as you get there. They need a strong role model right now."

"Yeah, I'll absolutely do that." She loved Ben that much more for giving her a hint of hope, a purpose amidst all that was happening around them.

"I'm glad to hear it." He stood, offering her a hug.

Saff readily accepted it. "You know, I promised you a long time ago that I'd try to make up for the whole almost-getting-you-killed thing. I'm going to do everything I can to help with this war, so we can move on and you guys can stop pushing back the wedding."

He squeezed her tighter. "You're the best. It'll happen."

She reminded him as he left the cottage, "Make sure to get me Heather's parents' phone number. And stay safe. Love you, Ben."

"Love you too, little sis."

She smiled again as he closed the door. 'Little sis'—all of her brothers called her that. Sure, they were technically all the same age, and none of the twelve boys had even sprouted until two weeks after the girls, but she'd earned that title in their family as the last to return home. At times, it was annoying. But mostly, it was endearing.

She gazed at the main focal point of the living room, sitting back down on the sofa. Hanging on the wall was a large painting that her Seeder mom, Murial, had painted for Saff and Devin—a portrait of their wedding day. Heather had giddily talked about how much she was looking forward to theirs someday, back when they first got engaged. But no one was giddy right now. Seeder weddings continued, but in border villages like theirs, they could maybe manage the equivalent of a rushed courthouse wedding, at best.

Saff took a deep breath, standing up and getting back to cleaning the kitchen. She'd meant what she'd told Ben. She was going to do everything in her power so they could have a proper wedding, sooner rather than later. Every bride and groom deserved a special day. And *everyone* deserved to feel safe in their own home.

Chapter 15

RACHEL WOKE TO THE QUIET clink of glass against metal and a muted rustling sound. Her body was half-numb. Her head screamed, and her eyes were puffy, almost swollen shut. She pried her eyelids open to check her surroundings. A brunette woman in her early to midtwenties tidied up a tray across the room. She wore a simple long tan dress with a dark belt. The room itself … was breathtakingly ornate. The walls had striped wainscoting, and above that, nature-themed murals.

Rachel shifted her body to be more comfortable, unintentionally alerting the woman to her conscious state when the clang of handcuffs rattled against the metal headboard of the bed she was on. The woman opened the door and poked her head out.

"Alert Prince Soren. She's awake."

A male's voice responded, "Yes, ma'am."

Closing the door, the woman turned to face Rachel, frowning. "You must be feeling miserable. I'm so sorry."

"Where am I? What happened?" Rachel asked. She glanced back up at the ceiling, more closely scrutinizing the painted mural above her. Her stomach dropped—a plethora of ivy vines were featured in the design.

The woman wore a forced smile. "You're at the palace. You'll have more answers soon enough. Just focus on healing yourself and building up your strength, okay?"

Rachel looked down—she was still in her prom dress; one of her ankles was strapped to the railing at the end of the bed with vines. Her immobilized foot had an IV in it. She glanced at her hands, both secured to the headboard with handcuffs. Her arms had faint bruising where vines had wrapped tight during the attack.

"How long have I been here?" she asked.

The woman still stood across the room, holding her hands casually in front of her. "Two days."

Rachel's heart sank. Everyone back home had to be panicked. She imagined her mom crying, Rob trying to comfort her. Meg pacing the floor with Eric. Wait, no Eric. *Poor Meg.* And… Well, David certainly didn't seem like he would be at home or worried about her in the slightest.

The door opened, and the devil himself walked in. The woman nervously curtsied. Gone was the prom tuxedo; he now wore tailored black slacks and a long-sleeved silky black button-up shirt. The only color in his ensemble was a green ombre stripe around one of his upper sleeves and grass-green decorative stitching around the hem.

The door closed behind him, and he gave Rachel a sympathetic frown. "Gosh, look at you." He walked to her side and sat next to her on the bed. "How are you doing? It looks like they were a little rough on you." Reaching up, he gingerly moved a wisp of bangs from her face, and she jerked her head away.

"It's okay. I know I betrayed your trust … again." He looked her over. "And the dress got torn. That's probably not easy to fix, is it?"

She didn't say a word, breathing slowly, trying to figure out his game.

"You couldn't even clean her up?" he barked over his shoulder, causing both the woman in tan and Rachel to flinch. "Bring me a wet cloth."

The woman scurried to the tray she'd been tidying when Rachel woke up, and dipped a white washcloth into a bowl of water before wringing it out. She handed it to David with a bow, avoiding eye contact with him, but catching Rachel's eyes for just a moment.

He was aiming the cloth at Rachel's neck when she tried to dodge him again. "Really? What am I going to do to hurt you with a wet cloth?"

She sat tight-lipped, glaring and remaining silent.

He raised his eyebrows and spoke softly. "Just let me clean it up, okay?"

As he moved his hand again, she stayed still. Her body involuntarily shuddered at his touch, but calmed more as he wiped around her neck. Luckily, it didn't sting anymore, but there was a decent amount of blood staining the rag when he pulled it back. Folding it over revealed a clean spot, and he finished scrubbing off the dried blood where sharpened leaves had pierced her in the ambush.

Putting a hand under her chin, he caressed her cheek while gazing into her eyes. "There you go. That's my girl."

Rachel clenched her teeth. She was not now, nor would she ever again be, *his* girl.

"Was that so hard?" he snapped at the woman again.

She rushed over, bowing and taking the soiled cloth from his hands, giving him a new one to wipe his hands clean. "My apologies, Your Highness."

He threw the second cloth at the woman after he was done with it. David looked Rachel over again. "I bet you'd like… Yeah, let's…" He snapped his fingers at the woman. "A glass of water for her, and take out the IV." He smiled at Rachel. "I bet you'll like that."

The woman brought the water over and then went to Rachel's immobilized leg, removing the needle.

With her hands still secured above her head, Rachel had to rely on David to tip the glass up to her lips. She only realized how parched she really was once she started to guzzle it down.

He took the empty glass and got up, refilling it for her. "I hope you can understand it had to be done this way. We couldn't risk you not coming." He returned to the bed and sat down again. "Come on. You're perfectly capable of holding a conversation. I'm sure you have something you want to say."

She squinted at him in loathing. "So this is who you really are? A psychotic, self-important jackass?"

He again surprised her as his hand shot to her face, painfully grasping her jaw. He stared into her eyes. "I am a *prince*. And I deserve more respect than that from a stupid—peasant—weed." He enunciated each word. His fingers dug into her skin painfully, only releasing when her eyes teared up.

He inhaled deeply, then exhaled slowly. "Plus, there's a difference between psychotic, psychopathic, and sociopathic. Your human public education system is *grossly* insufficient."

His eyes moved from her face down to her restrained ankle. "Nurse, when did you last check her progress?"

"This morning, Your Highness."

"Show me."

The woman approached Rachel's immobile foot, holding a short tool with a rounded metal tip. She looked Rachel in the eyes apologetically before putting it against the arch of her foot and clicking a button.

The instant surge of pain caused Rachel to scream and writhe. David set the glass of water down and casually leaned over, studying her ankles, which were now exposing her Seeder roots.

"Okay, that's enough," he said. "Any time now," he reassuringly reported to Rachel while rubbing her calf, as if to comfort her or wipe away the pain from the stun gun. "And then, we can get you out of this room. That'll be a refreshing change of scenery!"

She scowled, still shaking, her breath and heartbeat racing. "I prefer the scenery back home. Please, just let me go." Her voice squeaked.

He pursed his lips. "Oh, that's cute. No. Sorry. We can't do that. That would mean a lot of wasted time. And my time is worth a lot." He adjusted his seat on the bed. "You should consider yourself extremely lucky. How many girls get to date a prince?"

She bit her tongue, wanting to say a few choice words, but not wanting him to hurt her again.

He looked her over with a lusty smile. "I really should have waited until *after* prom night. Then again, only one person stood between me and getting what I wanted out of you. And they're not here right now." He started to slide his hand up her leg, under her dress.

She struggled as much as she could to get his filthy hand off of her, but she wasn't able to move much. He tightened his grip.

"I should be repulsed by you." He stared into her eyes with a cold gaze. "Sleeping with a human was boring. But a Seeder… That's gotta be interesting. Why don't we check that box?"

His hand was halfway up her thigh.

"Your Highness…" the nurse interrupted.

His entire countenance changed to livid at the interruption, but he stopped moving his hand. "Get out!"

Rachel's breathing intensified as she focused on the nurse. Begging, pleading with her eyes for her to stay, to help.

The woman frowned and looked down. "Your Highness, your uncle…"

His eyes narrowed. "Did I stutter?"

The door swung open, catching everyone off guard. "Your Highness, we have an update."

David huffed and pulled his hand away, then straightened the hemline of Rachel's dress. He shook his head. "It's never the right time for us, is it?" He stood and glanced down at her. "It's okay. I always knew I'd get you in bed." He winked and gestured at the bed with open palms, smiling in grotesque mockery of her current place of captivity.

Before leaving the room, he turned to the nurse. "Next time you interrupt me or disobey one of my orders, you're going to *wish* you were in her position."

The woman kept her eyes trained on the floor. "My apologies, Your Highness."

He scowled. "Keep her hydrated and send for me once the rooting is completed."

Rachel was determined to have the last word as the door was shutting. "GO TO HELL!" she screamed at the top of her lungs.

The door closed without any hesitation at her outburst.

The nurse glanced at the door nervously before walking over to Rachel. "Let me help you drink some more. I promise you—you'll need everything you have, to heal up."

After draining another glass, Rachel met the woman's hazel eyes. "Thank you. What's your name?"

"Olivia. And they said your name is Rachel?"

She nodded.

"I'm so sorry, Rachel," Olivia whispered.

"Thanks."

Olivia returned to her position, holding her hands in front of her, standing in the corner of the room. After a couple of hours, she approached Rachel with another glass of water. She looked over her shoulder at the door before whispering, "Don't fight in here. Once they move you to the next phase, that's when you need to resist." She then stood and went back to her position in the room. An hour later, another nurse took her place, her expressions decidedly much less compassionate than Olivia's.

Chapter 16

RACHEL LEARNED QUICKLY OVER THE next couple of days to voluntarily reveal her Seeder roots when she saw the nurses approaching with the stun gun. They wouldn't even bother to ask her to do it; they would just force the transformation. Though she would get no warning when she had fallen asleep and they decided to prod her, sending her into a state of panic and agony, the high voltage surging through her body.

She had no other visitors over that time. Granted, after David's last visit, she wasn't that keen on having any. Rachel knew for certain she was still in the Green Lands—the energy helped her heal, and she could feel it coursing through her just as much as the first time David had brought her through a rift. She was still unsure as to what his plan was; the nurses were tight-lipped, and she was sad to not see Olivia report for duty.

Rachel didn't need a nurse to confirm when her rooting had finalized. She could feel the pull to this realm. Like every Seeder teenage girl, her legs—when transformed—were covered in a web of nearly-flesh-colored roots. The pattern was as unique to each Seeder as their fingerprints. At the onset of her bloom, they'd begun at her hips, and with each passing day, had inched down her legs. Once they reached her ankles and wrapped around, the rooting was complete—she was forever tied to the realm she was currently located in. Having rooted in the Green Lands, Rachel experienced a surge in her capacity to wield energy. It also meant she could never call the human world home again.

It was more emotional for her than she had expected it to be. It was a disgraceful and isolated way of leaving behind the world and family she loved. She didn't have a single hope anyone would come for her after the way she'd disappeared into thin air.

Nonetheless, a nurse checked and confirmed her rooting, and to Rachel's dismay, that meant she would be seeing David again.

"As lovely as ever!" He beamed upon entering the room. He confirmed the rooting for himself and ordered guards to escort her out. They first restrained her with vines, then unlocked the handcuffs and sliced off the vines restraining her foot. "Not even weed blades can cut through metal cuffs." He smiled again.

They led her through a series of hallways and into a small room. The only furniture in the room was a tall chair. Like the hallways in the palace, this room was completely built out of marbled stone. Despite her attempts to avoid their demands, she was easily overpowered. Guards strapped her into the chair with vines, and a nurse appeared. Rachel kept wondering what Olivia had meant about struggling in the 'next phase.' Maybe she should have tried to escape while being transferred between rooms? There had been far too many guards for her to have any hope.

"Just enough to numb for now," David instructed. "I want her lucid enough to chat once it's done."

The nurse bowed and approached, extending a vine and wrapping it around one of Rachel's wrists. Rachel winced as the leaf blades dug in, but quickly succumbed to a haze that clouded her mind, weakening her. She remembered blinking a lot, and her head bobbing, and the shuffling of feet, something about 'Your Majesty.' David's voice said 'Mother.' And then Rachel was aware of a new set of razor-sharp vines digging into her flesh. The searing sensation lasted just a moment before a new frightening horror took center stage.

It was as if someone had opened a black hole in the center of her heart. Whatever they were doing, it was siphoning off her Seeder energy. Soon thereafter, there was more shuffling of feet, mumbling, and the door clicked closed.

It could have been minutes or hours for all Rachel knew, but her clarity of mind returned as the pain of the vines puncturing her skin grew. She opened her eyes. David stood in front of her, leaning back against the wall, his arms crossed.

"And she's back! Modern human medicine is so overrated when you can go with something as natural as our poison, right?" He gave her a smile teeming with genuine pride. "And it's a shame you didn't get to properly meet my mother." He shrugged. "I mean, not that she cares to meet someone like you, but it would have been a great honor for you if you hadn't been drugged up."

He silently nodded, as if waiting for Rachel to say something. "Okay, so this isn't just going to be a one-way conversation. But to start it off, I would like to apologize for my rudeness the other day. I don't think I properly introduced myself. The name is Soren; I believe I mentioned the 'Prince' part. Commoner Ivies, or even your Seeder brothers, like Jeff—"

Her eyes grew wide at hearing Jeff's name. It probably hadn't been that hard to guess, given their relationship back home, but she had never betrayed him.

"Well, they can go with boring names like that," David continued. "Royalty needs a little more anonymity when we're in the field, if you know what I mean.

"Anyway, I asked myself if I went over the line when I brought you here earlier than necessary, depriving you of prom. It was kind of poetic, but maybe not in the best of taste. I'm not a savage, after all. So, I've decided to let you ask me any five questions you'd like.

I'm sure this is all very confusing for you." He lifted his eyebrows in anticipation.

She frowned. "What are you doing to me? Why am I here?"

"That's two questions." He raised a finger. "Just to be clear, I'm counting. We are … using your innate abilities as … green energy." He busted out laughing, slapping his leg. "Come on. Don't you get it? I don't know why I didn't think of that one earlier. But, you know, back in the human world, it's considered 'green' if it's natural. We're in the Green Lands, we draw energy from nature … so … you are *literally* green energy."

He rolled his eyes in disappointment. "You were always boring and whiny when you were drugged. Anyway… Oh yeah. Why are you here? Because, good news for you, you're not nearly as much of a pathetic weakling as you thought. Just like any other weed girl out there, you're a D battery to our double- or triple-A. It's doing *astonishing* things for our War Vines, which just so happen to be *shredding* up your borders as we speak."

"But no one can take our energy without our permission," she shot back.

He squinted at her. "Now, that was not a question. But I feel like you want a response. Do you? Okay, yeah, we're deducting a question for that. Things are rarely as cut-and-dried as people make them out to be. Can I just walk up, touch your hand," he did just that, stroking her hand, "and use your energy? No. Can I access it through enough contact with your blood?" He smiled. "Apparently, that's a yes."

She remembered both times he'd brought her through a rift, cutting her wrists in the process and acting apologetic about it. She was sick to her stomach—that she had ever believed him, that she'd given him the chance to do this to her, that her pain was causing suffering to her own people.

"That leaves you with two more."

Rachel hadn't prepared for a Q&A session, and doubted he'd be completely forthcoming, anyway. She had held out the tiniest of hope that things weren't as bad as they seemed—but they were. Her heart hollow from the pull of the War Vines, she had nothing left. "Did you ever even care about me at all?"

"Yeah, of course," he professed adamantly, before pausing. "Well, wait. I guess that depends on your definition. I think we know how much I appreciated the physical attention you gave me over the years. And you're as pretty as any human," he waved his hand around, "as long as you don't go all green-eyed."

She fought the urge to vomit.

"But when it comes down to it, I think the cat *always* enjoys hunting the mouse and playing with it a little bit." He grinned without an ounce of remorse.

She closed her eyes, willing herself to not cry. Not that she cared one iota about his opinion anymore, but it hurt nonetheless.

"Come on. Don't cry on me. What did you really expect me to say?" After no response, he spoke again. "One last question, then I've got to be on my way."

"Have you ever been honest with me about *anything?*"

"That is a fair question." He squinted at the ceiling, as if searching his memories. "There were tons of technicalities, like some of my favorite foods, but I sense you don't mean that. Oh, I know. I *do* want to end this war, just maybe not the way I was letting on. And I *was* honest about there being a group of dissenter scum out there. But they're a tiny nuisance that'll be taken care of soon enough."

He took a deep breath. "There, I feel better. It's kind of nice to just get it all out there, isn't it? Here's a bonus one to cheer you up. I lied when I said you gave yourself away as a Seeder. We had you pegged *way* before that." He smirked. "But I won't spoil the fun— someone else will share that story with you at another time."

He crouched down in front of her. "Now, I have one question I need you to answer for me. Just one. I feel like that's a fair exchange for what I just gave you." He surveyed Rachel's face. "Do you know where Meg is?"

Rachel's heart sank. He really *was* after Meg. Just like his lie about the rebellion, he had put a spin on that truth to lure Rachel in. While he'd chastised her for being irrational about his inquiry back home, she was now glad she'd stuck to her guns and hadn't told him anything about Meg and Eric's breakup—in case it somehow mattered. Meg *had* to be one of her sisters, right? Another Seeder girl to strap in a chair just like this.

"So?" he asked.

Rachel scowled. "How would I know? I don't know where anyone is, outside of this room."

He closed one eye skeptically. "You're sure? Girls talk. Maybe something she said was inconsequential to you, but it means something to me."

"Even if I knew, why would I tell you?"

He gently placed his hands on her knees. "Hmm. I could give you some incentive. How about a full night's sleep? You're going to miss those."

She glared and kept her mouth shut. All she knew about Meg was that she'd been distant since the breakup. Rachel didn't have anything useful, and even if she did, there was nothing he could do to coax it out of her.

"Well, if you remember anything or get to the point that you feel like you'd rather die than stay here, let a guard or nurse know you're ready to talk, okay?"

He stood. "You know, one last offer." He wore a menacing smile. "None of the other girls have gotten these generous options. But I'd even be willing to let you have an *entire* day out of this chair, if you wanted to spend it with me in my chambers."

"You're sick. Screw you!"

"Well…"

"Piss off."

He let out a frustrated sigh. "Fine. But it's a limited-time offer, because I don't want you when you're all pathetic and useless. You still have some spunk right now."

He approached the side of her chair, moving her hair to one side. Rachel tried to lean away from him, but she barely had any mobility. He gently caressed her neck and then kissed her on the lips. Despite her refusing to kiss back, he forced his tongue into her mouth.

"Come on, once for old times' sake," he begged, pulling back. "A nice goodbye. Unless you'd prefer something else." His eyes explored her body as he smiled.

As her chest rose and fell with rapid breaths, she dreaded his advances again. "I'll kiss you."

He took great pleasure at her acceptance, moaning and playfully pressing his lips against hers, ever so gently, his hands supporting her head.

Rachel clamped down on his lower lip. His warm, metallic blood pooled in her mouth. He grunted in pain, and a leaf tip burrowed into her forehead. When the searing pain was too much, she finally released his lip with a bloodcurdling scream.

"You bitch!" he belted while backing up.

She spat his own blood at him as he touched his lip. Blood trickled down her face, stinging as some of it reached her eye.

"Shit, Rachel! What am I supposed to tell my fiancée?" He kept touching his lip to see how badly it was bleeding.

Her voice trembled through her clenched teeth. "Don't ever touch me again!"

He glared at her. "Next time I visit, you'll be plenty medicated. It would be a pity to die a virgin. We'll see how you feel about things then."

He turned his head. "Take care of this for me and send someone back to stitch her up. No numbing tonight," he ordered a nurse who had apparently been in a corner of the room for the entire duration of their exchange.

"Yes, Your Highness. Follow me, please."

Leaving with the woman, he slammed the door on his way out. Another nurse appeared shortly after his departure and stitched up

Rachel's forehead without an ounce of mercy or compassion. Other than sparing a few words to scold Rachel for flinching, the nurse said nothing. Rachel's head throbbed with each beat of her heart for the rest of the night. She became increasingly painfully aware of each and every leaf puncturing her arms, sitting in agony for hours, all alone.

Chapter 17

BY THE TIME SAFF, DEVIN, and Simon arrived in the human world, Rachel and David had been missing for over a week. Saff wasn't really sure what to expect—this type of investigation wasn't something any of them had done before. They interviewed Samantha and Rob, then split up, each taking on specific assignments, hoping to get to the bottom of the situation.

While Seeders often made friends in high places for the purposes of faked identities and deaths, and other disappearance cover stories, they'd still needed to call the local human authorities. Someone was bound to report the teens missing, and they wouldn't want suspicion to fall on Samantha and Rob. The trail died when the police found the known address for David now vacant. After an anonymous tip came in, they discovered David's studio apartment, complete with a letter that the two had run off together. Being seventeen or older, neither of them faced legal repercussions as runaways. Which was all well and good, as it meant the human authorities were keeping their noses out anyway, the Seeders decided.

Samantha and Rob refused to believe Rachel would run away like that—no warning, not taking anything. It didn't make any sense.

Given her vulnerable situation as a Seeder and David's apparent lack of parents, they knew something more disturbing had happened. He'd been vetted years ago, as had his parents. But Seeders knew Ivies crafted just as good of covers as Seeder family networks did.

Saff couldn't help but feel like they were being watched. She tried to shake away her anxieties, tried to shake away the memories of Ivy attacks on her and her family a few years prior in the human world. In this same town.

Jeff had caught a breeze after a couple of days without any word, leaving to report to his family and get help from the village. Rob couldn't handle just sitting there and doing nothing. He took his car and left, searching for signs of Rachel and David, trying to check every place he knew them to have gone for dates or hangouts. He'd left the day after Jeff.

And he hadn't come back. After just one day, Rob's phone went to voicemail and texts remained unanswered.

Meg hadn't been seen by anyone since before prom, nor had her parents. A letter was found saying they took an impromptu trip to Cancun—return date undetermined.

Eric was almost as much of a wreck as Samantha was. He was clearly still in love with Meg and didn't buy the random Cancun story; having her go missing was a huge blow. Either he was a great actor, or he also really cared about Rachel and David, even after the breakup. He was terrified out of his mind when Devin and Simon essentially kidnapped and interrogated him. Once they were satisfied he really was in the dark, they promised they'd let him know if there were any updates. He was still seemingly clueless about the green-folk side of the equation.

Saff followed Ben's advice, meeting up with the Seeder girls in Rachel's family. Immediately following Rachel's disappearance, all of her sisters had been pulled from their host homes and taken to a nearby undisclosed location. Rachel still had three sisters remaining in the human world; two had gone through their bloom and were left without a trainer after Jeff's departure. Saff trained with them from morning to night for three days straight. She did everything she could to get them ready to catch a breeze; they needed to be prepared to evacuate as soon as possible.

Samantha remained at home, available for questions from the police on the case of her now-missing husband. Devin and Simon did as much legwork as they could, tearing up David's apartment floor-to-ceiling, and even breaking into and searching around Meg's place.

There was some satisfaction on Saff's part about being able to train Rachel's sisters, as Ben had recommended. But the rest of it was pure frustration. They'd be leaving with more questions than they'd arrived with, their investigation not giving them any direction.

Saff was nearly ready to turn in for the night before heading home to the Green Lands. They were confident enough in one of the girls' progress that Saff would guide her through a rift the next night. Devin and Simon would return once Saff sent Jeff or one of his brothers back to work with the last two sisters.

While trying to help Samantha out by washing the dishes, Saff was startled when the doorbell rang. She looked through the peephole at an unfamiliar man in his twenties. Preparing for the worst, she opened the door.

"Hi. Uh, are you … Samantha?" he asked.

"She's not available. Can I help you?"

"Well, I've been doing rideshare for a month now and this is the first time someone paid me to transport a letter." He pulled a small envelope from his hoodie. "But instructions said I could only hand it to someone named Samantha."

"Let me go get her." Saff closed the door, bolting it, and then roused Samantha, who had passed out on the couch.

Groggy and puffy-eyed, Samantha opened the door, and he gave her the envelope. The driver turned to leave.

"Wait! Don't leave yet," Saff ordered.

He held up his hands. "I'm not in the courier service, ya know? The instructions said I'd get a good tip as long as I gave her the envelope and left. I don't know anything else."

"But who gave it to you?"

He shrugged. "No one. The pick-up instructions told me where it was tucked away at a bus stop." He started to look concerned. "Excuse me, but I'm going to take off. I didn't sign up for this double-o-seven nonsense, and I'm starting to think it wasn't worth the promised tip."

Samantha closed the door and tore open the envelope, while Saff spared a quick glance out of a small window by the door to see that he'd returned to his car.

"She'll be in the Neutral Woods. At sunrise, one mile west and two days after the blue fireworks."

Saff called Devin right away, and the men came back to look.

"It's talking about Rachel, right?" Saff asked. "It doesn't say her name, but it has to be. What's it supposed to mean? It doesn't mention a ransom, threats, or demands."

Samantha was in hysterics. "Does this mean she's alive? It doesn't say! And what about Rob?"

Simon tried to calm her down, reassuring her this was a good sign—the first lead they'd had since it all began.

"What's this, down at the bottom?" Saff asked.

Devin furrowed his brow. "Unitas." They did a quick search online. "Pronounced oo-knee-tas. It's Latin for 'Unity.'"

"And the symbol? Do you recognize that?" she asked.

Neither Devin nor Simon did. It was an image of a blossom in front of an ivy leaf.

Saff took Devin to the side. "So, what does this mean?"

He rubbed his eyebrow with a knuckle. "It means you and I need to get home and look for fireworks. And be prepared for an ambush, or…" Devin lowered his voice even more, glancing over at Samantha and Simon. "Or for worse news."

Chapter 18

AFTER HOURS OF PAINFUL SOLITUDE, guards and a nurse arrived to extract Rachel from the energy-draining chair and take her back to the room she'd originally woken up in. They pumped her full of IV fluids and the nurse tended to her wounds. Rachel was able to eat and use the restroom, then was handcuffed to the bed and allowed to sleep for five hours before the torture started up again.

The War Vines had already been activated by the queen—apparently, she had no need to revisit, because she never did. Now, it was a simple plug and play. The nurse gave Rachel a strong dose of poison to make the initial insertion of leaf blades tolerable. She rested the War Vines on Rachel's arms and they burrowed into her skin. Every four to five hours, a nurse would drop by, giving Rachel a small dose to keep her in a haze. It was a lot more manageable than the first night when David—Prince Soren—had punished her by forbidding any numbing. Olivia was her nurse a few times, but she seemed too afraid to talk again.

When it was close to dosing time, Rachel would remember what Olivia had said about this being the time to resist. But she couldn't. Even being dizzy and nauseous, she felt better being half out of it than being lucid with the physical and mental pain. She tried once to put all her focus into locking in her energy, keeping it centered in her heart. But she didn't last long—it was like trying to hold back floodwaters with a sieve.

After two more days of this routine—drugs, minimal recuperation time, torture—her vision began clearing and the pain of the process was seeping into the forefront of her awareness. Her neck was limp, her head leaning to one side as she fluttered her eyes at the creak of a door opening.

Olivia crouched down next to her and whispered, "You're going to need to pretend you're more medicated than you are." She wrapped her vines around Rachel's wrist, but didn't squeeze tight enough to break the skin. "She's good for a few more hours," Olivia reported to the guards as she left.

***

"She's alert enough to talk?" a familiar male voice asked a few hours later.

Rachel remembered Olivia's warning and closed her eyes, preparing to drawl and stare off into the distance, and also willing herself to not wince at the excruciating pain she was enduring in her current state.

"Yes, Your Grace." It was Olivia again.

The man stood in front of Rachel. She hadn't thought it was possible to hurt more, but her heart shattered. She'd hoped she was wrong about the owner of the familiar voice, but she had guessed right—and it took everything she had to not react as much as she wanted to. Rob. He was dressed in similar attire to what Prince Soren had been wearing.

"There you are. Sorry it took so long to visit," he said. "I'm assuming you're pretty familiar with everything going on around you?"

He raised his eyebrows the same way he had when she got in trouble back home. "Prince Soren told me he's not too fond of you right now."

She wanted to smirk at the memory of his bloody lip, but stayed droopy, as though she were still coming out of a haze from the fresh dose that Olivia *hadn't* given her.

"You're looking good. Useful and properly hopeless, just like any livestock doing its job."

Her blood began to boil. Never in all of his years as her stepfather had he said anything remotely unkind, not like this.

"I won't be here forever," she asserted, perhaps a little too forcefully for her acting job.

"No, I imagine not. But I'm guessing you mean you're leaving this place alive? Who will come for you?" He cocked his head to the side. "Your mother, who can't even enter the Green Lands? Or your boyfriend? Oh wait, we've already discussed his indifference. Perhaps your overworked and incompetent brother, who thinks you're a massive disappointment?" He paused, taking a deep breath. "But what about your best friend, Meg?"

Her heart ached at hearing Meg's name again; she still wasn't sure what had become of her.

He cleared his throat. "Do you remember if Meg told you anything about leaving? Going on vacation, or anything like that, before you left? Her family is really worried about her."

Rachel furrowed her brow in confusion and anger.

"Yeah, you're useless." He crossed his arms. "But what if she comes to save the day for you, right? Dang it, that's still a no. I mean, I'm guessing not, since she was the one poisoning you the whole time."

Rachel couldn't hide the shock on her face. He had to be lying. Meg would *never* do something like that.

He didn't even try to hide his joy at her slipped expression. "I really shouldn't wag my tongue so much, but anonymous artists are cliché. *Everyone* wants credit for their clever plans and hard work."

His smile brightened. "Your dear friend Meg—she's one of us. Have you ever heard of microdosing? Just enough to get the job done. A smidgen to weaken your energy, leaving you no alternative but to find your way home with your *knight in shining armor*. All delivered with a piping hot cup and a smile on the bottom."

Rachel cried. Had anyone in her life ever genuinely loved her?

"Well, that's why I ask. We're worried about her, too. Prince Soren wants to know where his sister is, and she just so happens to be missing. So, if you know anything, we'd really appreciate your cooperation."

"Then I hope you find her rotting in a ditch somewhere," Rachel seethed in anger.

His face flushed red. "If you know something you're not telling me, that may be exactly how they find your mother."

"I don't know anything!" she blurted. "Don't hurt her!"

He calmed, adjusting the hem of his shirt. "It's okay. Your mother is perfectly fine. For now. After years over there, you kind of get attached to people. I mean, not you—you're just a filthy weed. But your mother... I kind of liked her. If she weren't a useless human, I definitely would have considered bringing her here." He clasped his hands together. "And just so you feel better, assuming you cooperate and we don't have to hurt her, my lawyer has divorce papers drafted. She'll be free to move on to her next failure of a marriage. There's some incentive."

"Her only failure was trusting a leech like you!"

He glanced at Olivia. "She seems far too alert. Make sure you check back on her more frequently, or adjust her doses."

Olivia bowed, looking at the ground. "Yes, Your Grace. My deepest apologies, Your Grace."

He turned back to Rachel. "I'm sorry I couldn't be the father you wanted. But was I really that bad? Compared to a dad that left you to a naïve stranger, and a dad that left you as a young child without a word? I was good to you. It had a purpose, but still..."

She was determined not to cry more. He was right—she'd had the longest relationship with him out of any of them. Staring at the ground, her eyes glazed over in defeat.

"I know you're hurting, but maybe this will help you find some closure about Brad." Brad, of course, was the dad that had deserted Rachel and her mom before they'd met Rob. "You know what, I'm not all about crushing your hopes and dreams any more than we have to, so I'm going to give you a multiple choice, and you get to choose which one you want to believe. He either left because learning your true nature as a weed was too disturbing for him, or we had him permanently removed from your life, and … his own life."

He likely accomplished what he was looking for—her eyes stung once more with tears.

Rob's voice deepened, abandoning his flippant mocking. "Just remember how *worthless* your existence is, next time we ask you a question and want an answer, or the next time you remember something about dear Meg and try to forget to tell us. You literally serve *one* function in this life, and you are doing a *fantastic* job at it right now. I'd hate to shorten your usefulness by keeping you attached without any breaks and without medication."

He calmly clasped his hands in front of him once more. "So, I'm going to ask you one more time, where—" He was cut off by a knock at the door.

"My apologies for the interruption, Your Grace. We have news of Princess Kaylah," a man announced after opening the door.

Rob squinted with curiosity, heading to the door and closing it behind him. Rachel tried eavesdropping to see if this 'Princess Kaylah' they were talking about was Meg. Maybe the Seeders had her, and maybe she'd make a good prisoner exchange.

No words filtered through the door, only a gasp, some shuffling, a *thud*, and a *thwack*.

The door burst open.

Olivia stood alert with her head held high. A hooded figure entered, wearing all black and holding a machete dripping with blood. The figure pulled off the hood, and Rachel's eyes grew wide. Her best friend looked back at her. Replacing her usual messy bun was a braided updo. Instead of her warm, casual smile, her face showed fierce determination and blood spatter.

"Jon, gag her," Meg ordered. "Guillen, take care of that." She nodded in the direction of the door.

One of the guards, a brunet in his thirties, quickly approached Rachel, following Meg's orders.

Meg looked Rachel directly in the eyes while wiping at her own face. "I need you to listen to me. If you make noise or fight back, you'll probably die. You need to focus everything you have on healing. Do you understand me?"

Rachel's heart raced. She nodded that she would comply, the gag now in place.

"Jon, stand guard. Olivia, help me cut her loose."

Meg began slicing through the vines restricting Rachel's movement with her machete, and Olivia unwound them, carefully but speedily tugging them from Rachel's skin. Unable to easily slice through the War Vines, they gently wiggled them free. Essentially unmedicated, Rachel was grateful to have the gag to bite down on as embedded razor blades were plucked from her arms, one by one. As Rachel winced, she could make out the sound of something dragging across the floor from over her shoulder, and then a stomach-turning *thwack* and a *clang* as sharp metal hit the stone floor.

"I can only imagine what they told you about me. But if you ever valued our friendship, I need you to trust me right now," Meg said as they finished with the vines. "Take a deep breath. Put everything you have right now into getting enough strength to walk." She turned to the door. "How are we, Jon?"

"Still clear."

"Okay, we're going out the way we came in." Meg surveyed her party. "Me, Rachel, Jon, Olivia. Guillen at the back."

Meg and Olivia helped Rachel to stand. "Let's get a move on."

The men stepped out into the hallway. Meg marched over to what was now a beheaded Rob, giving his corpse a swift, hard kick. She rejoined Olivia to help Rachel walk. They followed Jon. The door clicked behind them and Rachel turned to look. Another hooded figure, the one Meg had called Guillen, joined them.

Walking down a couple of unfamiliar halls, they stepped over guards' bodies along the way. The group filed into a small room with what looked like a stone well; several giant vines were growing out of it and connecting to other parts of the room.

"We're going down," Meg said. "I can help stabilize you from below with my vines, and Jon from above with his."

They climbed down the chute, barely large enough for one person at a time. Rachel found it hard to climb down the metal rungs, as her knees wanted to buckle. At least once, Jon saved her from falling with his vines wrapped firmly around her upper arm. They reached solid ground in another room, similar to the one at the top of the well, but taller.

Meg turned to Rachel. "You promise you won't scream if I take the gag off?"

Rachel nodded.

After Meg removed the gag, Jon carefully peeked out of a door and announced the all-clear. They raced down a corridor, stopping in front of a side door. Meg motioned with her head for Jon to move forward, and they breached the door together, taking out a guard on the other side before he could sound the alarm.

They filed out of the door, and shut it behind them.

"Olivia, you'll come with me." Meg looked Rachel over; she was still in her prom dress. Closing her eyes, Meg shook her head. "Soren," she muttered. Opening her eyes, she sighed, looking at the men. "Get her some new clothes as soon as you're able to."

She now addressed Rachel. "I'm *so* sorry. They're going to take you home. Do as they say. I trust them with my life. And you can trust them, more than you were ever able to trust me."

Chapter 19

THE PALACE HORNS RANG THROUGH the damp evening air and Rachel ran as fast as she could in their escape, but her group was separated in no time and she fell behind, still weak from the torture she had been subjected to the last few days. Every muscle in her body throbbed.

She hardly even felt the vine that wrapped her ankle, causing her to lose her footing. Emerging from the host of guards, David appeared. Putting his hand over her mouth, he again dug a razor-sharp leaf into her forehead. Pushed past her pain threshold, Rachel screamed.

Her heart racing, her breathing rapid and forceful, she opened her eyes. She was in a cave. A clean-shaven brunet in his early twenties had his hand over her mouth. She looked up in terror and confusion, eyes warm, no doubt glowing green.

"It's okay. It's okay! It was just a dream," Guillen quickly whispered. "You need to be quiet."

She swallowed and tried to calm her breathing, ripping his hand from her mouth. She felt her forehead with a shaky hand, confirming it was coated in sweat, not blood, and the stitches were still there.

Sitting up, she moved further away from the man, cowering against the cold stone wall. She didn't even remember walking in there.

Jon loomed at the entrance of the cave, keeping guard and likely making sure her outburst hadn't drawn any attention.

Guillen watched Rachel, crouching nearby. "You passed out. You're okay. We're safe for now. Just take a second to breathe," he coached.

Her eyes were glued on him, their glow slowly fading. "Meg? Rob? David?"

Jon joined them, still positioned closest to the entrance, sparing an extra glance over his shoulder. "I'm sure the princess is fine. We're not sure where the prince is. And, uh … Rob, yeah—Duke Nuren is out of the picture."

Rachel had a staring contest with the cave floor, sorting through her thoughts. *Nuren. Rob was Nuren?* She'd actually wondered, in her rare moments of lucidity, if Jeff had gotten the name wrong. That it was Soren, not Nuren, the Seeders were searching for. But it had been Rob…

Her concentration broke when something rustled a few feet away. Guillen approached her with food and a canteen. She eyed it, still on edge about everything that had transpired.

"At least drink some water," he calmly insisted. "That will help with your healing."

She glanced down at her arms; the blood was crusting at each point of leaf insertion. She guzzled down the water, then sat with her head against the wall, her eyes closed.

"So, Meg and David, they're … really brother and sister?" she asked.

"Yes," Jon answered.

"And Rob, you said Duke?"

"Yes. Their uncle."

"They're all Ivy?"

"Yes."

She looked both of the men over. "And you are both…"

Jon continued to answer. "Ivy as well. But we're friendly."

She quietly scoffed. "Yeah, I've been told that before." She gnawed at her bottom lip. "And me? Why me?"

The men glanced at each other.

"That's a broad question, not sure how to answer that," Jon said.

"Like, I get why they had me hooked up, but why did they pick me? Why am I here right now?"

Guillen spoke up. "We don't know all the details. We mostly just know about the Unitas efforts."

"Unitas?" She studied his face.

"Yeah. The movement Kaylah started."

"Do you mean the rebellion?"

Jon chuckled. "Only the *oppressor* calls those in an opposing movement 'rebels' or 'dissidents.'"

Guillen glanced between the two of them. "But yes. Essentially. And Kaylah made you the priority."

"You should consider yourself lucky," Jon said while cleaning under his fingernails. "You're the last to be taken, the first to be freed."

"How many of my people do they have?"

"At least five others that we're aware of."

She swallowed a lump in her throat. "Kaylah—the princess, right? I know her as Meg? Is it true what Rob said about her? About the role she played in getting me here in the first place?"

Jon looked away.

Guillen pursed his lips. "I don't know what all they told you, but you need to remember she had orders to follow. And that Soren and Nuren often twist the truth to get what they want. When she went missing, they knew she'd defected, and they're desperate to get her back." He stressed, "Focus on what she's doing for you right now."

Rachel hesitantly decided to give the food a go, unwrapping a fruit-and-nut bar from a large grape leaf. The tartness of the dried fruit made her mouth water. "Where are we? What's the plan?"

"This cave is well hidden," Guillen said. "No one in the palace even knows about it. Kaylah and I discovered it as kids. Once you're up to it, we can move on and get you to your borders."

"Am I… Is this a hostage sort of thing? Why are you doing this?" she asked, still not sure they could be trusted.

Jon rolled his eyes. "We're risking our lives to get you home because we've pledged our allegiance to the princess. You'll have to ask her yourself about all the details."

She nodded. This was obviously a rescue, but with every shred of her identity and trust having been defiled, it was hard to know where to draw the line. This could just be another colorful deception, like David and Rob … and Meg … were clearly so good at. But when it came down to it, this beat life-sucking torture.

Jon informed her of their plan; there would be several days of walking, and she should get as well-rested as possible, healing up and gaining strength. They would need to be swift once they emerged from the cave. If they left before she was ready, she'd only be a liability.

"Why don't we just go through a rift and take me back to my people?" she asked.

Jon and Guillen exchanged a knowing glance.

"There are a few reasons we can't do that," Jon answered. "One being, we can't actually rift into Seeder territory. You can only rift in and out between the worlds, not within them. And even with your border walls compromised, we've never been able to get past the Neutral Woods. Plus, the princess gave orders about one of the stops we need to take on the way. And," his eyes jumped back to Guillen for a second before returning to Rachel, "there are other reasons. Just know it's not a possibility."

"Okay." She frowned, tilting her head to the side. "I used my energy to boost David, or, uh, Soren, to help get me through one of your rifts. That wouldn't make a difference, would it?"

"No. No rifts." Jon cleared his throat. "How about you finish up that water and see if you can get some more sleep. We'll take turns keeping watch throughout the day. By nightfall, we'll be needing to take off."

"Alright. What time is it? How long was I out earlier?" she asked.

"It's been a few hours," said Guillen. "The sun will be up soon, but this cave's hidden well enough that we're not too worried about them finding it. We'll still have our things ready to go in case we need to leave in a hurry."

Rachel finished off the water, every minute feeling the smallest degree better. The Green Lands were starting to replenish her strength, like an IV, one drop at a time. She lay down and recalled her parting with Meg—Kaylah. Rachel hadn't wanted to go with these two men, having to leave Kaylah and Olivia. Kaylah had firmly insisted that Rachel follow her orders, that she and Olivia would be creating a false trail for the guards to follow, then attending to 'other business.' Then the horns blew—the whole palace had been put on alert.

Another horrifying scene tore through Rachel's dreams, and she woke again, screaming. She quickly made out her surroundings. Jon stood nearby. She woke up faster this time, before he could rush over and muffle the sound. Guillen ran back in to check on things. Her eyes met theirs as she slowed her breathing.

"Sorry," she whispered, closing her eyes. She did her best to suppress any noises, but there was really no way to hide the movement of her whole body shaking as tears slipped between the edges of her eyelids.

The next time she woke, she was still breathing hard, but she was calmer. Sitting up, she spotted more food and water placed next to her. Both of the men were in view, eating a meal and whispering. They stopped chatting and greeted her once they noticed she was up.

Rachel looked at the tracks on her arms and, one by one, slowly ran a glowing finger over each wound, then scratched at it to flake off the dried blood. Once she'd finished, she realized she had an audience.

"That's pretty cool," Jon said with eyebrows lifted.

"Impressive," Guillen added with a smile.

She sized up the men. "Have you guys never seen our powers?"

"You're actually the first Seeder I've ever seen," Guillen shyly confessed.

"I've seen your kind, just never that," Jon said.

"Really? I mean, I guess that makes sense. But you've never seen one of us at all, Guillen?"

He shook his head.

She felt her forehead and finished healing up that last wound.

"So, Jon, you've dealt with Seeders." Her recollection was hazy, but she'd seen him more than once during her time in the palace. "What kind of damage did you cause before joining this 'Unitas'?" she asked casually.

He glared at the accusation. "I've never hurt a Seeder. I made my way up the chain peacefully and did a couple-year stint with the humans. Then I proved I was up to snuff for palace detail. I haven't taken any active roles in this current war."

She sighed. "Well, that's good to know."

"I could have, if I'd wanted to," he stressed. "Getting into palace work is hard; volunteering for the front lines is something *anyone* can do. Remember that, when you question my motives and integrity next. I've destroyed an elite career on the chance it will make a permanent difference."

Biting the insides of her cheeks, she looked down. "Thanks."

He took a deep breath. "Actually, I rightly guessed a Seeder girl at the high school where I was stationed back in my day." He sipped from a canteen. "I, uh, delayed reporting it for too long and she made it home. I told myself my hesitation was because I'd wanted to be certain first, but when I look back, I don't think my heart was really in it."

Rachel gave him a nod of approval. Jon was still in his guard uniform, but Guillen was in less formal combat gear. "If you've never seen a Seeder, what kind of assignment do you have?"

Guillen looked at her, squinting. "Is something on your forehead bugging you?"

"Oh." She had been rubbing her hand over the suture wisps the whole time. "Yeah, stitches. These are going to drive me crazy."

He grabbed something from his bag and approached her. "I can help with that." Unrolling a set of small tools, he grabbed tweezers and a sharp blade. "Just hold still and I can get those out." He drew close to her face, squinting in the shadows of the cave.

Being this close, Rachel could take in his pale-blue eyes and a large scar on his temple. His hair was brown and his breath still smelled of the mint leaves she'd seen him chew on after his meal.

Guillen carefully lifted the stitches away from her skin and cut through the sutures, pulling them out. "Good as new." He smiled.

She rubbed her forehead. "Thanks. You're quite the Boy Scout to have all those tools."

He read her face with a subtle narrowing of the eyes, as if he hadn't understood the reference.

It was more than a smidge unlikely that there would be a 'Boy Scouts of the Ivy Kingdom' troop for him to understand what she'd meant. "Oh, um, that's a human reference to being resourceful, prepared."

A spark of recognition shone in his eyes. "Glad I could be of assistance. Any others you need help with?"

She glanced down again at her arms and legs. "Nope, I only injured the prince enough to earn stitches the one time." She beamed at the memory of his bloody lip.

Guillen grinned. "Good for you."

Chapter 20

GUILLEN ROLLED UP HIS TOOLS. "That's a pretty dress. What's the occasion?"

Rachel examined the sad thing with rips and dirt disgracing it. She smirked. "Naturally, I got all dolled up to be kidnapped."

He chuckled.

"No, it was for a school dance." She sighed. "It's kind of a big deal back home. And just like saying goodbye to my family, I missed it." She shook her head. "All because I was stupid enough to trust an I—" She pursed her lips. "To trust the prince."

He gave a look acknowledging he knew what she had meant to say before she'd caught herself—'stupid enough to trust an Ivy.'

She was still regaining her strength, and since healing always ate up so much energy, Rachel happily went back to napping while the men took turns keeping a lookout. When she woke next, Jon was in the cave with her and Guillen was out taking a turn at watch. She sat up against the cave wall, sipping on water.

"I think I'm going to go stir-crazy. Any chance I can stretch my legs outside if I stay close?"

Jon looked her over. "I don't think that dress is the best camouflage. But you could explore the cave if you'd like. It's sound, and there's enough light to avoid tripping if you're careful." He pointed with his chin. "Keep to the left—there's some parts where daylight peeks through. Probably old rabbit burrowing holes."

She took his advice and looked around. The stone was brown, slightly reddish. A sapling was trying to make a home for itself in a crack halfway through the tunnel. Following Jon's instructions, she took the path to the left when there was a division; the narrow dark opening to the right appeared more foreboding, anyway. She was particularly intrigued when she came to the end of the cave. Leaning against the wall were a handful of wooden sticks and staves. Nearby, Rachel could just barely discern something carved into the rock in the shadows. Experimenting, she channeled energy to her hand, holding it up to look at the carving.

"That's pretty cool, too."

The break in the silence startled her, and she turned. Guillen was approaching from the main cave chamber. Despite how nice he'd been, she didn't like the feeling of being cornered. She started to back away in the direction of the staves.

Picking up on her body language, he moved back, raising his hands. "Sorry, just switched with Jon and wanted to make sure you were okay back here."

She relaxed a little at his soothing reassurance. "Yeah, doing good, thanks. You said you've been in these caves before? What do these symbols etched into the wall mean?"

He walked closer to get a good look, squinting. "You know, I forgot about those. I'm not sure."

"Hmm … Now that's going to drive me crazy, not knowing." She continued to stare at the carving. Her glance shifted to the staves. "What about these?"

"Training tools." He grinned. "I'm the one who taught Kaylah how to use that machete of hers."

Rachel's eyes widened. "I, uh … I guess you're good at what you do?"

He gave a gentle nod. "I'm *very* good at what I do." His expression softened as he searched her face. "But I would never hurt you. And neither would Jon. You're safe with us."

She bit her lip. "He was there—one of the guards that handled my transfers. Did you know that?"

Guillen frowned. "He's been on the right side of things for a while now. We needed help from the inside."

She fidgeted with her hands. "What kinds of weapons do I need to be worried about? I was under the impression green folk relied on their natural abilities for fighting. Why would Meg even need to use a machete?" She glanced at Guillen's belt; he carried his own machete and other knives.

He leaned back against the cave wall. "You're right. Most people around here *do* only focus on training with green folk abilities. Kind of stupid though, isn't it? A bit arrogant, too."

She gave him a half-smile. Something about Guillen was … refreshing, calming. He was more forthcoming than she'd expected, with him being so quiet earlier. She decided to try and get a better picture of the situation.

"Tell me about the royal family. Princess Kaylah… Prince Soren…"

He obliged without hesitation. "The queen and king have four children. Only one daughter. Soren's the oldest. Kaylah came a year later."

"Ivy society is matriarchal too, right? Like Seeder society?"

"Yes. Kaylah's the crown princess—heir to the throne."

Rachel shook her head. That was … not the girl she'd had silly sleepovers with, or gawked at cute boys with, or … consoled on the school bathroom floor after a breakup. And she wasn't just *a* princess. She was *the* princess. "So, you've been friends with the princess for a long time? You used to play here?"

"Yeah. I've known her all her life." He smiled. "She's always been generous and kind," he said with a fondness in his voice.

"That's the Meg I know. Or, I guess I should start to say Kaylah? I noticed you don't call her the princess like Jon does—why is that?"

"She *does* prefer Kaylah over Meg. And… I probably should call her by her title. But we've always been real close. She's my cousin."

Rachel swallowed hard, sizing him up. Cousin… He wasn't just an Ivy. He was royalty, too.

He narrowed his eyes. "No relation to Duke Nuren—he was the king's brother. My mother is the queen's sister. And we don't really have any part in palace life."

She studied Guillen's face. He was much more like the Meg she'd known growing up than the cocky and crass David she had become accustomed to. "So, if you're a member of the royal family, what's your title?"

He crossed his arms. "I think a person's choices and actions matter more than their title. Don't you?"

As she crossed her arms to match him, the light in her hand went out. "I think that's a fair assertion." She grinned. "So, I don't have to curtsy every time you pass?"

He laughed loudly before stifling it. "I won't bow if you won't curtsy."

She smiled wide. "Deal."

"Well, I, uh… I'm going to head back." He nodded in the direction they'd both come from.

"Not a bad idea."

After making their way back to the main chamber of the cave, Guillen suggested she try to get more rest before they headed out in a few hours. Before she drifted off to sleep, Rachel made herself a promise that she was going to see this through. She refused to allow herself to become a cowering victim. She was going to survive this. She was going to see her mom again and be there for her. She was going to help her people, and, if possible, play a part in ending this damned war.

***

Rachel woke to Guillen gently nudging her shoulder and whispering her name. Her eyes shot right open, but softened once she realized it was him.

"We're going to head out soon. Let's have you fill up on food and water before we slip out."

She snacked on some of the sunflower oatcake rations they provided and shook away the grogginess before they left the safety of the cave. The mountainous area surrounding the palace was heavily forested, which would provide great cover as they traveled. Jeff had once drawn Rachel a map of the Green Lands. The Ivy Kingdom occupied the entire eastern sector, and their palace was pretty far south. That was all he'd really shown her, as neither of them had ever expected to actually step foot in Ivy territory.

When Rachel had been rescued, she hadn't been wearing shoes. Her dress heels were hardly useful, and they hadn't cared to cover her feet in the palace, since they would put in an IV during her limited recuperation hours. Until Jon or Guillen could get her a change of clothes, she had to suck it up and watch her step, as her feet were now wrapped in only a pair of cotton bandanas.

After hours of walking in the dark, Jon announced they'd found their stopping point for the night. Jon did most of the navigating, and Guillen had kindly answered Rachel's questions along the way, including naming unfamiliar flora and fauna. Having reached their camping ground, Rachel happily lay on the forest floor and unwrapped her muddy feet, massaging and healing them. Shortly after, she allowed the crickets to sing her to sleep.

Rachel woke to whispering again. The men offered food and water.

"I've got connections in this area. I'll grab you a change of clothes and some shoes, along with extra provisions," Jon announced once she was up. He looked at Guillen while tightening a strap on his pack. "We're clear on what to do if we get separated?"

"We're set."

Guillen explained that Jon had grown up in this region and knew the lay of the land better, which would help him stay hidden along the way. They had a connection on the edge of the nearest city that could help them get what they needed. For several hours, Rachel entertained Guillen with information about the 'ball' she'd missed and other things unique to the human world. She was surprised how much he didn't seem to know, but then again, he hadn't been deployed as an assassin; maybe Ivies were just extra selective in their education on the human world.

"You never answered my question about what you do for work," she remarked over more sunflower oatcakes for lunch.

He shook his head. "No. I guess I didn't."

She waited with eyebrows lifted. "And...?"

He feigned not having understood she wanted an answer. "Oh, you wanted me to tell you?"

She rolled her eyes and picked up a small pebble, chucking it at him. He caught it with quick reflexes.

She smiled. "Impressive. Do you not need to have a job, being part of the royal family?"

He shook his head. "Not likely. I ... do construction work." He twisted his mouth, looking away.

"That's cool. There's no shame in working with your hands." She furrowed her brow at his reaction. "Do you not like it?"

"Not exactly a highly respected position in these parts. What kind of people have to do construction in the human world?"

"Have to? Well, no one really *has* to. I think..." She glanced at the sky in thought. "I guess people who just like to create and be active, and maybe don't like to go through as much formal schooling. There's a good fit for each person and each job. If you don't like it, why don't you try something new?"

He gave her a half-hearted smile. "That sounds nice, to be able to choose. For now, I try not to focus too much on what I can't have." He stood and brushed himself off. "I'm going to do a quick patrol of the area. Stay here and stay quiet, okay?"

Rachel stayed put, pondering their conversation. She realized how little she really knew about either culture in the Green Lands. Having grown up in a nation where she would have been free to choose her own career, she took that for granted.

Once Guillen returned, he sat and took out a couple of knives, throwing them with astounding precision at a log, and then sharpened them.

"Sorry for bringing up work," she said.

He gave her a polite smile. "No apologies necessary." Guillen wasn't exactly timid … but he was quiet, and there was something hidden there—something under the surface she wished she knew more about.

"So … you guys can't go over the nitty-gritty of strategy, but what's the end goal of Kaylah's movement? And what are you personally hoping for?"

"I have hope for old ways and new answers." He wore a genuine smile this time. "Kaylah has actually done a lot of research in the old archives. Things forgotten or hidden from our people. About how our powers work, both Ivy and Seeder. About our similarities. She really has a vision that could end this, once and for all, and make vast improvements for both sides." He sheathed his knives. "I'd give anything to have things the way she envisions them. This cause means a lot to me, personally. And once we expose the lies, take away the ignorance, and embrace the best parts of our pasts and people, no other decent person could reject her plans."

Rachel marveled at his speech. "That's pretty poetic. You're really dedicated, aren't you?"

He met her gaze. "One hundred percent."

"How big is the movement? David … or … Soren… I'm not sure if I want to call him either name…" Her stomach hurt just thinking about him.

Guillen chuckled. "There are a lot of less polite words that might fit him better."

She joined in with a laugh. "Amen to that. Anyway, he said, at least after he brought me here, that it's really small … that there's not much hope."

Guillen hesitantly nodded once. "We're still working on that. But we're gaining strength. We can only do so much on our side without your people's help." He raised his eyebrows. "You're going to be key in that."

Swallowing hard, she nervously wrung her hands. "I, uh…" She took a deep breath. "I'm not exactly a phenomenal specimen for this sort of thing. I'm way behind others in training. They either think I ran away or know I allowed myself to get kidnapped. Not sure what good I can do." She frowned and fought tears. Poisoned to destroy her confidence. Fake relationships. Everything was turned upside down. She was no leader.

He mirrored her frown. "From what Kaylah tells me, you've got more going for you than you give yourself credit for. I don't know what all they did to you, but every time her 'parents' would take her on 'vacation' over the years, she was back here. She always tried to carve out some time to visit with me, and she told me all about her best friend." He made it a point to meet her eyes. "It started out as an assignment, but she was just a kid. You softened her heart. If anything, you made this movement possible. Don't discount that."

Rachel wiped away tears. "Well, now you're going to make me blush." She chuckled. "But that's true? She talked about me?"

"Yeah. She started to get busier as you two got older, so I didn't get to see her as much on account of that. But I know she felt guilty about what she had to do to you."

"Thanks. That means a lot." She sniffled. "So, what do you guys need me to do?"

"We'll have more details by the time we get you back to Seeder borders. For now, stay alive. As long as it doesn't slow you down, I'd recommend focusing as much energy as possible on preparing to catch a breeze back to the human world after we get you home."

Tilting her head, she squinted. "Back to the human world?" He talked about Seeder lands as if they were her home. But wasn't her home really with her mom back in the human world? A place she could no longer survive long-term?

"Yeah. The human world. We'll go over that once we're closer to your borders."

She didn't hate the idea of a visit, even if it couldn't last more than a week. "And you're sure we can't just use a tree rift? I have to *fly* back to the human world?"

He nodded. "Things will work out. Have some faith."

Chapter 21

JON FINALLY CAME BACK TO camp with a whistle to announce his return. He was now dressed similarly to Guillen, having ditched his palace guard uniform.

"Thought we'd lost you," Guillen said, then scrunched his face comically, "to the pub."

Jon rolled his eyes. "Next time, maybe *you* get to head into town."

With both his hands and vines, Jon reached into his pack and pulled out clothes and shoes for Rachel. "Here, I tried my best, but they might be a bit big." They were similar to what Kaylah had worn, and to what her travel companions were wearing. All black, combat style.

"Do you want me to get dinner ready, or would you rather I show her the lake?" Guillen asked.

"I'll stay here. I've done enough walking today." Jon grunted as he plopped down on a tree stump. "And I don't need to be poisoned by your cooking."

Guillen shot him a dirty look.

"Oh, uh." Jon looked at Rachel. "That was maybe not the most tactful thing to say, sorry."

She stood, choosing to ignore the insensitive comment. "I'm more than ready to clean up and get rid of the memory of this dress. Let's find that lake."

It was a mere ten-minute hike to the beautiful lake. The shallows were home to a variety of minnows and aquatic plants. Her favorite were the large lily pads with giant vibrant purple blossoms. The central part of the lake was crystal clear.

They first refilled everyone's canteens, and then Guillen showed Rachel the best place to get in, and told her where he'd be waiting so she could have some privacy. The water was frigid, but she discovered she could heat herself up a little by expending some Seeder energy. It felt like heaven to scrub away the dirt and sweat and tears. She took her time soaking, mesmerized by the ripples in the water. She could have stayed there forever, allowing the lake to not only wash away the grime, but all of the hurt, the confusion, the hate. But even in the Green Lands, nature could only do so much.

After grabbing her bandanas and underwear from the bank, she hand-washed them. She hastily toweled off after emerging from the lake, and got dressed in the new clothes, which ended up being a bit baggy for her. The shoes fit decently well—Jon had measured her feet before leaving for town. She returned to where Guillen was waiting, her arms clutching the massacred dress. He was back to tossing a throwing knife with exceptional accuracy at the same spot in the ground over and over.

"Sorry that took so long," she said. "But it felt *so* good."

Picking up his knife, Guillen wiped off any dirt before sheathing it. "Then I'm happy to hear it. We've got nothing else on the agenda tonight. Now, about that dress…"

It was ripped in several places, with dirt and detritus all over it. More than the damage, she hated the memories it brought—a prom she'd never get to have, a horror she wished she'd never endured. Even after allowing her to clean up and use the facilities, she'd been forced to redress in it, per Soren's orders. "Can we burn it?" she asked.

Guillen smirked. "Mmm, best not to. But we do need to lose it. Let's go sink it in the lake."

They headed back to the lake together. Finding an ideal spot with seaweed and lily pads, he rolled up his pant legs, taking off his boots to wade out to it. She tossed him the dress and picked up a couple of large rocks he pointed out to weigh it down. She bent down, self-consciously clutching an arm over her chest, picking the rocks up one at a time. Once he got back out, he dried his legs and feet with a small rag, replacing his boots.

"I'm not going to miss that, or what it represents." She let out a short breathy chuckle. "You know, I could have spent more on it. Rob said I could. I wish I would have taken him for every penny he had. Then again, I'm hoping my mom has access to his money now." Vicious homesickness washed over her as she worried about her mom. Jon and Guillen had confirmed, to the best of their knowledge, her mom was still safe, that Nuren hadn't lied about that. "Do you think she can make a life insurance claim if he died in a different realm?"

Guillen shrugged. "That's way over my head. But I'm sure your people will do everything they can to take good care of her. And ours will, too." He lifted an eyebrow. "Well, when I say 'our' people … you know, those united in the cause."

She frowned. "Yeah. She's tough. I miss her."

"Just remember." He smiled reassuringly. "Part of your job is to get back there once we return you. There's work to be done, but I'm sure seeing your mother can be part of it."

She smiled at his constant words of encouragement. "Yeah. I'll keep that motivation in mind, thanks."

"All ready to head back and see if Jon is capable of making something edible?"

"Almost ready." She thought of the soggy contents of her pants pockets. "Is there, uh, a discreet place I could hang something to dry?" she asked, avoiding eye contact.

He furrowed his brow. "What would you need to—" He went silent, his mouth opening as his eyes settled on her arms, still clutched across her chest. "Oh."

"Jon only got me new outer clothes." She blushed.

"Yeah, we can find somewhere to let them dry overnight."

They found a nice hidden area by the lake in some bushes, and he told her they'd come back to pick them up and fill their canteens the next day before heading out.

Walking back to their campsite in relative silence, Rachel continued to take in the scenery. The variety of greenery was astounding. Green bananas grew high overhead, and just yards away, huckleberry bushes were bursting, full of fruit. Her brother Jeff had explained that unique aspect of the Green Lands, that plant life intermingled much more here than it did in the human world.

Rachel found it soothing—the chirp and buzz of bugs and birds, the rustle of leaves as little lizards chased each other. The air was crisp and their surroundings untouched by the destruction of modern man.

As they foraged sorrel, mushrooms, nuts, and berries along the way to supplement whatever Jon was preparing, Rachel pondered on another cultural lesson from her brother.

"Your kingdom is really beautiful," she said. "I was taught it's a wasteland."

Guillen met her eyes while plucking a few more berries. "Yeah. We're still close to the palace. It's not all this way."

"Do you live close to the palace?"

Looking back down, Guillen shook his head. "Well, kind of. A few days walk away. I've moved around a bit over the last few years."

With bandanas and pockets full, they approached their small clearing.

"Does your family know you're doing this?" she asked Guillen.

"No," he answered softly.

Scanning his face, she dared to pry a little more. "They wouldn't approve of you helping a Seeder?"

He glanced her way with a smile. "I don't really worry about trying to make them proud. My family's kind of a mixed bag, anyway. We're all individuals, right?"

She nodded as they reached Jon and started unloading the ingredients they'd scavenged.

"Any garlic or onion bulbs?" Jon asked.

"No, sorry," Guillen said.

"We'll make do." Jon finished stirring a stew of some kind.

Apparently, Jon was capable of turning out some decent food with the fresh produce he'd brought back from his side trip. They settled down for the night with full stomachs, waking at first light.

"We're going to risk travel in daylight today," Jon explained, "since these woods aren't likely to be patrolled heavily, and our next stop isn't too far away."

"Rachel and I will go top up the canteens, if you want to clean up the rest of camp?" Guillen offered.

"Works for me," Jon said, organizing his pack.

Once Guillen and Rachel arrived at the lake, he offered to fill their canteens while she picked up her delicates and changed.

She'd just finished putting on her bra when a hand slipped over her mouth and an arm wrapped around her, pulling her down to the ground.

"Shh! Quiet!" Guillen hissed in her ear.

She could've had a heart attack with the way he'd surprised her so unceremoniously. She quickly gathered her thoughts and controlled her breathing. Male voices grew louder past the bushes, approaching the lake. Sure, Guillen was protecting her, but she could have happily spent every day of the rest of her life never having a man cover her mouth like that again. And tackling her half-dressed, to boot.

She pried his hands from her mouth and midriff, turning quietly to face him. Giving him a frustrated look, she indicated she understood the stakes by throwing a glance in the direction of the voices. They stayed on the ground in silence for a while. Several minutes passed before the voices faded away. Guillen's eyes wandered once, then he averted his gaze and blushed. She reached for her shirt and held it over her chest.

"Sorry," he whispered. "I'll go check it out and leave you to finish up here."

She quickly finished getting dressed and reemerged, joining Guillen at the lakeside where he was filling the canteens.

"What about Jon?" She couldn't get herself to make eye contact.

"I'm sure he's fine."

They cautiously snuck back to the campsite, where Jon was nowhere to be seen.

"What if something happened to him? What if they saw him?" she asked.

"He can take care of himself. I'm sure he's just hiding out, or trying to get some intel by following them."

"I thought this area wasn't supposed to be patrolled!"

Guillen tilted his head. "We were bound to run across soldiers at some point. Let's hope it's out of the way now. Either way, we wait here for an hour—if he doesn't show, the plan is to meet up at the next location."

She fidgeted with her hands, still uneasy at the close encounter. "And what happens if *I* get separated like this along the way? I don't know where I'm going."

"I promise you—we won't let that happen."

She sat on a stump. "Then I guess we wait."

A half hour passed in silence; all eyes were trained on the perimeter, looking for Jon's return and any additional trouble.

"How long have you known Jon?" she asked.

"Only a few months. Kaylah made the introduction."

"How do you know he can be trusted? Couldn't he have tipped them off in town to come out here?"

Guillen's voice was firm. "If Kaylah trusts him, I trust him."

Rachel shook her head, her stomach in worried knots. "You might think I'm paranoid, but I earned my right to have trust issues."

"I get it. I really do. Either one of us could deceive you." He quickly added, "Well, not me. I wouldn't." He sighed. "I'm just saying, she handpicked us for a reason. But I'll keep an eye on him, okay? Just to be extra cautious?"

"Thanks." She smiled. "But who will keep an eye on you?"

He grinned. "You can." He winked.

Promptly breaking eye contact, she swallowed a few times. She stared blankly at the ground, wringing her hands. He was flirting. That was just … too soon, and complicated, and too much to process right now.

"Hey…" he started.

Jon's whistle of return claimed their attention; they went back to surveying the area.

"Took you long enough," Guillen complained.

"Well, I'm glad you're okay, too," Jon said gruffly. "They've moved on. I wasn't able to hear anything worthwhile before I stopped tailing them. But we should get going."

They headed away from the lake, giving the path the soldiers had taken when passing their camp a wide berth. Other than chatter about the movement of troops, the trek was relatively quiet. Rachel avoided Guillen's gaze, walking with Jon between them for the most part. When they settled down to eat lunch, Guillen asked Rachel if they could talk in private for a moment.

They stepped a few yards away, Jon curiously looking after them.

Guillen's hands were in his pockets, his arms rigid. "I just wanted to apologize. I didn't mean anything by that. You've been through a hell of a lot, and that was … uncalled for. Okay?"

She hugged herself. "It's alright, not a big deal." She looked at his apologetic eyes. "You're really nice. I just … ya know…" *Went through the realm's worst breakup…*

"Yes. I know." He raised his eyebrows. "I don't know *everything*, and that's fine. You don't have to talk about it if you don't want to. But I know what kind of person Soren is; I'm sorry you had to get wrapped up in all of this. I didn't mean to be insensitive back there."

"Thanks." She wore a soft smile. "It was just a twitch anyway, right?"

He smiled back. "Yep, darn eye." He winked again. "Dang it, I should get that checked out."

She chuckled.

"But really, if you ever want to talk—I'm willing to listen. Jon might know more about our training on manipulation tactics, but I know more about Soren, personally."

"Thanks. I have been wondering… Is it true what Soren said, that he's engaged?"

Guillen winced, rubbing the back of his neck. "Yeah, they announced it as soon as he came back."

"How long has it been in the works?"

He arched an eyebrow. "You're sure you want to know these details?"

She nodded.

"They've dated for years. Sorry if that's hard to hear."

She shook her head. "Don't feel sorry for me. Someday, the fog will clear. And I'll be surrounded by people that are actually honest and care about me. I have to believe that." She wanted to add an extra level of assurance. "I don't pine for David. The only thing I want from him right now is for him to get what he deserves, just like Rob did."

Guillen's voice was gentle. "And he will. Are we good?"

"We're good."

Returning to sit down with Jon, Rachel was grateful the tension had dispersed.

"Plotting my demise?" Jon asked lightheartedly.

"Yep," Guillen said with a straight face.

Rachel tapped her fingertips together menacingly.

Jon casually responded, "Sounds good. Hurry up so we can get moving."

***

With at least a couple of hours before the sun would even start to set, Jon announced they were approaching their stopping point for the night. Rachel's heart dropped to see a tiny worn-down log cabin—another thing she would happily never have contact with again. *Why did David have to ruin everything?* She glanced around at the trees nearby—a few of them were dead, looking as though they'd been used by an Ivy to form rifts to the human world. She stood back, fidgeting with her hands. Her apprehension was evident, her anxiety plastered on her face.

Jon offered to clear the building. She could inspect from outside with the door open before entering.

"We can't just keep going? I don't mind walking more, getting more distance in tonight," she suggested.

"The princess gave explicit instructions about stopping here."

Hesitantly, Rachel entered the cabin, curious at the insistence on this location. Essentially one small room, it was crowded with abandoned items, looking like it hadn't seen much use over the years. After shutting the door behind them, they all found a place to sit.

"Why did she say we needed to come here?" Rachel asked.

"She didn't say." Jon shrugged. "She just said it would be helpful for you. Does it spark any memories? Anything jump out at you?"

"No." Scrutinizing the room, Rachel tried to figure out why this place would matter. And then she spotted it, tucked behind some dusty books—a coffee cup, from the shop Kaylah used to work at back home.

Rachel wanted to run up and grab it, but instead made sure to not let her eyes linger too long. She didn't understand the need for this cloak-and-dagger approach if Kaylah really trusted these men, but either way, it was clearly meant to be private. She'd wait to get a closer look.

Chapter 22

RACHEL TOOK IN HER DUSTY surroundings. "How is it you have all these random decrepit cabins in the Neutral Woods?"

"They're from the old days, before our people withdrew and the current boundaries were set in treaty," Jon said. "These are part of the property they abandoned." Their little group had officially left Ivy Kingdom borders a while back and were now in neutral territory.

"Really?" She raised her eyebrows in disbelief. "They're in sad shape, but they've been unoccupied for over two hundred years?"

Guillen shrugged, taking a swig from his canteen.

Jon smirked, balancing his pack on the back edge of a sun-faded love seat. "I forget you haven't really lived in the Green Lands yet. Even if the tree is dead—used for lumber, or paper in books—it doesn't degrade as quickly here. Not like in the human world."

Rachel nodded in approval. "This place is pretty amazing."

She decided to wait until Jon took a turn resting before she would go look at the clue Kaylah had left for her. He encouraged Rachel to try and get some shut-eye as well, so they could be on their way before first light. She told him she would, but she just needed a few minutes to wind down first. Guillen stood at the front window, keeping watch. After Jon's quiet snoring began, Rachel meandered around the room, picking up and examining random items. Reaching the table with the coffee cup, she glanced over her shoulder to make sure Guillen was still focused elsewhere.

Opening the lid, she looked inside—nothing. Flipping it over, she was happy to see a picture of a smiling sun staring back at her. A sweet reminder of back home, she thought, until the fond memory grew tainted with the reminder that her best friend had been poisoning her to screw with her mind. Either way, what was the purpose?

She gave it another look-over, turning and searching for any marks or messages. Scrutinizing the bottom of the cup, she found what she was looking for—one of the rays on the sun was touching the edge of the cup, but it didn't perfectly line up. There was a false bottom.

Picking at it with her fingernail, she popped the bottom off. On the other side of the sun was a message in Kaylah's handwriting. "Memorize. Destroy. Itiner."

Itiner? What's that supposed—

A floorboard creaked behind her, and she quickly folded the note, palming it.

"Find anything fascinating over here?" Guillen whispered, now much closer.

Rachel picked up one of the dusty books. "Just fancied some light reading."

He tilted his head to read the spine of the book. "Recipes? Should we have you take over cooking?"

She set it back down. "I think we'll manage without my attempts. I'm going to turn in."

Noticing the coffee cup, he picked it up, looking at it curiously. "Hmm."

Having stirred up some dust when she'd picked up the book, Rachel fought an oncoming sneeze. Unable to control it, she sneezed into her shoulder. Jon snorted out a loud snore, shifting positions and returning to his quieter breathing.

"Sorry," Rachel whispered.

"Good health," Guillen said, setting the coffee cup down.

Rachel scanned his face. "Good health?"

Guillen studied her face in turn. "Yeah, you sneezed. Do Seeders not … say that?"

Smiling, Rachel now understood. The way he'd said it, with a curious innocence, was undeniably cute. "Well, I honestly don't know what Seeders say for sneezes, since the only ones I've met were pretending to be human. But where I'm from we say 'Bless you.'"

His eyes narrowed slightly. "Is that a power I've never heard of? Can humans bless others with health?"

She bit the insides of her cheeks to suppress a smile. "No. It's just a saying."

He shyly averted his gaze. "Right. Okay."

"Well, I'm going to go lie down now." She settled onto the lumpy old couch to sleep. Once he went back to the window, she carefully tucked the note in her pocket. Struggling to fall asleep, she racked her brain about what she was supposed to use this for. Finally, not long after Jon and Guillen switched places, she found rest.

She woke up to Jon's hand over her mouth this time, a scream ringing in her ears. The warmth of her own breath was trapped by his large hand. Feeling like she could suffocate, she ripped it from her mouth. "Keep your hands off me. Everyone!"

Jon scowled. "I get you've gone through a lot, but you could show a little gratitude. Or should I just let you scream it out and *hope* soldiers aren't nearby next time you have a bad dream?"

Rachel sat up, pinching the bridge of her nose. She was cranky from too little sleep. And the sleep she *had* gotten had felt like a marathon. All. Night. Long. Running for her life, trying to figure out how to hide her little piece of paper. "I'm sorry," she whispered.

It was still dark out, but since they were all up, Jon recommended they take advantage of the cover of night. "Did you figure out … why we're here?" he asked.

"You've got your orders, and I've got mine," she replied, securing the strap of her pack closed.

"Spoken like a true covert operative." Jon flung his pack over his shoulder. "We might just make you one of us yet."

***

The further they traveled from the palace, the less dense and lush the woods became. They made it a point to travel at night and find a well-hidden space to rest up during the day. Rachel ingrained Kaylah's message into her brain and carefully tore up the paper, hiding small pieces of it in the dirt as they would go, until it was all gone.

After four more nights of walking due west, Jon announced they would be staying a little longer; he'd swing by a local outpost and pick up more supplies to get them through the rest of their trip to Seeder borders.

Rachel woke midday to a haggard-looking Guillen. The split sleeping schedule was taking its toll on both of the men. Rachel got up, then sat next to Guillen on a fallen tree. "How about I take a turn keeping watch? You're looking worn out. Grab some more sleep before he comes back."

Guillen took a deep breath, rubbing the back of his neck. "No, it's fine."

"Maybe… But if you get more sleep now, maybe he can get more sleep, too, and you will both be the better for it."

He looked hesitant to accept the offer.

"I can handle it. I'm healed up. I'm well rested. I've got these guys down." She extended her Seeder blades, and he eyed them. He hadn't yet seen her transform all the way. "And I can stay right next to you. If there's any noise or problem, I can wake you up right away."

He yawned. "Only for a little while. Don't let me sleep too long. And anything suspicious, get me up right away."

"Okay. I promise."

He curled up nearby and soon drifted off, his breathing slowed. She smiled, watching him peacefully sleep. It suited him with how calming he was. She wished she could sleep that well right now.

While the scenery was beautiful, Rachel's eyes wandered to Guillen's sleeping figure more often than not. He was handsome, and sweet, and innocent, and strong. Unlike Jon, who'd let his beard scruff take over the last few days, Guillen made it a point to do a quick shave with his sharp blades every couple of days.

Probably an hour or more passed and, as promised, she was still sitting next to him, her eyes focused now on his belt and the knives attached to it. The only thing that had stirred during his nap was an adorable chipmunk that scurried past them into a bush.

"Had any training with knives?" Guillen asked, startling her. "Other than your own blades?"

"No."

He sat up. "I could show you a thing or two."

She smirked, sneaking a quick glance back at his belt. "Are you trying to offer to let me … check out your … tools?"

His jaw dropped. "You … just went there. Was that a joke about…"

She giggled, thinking it was only fair after he stole a peek at her chest by the lake. "Sorry. Just having some fun." She cleared her throat. "I'd love to learn more about your mad skills. Anything that would help with defense is good."

Grinning, he scanned her face. "I like seeing you smile more. Real smiles."

She blushed. Despite all the chaos she'd been through, his smiles were something she was enjoying, too.

He unsheathed a knife for each of them, then demonstrated his technique on holding it for best control in fighting, then how to throw it to stick it in the ground where he wanted. He had amazing accuracy. She … needed practice.

Rachel turned the blade in her hand after a while spent chucking it haphazardly. "How do you know when it's dull enough to need sharpening?" Running her finger along the edge of the blade, she winced as she cut herself.

He held his hand out, and she surrendered the knife. "Well, that's not exactly how I would recommend going about it."

She stared at her finger, oddly entranced. As the blood seeped to the surface, she remembered some of her darkest days. Probably caused by Kaylah, but also ended by her, when she'd caught her with the needle. Rachel moved another finger over the blood and focused on healing it.

"You okay? You had one of your looks, like you left for a while."

She continued to stare at the now-healed finger. "Wouldn't it be nice if I could heal my heart and mind, the same way I can my skin?" Her melancholy tone matched the numbness inside her.

His voice was soft. "Even in the Green Lands, with all of our accelerated healing, we all have scars. Most of them just aren't visible."

Snapping out of her trance, Rachel took her canteen and washed off the blood. "Speaking of, I was curious about trying something. Could I look at your hand?"

"Sure…" He offered both hands.

She selected the one bearing a large scar on the back of it, near the wrist—the scar still seemed fresh; it was pink.

"I don't know if it works for old wounds." She placed a healing touch on the scar, smiling internally at the warmth of his hand. Her mind wandered again to their encounter at the lake, and she fought a grin while focusing on her experiment. She checked it twice before calling it done, feeling a significant drain. She'd expected it to heal faster, like Soren's cut that she'd taken care of, especially with the energy of the Green Lands. But she'd never tried healing something that was technically already healed. After a few minutes, she revealed it. It had faded enough to be noticeable.

"That's impressive." He ran his fingers over it.

She raised her hand to the larger scar on his temple. "If you'd like—"

Guillen intercepted her hand, guiding it down. "Some scars we earn, and they become part of our story." His piercing eyes conveyed the importance this one must hold for him. "Plus, I know that takes a lot out of you. Best to use it on fresh things, not focusing on something from the past."

"Okay."

He knew how to say the right things. He wasn't manipulative or flattering the way David was. His words held genuine kindness and wisdom from what must have been years of introspection.

"Can I practice more?" She glanced down at her hand—he was still holding it after preventing her from healing his scar.

"Are you done trying to filet yourself?" He wore a playful grin.

She scrunched her face in defiance before he handed the knife back to her with a softer smile.

He corrected her technique every so often, and she slowly saw improvement in how well she could aim. He then showed her how to sharpen the knives they'd been practicing with.

"Your skills are pretty impressive," she complimented. "You've obviously dedicated a lot of time to learning."

"Your Seeder skills are pretty impressive, as well," he returned.

She carefully made another pass with a sharpening stone. "Yeah, but yours is a learned skill, on top of any natural botanical powers. The sum of what I can demonstrate is seriously insufficient natural ability."

"I *wish* my practice added to natural abilities." He looked down after their eyes met.

"What do you mean?"

He drew a deep breath and met her gaze. "Have you ever seen my vines?"

She searched her memories. It wasn't like Jon had pulled his out often, but she'd seen them. It wasn't exactly something she had fixated on, but now that she thought about it… "No, I guess I haven't."

"That's because I don't have any."

Chapter 23

RACHEL SURVEYED GUILLEN, CONFUSED. "What do you mean? Don't all Ivies have vines?"

Guillen raised his eyebrows. "Not if you're a stunt."

She narrowed her eyes, never having heard that as green folk terminology. "Like … 'I do my own stunts'? It's from an injury?"

He shook his head. "No. Kaylah once said humans might classify us as 'disabled'?"

Her eyes widened. "Oh."

"Not something I always bring up." Guillen pressed his lips together.

She bit her lip. "You don't have to talk about it, if you don't want to…"

"It's okay. It's probably better you know the limitations of someone you're working with, anyway. Jon knows. I guess you could call it a birth defect. It's pretty rare, but I can't do anything a normal Ivy can. I'm just," he shrugged, "this. I'm essentially human."

Her mouth hung open. "I … hadn't thought about something like that."

He smiled, though the warmth didn't reach his eyes. "I wish I didn't have to think about it. Stunts are… Well, let's just say there's not a lot of respect for my kind. They group us together, in our own communities, at the back end of our territories—for our own 'safety.' We don't get the same kind of education, since it's not necessary for us to learn to use vines, or create rifts, or how to blend in with humans." He shifted slightly on the fallen tree he'd been sitting on. "We're tasked with the menial work others in more respectable positions don't want to do—so we can feel 'pride' in contributing to the kingdom. We're even forbidden from having kids so we don't pass on our bad genes."

She frowned. "That's so horrible. I'm sorry."

"Thanks. But I try not to let myself dwell on it too much. I'm pretty lucky, honestly." He rolled up one of his sleeves. While his toned arms were impressive, Rachel immediately spotted what he was trying to show her—a tattoo.

"That's neat."

"That's one way of looking at it."

It was the outline of an ivy leaf, and in the middle was a crown symbol.

"Can I?" she asked as she moved closer, running her thumb over it. "What does it mean to you?"

"The middle symbol permits me to move around undocumented. It allows me to have some semblance of normalcy despite my nature. If you're not close in the royal bloodline like I am, you have a number in the middle of the leaf. That signifies the community you're assigned to."

She looked into his eyes, horrified. As if she'd gotten the wind knocked out of her, she stuttered. "They… They … tattoo *numbers* on your people, just because they don't have the same powers?!"

He took her hand from his arm and unrolled his sleeve to cover the tattoo. "I don't want you to look at me that way." Shaking his head, he looked away. "I don't like people feeling sorry for me. This is just the way it is for my people. I have no room to complain—I still get a lot of freedom. I get to choose which of the communities I live in." He shrugged. "I got extra tutors and was given the choice to live with my family until I was eighteen."

Her heart ached. "Guillen, I know you didn't learn about human history, but ... this is the kind of thing that was done by one of the *worst* rulers over there. It's despicable!"

He looked slightly confused. "When the only thing that differentiates you from your enemy is a demonstration of powers, how do you ensure they're not infiltrating your land under the guise of being a stunt?"

She crossed her arms, scowling at the ground, pondering his question. "I don't know." She lifted her head to look at him again. "But it's still wrong!"

He studied her face. "There are good and bad people in every society, aren't there? I bet you never thought you'd feel sorry for a group of Ivies."

She sighed at the irony. "I guess you're right. I just can't believe they'd do this to their own people."

Guillen blew out a long puff of air. "That's what hate does to us. It makes us forget how much we have in common, and that we all have our own struggles. But like I said, with my ties to the palace, I'm not treated as much like a pariah as most are. And Kaylah's always been a good cheerleader. And she's pretty impressive with a dagger and machete, from years of sparring with me. I couldn't be a military man, but that didn't mean I wasn't capable of learning new skills."

Rachel smiled, finding herself admiring him more each day. "I'd say 'capable' is an understatement. And honestly, humans live every single day without abilities like we have in the Green Lands. They're blissfully ignorant, living their lives over there. Granted, for them it's normal. I bet you'd love it there, not being treated the way you are in your kingdom."

"I'm sure I would..." he said wistfully.

The conversation lit a light bulb for her. "Do you know … about *my* people? I haven't heard about this kind of thing before, but I can only imagine some of our people might have a condition like this."

"No. Not a lot of cultural information comes our way from your side. It would be interesting to learn about, though. When you're back there, you'll have to find out."

"I'll do that, for sure." She smiled.

"Great. I expect to see you again someday or get a note all about it."

Her smile widened, then shrank with another question. "What does 'stunt' actually mean?"

"Ah, yes, that. It's short for 'stunted.'"

She'd had a feeling he'd say something like that. It made her sick. "That's not right."

Guillen shrugged. "It's the politest term I've ever heard for us."

Rachel frowned. "Really? You don't have anything else you call yourself?"

He smirked, picking up a pine cone. "I thought you knew—*I* call myself Guillen."

She chuckled. "I think you know that's not what I meant, but I'll take it."

He tossed the pine cone back to the forest floor. "Just do me a favor?"

"What's that?"

"I *really* don't want any pity."

"There's nothing pitiful about you, Guillen." She looked into his stormy eyes, which softened, warming her heart.

She took a sharp breath. "So … Jon… We're still thinking he's on the up-and-up? Why is he the one that disappears for hours at a time and you get the babysitting duty?"

Guillen chuckled, then took a drink from his canteen. "Honestly, he's become a palace boy. I sense he's not quite as fond of the nomadic camping lifestyle. Signs of civilization seem to keep him sane." He smirked again, holding up his canteen. "So, I suffer, taking on this monumental task, watching this beautiful and kind girl. I just don't know how I'll make it through the next few days."

She flashed him a toothy smile. "I guess we'll just have to make do." She bit her lip. "Honestly, I haven't gone camping since … Brad." Her high spirits began to deflate. Had Rob been honest about Brad leaving, just because he'd found out she was a Seeder? Or that Rob had killed him? Or was he just trying to get to her? None of the options brought her any comfort.

She tried to stop the mental train wreck in progress. "I need to stretch my legs. I saw a patch of wildflowers growing not that far from here. How about a walk to go take a look?"

***

After Jon returned to camp with fresh supplies, they let him rest up and then pressed on after nightfall. They anticipated at least three more days of travel, and then things would get a little more interesting.

"We don't actually know which village you belong to, or where it's located along the border," Jon said. "But your people should have gotten word about your return with plenty of time to have eyes looking out for the signal."

Over the hours and days of their travels, Rachel had a lot to take in and sort through. The exchange of information, hopes, and dreams between green folk that would usually be enemies was thrilling. Rachel had more than enough time to try and make something out of the jumble of mental chaos that had been inflicted on her. Her healing journey was far from complete, but she had a new resolve, and greater perspective on who she was and who she wanted to be from here on out. The energy of the Green Lands, the understanding companions to talk to, the quiet away from chaos—she reaped the rewards, bit by bit.

Initially, starting the journey back to her ancestral home, she'd been bogged down by despair and pain. Over time, it had transformed into hope, and now, unfortunately, building anxiety. The closer they got to Seeder lands, the more she realized how much pressure would be placed on her, how much things would be changing again. She stressed over how she would be received by her new family and people. The shame she felt for allowing herself to become a victim. And not only that, but one that had helped the enemy in their attack. Not willingly, of course, but the fact that they'd had her in the first place to be able to steal her energy…

She also worried about her role in this war. She was now consigned to this world permanently—Soren and Nuren had taken that choice from her by making sure she'd rooted here. But where does one start a new life when they arrive in the middle of a bloodbath?

And Kaylah. The 'rebellion.' Her expectations were more than cryptic, but nonetheless, she had expectations. The quicker Rachel could get back to the human world, the better. Ignoring the request of your best friend/revolution leader/rescuer/princess was hardly an option on the table. And it was getting late in the season, even for an experienced female Seeder, to catch a breeze to the human world.

***

Rachel woke one morning to birds chirping in the trees. Rolling onto her stomach, she rested her chin on the back of her hands. Thinking of her mom, she ached. How many people willingly took in someone else's child? And to be betrayed like that, being left by two men. Did her mom even know about Rob's betrayal? Did she think her daughter was dead?

An iridescent beetle strolled by, giving Rachel cause to smile. Guillen and Jon were whispering again. This time, Jon said he'd be off relieving himself past some trees. Rachel reached out, moving a twig out of the beetle's path.

"So, you *are* awake," Guillen said.

Rachel took a deep breath. The crispness of the air and the babble of a nearby brook were enchanting. "Even the bugs are pretty here."

Dirt and gravel crunched under his boots as he drew near. He sat a few feet in front of her, tilting his head to the side with a hint of a smile. "Not afraid of the pretty little bugs?"

She propped herself up on her elbows. "Spiders are different. Unless maybe you have rainbow spiders?"

He grinned. "Not that I'm aware of."

Rachel picked herself up, sitting cross-legged facing Guillen and taking a drink of water from her canteen. "I appreciate you and Jon helping me. And Meg … Kaylah … said I could trust the two of you."

"Yes."

Looking down at her hands, Rachel picked at her chipped prom manicure. "But how do I know I can trust *her*?"

Guillen frowned when she looked back up. "I don't know how to convince you. All I can say is that I know you can. Kaylah's been lied to, probably as much as you have been. She hardly knows who to trust, herself."

Rachel's eyes narrowed. "Really?"

He nodded. "From what she told me over the years—and I've never known her to lie to me—this whole thing was Nuren's plan, and Soren volunteered to help. Kaylah was the only one not given the choice."

She studied his face. "Why would the future queen spend her youth in the human world? Wasting so much time on a nobody like me?"

He raised his eyebrows in disapproval. "You're not a nobody."

She shrugged. "But I'm not special."

Smiling, he broke eye contact. "I suppose that depends on how you classify 'special.'" He cleared his throat, picking up a pebble and rolling it across his hand. "But you want to know why the queen and king would ship her off like that?" He shrugged. "Because Nuren had trust issues and wanted a girl he could keep under his thumb to befriend you? He had the queen and king's ear. Supposedly, sending their older kids off on this mission could earn them the pride of the kingdom—examples of successful covert operatives as a notch in their belt."

Guillen sighed. "She was constantly kept in the dark. For the first several years, they lied to her, telling her you were a human. She thought she was brought there to study human society."

Rachel's eyes narrowed again in surprise. "Really?"

"Really. Just … give her a chance. And cut her a little slack. She's so used to putting on an act that sometimes it can take a while for her to really open up about her struggles."

Rachel wore a contented smile. "I'll think about all of that. Thank you. I'm glad she has someone like you to talk to."

He grinned.

Rachel's mind drifted to the coffee cup clue. "If she trusts the two of you, why did we need to stop at the cabin for me to find something? You don't know what she left for me there?"

Shaking his head, he leaned back with his hands propping him up. "It's best to break up intel. That's one less thing they could torture out of Jon and me if we got caught."

Rachel swallowed hard. "Right."

"Did I miss anything important?" Jon asked as he returned.

Guillen looked up. "Just talking about how Rachel can know whether to trust Kaylah."

Rachel craned her neck to see Jon's face.

He dropped his pack on the ground. "You seem like you possess more than half a brain. I'm sure you'll figure it out."

Choking back a laugh, Rachel put a hand over her heart. "Jon, you are just *so* sweet!"

He rolled his eyes, showing the smallest hint of a smile. "Are we ready to move on?"

Chapter 24

WHILE THE WOODS BETWEEN THE Ivy palace and neutral territory were somewhat sparse, they grew denser again as Rachel and her escorts approached their target. Despite having more trees for cover, they had to be more alert than ever—this area was crawling with soldiers, most of them Ivy. And with two Ivies accompanying her, it wouldn't be ideal if they were caught by either side at this point.

"This is where we start the final phase," Jon announced. He pulled out some items from his pack and handed them to Rachel. First, a rolled letter, sealed. "That is for you, you can read it when you're ready." Another sealed letter, with a gold ring tied to it. "That is for your people once you're safely on the other side. Guard them with your life."

Guillen spoke up. "The last thing Kaylah needed you to know was 13310 North Maplewood. You'll want to remember that."

Rachel repeated it in her mind until it was permanent, adding it to the other clue. *Itiner. 13310 North Maplewood.*

"Guillen is going to go tonight. Don't be startled by fireworks in the sky," Jon said.

Rachel's eyes darted to Guillen. "You're going?" Her heart was heavy at having to say goodbye already.

He gave her a gentle smile. "I'll be back. You're not getting rid of me yet."

They found shelter in a densely wooded area that, according to their latest contacts, was not heavily patrolled right now. Guillen snuck out before sundown, leaving Rachel and Jon to silently keep watch. Rachel took the opportunity to open her letter from Kaylah.

I hope you can forgive me. I need you to put everything behind you that David and Rob have ever said or done to you. I'm not without fault, and I'm sorry for that. I wish I could undo so many choices, but that's the past. What I can do now, and what you can do, is work together for our people. This is Unitas, the Unity Movement. Change can happen when enough people learn the truth and question the propaganda. It takes strong people like you to get the job done. I need you to meet with me, to provide an introduction. I can explain more when you come. Stay safe. I look forward to seeing you soon. Love you.

Rachel looked up; Jon was watching. "Do you know what's in here?"

He shook his head. "I don't need to know."

"So, when we part ways, what's next for you and Guillen?"

"Well, now that we took out the duke, I'd say we're pretty set on our paths. We have our orders once you're safely back. We each have our specialties and connections; we'll keep growing the movement."

"Will I have any way of contacting you guys?"

"Not that I know of. This assignment will be over. And you'll have plenty to work on, too."

She frowned. If this had been the human world, she'd happily exchange numbers with both of them, to keep in touch. But there were trade-offs for life in the Green Lands, one of them being the lack of electricity.

At least two hours passed before they heard any noise from outside of their shelter. An explosion tore through the night sky, shattering the silence. Jon confirmed the first sign had been deployed—red fireworks.

While anxiously awaiting Guillen's return, Rachel decided to try and get to know Jon better.

"I'd love to hear more about you, your story." She barely spoke above a whisper. "If you're willing to share." More than wanting to calm her nerves, she knew any witness who could speak for the movement may be helpful.

"My story, huh?"

The moon was bright, the sky clear. Jon's shadowed face darkened in his hesitancy to talk.

"Yeah. Why you decided to make the sacrifice and join Unitas."

He nodded. "Our people don't know what's going on at the palace, you know?"

She furrowed her brow. "Really? You mean what they're doing to my people?"

He nodded again. "That's the main thing. It's against orders to talk about it. Some people in the palace don't even know, like servants in the kitchens." He pulled out a flask and took a swig. "People don't want to know the truth. They want to be told *what* to want, and then told *how* to get it. They don't think for themselves."

There was a reason he didn't talk much about anything other than strategy. There was an altogether different tone to his delivery.

"So," he cleared his throat, "the first girl. That was…" He paused. "Sickening. Unbelievable. Horrifying. Especially as they worked things out. Trying to figure out how to tune things, how to balance giving her breaks." He took another drink from his flask. "My least favorite assignment, by far, having to play any part in that."

The full weight of his story sank in for Rachel as he drew a deep breath. She hadn't been an early guinea pig—it could have been worse.

"So, when they bring a second one around," Jon continued, "I see Princess Kaylah come back for a visit. And we shared a look. You don't get cozy with the royal family; we'd never formally met. So, it was a bit terrifying when she sought me out privately. Thinking I'd be dismissed, or worse, for showing weakness."

He let out a breathy chuckle. "Boy, was I wrong about her. It didn't take much convincing to join her little group. She put me to work almost immediately."

Shifting his position, he settled in with more ease as he talked. "It actually wasn't that hard to do my part. You just happen to accidentally, cautiously, be loose-lipped to the right people. You see what their reaction is about what's happening at the palace, gauge their feelings, see where they fall on the spectrum of potential allies."

"That's really neat," Rachel said. They'd been thinking this out and working on it for some time. Of course, this was all just from when Jon had joined. She didn't know how long Kaylah had actively been working on things.

He sighed. "It doesn't come without a cost. Sometimes, you wish you could go back to being ignorant about what people really think."

She frowned. What had his personal cost been? "Do you have a family?"

He arched an eyebrow. "Everyone has a family."

She picked up a twig, starting to draw in the dirt with it. "You know what I mean."

"No. Not one of my own," he said. "My, uh … partner, of five years—she's one of those I wish I'd never said anything to. Around the time I realized she wasn't likely to come around, Princess Kaylah was starting to ask more of me. I gave Sheila some crap excuse when I decided to move out."

"I'm sorry." Five years—that was a decent investment. At least Ivies weren't stuck mating for life like Seeders were. "You'll find someone that's better for you someday."

He shook his head. "We'll see. I still love her. If I could just change that *one part*... But I can't blame her. *I'm* the one who changed." He took another deep breath, capping his flask and tucking it away. "Doesn't really matter now, anyway. Once they got you, and the princess reached out… I'm as good as burned."

He chuckled. "You're gone. We left bodies. And I didn't show up for work the next day. I think it's safe to say they might have put two and two together."

"Yeah. I guess you're right." She poked at the ground with her twig, feeling a bit guilty, and still nervous to see Guillen return. "What about Guillen and his kind?"

"Good ol' Guillen," he said. "Never lived near his communities. And his kind do their best to blend in when given permission to visit normal cities, so I can't say I've knowingly met one before."

Rachel stayed silent, feeling protective of Guillen. She found herself frustrated that Jon didn't seem to carry equal passion about that particular domestic agenda.

"I was a little nervous to be working with him. Being without … well, you know. But I was surprised. He's really competent, brings a good mix of skills."

After a moment of silence, she decided she'd rather go back to listening for Guillen's return. "Thanks for sharing all that with me."

"No problem."

The quiet helped her mind wander, helped her worry. "What would we do, if we came across a huge ambush out here?"

"Depends on who it is and how bad," he said. "If it's your kind, we surrender and hope for the best. If it's ours, we fight. If there's too many, you're the priority. We both know that."

Her chest tightened, glancing at the trees surrounding them. "Are you capable of taking Guillen's kind through a rift? Like Soren did with me?"

Jon shook his head. "Only Seeder females can do that trick—the only beings in the Green Lands capable of sharing energy."

She'd worried about that. It wasn't just that Guillen couldn't create his own rift because he didn't have vines. He couldn't rift *at all*. While Jon couldn't rift Rachel safely into Seeder lands, he *could* take her back to the human world to get out of immediate danger, and then try to come back from a new place. Guillen would be left alone.

Every moment Guillen was in these woods escorting Rachel back was one of incredible danger. "I… If we find a good clearing, I should be able to catch a breeze and get home on my own this close to our borders, right?"

"No. We're following the plan. Your people will escort you back safely."

She didn't hate the idea of more time spent with Guillen. A day more, even a second more. But she realized that was beyond selfish. "But it would be safer for … both of you … if I went the rest of the way on my own."

"The princess is worried about arrows."

"Wait. I thought Ivies primarily used vines to fight."

With a heavier sigh that seemed to carry frustration, Jon shifted his position again. "As a point of pride and practicality, archers are only stationed at the palace. Your people have projectiles and can fly. We have to be able to combat that. Nuren petitioned the queen for years, saying we ought to send archers into the woods, too. Now that he's dead, the princess wants to be prepared for any unintended consequences."

Rachel left it at that. There was no winning.

***

Three hours passed without sign of Guillen. The knots in Rachel's stomach grew tighter with the nerve-racking silence.

"He'll be fine. It's likely to take longer to return. He has to avoid being followed, and that thing," he pointed to the night sky where the fireworks had previously lit up, "is drawing a lot of attention right now."

Jon was right—she was able to breathe a sigh of relief not much later as Guillen returned. The next night, it was Jon's turn to go out. It was only an hour or so before green fireworks rained down, another decoy.

On the third night, Guillen took off in a different direction, this time taking three or four hours before brilliant blue sparks lit up the sky.

"The finale," Jon whispered.

It was late into the night before Guillen returned. Jon offered to let him sleep, but Guillen insisted he wasn't tired yet and would take over the watch. Rachel tried her best to get some shut-eye, but her mind was playing every possible scenario that could happen over the next few days. Her eyes met with Guillen's in the moonlight and he moved closer, crouching down in front of her.

"Not able to sleep?"

As she shook her head, a wisp of hair fell in front of her eyes.

He tucked it behind her ear, smiling. "How about I sit here next to you?" He did just that, placing his hand on her shoulder, softly rubbing it. "Just until you fall asleep."

She wore a contented grin. "Then I might choose to never fall asleep."

He met her remark with a gentle squeeze of the shoulder, to which she replied by moving her other hand to meet his, intertwining their fingers. She didn't remember falling asleep, but she did remember having the most peaceful rest she'd had in an insanely long time.

When she woke, Jon was anxiously staring at something outside of their hiding place. Guillen was sleeping on the ground, not far from Rachel. When Jon spotted her gaze, he put a finger to his lips and indicated with a nod that there might be danger nearby. Staying still, she listened quietly. There was a faint rustling of foliage, and then whispering voices. Jon pointed to Guillen. Since Rachel was closer, she would be the one to carefully wake him up. Should they be discovered, they would need to be ready.

She cautiously moved over to him, leaning over and covering his mouth, whispering into his ear, "Guillen. We've got trouble."

He reflexively reached for his belt, but the tension in his face and arms melted away once he realized it was Rachel, who now had a finger to her lips. She slowly removed her hand and nodded at Jon. Guillen quietly sat up and listened. They couldn't give away their position, especially now that the final fireworks had gone out. If they had to move, the location wouldn't be accurate for the Seeders to find Rachel.

While the soldiers passed uncomfortably close, it appeared the Unitas party remained undetected.

As they ate their lunch later in the day, Rachel asked with a cocky smile, "So, how do *you* like it? Waking up with someone's hand on your mouth? Not the best feeling, is it?"

Guillen grinned and did a quick up-down look at her. "I'd be okay waking up seeing *that* every day." He winked.

She blushed, having walked right into that.

The rest of the afternoon passed by in cautious silence. They only had a few hours left before they went their separate ways. All three of them were on edge as they bided their time.

More than once, Rachel caught Guillen's gaze. More than once, he also caught her checking him out. Each time their eyes met, they exchanged a shy smile. But no one talked. She didn't know what to say. And they needed to be vigilant about monitoring their surroundings.

What would they have to say, anyway? What could she and Guillen have even hoped for out of this, on a personal level?

The pain and fear mounted as Jon and Guillen packed up their things. They planned to leave before dark to put a good amount of distance between them and Rachel. White fireworks would go up in the sky that night, and they wouldn't be returning.

Guillen approached her first. "You'll do great things." He handed her one of his knives, smiling. His hand lingered as it touched hers in the exchange. "Because you don't have to just rely on natural abilities, right?" He bit his lip, meeting her gaze. "And maybe it's something you can remember me by."

Rachel's heart was screaming that she didn't need anything to remember him by, not if he stayed with her. He could stay; they could figure things out. She could be happy with him by her side. He could be happy in Seeder lands, not being treated as a nobody.

But she knew she couldn't be selfish. It would risk his life further, and they both had work to do. She wasn't even sure if his kind would be immune to the poison that haunted Seeder lands—being there with her might actually carry a death sentence for an Ivy 'stunt,' a being without powers.

She lunged at him with a hug, squeezing tight. "I'll do my research, as promised. And I expect to see you again, so take care."

He wrapped his arms around her, whispering back, "You too."

Releasing Guillen, she gave him a kiss on the cheek.

Jon snickered. "I see what happens when I leave to get supplies."

She turned to Jon, smiling, and opened her arms for a hug.

He held out his hand for a firm handshake. "It's been my pleasure. Do your best to not need saving again, okay?"

"I'll do what I can."

"And don't let down the princess. Everyone's counting on you."

And with that ominous reminder, they left.

Chapter 25

MINUTES TICKED BY. THE HOURS drew long. Finally, the sign came—a shower of lights in the night sky. Jon and Guillen were still alright, and they were keeping Rachel safe. There was no going back, nowhere to go. Now, she just had to wait.

Rachel stayed alert all night, fidgeting with Guillen's knife and Kaylah's letter for comfort. She rehearsed the clues she'd been given to memorize. She practiced reading and manipulating the surrounding air, something she would need to master quickly to catch a breeze.

Just before the sun rose in the sky, the crack of a twig nearby caught her attention.

"Don't worry, we'll find her," a male voice whispered.

"Rachel?" a female called out in a hushed tone.

Rachel peeked out from her cover. Two sets of glowing green eyes searched the area. She lit hers up to give her position.

"Rachel? Is that you? Are you okay?" the man asked.

She emerged from the bushes. "Yeah."

The strangers reached her, giving her a tight hug.

"We've got everyone out looking for you! My name is Saff. This is my husband, Devin. We're going to take you home."

As they quietly and cautiously made their way through the Neutral Woods to Seeder territory, they ran across two more searchers—one being Jeff. Jeff and Rachel shared an awkward hug before approaching the Outer Wall. Once they made it through the Outer Wall, Devin gave a signal and a trumpet blew, recalling the rest of the search parties.

***

The first day and night were overwhelming, to say the least, as she was taken to the family she'd never known. It would have been a decent walk back to her village, but Rachel insisted she wanted to catch a breeze to cut down the time. She needed more practice if she was going to do what Kaylah expected of her. She was a bit wobbly, and thoroughly embarrassed by her technique, but the new energy coursing through her—now that she was rooted in the Green Lands—helped her complete the trip without incident.

While flying over Seeder territory, Rachel spotted similar plant life to the lush growth she'd seen near the Ivy palace. But this time, she got to see dozens, even hundreds, of Seeder homes. Footpaths leading to every part of the landscape were covered by people going about their tasks and meeting at outdoor markets. It was beautiful, but bustling. Nervous, part of her didn't want to land, didn't want to be around more new people, didn't want to leave the serenity she'd enjoyed with a couple of kind companions in the Neutral Woods. But land she did.

Her Seeder family's warm reception was filled with tears of relief, though not even half of them were present. Most were fighting or still in the human world. Rachel met one-on-one with her birth mom, Lyza. Lyza was thin, with much darker hair than Rachel. They really didn't look much alike, though Rachel had learned that most Seeders didn't carry a strong family resemblance. Before her true Seeder identity had been revealed, she'd always grown up knowing she was adopted, and had secretly painted a picture in her mind of how her parents looked. She imagined she might have shared their eyes or nose, or something distinct. But Lyza looked like a complete stranger. Rachel still hadn't met her Seeder father, but from the pictures Lyza showed her, she didn't seem to share any jump-out-at-you traits with him either.

During their initial exchange, Lyza shared with Rachel the Seeder name she'd been assigned, as was customary in their family upon a girl's return home. Luckily, Rachel didn't feel pressured to accept it right away.

She found herself increasingly shy as all those able to be present sat down to a picnic in their family lot to celebrate her return. Everyone tiptoed around the topic, asking her how she was, but never addressing the elephant in the room.

A new sister she recognized from her high school sat down next to Rachel, offering her a bowl of blackberries. "We're all really glad you're home safe." She gave a cautious smile.

Rachel picked out a few berries. "Thanks." Surveying her family, she tried to hide a frown. The odd glance was thrown her way now and then, eating at her. *What do they know? Is it public knowledge that I was so stupid to not see the signs, and allowed myself to get taken? Did the power drained from me cause anyone harm, or worse? Do they blame me?*

One of her brothers approached, crouching next to Rachel. "Hey there."

She forced a smile. "Hi, um…" She blanked on his name. There were too many new names to keep track of.

He gave an understanding grin. "Patrick."

"Right. Sorry."

He waved a dismissive hand in the air. "No need to apologize. I'm sure there's a lot for you to take in."

Rachel nodded.

"I'm going to head out in a couple hours, to let Samantha know you're back safe. Do you want to write her a letter?"

Rachel choked on her words as she unsuccessfully fought tears. "Yeah, um, definitely."

He frowned, moving his hand up to her shoulder. "No rush. Just let me know when you're ready."

She tried to subtly and quickly wipe the tears from the corners of her eyes. "I, uh… Does she know what all happened?"

He pursed his lips. "I was told you went missing. And your boyfriend, and stepdad, and best friend and her parents. Sounds like everything kinda hit the fan at once." He looked down. "As far as I know, that's what she knows."

Rachel's heart dropped. *She* would have to be the one to break the news to her mom about her husband having betrayed them both.

Patrick met her gaze, seemingly hesitant to speak again. "She, uh… Well, maybe don't take too long to write that letter. They found a note that was supposed to be from you and your boyfriend, that you'd run away together."

Rachel looked down, shaking her head. *Soren.*

"And then another note came, I guess, that apparently led us to you?"

She cracked a tiny smile. *Kaylah.*

"I'm just saying, there was some conflicting information, you know? I think she'd feel a ton better knowing for sure that you *are* actually alive."

Rachel immediately looked up. "Where's some paper?"

After taking time to write her letter, Rachel handed it over to Patrick and walked down the lane with him, watching as he caught a breeze.

That night, she slept soundly in a comfortable bed, safe from harm. The next day, however, would not be so easy.

***

Rachel was asked to meet with the village council for debriefing. Saff, her welcoming mentor, picked her up in the morning. As they walked down the lane together, Rachel bobbed along in silence.

"How are you doing?" Saff asked.

Rachel shrugged. "Good. It was nice to sleep indoors again and get a proper shower."

As they approached the main lane toward their destination, Rachel's heartbeat quickened at the sight of the crowds. "Do we have to take this path?"

Saff frowned. "It's the fastest way to get there. Plus, I figured it would be nice to give you the grand tour of our home village today."

Rachel stayed silent, still not wanting to go that way.

"And we can grab you some lunch from the vendors on the way. It's not usually this busy, we're just crowded with the…" Saff looked down. "With the Vine attacks."

Swallowing hard, Rachel scanned the street. Yards away, near a vendor's handcart full of oranges and cabbage, a pair of girls around her age huddled as though gossiping. In unison, their gazes reached Rachel, and they continued to chatter.

"I can skip lunch," she said, wanting to be anywhere but there right now. "I don't want to go down this street." Right after she'd said it, a little boy bumped into her, being chased by what was probably a brother. Her breathing picking up, she turned to Saff, pleading. "Please, can we go a different way?"

Saff nodded with a sympathetic frown. "Yeah, let's go down a less busy lane." Wrapping her arm around Rachel's shoulder, she guided her off of the main path. "How about I circle back and bring you some lunch when I come to pick you up from your council meeting?"

"Yeah. Thanks."

Joining the local council at a large oval wooden table in a public meeting room, Rachel was drilled about the locations, tactics, strategies, and really anything she'd picked up from being in Ivy territory. She was grateful no open accusations or shame were being thrown her way. They asked how she'd been kidnapped, how the Ivies had targeted her. She chose not to tell them she *willingly* went with Prince Soren—she carried enough guilt over the situation. From what she gleaned, the other five girls had probably been kidnapped in different ways.

Rachel handed over the sealed letter Jon had given her. They unrolled it and read it aloud.

To the Honorable Leaders of the Seeder People,

As a gesture of goodwill, and sincerity in extending a hand in friendship, we bring you safely back one of your own and present you with the ring of Duke Nuren. Desiring to forge an alliance as a means of ending the current hostility and pointless bloodshed, I request an audience with a small delegation of leadership. My only requirements are an agreement of peaceful parley, and that Rachel accompany the group, as she knows how to find the location. Understanding the urgency for your people, I guarantee safe and swift passage for any Seeder coming at my invitation, including a prompt return to the Neutral Woods, at our expense, upon the completion of negotiations. In so doing, I denounce the ways of the current Ivy leadership. My goal is peace and equality, the kind our peoples have not seen for centuries.

Kaylah Elonta, Crown Princess of the Mountain Palace and Ivy Kingdom, Leader of the Unitas Movement.

Rachel was ready to go. The Seeders were not. They deliberated for hours. They'd only heard faint rumors of such a rebellion happening on the other side, and even though Kaylah had offered a token with the duke's head on a platter, and Rachel's safe return, they wouldn't budge.

"It's not big enough to waste our time on," they said.

"Maybe when they've proven they can do more," they reasoned.

"We could just as easily be walking into another one of their traps," they warned.

"If you give us her location, we can send some men to check it out ourselves," they tried.

"I don't have an address to give you," Rachel lied. "I'd need to go, too, if you want to find her."

A councilwoman narrowed her eyes. "Why would the princess say you knew how to find her and then not give you any indication of where she would be? Why would it make a difference if you were there?"

Rachel swallowed hard. "The only address I know of is her house in the human world. Maybe she left a clue there that only I would recognize?" Her heart raced. She refused to be cut out of this part of the equation. She wasn't going to send Seeder soldiers to kidnap or kill Kaylah.

The councilwoman gave a polite smile, folding her hands on the table. "I hate to be indelicate, Rachel. But do you know what grooming is? Conditioning?"

Rachel glanced down, her stomach knotting. "I want what's best for our people."

The woman sighed. "I hope that's true. I think it's important to remember who has your best interests at heart. They've prepared you to trust the wrong people from a young age. I understand you might be conflicted."

Looking up and staring at the woman, Rachel remained silent.

"How about we start with a show of trust from our side? We'll dispatch some soldiers to her last known residence in the human world. They'll thoroughly photograph everything and bring it back for you to look at. We'll see if anything comes from that." The woman tilted her head to the side.

Rachel read the faces of those in the room, all focused on her. "Yeah. We can start there. Like I said—I want to help."

Rachel knew she would need to win them over, and she *would* be going.

After being dismissed by the council, she was sent to live with her new family permanently and to take lessons, finding a place to help in village defense. It wasn't that her family wasn't kind, or didn't try, but these people still didn't feel like family. She could hardly even look at Jeff. When she'd originally chosen this life, it was because of the insistence of her human mother, who was now, no doubt, devastated, and a stepfather, who she now knew had orchestrated every moment of her life for the last decade, to lead to her demise.

When she had planned on coming here, to be with these people, she'd imagined being part of this wonderful rebellion the prince had painted in her mind, that she could play a part in making things better. And she wouldn't have been alone, like she was now.

Rachel's eighteenth birthday came quickly. Though … she learned it had never really been her birthday, after all. Technically, the anniversary of her sprouting reveal had already passed—the first day of spring, just like every other Seeder. She sat in bed at the beginning of the day, mulling things over.

No one had even mentioned her 'fake' birthday. Not that she'd expected them to. It was wartime, and the date was just a falsehood created to keep everyone from wondering why a dozen girls in school had the exact same birthday.

Before lessons, she'd be visiting the temple. Before that, she had some extra time to herself.

She'd taken to journaling—trying to process the nightmare she'd just lived through, and trying to find a purpose. Daydreaming of Guillen, she yearned to hear his sweet encouragements. Rachel thought about Kaylah. She hated her. And loved her. She really had to come to terms with her part in all of this. But reason won out. Despite the horrible part Kaylah had played in Rachel's trauma, she couldn't deny that Kaylah had saved her life, that she'd only hurt Rachel because she'd had to.

Rachel frowned. Kaylah had probably remembered it was her birthday, wherever she was. She always did.

Glancing around her new bedroom, Rachel mentally compared her experience thus far to what she'd had described to her. Seeder life was simple, charming. There was a stark contrast between her current surroundings and back home in the human world. Outside, asphalt and cement were replaced with dirt and cobblestones. The plant growth in Seeder territory was nothing short of a paradise. No cars, internet, or any modern technology. The only thing that resembled electricity thus far was the stun gun she'd been subjected to at the palace.

Despite her struggle to feel at home, Rachel was surprised to find how easily she'd transitioned to such a foreign setting. Most Seeder homes were made of wood; they rarely painted anything, instead focusing on the simpler, more natural look of it all. And they weren't a wasteful people—she appreciated that. Her mom might have liked it here. The mom she'd grown up with, at least… The one she'd met upon coming here was nice enough, but still…

Rachel closed her journal with a sigh. She needed to get out of the house. After making her bed, she left her room. In their family housing, the girls and guys each had their own level. Each child had a tiny room, but shared common spaces. It was like a rustic version of dorm rooms. The rest of the house was quiet, everyone off already to fulfill duties, go to classes, spend time with others.

Getting ready for the day, she dressed, then cut a slice of bread off of a fresh loaf one of her sisters had made that morning, slathering it with a honey coconut cream. Grabbing a wooden bowl, Rachel headed outside and walked a few yards to their family garden, then proceeded to pick a mound of raspberries and something a sister had called 'pimple berries'—they were white, sweet, and creamy. Pretty delicious if you could get over their name and the association. She sat at a little outdoor table and did some energy-bathing. A lot of things were tainted, and not ideal at the moment. But the sun was still warm, the air was still fresh, and the energy of the Green Lands was still invigorating.

After enjoying her breakfast, Rachel set out for her daily walk to the temple. She'd been given a certain amount of freedom on things like temple deposits, with her people understanding the trauma she'd been through. But she wanted to do her part—it was worth it.

As she approached the temple, she thought of Guillen again, amidst the heavy traffic of Seeders showing their green eyes and purple hair tips, identifying themselves.

Standing in line, Rachel pondered on the history behind these temples, these walls, this war. Like the current attack, the biological warfare that had poisoned their lands had been a new tactic that took

Seeders by surprise. Not only did they lose a whole generation of their women in the Great Poisoning, they'd essentially lost that many men before they'd created the thicket walls in the first place. Fighting had been brutal, and matriarchs from every village had given everything they had to erect these walls, keeping them safe from further attacks. The men had fought valiantly, at a high cost, giving their women the time required to complete such an enormous task.

They were quick thinkers; they were people that had sacrificed so much. Rachel frowned. She wanted to go back and chastise her people for giving up. For settling on the human world as an alternate way to raise half of their kids. Sure, it was a great stopgap. But this had gone on far too long.

She sighed. She had no right to judge them. They'd frozen; they'd just had their way of life ripped from them. They'd done the best they could at the time.

When her turn finally came up, Rachel stood at the jade well, placing her hands on the emerging knotted roots. Closing her eyes, she took a deep breath. Envisioning the energy and warmth in her heart, she pushed it down to her hands to do her part in strengthening the walls. She had to exert extra effort to get the energy to move past her forearms. It initially lingered there, she assumed, probably because of her mind getting distracted. She could only hope that eventually things wouldn't be this hard. That it wasn't just muscle memory, her body remembering the energy should drain to leaves drilled into her arms. She stood straighter, willing the energy to make it all the way down. Feeling it leave her body, she opened her eyes.

Emma, one of her sisters, waved at her from a distance. Rachel joined her, walking in the direction of her classes. Emma was one of the sisters she'd met in the human world with Jeff.

"How are you doing today?" Emma asked.

"About like usual." Rachel gave her a half-smile.

"Did you hear the good news?" Emma asked cheerfully.

Rachel's eyebrows lifted. "No. What?"

"Everyone in the family will finally be back soon! Our last sister is blooming now."

Rachel was a little disappointed it wasn't something bigger. "Cool."

"Then Dad and everyone can be here to help at the borders against the leeches." She smiled.

Rachel bit her tongue. The moment Saff and Devin had guided her home, she'd realized how odd it was for her to be around her own kind. Other than Jeff and a couple of sisters, until arriving at their borders, she'd met significantly more Ivies than Seeders. She'd sworn off using the term 'leeches' for Ivies. Maybe still for people like Soren … but generally speaking, it didn't sit right with her anymore. Not after meeting Guillen, Jon, and Olivia.

Emma was kind, as they all were, in trying to make her feel welcome, trying to lift her spirits. But Rachel started to fear that, even *if* the council came around to joining Unitas, the Seeders might not be willing to reconcile. After generations at war, even *if* they weren't at fault in any way, there was equal hatred. She could only hope that when the time came, her people would be able to welcome peace and show compassion, that they'd stick to their beliefs about wanting to live peacefully, being left alone.

Rachel bolstered her courage. Unlike Jon, she didn't have to carefully tiptoe around with her opinions to help the cause. Even if her fellow Seeders disagreed, no one here would harm her for sympathizing with the Ivies. They might not trust her, and they might ostracize her, but she really didn't care. Even if she wasn't able to fulfill Kaylah's request at the moment, she could be a voice.

"You should stop calling them that," she told Emma. "Let me tell you what I know about how things work over there."

Chapter 26

FOR NOW, RACHEL FOCUSED ON lessons with Saff—her assigned welcoming mentor. Like most days, they trained in a small portion of a field near the local Seeder school. The sun was warm, but not nearly as heated as their disagreement.

"I get it, Rachel—I heard about the letter. You've been through a lot and you want to see your mom. But you're going to have to wait until next spring. We need you focusing on healing and fighting, *not* catching a breeze," Saff argued while they took a break.

Rachel shook her head. "You don't get it. One way or another, I'm going. And soon."

Saff shot her hands up, exasperated. "What will you accomplish over there? Can't you see it's just playing into their hands? At best, it's a distraction. At worst, it's a death sentence! What happens if you manage to make it to the human world? It's late in the season—I don't even know that *I* could make it back home!

"But you want to rely on the enemy, who's deceived you before. You have one week before you start to die over there from root rot. *One week.* And that's maybe the merciful route compared to them bringing you back to their lands as a battery in their war machine, all over again." She stared at Rachel, her frustration obviously growing.

Rachel crossed her arms, stone-faced. "If you don't want to train me, that's fine. Even if I have to go by myself, I'm going. I was close enough to catching a breeze before I was brought here. And leaving from here is easier than returning." There was the small detail that Rachel had never been through a Seeder rift. She had no idea how or where to make one … other than the vague knowledge that Seeders created them in the sky.

Rachel appreciated how much Saff had taught her. She was a great teacher. Not always such a great cheerleader. Saff was beyond stubborn. She was just like the council and every other Seeder Rachel had met thus far.

"Don't be selfish," Saff chastised. "Our people are dying *every day*. We need your help at the temples, as a healer, even in combat," she pleaded.

Rachel was tired of being treated like a foolish child. She'd grown up fast—the harsh realities of this war had hit her just as much as anyone else.

"I'm *trying* to help! Maybe the Ivies are right that *we're* the prideful ones. Not willing to even hear out the princess. I'm willing to risk it, because I believe in this cause. You might not think it's worth it, but you weren't there."

Saff sighed, pausing with a pensive look and tightening her ponytail. "You know how people grow up," she started with a softer tone, "and they have the horror of realizing they just said something that would have come out of their parents' mouths?" She gave a weak smile. "Not my parents, but my brother, Ben. After my cover was compromised, like you, back in the world we grew up in—I took some risks. I put other people in danger, myself in danger. I remember yelling at my brother that we all get to be selfish sometimes. But there are limits. I'll try to carve out some extra time for the training you want, but no one here is going to risk their lives, or yours. Not without more evidence to back up her claims."

Rachel huffed. "What if I'm right? Haven't you ever wished our people tried something different to change things? What if *this* is it?"

Saff gently raised her eyebrows. "Of course I've thought about it. And I'm doing the best I can. We're all doing the best we can. I gave up visiting my human parents this year because of this war, and to help your mom and sisters. I'm trying."

Rachel frowned and nodded, accepting the lean olive twig to possibly train more, taking what she could get.

***

After another hour of training in energy exercises, Saff dismissed Rachel for the rest of the day. They stretched, and Rachel was the first to walk away. After setting down her water bottle, Saff shook her head, watching Rachel go.

Rachel was brainwashed—plain and simple. She was too naïve to see what the Ivies had done to her. She needed protection, possibly even from herself. This poor girl genuinely trusted the very people who had ruined her life. The proof was right in front of Rachel, but she refused to see the danger. Saff knew that danger—intimately. The Seeders were worn thin. She and her family had experienced Ivy brutality firsthand back in the human world. She wished, more than anything, that she knew how to get through to Rachel.

Having been briefed by the council before being assigned as her mentor, Saff had thought she was up to the challenge of helping this girl find her way. But Rachel was just as stubborn as Saff. The big difference was, Saff hadn't been raised by one of the enemy. She didn't have the blurred lines Rachel did. And Rachel hadn't been here the last year to see the devastation that had fallen on their village, on their entire people. She didn't have a mental tally of the dead running through her mind daily.

Sighing, Saff frowned. She wanted to do right by Rachel. And she knew why she was so protective of her, but couldn't bring herself to mention it. It wasn't just that Rachel was another new return, or because she was from Saff's hometown and home village. The moment Saff had heard that name again—Nuren—she'd realized their fates had been intertwined. In the blur of her own thwarted assassination, one of the attackers had referenced that name. Nuren had been hiding out in her own city the whole time. Saff could have easily been in Rachel's position if her brother, Ben, hadn't saved her.

She had a personal obligation to protect Rachel from further harm.

"Rough day?"

Saff looked to her right, spotting none other than Ben himself. "You could say that."

He crossed the field to join her. "What's up?"

She pointed at Rachel, who was still walking away in the distance, now hugging herself as she approached the crowded lane. "That one will be the death of me."

Ben grinned. "You can handle a classroom full of little boys, but one teenage girl will be your downfall?"

Saff chuckled. "You clearly don't know how much trouble teenage girls are."

He raised both eyebrows, tilting his head to the side. "I was your protector, wasn't I? I think I know *precisely* how much trouble teenage girls can be."

Poking him in the arm, she fought a smile. "But you loved every moment of being my protector!"

Ben busted out laughing. "Whatever you want to believe."

Saff rolled her eyes. "Come on, you. I'm headed home. I assume you're headed that way, too?"

"Yeah, c'mon." He nodded, heading in the direction of their homes. He often dropped her off at her and Devin's cottage on his way to the family home, when their schedules aligned.

Saff snatched up her water bottle from the grass, and followed after him. "You know, she's actually really talented."

"Yeah?"

"Yeah. Then again, she probably had to work at least twice as hard as other Seeder girls have to after they bloom, just to make any progress in her training in the human world."

"I bet." He shuddered. "I can't imagine being poisoned like that."

As they hit the bustling long lane, Saff's anxiety grew. It was so crowded these days.

Ben must have noticed her uneasiness, nudging her arm. "Not exactly the calm path we used to take to skip rocks at Glass Lake, is it?"

Saff looked down, shaking her head. "Why can't things be the way they used to be? Simpler? Happier?" They used to skip rocks and chat all the time, multiple times a week. Even after she'd gotten married.

Wrapping his arm around her as they pressed forward into the sea of bodies, Ben gave her a squeeze. "Things will calm down again. I promise."

Only a few yards down the lane, Ben quietly gasped.

"What?!"

He pointed at a passing purple butterfly. "Do you know what that one's called?" His voice was full of awe.

"No…"

"It's a hope butterfly, Saff. If you smile when one crosses your path, you'll have good luck."

She couldn't resist smiling. "You're such a liar."

He winked. "But it worked."

***

Graduation was about to happen in the human world. Summer was coming soon. Being deeply rooted in the Green Lands, Seeder women best managed short trips in the spring. Summer was iffy—fall was nigh to impossible—winter had never happened. Not a round trip, at least. But Rachel didn't need a return; she knew she could get back with Ivy help. Assuming she was right, that things were on the up-and-up… For now, she trained and kept her ear to the ground.

After a couple more weeks of intensive one-on-one training with Saff, Rachel was called in again to speak with the war council. They'd already shown her pictures of Kaylah's old place. Unsurprisingly, she didn't have any great revelations they'd found helpful. That was all a bluff on Rachel's part, anyway. All it had done was make Rachel homesick. After further deliberation amongst the senior council members, Rachel was pressed for more details on her time at the palace and her journey back.

Her people didn't completely disregard what she had to offer in the way of ideas and suggestions. Rachel helped, wanting the rest of the girls still held captive at the palace to be freed, but her heart wasn't fully in it. She objected to their proposed strategies, the way they planned to use her information—stressing that her rescue had been facilitated by multiple insiders.

"We may not have an inside man, but we've got the numbers, training, and strategy," the elected war council leader said. "We need to hit them and get our girls back before another one comes to fill Rachel's place. It's our time to take the battle to them. It's our turn to cross the Neutral Woods. We can draw them away from the palace and send in a team to extract them."

With Rachel's protests ignored, her stomach was in knots. Surely they had to know the palace would have added extra security after Nuren's death and Rachel's escape. She remembered the questions posed to her—about her loyalty and priorities, and her own judgment and state of mind. She thought she'd finally seen things clearly after meeting Guillen and Jon. But maybe that had been Kaylah's plan all along, lulling her into another false sense of security.

With more than a little hesitance, Rachel accepted the Seeder council's plan. Not that they cared for her approval. At least the Seeders were finally striking back, not just hiding behind their borders and skulking around in the human world. Even if all they did was get the other girls back from the palace, Rachel could perhaps sleep more peacefully.

***

Another week passed. Battle plans were made and orders issued. As a couple with a female as powerful as Saff, she and Devin could do some damage. But it had been decided that no female Seeders would be approaching the palace for extraction. The possibility of one being captured and falling to the torture they were trying to stop was not a risk the Seeders were willing to take.

Saff had been willing to go. Remembering her high school self—barely surviving Ivy attacks and hardly contributing to her own safety back in the human world—she'd wanted to redeem herself.

With the extraction team being all male, Saff and Devin planned on deploying to the Neutral Woods, especially now that they'd done some recon while collecting Rachel. But plans changed. Saff was asked to manage a triage clinic on the border between their village and the next. They'd just had some new girls return home and she could get them up to speed on healing near the walls. Rachel would join them. Devin was still assigned to the Neutral Woods. Saff's anxiety was through the roof at the thought of Devin working out there without her by his side. But she had to trust her people, and Devin's abilities.

Taking a rare opportunity, Saff and Devin's families gathered for a joint family dinner on Thod and Murial's lot. Their parents were still neighbors and many of the kids had consolidated their spaces, still living in the kids' housing in the back.

Sitting on a picnic blanket next to Devin, Saff surveyed the group of over fifty people. Some of their siblings had brought new spouses or significant others. Her closest sister, Tabatha, winked at Saff from several yards away, then snuck a kiss from her boyfriend. Saff smiled.

While chewing a bite of her buckwheat-and-green-apple salad, Saff's heart swelled at taking in the sight of so many loved ones. Their families had fought off a small army of Ivy assassins that had been after her in high school. Her family and in-laws were capable. They were supportive. They were great. But how long would the statistics swing in their favor, that none of them would be lost?

"You look worried," Devin said, bringing her back from her musings.

She gave him a half-smile. "I'm always worried nowadays."

Frowning sympathetically, he leaned over and gave her a sweet kiss on the cheek. He then whispered in her ear, "Even when we're together?"

She quickly matched his grin. "Together-together? I think I'm sufficiently in the moment for those times."

"Mmm. Then I guess we need more of those times."

Laughing, Saff leaned over and reciprocated with a kiss on his cheek. "With the enormous amounts of free time we have, right?"

Devin frowned again, then spared a glance past Saff. "I wish they'd just get it over with and get married. Then they'd have what you and I get to share."

Turning to look, she knew exactly who he was talking about. Ben and Heather. They sported googly eyes for each other, like any engaged couple would. Saff sighed. At this point, she was starting to agree with Devin. Heather wanted a traditional wedding, not a rushed one. But how long would they have to wait for things to calm down? Finding strength in the council's plans to be more proactive, Saff allowed herself to smile. "Hopefully not long now."

Ben would remain at his post on the Outer Wall. He'd requested to be part of the extraction team. But with older and more experienced Seeders willing to sign up for the elite team, he'd been overlooked. Saff knew how much he wanted to contribute, but she was secretly happy to have him safer, closer to home. Heather would be stationed at the temples—close by for energy deposits and directing traffic, as well as healing.

Every Seeder had a role to play. They were a peaceful people. That was what they'd always wanted. But everyone has their limits, and they had found theirs. The Seeders were ready to end this war.

***

"It's nice to meet all of you girls. I wish it were under better circumstances," Saff introduced herself to scared girls who had just recently learned their identities and were thrown into a war. The longer the war raged, the more girls were choosing to become human, fearful to commit to something so wholly foreign to them. She couldn't blame them, and probably would have made the same choice if the Green Lands had been in this shape when she'd come of age.

"Knowing how to save a life is not as simple as knowing how to heal. We're going to have a crash course on anatomy, so you'll know what we need to focus on. Don't expend energy and time healing up a flesh wound when someone else is dying from a deep gash or stab. And knowing how to heal is not as important as knowing how to heal *efficiently*."

They dedicated one day in their makeshift clinic made of wood and canvas. There were still wounded trickling in from regular fighting on the borders, so they had some practice, but these girls' lives would never be the same once the real push came.

"Wipe up the blood first, if you can—it'll minimize cleanup time between patients," Saff continued. "Don't put your whole hand on a wound if you can concentrate your energy by covering it with just a finger or two. If they have multiple serious wounds, it's best to let your efforts emanate from a central part of the area. If you're unsure what to do or what the problem is—call for me."

Most of these girls were fresh returns to the Green Lands and had just cancelled their plans to hang out with their besties in the human world for the summer break.

Rachel was visibly stressed. "You're sure we can't convince them to wait a few days, try to at least get extra help or intel from the princess before we make our attack?"

"That defeats the element of surprise. We're doing this on our own."

***

The morning started slowly at the healing clinic. Rachel tidied up a stack of sterile cloths absentmindedly. Guillen consumed her thoughts—his calming presence, his sweet smile. Why had she let him go? *Right, the big picture.* And Kaylah—did she know by now that her request was being denied? Would she extend the same offer after this strike?

Rachel's stomach growled loudly, and she regretted having skipped breakfast. She'd struggled to eat and sleep lately, her anxiety growing as the time was fast approaching for what she considered an ill-prepared Seeder strategy.

~

Saff scanned the triage tent, packed with cots for the wounded, and several nervous girls. Closing her eyes and taking a deep breath, she tried to prioritize. She couldn't help these girls, couldn't save soldiers' lives, if her mind was out in the Neutral Woods with Devin, was out with all of her family members at their positions. She needed to be here, in the moment.

She didn't have to stew in her thoughts for long. The wounded started to file in, and Saff busied herself with assigning girls to the incoming soldiers. Since the learning clinic was full of new girls, it wasn't the first location for the severely wounded to be sent to. Ideally, women in the woods could heal as needed. But some were brought home and healed at the walls, and once things piled up, the clinic saw more serious cases. Green folk didn't have huge industrial manufacturing plants. They didn't have nuclear bombs. They didn't use planes. But the lack of advanced technology had never stopped a man from taking a life.

The return through neutral territory that had taken Rachel and her companions well over a week could be covered by healthy, trained troops faster. The freshly deployed Seeder troops had no need to get new clothes, or hide to avoid being spotted. They would take out anyone in their path. Those in the woods were starting to draw more and more troops to the Seeder borders.

***

Saff's heart would only ever calm at night, each time Devin would come home alive. He was out of action for a couple of days at one point, healing after a particularly nasty ambush, but he went back out there fighting for his people as soon as possible. Saff thought fondly of something he'd told her before she'd left his side to return to the Green Lands years ago. 'Nothing is more important to Seeders than family.'

Daily, she counted her blessings, grateful for her family, and that they'd been spared thus far. Many families in her village weren't so lucky. And her dad and brothers were almost all stationed in the woods or at one of the walls—none of them marched on the Ivy palace. With no women allowed to take on the palace, there would be no healing for those men. Those who had signed up knew what the risks were.

To ensure everyone was easily accounted for, and so information could disseminate quickly amongst their families, Saff and Devin's siblings would stop by their parents' houses first, before heading to their individual homes at the end of each day.

Shuffling along in exhaustion, Saff made her way to Thod and Murial's house. It was later than usual and she expected some of her siblings to already have reported in for the night. They were waiting to hear of a triumphant return any time now, to see the War Vines breaching their walls shrink and recede. Every time she twisted that doorknob, she hoped for good news and prayed away the bad.

Saff opened the door at her in-laws' house. Devin's mom and one of his brothers were huddled in a corner. At Saff's arrival, they turned to look at her, revealing Heather—covered in blood, sobbing.

Saff stood frozen in place. "Where's Devin? Where's Ben?"

Devin came bounding from another room.

"Where's Ben?!" Her voice trembled.

No one spoke up.

Devin grabbed her and pulled her in tight; she fought to get out of his arms, thrashing with what little energy she had left.

"No! Where is he? I want to help! I can help!" she screamed while fighting for air.

"It's too late," Devin whispered in her ear. "I'm sorry, Saff. It's too late."

She crumpled to the floor, heaving. "It's a mistake. He's fine. It can't be Ben. He's smart. And strong. And… It can't be."

Devin held her, quietly shedding tears of his own. "I'm so sorry."

Chapter 27

SAFF LAY IN BED, RESTLESS. In shock. Still half expecting Ben and Heather to drop by sometime that week. But that wouldn't happen. It couldn't. Ben was dead. She tried to control her breathing.

He was dead. Nothing could change that. His burial was already scheduled for the next day. More tears wetted her pillow as she dwelled on her memories of him. Meeting him when he was undercover in the human world, pretending to be her foster brother. Him saving her life from Ivy assassins, more than once. Skipping rocks at a local lake after they'd both returned to the Green Lands. His proposal to Heather…

Saff sniffled, struggling not to spiral in a sea of hopelessness. The sun was just starting to rise. Maybe going to work that day would help distract her? But she didn't want to be at that clinic, surrounded by blood, injuries, and death. Her mind lingering on Ben, on his injuries, on her work at the clinic, Saff's thoughts turned to Rachel. What was it Rachel had said about going to meet with the leech princess? 'Haven't you ever wished our people tried something different to change things? What if this is it?'

Wiping away her tears, Saff slipped out of bed, quietly opening a dresser drawer to change.

"What are you doing?" Devin asked, now awake.

She turned to face him after pulling a shirt over her head. "Um… Just going to walk to the clinic."

He frowned, his eyes starting to glow green. "We're allowed to take the day off. I… I think we should spend the day together."

Swallowing hard, she paused. "Yeah, I agree. I just…" She looked away, grabbing a long skirt to change into. "I just want to make sure the girls at the clinic know I won't be there for a couple days."

Devin rolled over in bed to follow her movement as she crossed the room. "Other people can tell them. Come back to bed."

Saff didn't respond as she finished changing. She wasn't accustomed to lying to Devin. After putting her hair up in a ponytail, she sat on the bed next to him, forcing a small smile. "I really need to go for a walk, okay? Alone. Just something to clear my mind. And I'll stop by the temple on the way there." She caressed his face. "I promise. I won't be gone long."

"Okay," he whispered.

Leaning down, she gave him a soft kiss. "I'll be back before you know it. Love you."

"Love you, too."

Leaving the cottage in the direction of the clinic, Saff avoided eye contact with everyone in her path. *This time tomorrow, I'll be getting ready for a … burial.* She'd never been to a funeral in the human world, and had never attended one in the Green Lands of someone so close to her. She picked up the pace, sniffling and wiping away tears as she walked. How was she supposed to handle being at the graveyard? See Ben like that? See their families like that? She didn't think she could bear any of it.

***

Rachel scraped herself out of bed and made her way to work for the day. The year-round utopia of the realm was dimmed by the downtrodden spirits of those she passed, and the neglect of aesthetic attention Seeders usually gave to their homes and streets. Yards were unkempt. Flowers—not necessary for food—lay wilted in flowerbeds. This had not been in the brochure. As she arrived at the clinic, it was quieter than usual. Saff was alone, flicking Seeder darts into the wall.

"Where are the other girls?" Rachel asked.

Saff turned, her eyes puffy, jaw clenched.

Rachel tilted her head, worried, nervous. "Did something happen? Is there news from the palace?"

"Do you really trust your friend? That she would still meet with us? That she can guarantee we would get home safely?"

"Yeah… I do. Did the council change their mind?"

"And you realize going could mean a death sentence for us? If we don't come back within a week, we rooted women die in the human world? And we might not be able to come home on our own this late in the year?"

Rachel recalled what she'd been taught about the limitations of Seeder women's powers, their reliance on the energy of the Green Lands. "Yes, I understand how it works."

"And you're sure you know how to find her?"

Scanning Saff's face, Rachel hesitated. Why did it seem like Saff might be willing to help now? What could the council have done to tick her off? Cautiously, she answered, "Yes."

Saff took a deep, shaky breath, then blew it out. "Then go home. Rest up. You and I are going tomorrow."

Rachel's heart lit with hope. But this wasn't exactly how she'd expected it to go. "Just you and me? *None* of the leaders? I know you're respected in our village, but—"

Saff raised her eyebrows. "Do you want to go?"

"Yes."

"Then let's make the introduction. Go home," Saff ordered. "We're leaving at first light. Best to keep this between us for now." She followed Rachel out, walking back to their village together.

***

Saff hardly slept a wink that night. She and Devin had been given a couple of days off to mourn Ben's loss. She lay in bed with Devin's arm wrapped around her. Exhausted, he slept peacefully.

She mulled over her plan, her promise to Rachel. Saff had gotten to know Rachel plenty over the last few weeks of training and at the healing clinic. Rachel knew more than she was letting on to the council. And Saff had been right about that, with Rachel willingly taking her to the Ivy princess now. Not yet daring to ask herself if this was the wisest decision, Saff had to ask herself if she could even keep her promise.

Rooted Seeder women their age could only manage one round trip to the human world each year, preferably in spring. It seemed like such an arbitrary restriction. After learning from Devin years ago that Seeders didn't understand all of the aspects of their powers, especially rifts, Saff had asked around and done some research. It was true—it was physically impossible for a rooted female Seeder to make a second trip through a rift in a year.

All accounts she'd heard gave the same answer. The women could obviously still catch a breeze all they wanted. They could harness the energy of the realm and fly with ease. They could even *open* a rift. They just couldn't manage to travel through it. Doubting girls tried all the time. All reports followed the same general description. After entering a second rift, the girls experienced a crushing pain, centered in their chests—and instead of emerging in the human world, they just ... kept flying, in a straight path, still in the Green Lands. Time and time again, after each approach, it was the same. They were tied to the Green Lands, the energy that flowed there. No one quite knew how.

The only sliver of hope Saff now held was that she hadn't ever foolishly made a second yearly attempt before. And she wasn't exactly the average Seeder. While she was tired of hearing it, the fact remained—Saff was different. She could harness almost as much energy as a fully-rooted matriarch. Having the extra power, but not the same limitations as a matriarch, maybe, just maybe, she could slip through the crack. Because just like their ties to the energy of the Green Lands, no one had a concrete explanation for Saff's ability to harness that extra power.

Yes, she'd concluded that it had something to do with an immunity to Ivy poison, but there were too many unknowns, too few stories to corroborate.

Rolling over in bed, Saff admired the man she loved. Even if she were *capable* of an impossible feat like this, she had to ask herself if she *should* be doing it. She'd done her best to follow orders in the Green Lands. Her blunders in the human world after her botched bloom had proven that she needed to trust her people. Ben himself had even challenged her to try and keep a few rules, since she'd been such a thorn in his side. But then again, she had been right about her best friend, Zach, being a human. Even if no one else trusted her judgment, she wasn't *completely* off her rocker to entertain this plan.

Devin shifted slightly in bed, still asleep. Saff frowned—he would never approve. He had tried to stop her from her earlier visit to the human world. But he himself had said years ago that he wished they could find a way to end this war—he just didn't know how. And things weren't nearly as bad back then.

Saff moved closer, placing a tender kiss on his lips. He drew a deep breath, barely cracking a smile. He reciprocated with a sweet, sleepy kiss, before letting out a soft moan and wrapping his arm and leg around her. His breathing slowed again as he promptly fell back asleep.

Ben and Heather deserved this. They were some of the best people Saff knew. And Ben shouldn't have died at the Outer Wall. More casualties were expected to tally from those marching on the

Ivy palace. The Outer Wall was much more dangerous than the Inner Wall inside their territory, but he still shouldn't have died. Seeders weren't safe anymore—not even in their own lands.

Something had to change.

If Ben had been willing to give his life for Saff, when he came to her rescue more than once in the human world, and for his people, then maybe it was Saff's turn.

And that was what this was. An impossible plan. A suicidal one.

She thought of how mad Ben would be. How livid he had been when they were teenagers in the human world and she would defy his orders, when all he was trying to do was protect her. But she was doing this *for* Ben. She was doing this for all of her brothers and sisters, and for her husband, and Heather, and her village, and everyone. She owed it to them. This much she could do.

What exactly she planned to do if she made it over, she wasn't sure. Maybe this princess could actually help. Maybe it would feel good to kill a leech right now. Maybe the leech princess would make a good bargaining tool.

She could figure things out later. But one thing was certain— Saff knew there would be no coming back for her unless this really paid off. Even if she could make it through a second rift that year, there couldn't possibly be a way back for her on her own. The energy in the human world was significantly weaker. And within a week, fatal root rot would set in. She had a week to live in the human world, maybe less. But Rachel was convinced the princess would keep her promise, helping them return through a rift with minimal energy drain. Even if Saff decided to trust this princess, would it work for Saff? This was all just an experiment. A potentially deadly one.

Setting her resolve, Saff savored Devin's embrace, not allowing herself to drift off again. A couple of hours later, she carefully pried herself from his grasp and got dressed. She penned a letter to him, leaving it on the kitchen table. Her heart heavy, she grabbed one last thing from a ceramic pot—a debit card. All Seeder families kept investments in the human world for visits. For burner phones, food, taxis. Slipping the card into her pants pocket, Saff looked around her cottage, her eyes glazing over. This was her home. Her family. Her people.

Under the light of the moon, Saff quietly closed the door behind her, heading down the dirt lane to meet up with Rachel.

***

Despite Saff's attempts to make time for Rachel's requests on how to catch a breeze, time and energy had become increasingly limited resources. Rachel approached their agreed-upon meeting spot—a small park nearly halfway between their homes. Rachel hugged herself. She was a bundle of nerves. Excited to visit home, to see Kaylah, to go through her first Seeder rift. Worried she hadn't trained enough, or could be wrong about this decision, or that Saff was somehow setting her up. What if the council had put her up to this as a way to prove that Rachel had been lying about knowing how to contact Kaylah?

Saff was already at the park, pacing. Rachel glanced around in the dark—it appeared they were alone.

"You're ready?" Saff asked.

Rachel nodded. "I don't have a family card yet. I couldn't really ask for one without them knowing I was planning to leave."

"That was smart. We'll be fine with mine." Saff studied Rachel's face. "You promise you know how to get in touch with the princess? Quickly?"

Rachel hesitated. "Yes."

Saff's eyes narrowed slightly. "Because if you don't, you'd better tell me now."

Rachel rolled her eyes. "I know how to. Are you sure you can guide me through? Didn't you already make your yearly trip?"

Saff tucked her hands into her pockets. "Yes. And yes."

"How's that possible? Did they lie to me about that? We can actually go back more often?"

Saff swallowed. "No. But I have a theory."

Rachel's heart dropped. "A theory? I guess I don't really need you to show me around on that side." She glanced at Saff's pockets, thinking of the card. Even if Saff only guided her to their rifting space, Rachel didn't know where to go from there. She didn't know how to find her bearings. And she had no human money. "But it's probably best I don't go alone. What's your theory?"

Saff rubbed her forehead. "Either I'll prove my theory right and we make it, or I'll be wrong and you're left to make yet another plea to the council." She raised her eyebrows. "If you're worried, I could go alone. If you give me the address and information you have."

Rachel shook her head. "We're going together."

"Okay. Let's do this."

***

Approaching their chosen takeoff location, Saff allowed herself to question her plan once more.

Her mind drifted to the last time she'd seen Ben, their last conversation. She envisioned herself standing in a graveyard later that day. Her knees weakened. She could barely breathe.

She'd made her choice.

Biting her tongue, she attempted to stave off fresh tears. She opened her eyes wide, not daring to wipe at the coating that blurred her eyes, fearing she might draw Rachel's attention.

Once she'd finally regained her composure, she cautioned Rachel. "Whether or not this works, I may get hurt going through this rift. Don't freak out—I'm sure I'll be fine."

Rachel nervously side-eyed her. "Are you sure this is a good idea? Would I somehow be at risk, too?"

Saff thought about it for a moment. "You would only get hurt if I didn't make it through. So, I'll form the rift, then fly through. Hang back. If I just keep flying, then don't go. If I disappear, then it's safe to go through." She hated outright lying to Rachel. There really wasn't any risk of Rachel getting hurt, but Saff wanted to make sure she didn't go alone, should Saff's hopes prove to be in vain.

Rachel cautiously nodded.

Saff had Rachel take off first. She was a pretty shaky beginner, not having been able to train nearly as much as she should have. Some of that was on Saff. But really, the Ivies were the ones to blame.

Saff leapt into the air, also catching a breeze and speeding to catch up. After a long journey to the closest rifting space, Saff gave the signal to Rachel to slow down and hang back. Saff's heart beating a mile a minute, her stomach twisted into knots. Bolstering her courage, she waved her hand in the air; a ripple in the sky signified a rift had been formed. Clenching her jaw in anticipation, she flew into it.

Chapter 28

SAFF FLEW THROUGH THE RIFT she'd created. Time passed slower. Panic set in with a telltale pain in her chest. The tether of her rooted energy was trying to keep her in the Green Lands. The crushing pain left her unable to breathe. The pain experienced by rooted females trying to leave too often, more than once a year. The pain felt by any fully-rooted matriarch that tried to leave the Green Lands at all.

Fighting with all she had, Saff pushed extra energy to her heart and ripped through the rift. Gasping, she plummeted.

Realizing she was clutching her chest instead of balancing in the breeze, Saff straightened herself out. Disoriented by the pain, the wind rushing past her, and the turbulence experienced from different energy levels between the worlds, Saff grunted, forcing herself to steady. Before dropping dangerously low, she recovered her trajectory.

Saff flew higher, focusing on her breathing as the pain lingered. The change in scenery and ambient energy was undeniable—she'd made it to the human world again. And she was on borrowed time.

***

Rachel's anxiety peaked before she approached the rift—her first Seeder rift. Saff had made it through just fine, from what she could tell. The journey had already been difficult on Rachel with so little practice, and it would be harder on the other side without the extra energy boost, but she circled back with resolve to the rift Saff had created.

Making it through with ease, Rachel was immensely grateful to not have an Ivy sucking her life-force to take her through a tree rift. The kind of rifts Seeders made in the air were so easy, as long as you could endure the flight.

Having emerged from the rift, Rachel was jostled about by the difference in energy and the sudden shift in wind direction. She focused and quickly recovered her balance. But there was a problem—Saff was nowhere to be seen.

Rachel's eyes darted around. Saff hadn't risen higher. She hadn't veered off to the side. Looking down, Rachel's eyes grew wide in horror. Saff was dropping in a freefall.

Her breathing rapid, Rachel frantically tried to figure out how to help. But it wasn't like she could catch Saff. Rachel was barely balancing on her own. Slowly and carefully, she shifted her trajectory down, in case she could somehow think of a way to help. Not much later, relief washed over her as Saff balanced herself and slowly climbed. Saff was grimacing, her face red.

Rachel followed Saff's nod for directions, trailing after her.

Between the time difference and extended travel, the sun was just coming down as they landed in a park of their human-world hometown. Rachel's landing was far from graceful—she panicked and thrust energy to her arms and legs to strengthen them, trying to avoid breaking anything. Curling into a ball at the last moment, she tumbled on the ground. Only bruised and a bit shaken, Rachel opened her eyes and scanned the grass for Saff.

Lying on her back with her hands on her chest, Saff was halfway across the park, not moving. Rachel jumped up and ran to her.

Saff was breathing hard, staring up toward the sky.

"Are you okay?" Rachel asked, checking her for injuries.

Saff winced, shifting her weight. "Yeah. Oodles of fun."

"What happened? And how did you even do it? You're sure you're okay?"

Giving her a forced smile, Saff sat up with a groan, then rubbed her chest. "Yeah. Just some bad turbulence."

Rachel raised an eyebrow in disbelief. "Right. Well, I guess mine wasn't so bad, just a few seconds later…" She offered a hand, helping Saff stand.

"Thanks." Saff brushed herself off. "Let's get going. We won't have time to see your mom, but you could call her."

Rachel frowned, hoping they might still be able to carve out time. But she understood the mission.

They entered a nearby gas station and asked for directions to the address Rachel had memorized. With Saff's debit card, they bought a burner phone and called a cab.

***

Rachel's palms were sweaty as their cab pulled up to the address she'd provided. The council could be right. This could be a trap.

"Alright, this is us. 13310 North Maplewood," Saff said. "Do you recognize this place?"

It was a standard-looking small house, likely just a couple of bedrooms, on the outskirts of their hometown.

"No. But let's check it out." Rachel swallowed nervously. "Hopefully they don't mind visitors this late at night." She'd never seen this place before and had no idea why Kaylah would have directed her there.

Knocking on the door, they glanced over their shoulders to watch out for suspicious characters. Lights turned on in the house and the door unlocked. A tall man with dark hair, looking to be in his forties, answered. Rachel didn't recognize him, and a momentary glance in Saff's direction confirmed that she didn't either.

"Can I help you?" he asked.

"Yeah, we're looking for a friend." Rachel tried to read his expression.

His face hinted at nothing. "Do you have a name?"

He could have meant Rachel's name or Kaylah's name, but Rachel assumed it had something to do with the coffee cup clue. "Itiner?"

He nodded in recognition. "Come in." Offering them a seat in his front room, he pulled out a small lockbox from a closet. "Will there be any more in your party?"

Rachel was just winging it at this point. "Um … Not with us. Just the people we're coming to meet, if that's what you mean?"

Not looking up, he continued to work on the lock. "Just want to make sure I'm not denying anyone else that trickles in, that should be pointed in that direction."

Rachel shook her head. "No, that was specifically given to me. No one else will be using it that I know of." She surveyed the room while waiting. A set of tall shelves was jam-packed with books. The furniture was a matching set. It felt as cozy as any other home she'd been in; it didn't exude any nefarious vibes.

"Alright." He reached into the lockbox, sorting through small pieces of paper.

~

"So, we're not meeting anyone here?" Saff asked, itching to get this over with and go home. The aching in her chest had mostly subsided. No matter how much she loved her human parents, she'd never try another trip like this again. Now she just had to see if she'd die from root rot, or if this was all an elaborate trap.

"Afraid not, it's safer for the network to have gatekeepers," he answered.

"And that network is…?" Saff asked.

He looked up, visibly suspicious at Saff's line of questioning.

~

"You can ignore her. She's new," Rachel responded, shooting a look at Saff to shut up. "But I *am* curious. I don't recognize you, are you a…" Rachel hoped he'd fill in the blank.

"A friend in Unitas?" He grinned.

Rachel smiled. "That's enough for me."

He handed Rachel a piece of paper. "Do you have a car?"

"No, but we can call the cab back," Saff replied.

"Okay. Just be prepared—this one's a two-hour drive."

Saff called the cab company again, and the man patiently waited with them until their car arrived. They tried carrying on with painfully awkward small talk, probably all wanting to be aloof given the circumstances. Once the cab pulled up, they bid him farewell, having never even learned the mystery man's name.

"You have to admit, this is kind of cool: secret meetings in the night and whatnot," Rachel remarked as they walked to the car. It felt good to be home, if she could really claim either world as home. She already missed the energy of the Green Lands, but the familiarity of the human world, mingled with adrenaline, was invigorating.

~

"Annoying is more like it." Saff was in no mood for games; she'd missed Ben's burial for this. She was risking her life for this. She remembered how she hadn't been much younger than Rachel when she, too, had found a thrill in covert operations, sneaking away with her boyfriend for training, and to relay information to the Seeder network. Those were different times.

As they ducked into the cab, it registered how her comment had hurt Rachel. Rachel's smile was gone, her posture deflated. She sat back and stared out the window after giving the driver the new address. Saff looked down, rubbing the knee of her jeans. The reality of her choice to come on this mission was starting to settle in. The rifting pain in her heart was replaced by an unwelcome yet familiar one. *Devin. My parents. What did I just do?*

And she'd just lost her job. A job she loved. Not that Seeder career positions were handled the same way they were amongst the humans she'd grown up around. But she was outright disobeying council orders. She was leading one of her mentees into potential danger. No matter what happened with this mission, there would be unpleasant repercussions for Saff. *I'm an idiot.*

But she couldn't allow herself to dwell on doubt and regrets right now. She couldn't take it back. The only way was forward. She glanced at Rachel, who was still frowning at the window. "Sorry."

Without moving a muscle, Rachel whispered, "It's fine."

***

After two hours of driving through the night, they arrived at the new address. Rachel hopped out of the car first, ready for the next step. This was a much larger off-white house with a two-car garage and a tidy yard—though nothing flashy. It took longer for someone to turn on the lights and answer the door at this house, but it was well worth the wait.

Greeted by a familiar blond, Rachel's jaw dropped. "Eric?!"

"Come in!" He rushed them in and closed the door behind them. "Rachel, it's so good to see you!" He swooped her up in a big hug and spun her around. "Gosh, it's good to see your face! Kaylah hoped you'd be here sooner. I was worried about you."

Rachel beamed. "So, you know? All of it? Her name? Who she is? What we are?" She furrowed her brow. "Wait, what are you?"

He grinned. "Humans can be in Unitas, too, ya know. You'd be surprised."

"So, everything's good with you two? Is she here?"

"No." He pulled a cell from his pocket. "Let me send a text and the network will get word to her that you're here. She's pretty busy."

She waited for him to send it off. "Sorry, let me introduce my travel companion."

He extended his hand to Saff with a smile, and she shook it. "We've met. She was at your mom's place after you and Meg—er,

Kaylah went missing, and… Gosh, Rach, I'm sorry about Rob and David. She told me about all that."

Rachel tucked her hands into her pockets. "Thanks. But I'd be happy never hearing those names again."

"Done. You won't hear them from me. Do you guys need something to eat? Or are you ready to rest up? I understand you've got to be tired, and we keep some beds ready at all times."

Rachel looked back to Saff. "I'd love to get caught up first, if that's okay."

Saff stood against the wall, scrutinizing the room. "I don't know how comfortable I'd feel sleeping here. Maybe we should get a hotel room for the night, and we'll come back when you call to tell us she's arrived."

Eric frowned. "You've met me. This is a safe space, a neutral space."

Saff met his frown. "No offense, but we don't know each other *that* well. And I don't know about neutral anything—you or this place. Your girlfriend is the Ivy princess? And who pays the mortgage here?"

He cocked his head to the side. "I care about Kaylah, and I care about Rachel. Maybe you didn't get the memo, but Kaylah's not exactly in the good graces of her parents right now."

Rachel furrowed her brow at Saff. "We came here to meet. Like you said: we can't waste time. We should be here when she arrives, not wasting time finding hotels and calling cabs."

Saff sighed, looking exhausted. "Fine. I'm not letting Rachel out of my sight, so I guess we're staying up for a little while."

Eric gave them a warm smile. "I'm all for it. Let me grab you both some water and get a coffeepot on. Take a seat."

Returning with water, he placed it on the coffee table in the humble living room. A pair of framed nature scene paintings hung on the wall as the only decor in the room. The furniture was a basic matching set that could easily be found at a standard department store. "It's not much, but it's home for now."

"You have to tell me everything, seriously!" Rachel gushed. "You're the *last* person I expected to see."

He laughed. "Is that because I'm human? Or because a princess broke my heart?"

"But you're obviously okay now…"

"Yeah. She wanted to make sure they wouldn't come after me when she went missing. She needed to put some distance between us. When she came back, she explained everything to me. To say it was all a shock is the understatement of the century."

Rachel picked from the millions of questions streaming through her mind. "How was graduation, and what are you doing out here in the middle of nowhere?"

"Can't you tell? I'm *hundreds* of miles away at school right now, taking summer courses." He winked. "If it's important to Kaylah, it's important to me. I can take classes remotely while I help."

Rachel sipped water. "And you said there are humans in the cause? Have you met both of our kind? What about the guy that gave us this address?"

Eric scratched his chin, settling down more comfortably on the couch. "His business is his own, so I can't answer that one. But humans, yeah—you can't send your sons and daughters to be raised and cared for, and then expect us to not care what happens to them. Or, you know, date and befriend us, and expect us to not worry when we learn the truth. We can only do so much on this side, but we're willing to help.

"There are actually several Ivies I've met on this side, too. Like Kaylah's parents. Well, I guess not really her parents, right? Nathan and Ginger. She sent them away for their safety when she went missing, but my understanding is they're actively involved right now. That couple was hand-selected by the queen and king to be her guardians while she lived over here. When she had a change of heart, they followed after her."

The news brought so much renewed hope to Rachel; she prayed it was reaching Saff as well. "So, is that it? You hold down the fort here, for a meeting place?"

Eric shrugged. "That's mostly it for now. It's a safe house for defectors, but Kaylah suspects it might get busier once the alliance is made with your people."

~

Saff smiled and shook her head.

"What's that about?" he asked.

"Oh, it's just funny. Last time I was in a safe house, I was in high school and a pair of Ivies had just tried to murder me. I never thought I'd see the day where Seeders and Ivies might consider sharing a safe house. And with humans in the loop."

"Sometimes seeing is believing, right?" he said.

"I guess we'll see," Saff replied, still thoroughly uneasy. "How long until she arrives?"

"Sorry, I can't answer that. It can take some time for someone to track her down in the field and for her to get back here."

"Well, maybe we should go to sleep," Rachel offered.

Eric showed them to a room down the hall. "A couple of beds in here for you two. Decoration isn't exactly a priority around here, but the beds are amazing. Humans may be limited in what they can do to help, but they do know how to open their wallets."

The guest room featured a window with blinds and a full-size mirror. The bedspreads were identical navy blue, and the pillows appeared welcoming and fluffy. He gestured to a large built-in wardrobe. "Lots of comfy clothes options, and there's a chute in the bathroom down the hall to the downstairs laundry room." He pointed to another room down the hallway. "That's mine. Wake me up if you need anything at all, day or night—I'm here to help."

"Thanks so much," Rachel said with a smile.

"Yes, thank you," Saff added.

"Sure thing," he said. "Oh yeah, and any toiletries you might need are in the bathroom, and have at anything in the kitchen if you get hungry."

Saff picked out a bed while Rachel gave Eric another huge hug.

Chapter 29

SAFF AND RACHEL HAD BOTH hoped to see Kaylah first thing in the morning. But they awoke to just the three of them, Eric playing their gracious host.

Saff's patience was growing thin while waiting. Having slept horribly did nothing to help the situation. She refused to admit that she regretted the decision to come already; her whole family had to be worried. And she still didn't know how root rot would affect her on a second trip. So far, she felt pretty much the same as previous trips, but she didn't have any desire to play chicken with an unknown deadline.

"It'll be okay," Rachel said, taking a break from getting caught up with Eric. "She'll be here."

Saff paced the open-concept entryway connecting the living room, kitchen, dining room and hallway. "She does understand we have a timeline, right?"

"She does," Eric assured her. "And I have emergency contacts—human and Ivy. If you needed an Ivy-assisted exit at any time, I could get you one in less than a day."

Saff was somewhat pacified to hear that, from a source she hoped was, at least, benign. And to hear it was a well-coordinated operation was promising. But it wasn't like she was anywhere close to trusting the leech princess. "And if things don't go her way?"

Rachel's tone became less friendly. "Would you calm down? She's been more professional and hospitable than any of *our* kind have been, while extending an olive branch."

Another night and day passed. Saff had tried to go for a walk to ease her anxiety. Had tried to appreciate a ladybug landing on a nearby flower when she spent some time in the backyard. Had tried to take a nap. But nothing helped. She was wound tighter than a clock.

"We have people dying back home that could use our help," Saff complained. "We're not going to wait much longer."

Eric attempted to alleviate the tension. "It should be any time now."

***

Rachel woke the next morning to Saff sitting on her own bed, ready for the day.

"We're wasting our time," Saff said.

"It's worth waiting for. Maybe we can get Eric to reach out for a better update," Rachel suggested while getting dressed.

Not long after they left their room, Eric came out of his to join them in the dining room. "Coffee's already on. Any requests for breakfast from you lovely ladies? Anything fancier than muffins and yogurt today?"

Rachel yawned. "They're all vegetarians back there. Even the Ivies. I would love you forever if you had bacon and eggs."

He poked around in the fridge. "I can actually make that happen."

"I love you, Eric. Remind me to kiss your feet."

He chuckled. "Maybe you should start with some coffee; sounds like you could use it."

~

Saff poured them each a cup and took a sip, cringing at the bitterness. She'd never really been a fan of the stuff, even if it was half sugar and creamer, and it wasn't likely to calm her nerves…

A shower turned on down the hallway, causing Saff and Rachel to share a glance.

"Is someone else here?" Saff furrowed her brow.

"Yeah, Kaylah got in late last night. We thought it best to let everyone rest. She'll be out in a few." A frying pan sizzled as he cracked eggs into it and got bacon going in another pan. Once the shower turned off, he went into his room for a couple of minutes before reappearing. "She'll just be a few more minutes. I let her know you're both awake."

~

Eric was making up some toast while Rachel gratefully sipped coffee; Saff had set down her coffee cup, now clutching a glass of water at the table. Eric's bedroom door opened and Kaylah stood in the doorway, pulling her hair into a messy bun like she always used to. It was weird for Rachel to see her looking this way—knowing she was a princess. And the last time she'd seen her, Kaylah had worn all black and carried a blood-covered machete. Kaylah was now dressed in cute and trendy clothes like she always had in high school, her makeup looking sharp.

~

Saff's first impression of Kaylah wasn't at all fond. Seeders knew the names and insignias of Ivy royalty, but they'd never known their code names or what they looked like. Save the likeness of the actual queen and king, the rest remained in the shadows, which made sense with how well they had pulled off this kind of operation and attack. Saff looked at Kaylah and saw a ridiculous spoiled teenager.

Kaylah closed her eyes and inhaled deeply, placing her hand over her heart. "There's nothing like bacon to bring people together."

Eric walked up to her, holding a spatula and giving her a kiss. "I'm almost done, then I can make a run to the store if you ladies would like some privacy in your discussions."

Kaylah pulled him in for another kiss. "As long as you're not gone *too* long."

He grinned, returning to the kitchen.

~

Rachel wanted to run up and hug her, but Kaylah seemed hesitant, unsure.

"Kaylah, this is Saff. She's from my village. Saff, this is Princess Kaylah."

"Nice to meet you," Kaylah said, nodding with the poise Rachel expected of a princess. "Should we eat some breakfast and talk about how things are going to go today?"

Saff glared. "I think we've wasted enough time already."

Kaylah raised her eyebrows. "Okay… I just figured we were waiting for more of your people to show up?"

"Um…" Rachel's expression was apologetic. "This is going to be it."

Kaylah pressed her lips into a straight line. "I won't lie, I hoped for more. Especially after how poorly your attack on the palace went."

Kaylah's demeanor immediately changed. She was wide-eyed, moving a hand to her pocket, the other wrist being positioned directly in front of her, facing out. She was staring directly at Saff. Rachel looked to Saff to see why Kaylah had reacted that way. Saff was livid—green eyes, yellow hair, blades extended, fists balled up.

Kaylah's nostrils flared, her tone deep and threatening. "I would caution you to watch how you posture yourself. I may not have brought guards on this visit, but I'm not a dainty little palace girl." Kaylah's eyes darted from Saff's face to her hands. "Even if you have something up your sleeve, I wouldn't risk your only shot here."

All green folk knew darts were inherently a male trait, but once a Seeder was old enough and mated, the females gained that lethal weapon as well, with a simple flick of the wrist. And there was no way of knowing who had that ability.

"Can you give us a minute, Kaylah?" Rachel gulped and stood, moving between them.

Kaylah kept her eyes trained on Saff. "Sure. Eric and I would love to take a short stroll."

Eric had quietly stayed in the kitchen. He turned off the stove and strode over to Kaylah, taking her by the hand. Walking behind her, between the women, he escorted her out the front door. "Ten minutes?" he asked over his shoulder.

"Make it fifteen," Rachel said.

Saff kept her eyes on Kaylah as they left.

Rachel turned her frustration on Saff as soon as the door shut. "I knew I should have questioned your motives when you agreed to come, but I didn't really care. But what the hell is wrong with you?"

Saff was seething, pointing at the front door. "Is this a joke? Look at her. How am I supposed to take anything she says seriously? I was right that this would be a waste of time!"

"You've got to be kidding me. Because, what? She's not wearing formal clothes and a flipping tiara? That's what matters here?"

"She kept us waiting while our families could be dying, and she *casually* mentions things are going badly back home? She's a spoiled brat that doesn't give a *shit* about our people!"

Rachel's jaw dropped. She shifted in her seat to face Saff better. "Seriously. What's going on?"

Saff clenched her jaw.

"Is your husband okay? Did you lose someone? Is that what this is about?"

Saff looked as though she would burst into tears.

Rachel frowned. "You should have said something. We could have handled this differently. I'm sorry." She wrapped her arms around Saff.

Saff initially stayed stiff but soon gave into the hug, sobbing. "My brother. He didn't deserve this. He was…" Her shaking whimpers took over.

Rachel held her for a few minutes before speaking again. "I'm sorry. I'm sure he meant a lot to you. But I really believe she's on our side. She wants to stop this from happening. You don't have a lot of reason to trust her, and you don't have a lot of reason to trust my judgment, either. But could you muster enough faith to just try?"

Saff sat back, looking blankly around the room and wiping tears from her cheeks. "I don't know how much more of this I can take. I really don't. They almost got Devin the other day, too. He was in pretty bad shape. I'm just … tired."

Rachel moved her head to get Saff's full attention with eye contact. "Then let's hear her out. A couple of days here could mean we save thousands of lives, even if there's just a small chance of everything working out."

Saff frowned, gesturing at the closed front door. "What is she even offering? She didn't really give us much to go on in her letter."

Rachel was strengthened by remembering Guillen's conviction and commitment to the cause. "I don't know the particulars of her plan. But she killed a high-ranking member of the royal family, her own uncle, just to save me. She's burned her bridges over there. She's taking a lot of risks to try and help."

Saff fidgeted with her hands, her appearance having returned to normal. "Yeah. But from what I understand, she was pretty instrumental in your kidnapping. And you trust her?"

Rachel matched her frown and drew a deep breath. Did she trust her? Seeing Meg—Kaylah—again had rekindled her trust. She could only hope she wasn't being an idiot right now by ignoring the Seeder council's warnings. "I do trust her. I have to live with what they put me through." Horrific flashbacks of the palace played through her mind as she wiped away a tear. "Even then … it's worth giving her a chance. And frankly, we need a different strategy. What we've been doing *isn't working*."

~

Saff stood and grabbed a tissue from a box on the kitchen counter, sopping up her tears and blowing her nose. "I'll listen to her. But she's on a short leash until I'm convinced we can really trust her. And the *moment* she starts to act like she has ulterior motives, is the moment her part in this war takes a different role."

"Fair enough. How about you give me some time to talk to her when she gets back? I think you could do with some fresh air."

Saff stared at Rachel, not wanting to leave her alone. She'd been reckless enough by allowing Rachel to come on this dangerous mission. But Saff knew she was shooting herself in the foot already if there was hope for change, and she desperately needed that change. She was going to need to place some trust in Rachel.

"Fine."

***

Saff was sitting in the living room by herself when the front door opened again. Eric cautiously poked his head in. "Are we, uh … good?"

Rachel addressed him from the dining room table. "Saff would like to go into town with you to grab a bite, if that works for you."

"There's a great little place nearby with fantastic omelets; I'd be happy to help." He walked in and shot Rachel a questioning glance.

She nodded, indicating it was safe for Kaylah to come in.

Kaylah followed after Eric, keeping her eyes on Saff, though not posturing aggressively. She moved over to allow Saff plenty of space to approach the door.

"Kaylah can contact me when you're ready for us to come back," Eric said while Saff met him and walked out the door.

The door shut, and Kaylah glanced awkwardly at Rachel. "Can I hug you? I'm not really sure where we stand with things right now…"

Rachel stood, opening her arms.

Kaylah squeezed her tight. "Gosh, I missed you. You had me worried sick! I mean, I trusted my men to get you home, but still…"

They sat at the table and Kaylah grabbed a piece of bacon from the pan Rachel had taken off the stove while waiting for them. "What's with her? What's with the delay, and it just being the two of you?"

"Her brother just got killed."

Kaylah gulped. "I'm sorry. I'll keep that in mind." She huffed. "She can take mine in return."

"I think it bothered her you seemed so casual."

Kaylah threw her hands into the air. "A girl just wants to wear comfortable clothes in a safe place. When Eric said there were just two of you, I assumed others were coming and… Well, I assumed." She sighed. "So, where do you and I stand? I don't even know what Soren and my uncle told you—some of it may not be true."

Rachel gnawed on her bottom lip. "Well, I think it's safe to say we both understand your mission was to take out a Seeder, from the moment we met?"

Kaylah frowned, setting the strip of bacon down on a plate. "We were just kids, Rach. I didn't understand everything."

"I get it. Just laying it all out there. And you were the one that recommended I date your brother."

Kaylah nodded, her frown deepening.

"And they said you were poisoning me to weaken me." Rachel shot a quick glance at Kaylah's wrists.

"Yeah," Kaylah whispered. "When they confirmed your bloom, Rob ordered it, so he could … control you. I'm sorry. I didn't want to do it. For most of our friendship, it was just that—enjoying being your friend."

Rachel shook her head. "I understand you had orders, but you walked out on everyone, just months later. You couldn't have taken a stand earlier? Not done it? Given me a heads-up about Soren so I wouldn't have given him a chance to take me?"

Kaylah huffed. "I did what I had to, and I tried my best. I'm sorry, but there was only so much I could juggle."

She continued to explain. "The poison doses were up and down, helping you feel better when you were with Soren, dragging you down to go back to him when you doubted yourself. Do you know what it's like, having to keep a smile on your face as you betray someone you love? It's a nightmare! And when I found you…" They shared a knowing look about the time Kaylah had caught Rachel hurting herself. "You probably don't remember the timeline, but after I found you that day, that killed me!"

Rachel furrowed her brow. *What timeline?*

"Do you remember what happened a few days later? You started to feel *better*, and then I showed up with a scarf around my neck. That was to cover bruising from my *own brother* strangling me for not doing my job well enough."

Rachel looked down. "Oh."

"And you have to believe me—I had *every* intention of taking you with me before Soren completed the plan. But the sadistic prick took you earlier than he was supposed to. I was gone coordinating Unitas. I did my best. I've had to deceive both sides for a while—I've been homeless for a long time in my heart." She sat back in her chair with a heavy sigh. "We extracted you as soon as we possibly could."

Rachel bit her lip, tears forming in her eyes. "Do you know what he did to me?"

"I… I'm not sure." Kaylah looked down at her lap. "I know what the War Vines do. And Olivia told me about his behavior in your recovery room…"

Rachel remained silent.

"I protested him being assigned to date you from the very beginning. He's … *literally* the worst person I know. And I tried, in my own way…" She rubbed her forehead, clearly flustered. "It wouldn't have mattered. One of my jobs was to coach him, to make sure you wouldn't dump him, to try and keep him in line."

Rachel envisioned another string in the hands of a puppeteer. That was all she was—a puppet. If it wasn't the Seeder lies of her childhood, it was the Ivy betrayals tugging at her every move. She imagined every conversation she'd had with her best friend about her boyfriend, shared in confidence. Her friend had turned around and told him about them, teaching him what to say, how to act. Rachel was growing increasingly nauseous. "I hate my life. I wish I were human."

Kaylah's face was painted with guilt. "Please don't say that."

Rachel picked at her fingernails. "I'm grateful you saved my life. And I appreciate what you're trying to do. I just… Meg… Kaylah… I almost slept with him, because I didn't know what he really was."

Kaylah's eyes searched Rachel's face. "But you didn't, right?"

"No. But that's not the point."

"I told him I'd have him killed if he slept with you."

Rachel's eyes narrowed as she recalled something Soren had said, about someone getting in his way. "Why would he answer to you? He choked you."

Kaylah shook her head. "He may be my older brother, and he may have been given too much power on this project, but I'm still the heir to the throne." She slid a hand forward on the dining table, reaching toward Rachel. "I had to draw a line somewhere. I couldn't let that happen to you. You never deserved that. That's why I suggested our pact years ago, about sharing with each other if we'd gone all the way, Rach. I'm serious—whether or not you'd wanted it, while you were in this world, if I had found out he'd done it…"

Rachel took a moment to respond. She'd forgotten that the Meg she once knew had been the one to suggest their pact. She could hate Kaylah as much as she did the rest of them. But Kaylah was the only one making amends, and making a difference. "I forgive you."

Kaylah's tough facade broke for the first time as tears rolled down her cheek. "Thank you."

Chapter 30

KAYLAH WIPED AWAY HER TEARS. "I don't know if it's much consolation, but the fact that Soren took you before I could, might have saved multiple members of your family from the same fate. He acted without my uncle's approval, and your family put all of your known siblings into hiding before the assassin network could get to them."

That comforted Rachel; she hadn't thought about the fact that her stepdad had known some of the other identities and would have naturally gone after them, too.

Taking a cleansing breath, Rachel was ready to move on. This wasn't all about her. This was about their world at war. "Let's not insult Eric by letting this amazing breakfast go to waste." Rachel scooped eggs onto her plate. "Speaking of… I'm happy to see you two together."

Kaylah almost had a glow to her. Not a literal one, of course—Ivies didn't do that. "I don't know what I would do without him, honestly. He's a good man." She poured herself a glass of orange juice. "I really, *really* love him. My visits here keep me sane."

Rachel wore a smirk. "Yeah, you do love him, don't you? Coming out of his bedroom like that—you guys have clearly made up."

Kaylah fought a grin, biting her lip. "We're adults in both worlds, you know. We can make our own choices, thank you very much."

"I'm curious though. Soren and I talked about it… That's not weird or anything? I mean, we're different… Is it races? Species? I don't know the difference, really. But still…"

Kaylah's expression grew even more mischievous. "Neither of us are complaining." She chuckled. "I know your people are even more different from humans than we are, with the whole rooting and giant batch of kids thing, but if you're not focused on reproduction or your weird transfer of powers, there's really no reason you can't have a completely happy relationship with an Ivy or a human."

"That's good to know. And I'm really happy for you guys."

"Why so curious?" Kaylah raised her eyebrows playfully while taking a sip of juice. "Guillen says hi."

Rachel's smile dropped as quickly as her heart did. "You've seen him? How long ago? He's okay?"

Kaylah beamed. "Oh my gosh. Girl, you really did fall for him! He's fine, totally fine."

Rachel drew a deep breath of gratitude.

"He's one of the most capable men I know, and I grew up around elite assassins." Kaylah began to butter some toast. "*And* he has the biggest heart. Those are hard to find." She rolled her eyes. "Especially in *my* family."

Rachel blushed. "Nothing happened. Dating isn't really a priority right now, if you know what I mean."

"You don't need a man to stand on your own two feet. I get that." Kaylah's tone was warm and encouraging. "And we're living through some ugly crap right now. I'm just saying, I give you permission to like him all you want." She pointed at Rachel with the butter knife. "And I'll tell him you said hi when I see him next."

"I'd like that." Rachel bit into a piece of crunchy bacon. Her mouth watered, having missed meat. The vegetarian lifestyle of the Green Lands had been harder to get used to than she'd expected. She savored the salty, smokey bite, barely holding herself back from moaning. "How's Guillen's work going? What's his mission right now?"

"Guillen is out scouting for me. He did want me to ask how your research was going on Seeder people like him."

Rachel frowned, guilt gnawing at her for not having put more focus on it. "I haven't had the time to ask around."

"Well, I recommend putting that high on the list when we get back. I could see myself assigning you two to work with Green Humans." Kaylah grimaced. "Is that a weird label? Ivies don't have any nice ways of referring to them. They're not stunted or disabled, they're just … unpowered?"

"I don't know. Maybe we'll run the title by them." Rachel huffed. "I really can't believe the way they treat his kind, though. That's horrible. And calling them 'stunts'?"

Kaylah flashed a sympathetic frown. "It's just one of the many things I hope we can fix."

They continued to eat their breakfast and catch up before approaching the reason for the reunion. "So, tell me about what's going on," Kaylah said, pushing away from the table. "Why have your people ignored my offer to meet? Who is this woman you brought with you?"

Rachel shrugged. "I tried—I really did. And honestly, you're lucky *we* even showed up. After the mind games your people have put me through, I'm still kind of waiting for the other shoe to drop."

Kaylah frowned again.

"I say your people, but you know what I mean."

"I know what you mean." Kaylah grabbed their plates, taking them to the kitchen sink. "But the Unitas Movement and Ivy Kingdom aren't mutually exclusive. They're still my people, I'm just trying to … do the impossible and change things."

Rachel sighed, twisting in her chair to face Kaylah. Even if she hadn't been manipulated for half of her life, she doubted she'd have been ambitious enough to try and end a centuries-old war, taking responsibility for millions of lives. "I'm glad I'm not in your shoes. Anyway, Saff—she's a good ally, she's just worn down, as are all of our people. Her brother's death is still fresh, so be patient with her."

"But what position does she hold? Downstairs, we have a big table set up because I expected maybe a half dozen of you."

"She works at the school, training, right now healing. They say she's possibly the most powerful woman in our village, at least for her age." Rachel flashed back to Saff's miraculous and seemingly perilous entrance into the human world. She'd actually made good on her promise to guide Rachel here. Somehow. Rachel had been too nervous to broach the subject with Saff again, with her being so antsy and grumpy. And Rachel had selfishly enjoyed too much time catching up with Eric, trying to ignore her own worries.

Kaylah turned on the tap, filling the frying pans to soak. "That's impressive, but she's not even on a leadership council? It sounds like this could be a waste of all our time if she can't even represent your people."

Rachel shook her head, at a loss for what more she could have done. "We had to try. It has to start somewhere. Win her over, and just like I made the introduction, she can introduce you to our leaders."

"We'll try. I'd hoped to do this in a more neutral location." Kaylah met her gaze. "If I could do this all on my own, I wouldn't have reached out to your people for help."

Rachel averted her eyes, wishing she could have been more convincing with the Seeder leadership.

Kaylah crossed her arms, leaning her hip against the counter. "How long have you been away? How many days do you have left here before it takes a toll on your health?"

Rachel was already feeling the slight dimming of her energy— the precursor to fatal root rot. "We really should get back as soon as possible. But we can spare a day or two if needed."

"That can be enough to get us started."

***

Eric came in the squeaky front door and greeted the girls. "She's just taking a minute to herself in the car before she comes in."

Rachel smiled as Kaylah met him at the door, giving him a kiss. "Thank you."

He took a few steps and peeked out the blinds in the living room. "Well, if she takes a while, you could find a way to *really* thank me." He walked back and pulled her close.

Rachel covered her eyes. "No honeymoon with others in the room, please."

Kaylah chuckled, giving him a couple more smooches. "Rain check."

Saff came in after a few minutes, much calmer than before.

Eric grabbed his keys again. "I'll head out and ... do something."

"You know what? Stay," Kaylah said, grabbing his hand. "If this is about bringing our people together, we should have a human here for this meeting. Wouldn't you agree, Saff?"

"I think that's a great idea," Saff conceded.

Eric slowly set his keys back down on the entryway ledge, his face clearly expressing his discomfort. No one had to say anything— Rachel knew how he must be feeling. What did a recent high school grad have to say about military strategy or brokering treaties? But this was the first ever meeting of the worlds like this in known history, and he would do fine as a layman representative.

Kaylah recommended they sit in the living room as the downstairs wasn't nearly as comfortable; she and Eric claimed the couch while Saff and Rachel took separate armchairs.

Kaylah first addressed Saff. "I'd like to start by offering my condolences. I'm very sorry for your loss. I'm hoping our working together can prevent more loss of lives."

"Thank you," Saff calmly replied. "But before hearing all of your plans, I'd like to be clear on what your end goal looks like. Our people have no need to get caught up in your internal affairs. If you're wanting our help to start your own civil war, or because you have delusions that Seeders will ever recognize the authority of Ivies over them, then this is a wasted meeting."

Kaylah's face showed frustration. "My motives aren't as self-serving as you imagine. Our people used to thrive together, embracing our differences. Imagine not having to use humans and their world as a battleground? Free passage, free commerce, freedom to be who we are without hiding, and fear, and secret identities."

Saff raised her eyebrows. "We're fond of humans—they've always been kind to us. But we don't have much need for Ivies. We're content to keep to ourselves, if your kind could learn to do the same."

Kaylah's lips formed a disingenuous smile. "Then I'd say Seeders are as bad as Ivies at teaching their people history."

Saff scowled. "I don't need to know the particulars, to know when my life is threatened. And I don't have to know every aspect of your culture to recognize you stand to gain a lot with our help, as next in line to be queen."

"I'm talking about things our people have lost—on both sides. Even before the wars. And tell me, Saff, how many years have you studied battle strategy? I didn't get to play with dolls as a child; I moved troops on a battle map!" Kaylah paused. "Your people have numbers and power, but they don't have the organization or tactical preparation. I can help with that. And more.

"I would never assume rulership over your people. And when my time comes, you'd better believe I'm shaking up things on our side as well. Do you think our people like the class system? Do you think they love living in the wastelands?"

"Your people did that to themselves! And I don't give a damn about your lands. I care about us losing good people every day because of something we never provoked!"

Kaylah raised her voice to match Saff's frustration. "I lost good men at the palace in your latest blunder! You got *one* more girl back, congratulations. *One. Of. Five.* How many of your people died in that attempt? How much better could that have gone if you'd had access to the contacts I still have on the inside?

"I'm practically giving you the keys to the kingdom if you'd learn to swallow your pride." Kaylah moved forward in her seat, pointing at Saff. "Don't talk to me about losing people—we've lost on our side, too, by the hand of Ivies *and* Seeders. And by now, our side and your side—they should be the same."

Eric sat silent, not making eye contact with anyone in the room.

Rachel grimaced, adjusting a throw pillow and deciding to take a turn. "I think we can argue about motivation and trust all day. I'd like to hear more concrete plans, and hear how you intend to actually carry them out. We need some validation."

Kaylah gave a heavy sigh. "Fair enough. Aside from my recent actions trying to prove myself, and my inside connections, and years of the best training, there's one more key reason why I'm uniquely qualified to lead this cause."

All eyes focused on her with curiosity.

"Have you never wondered why the royal family would focus three of its own, just for one Seeder? We have troops that can take care of that. We spent *years* preparing for this. Rachel perhaps wasn't ideal because she took longer to bloom than others." She glanced at Rachel. "No offense."

Rachel shrugged, and Kaylah continued.

"First, I think it just started as a way to infiltrate one of your networks. We'd never been able to do that before." Kaylah arched an eyebrow. "We didn't gain as much information as Nuren would have liked. Your people aren't exactly trusting…"

Rachel's lips formed a hint of a smile. No—trusting wasn't exactly high on the list of descriptors for Seeders. They only trusted who they had to. But then again, they *had* been oppressed and hunted for well over a century.

Kaylah continued to address Rachel. "Even when you became a teenager, your Seeder family only doled out the bare minimum needed to your parents, to keep you safe. My uncle only learned about the jade charms you use once they spotted you budding."

Rachel's heart sank. Soren had said as much—that their understanding of the charms was something they'd only recently learned about. If it was true that the Ivies had been in the dark about that tactic until recently, Rachel's family was at fault for endangering her entire species. No doubt, *every* Ivy assassin in the human world was now using that as a method to sort the humans from the blooming Seeders.

She recalled when Soren had asked her other questions, acting as though it were a fascination to learn all about her people. He'd asked if there were other tools they used. And where her family planned to have her catch a breeze to go home. She knew there had to have been other questions. She remembered feeling like her family had kept her in the dark about a lot of that kind of stuff. Which, in retrospect, had been wise. She prayed nothing she'd said had put more Seeders in harm's way.

Realizing the end game hadn't just been to kidnap Rachel, but to infiltrate and gain information, she reflected on the first point of Ivy insertion into her life. "Do you know how they discovered my identity when I was so young? And what ... happened to my dad? Brad?"

Kaylah frowned, shaking her head. "I'm sorry, I don't. They wouldn't tell me."

"I still don't get why the royal family dedicated three people to one Seeder," Saff said.

Kaylah shrugged. "My uncle wanted to make a name for himself. This was a unique opportunity. I just so happened to be dragged into it. As time went on, he wanted to maximize the use of the situation. He had theories; he'd done some perusing in the old archives. Rachel was intended to be the target to test out his brainchild—the War Vines. In a way, his actions will ultimately be the reason we win this. He let the wrong person get too close to his research—he let *me* get involved."

Saff sat up straighter. "Okay, we're listening. What does your research have to do with winning this thing and creating this utopia you're dreaming of?"

Kaylah leaned back in her seat and Eric slid his arm around her shoulder. "Ivies have been lied to for decades about our powers, about our potential. Our people don't realize what they've had stripped from them, how they've been manipulated to benefit the upper class and wage a senseless war. I understand that now."

Still seemingly skeptical and annoyed, Saff scoffed. "I don't see how your people learning they have more powers benefits my people."

"I haven't seen your archives." Kaylah squinted. "But from what I've learned, your people are missing out on some things, too. I know some of the reasons, but not all." She smiled. "We could teach our people together."

Saff rolled her eyes. "That's all well and good, learning more powers. But what does that do for us *right now*? I care more about how I can save lives than finding out I can sprout antennae or something like that."

Kaylah reached for Eric's hand before answering. "Duke Nuren misplaced his focus on what he was researching. What would you say if I told you Seeders would never have to send away their daughters again? And that we could safely bring them all back home, right now? Even the young ones?"

Saff and Rachel glanced at each other. Rachel didn't know all the specifics about Saff's story, and she certainly hadn't told Saff everything about her own, but they knew enough about each other's struggle.

Rachel spoke first. "Then I'd say we're interested in hearing more."

Chapter 31

SAFF SHOOK HER HEAD, ANNOYED at Kaylah's overly dramatic delivery. "You'll have to excuse me. I'm just trying to figure out if you're stupid, delusional, or a bad liar. If there were a way to keep our families together, we would have figured it out a long time ago!"

Kaylah glared. "Let's start with getting those back who have bloomed. We can provide instant transport to the Green Lands. They'll be safe from the hunt and able to train better in our realm." She raised her eyebrows. "And able to contribute energy to your borders."

"I guess I'll be experiencing that transportation firsthand? I can see how that could be beneficial," Saff conceded, knowing full well it was probably the only thing able to save her life at this point.

"Then to get the younger ones back … it'll take a lot more, but I'm confident we can do it. I'll need access to your temples and ancient texts."

Saff arched an eyebrow. "I don't know how much you'll find there. Maybe you're not aware of it—but your people happen to possess stolen knowledge from our archives. And killed off *thousands* of Seeders that might have been old enough to pass down a few tidbits. I think we'd be happy to have those books back. And you want access to even more?"

Kaylah frowned. "I only have part of the equation, but I'm almost there. I'll happily make reparations in regards to things like ancient artifacts and archives when things are righted, but that's not the focus right now. I'm talking about bringing your people home—I know there's a way to open a more permanent rift."

Saff pressed her lips together, reflecting on Ivy rifts and their wastelands. "Speaking of rifts. Even in wartime, we find it objectionable the way your kind destroys nature to punch your way through. What forest are we decimating for this?"

"I said per-ma-nent," Kaylah retorted. "We'll be going back via tree, but in the long run, we won't have to. And I'm not saying it's an overnight solution that just a couple of people can do. But it's been done before and can be done again."

Saff closed her eyes, rubbing her temples. Kaylah was making a lot of vague promises, but Saff had to admit that even the less far-fetched ones could be immensely helpful. She thought back to their trip getting there. Saff had accomplished something she shouldn't have been able to. She definitely *did* want to learn more about Seeder powers, but returning to the human world once more a year wasn't only excruciating—it wasn't all that useful. This was about saving lives. And that was what Kaylah was ultimately promising. Though… "I think we're forgetting something important—even if we can pull it off, where do you expect these young girls to live? You mentioned the unbloomed earlier. Have you forgotten the fact they were taken from our lands in the first place because of the poison? Even if we weren't attacked in the Neutral Woods, we're not that fond of having to give up our homes."

Kaylah acknowledged her words with a triumphant smile. "I think we're at the point I can actually demonstrate something to prove myself. Let's head to the backyard."

They all filed outside, and Kaylah knelt on the grass. Placing her hands on the ground, she extended vines into the soil. Taking in a deep breath, she closed her eyes. Radiating out from her vines, the healthy green grass started to fade, turning brown—a large patch surrounding her all wilted.

Saff wanted to say something, but kept it to herself. *Obviously,* they knew how to poison and destroy things.

~

Rachel, however, was in awe. And a bit sickened. That kind of poison had laced her drinks for months…

Kaylah took a moment to focus; the grass began to change again. Not only did it grow green again, it grew twice as vibrant and tall. Rachel and Saff stood with their mouths agape. Eric looked proud, like he'd seen this trick before. He helped Kaylah stand up, and everyone went back inside.

"You okay?" he asked as Kaylah sat down on the sofa.

"Yeah, thanks." She smiled.

"The growing thing is hard for her," he explained, clicking on an oscillating fan to help cool the room.

~

"So, you can really undo the damage to our lands?" Saff asked, still in awe but hesitant. "It's not even a poison we can see. We still have lots of lush plant growth—it's just latent in our soil and water, affecting our girls."

"It can be done. It'll take some training and a lot of help. But it can be done." Kaylah gave another weak smile. "My people don't realize how much they've been lied to, how much they've been weaponized. Our nurses administer crude medication, but good technique can refine how they dose people." She turned her gaze to Rachel. "You remember Olivia? She's learned to administer numbing without *any* of the negative side effects—the nausea, dizziness, all of that."

~

Rachel pondered if she would have even wanted Olivia to administer only numbing in the palace. Sure, it was to help so the vine insertion wasn't so brutal, and to keep her from resisting, but the haze of the poison they'd administered had helped her pass the time, numbing more than just her body.

Kaylah continued to lay out her plea. "Our abilities aren't just there to hurt others; we're actually capable of a lot of good things for nature and people. It's like nuclear power here in the human world; it can provide electricity, or it can kill without mercy—it's how you use it." She continued with a harder, resentful edge to her voice. "Don't even get me started on how our Mother Vines steal from our own communities. Our people were aiming for progress, instead we got prison. And most of them don't even realize what they've given up."

~

Saff furrowed her brow in thought. "What's the difference between your 'Mother Vines' and 'War Vines'? Our elders said the new attacks were probably a mutation of your Mother Vines."

Kaylah clicked her tongue. "That, yeah… Mother Vines stretch from our communities to our palace. Their abilities are varied and intended to support the entire kingdom, in theory at least. Only one person has their allegiance—the queen. The War Vines are a similar construction, but a newer experiment. And, well," she looked down, "we all know what their main purpose is, and how they work, right? They also answer only to the queen. My mother created them after my uncle's research and infiltration efforts earned him a position as advisor."

Saff was starting to soften at hearing Kaylah's disdain for the practices of her own people. And now that she'd witnessed a power she hadn't known Ivies possessed, she craved to know more. "You have my attention. Tell me more about these permanent rifts you mentioned."

Kaylah reached for a pad of paper and pen from the coffee table, drawing some symbols. "Have you ever seen anything like this?"

~

Rachel cocked her head in recognition. "The cave, by the palace. Guillen said he didn't know what those meant. But you do?"

Saff sat up straighter. "I've seen something like that in our temples, too. Decorative stuff. No one I've asked seems to know what they're supposed to mean."

Kaylah smirked, tossing the pad of paper back on the coffee table. "This is the ancient text of our peoples. This is the key."

Rachel lifted her eyebrows, the intrigue growing.

~

Saff was still struggling with diplomacy mode. "So, your people learn more powers." She cleared her throat. "Good ones. And undo what you've done to our lands, and get our girls back home… What's in this for you? And what do you expect from the Seeders?"

"Well, I need access to your temples and archives—so I need safe passage in your lands, and help in my research. Possibly, protection to allow Unitas members to train on new abilities. And when the power changes hands in my kingdom, negotiations for a peaceful resolution. Talk of lands, cooperation, trade."

"You expect our help to protect your little rebellion when we're not even able to protect ourselves?" Saff scoffed. "Seriously, the audacity."

"You'll have more resources to do so!" Kaylah shot back. "Each son and daughter of yours that we bring back helps. Each person that joins our cause from the Ivy side is one less enemy to fight. It will grow—but only if we can agree to unite."

Saff rubbed her eyebrow with a knuckle. "You talk about power changing hands. If you're intending a coup and plan to stop the war and fix society, why don't you just do it yourself? You stormed the castle once already."

"I never said it was a coup."

Saff squinted. "Then what are we even talking about?"

Kaylah sighed. "Your army, my intel—that's how we forge peace. There are a lot of ways we can make this happen, but I refuse to do any of it without trying negotiations first."

"Sounds like a waste of time," Saff said. "Negotiations have never worked before. If they fail, you'd concede to taking the throne and making good on your promises?"

~

Rachel swallowed a lump in her throat. Was Kaylah really going to have to kill her own parents? That kind of thing had happened throughout human history, and obviously, it would be for the greater good, but still… She tried to read her best friend's face to determine how she felt about it.

Kaylah wore the slightest frown. "One way or another, my mother's power will come to me. My parents may not be as sinister as you think, but… I understand the consequences if we can't find a peaceful resolution with them. Either way, we took out Duke Nuren—that was the first critical move. He's the one that shifted the power; we'll stand a much better chance now that he's out of the picture."

Her gaze moved between the two Seeders. "I get that you've lived your life in societies—both in the human world and Green Lands—that don't involve royalty, but it's not as simple as you're imagining, to just stand up as a new queen and command change. It's easier to kill off a usurper and put someone new in their place, than it is to win over a nation with drastic new ideas." She ran a finger back and forth over the knee of Eric's jeans. "All of my study and planning can be useful. Either as leverage to force my parents to change things, or if we can't get through to them and can't get my people's support to bend their will…" She clasped her hands together, resting them in her lap, then met Saff's gaze. "Then I will take care of it myself. Either way, as long as your people can demonstrate a little trust, we'll be changing the way things are being done."

Rachel was afraid to ask, but needed to speak up. "How will Soren play into your plans, whether or not your parents … you know?" *Have to die?*

Kaylah grinned. "He doesn't have any say or pull, politically. He's just spoiled and temperamental. Even if he's their favorite, he's not the heir—estranged or not, my opinion matters more; our society and powers dictate that." Her expression grew more serious. "I'll see to it that he pays for what he's done."

Rachel bit the insides of her cheeks, nodding.

~

Saff blew out a puff of air. "You know I'm not a politician. It sounds like all sorts of crazy plans, but maybe there's something here we can use." She looked down, focusing her thoughts, fighting to trust. Kaylah was still being too vague about what she had to offer. Maybe she was intentionally keeping details back, even if she was being honest about needing access to Seeder information. But this wasn't enough, not yet. If Saff was going to risk her life and defy council orders, she needed more proof that she'd made the right call to come.

Moving her hand up to where her jade charm usually would have rested, Saff considered the necklace. Trying to sneak out quietly, she'd left it in her bedroom at home. But she still wore it most days. She was gutted the Ivies now had another tool in their belt.

She then thought of her high school days. Devin had confessed that they didn't know how Ivy assassins managed to find Seeder networks in the human world. Seeders didn't understand everything about Ivy or Seeder rifting. She looked up. "If you're wanting us to trust you, we need more than campaign promises. I want to know *exactly* how your assassin network does their job. Everything. How do they find our girls?"

"They're not *my* assassins. They're my parents'."

Saff scowled. "Don't give me that shit."

Kaylah pursed her lips more humbly. "You do realize the vulnerable position I'm in, right? This is a give-and-take. Mutually beneficial. If I play all my cards right now, your people have no need to keep me alive."

Warmth grew in Saff's eyes as she tried to control her energy and anger. "Play your cards? I didn't realize this was a game to you. Your assassins are out there right now, fully aware of the most crucial tool we have to keep our girls safe. And you expect us to be okay with that, without anything in return? 'Give-and-take.' If you can't give us that, then *neither* of us are going to take you to a meeting with our council." She glanced at Rachel, daring her to side with Kaylah.

~

Rachel frowned, digging her fingernails into her palms. She could see both sides. Kaylah was risking everything to change things. She didn't want to just go down as a martyr, not that either side would even think of her that way at this point. But Saff was right. Every second Ivy assassins prowled human high school hallways with the new information was a second Seeder girls were at risk. "She's right, Kaylah."

Kaylah's shoulders dropped, her expression showing her heartache. "I'm not trying to be difficult. I know it's not a game. How do I know I can trust you? That I won't just be tortured, killed, or traded?"

Saff crossed her arms. "If you tell us what we want to know and return us to the Neutral Woods, I'll personally guarantee safe entry to our lands. Whether our people accept your proposals and what you want—that I can't say."

Kaylah slowly nodded. "I've already betrayed my family and kingdom. I hope your people take that into account when they decide whether they'll honor your promise of safety."

Saff glanced at her own hands. "I promised you safe *entry* to our lands, but I can only offer so much. The rest is up to you. Just remember that your ideas and actions are what will be earning you the ability to keep your life."

Kaylah narrowed her eyes in challenge. "*Your* people ignored my request to meet. It's late in the season. I understand that makes it more difficult to catch a breeze home. Just remember, getting home alive is by *my* hand—I hold those cards. I hope you're earnest about getting me in."

Saff flashed green eyes. "You'll get in."

Rachel shifted uncomfortably in her seat. It wasn't like there had been a class in high school on negotiations and confrontation of this sort. She respected Saff, and Saff was one of her kind. But, enemy or not, Kaylah was still her best friend. Witnessing them threatening each other knotted her stomach. Rachel looked down into her lap. Was she just being a pawn again? If push came to shove and Kaylah denied Saff entry back to the Green Lands, would Rachel be spared?

Kaylah sat back on the couch, closing her eyes. She took in a couple of deep breaths. "Ivy assassin networks. Let's talk about it over lunch."

***

Kaylah offered to order everyone delivery. It felt so odd for Saff, having become used to the Seeder way of life, to just use an app for someone to bring food to you. It also felt off to accept food from an Ivy, but she rested a little easier with the knowledge that they were ordering a family meal—they'd all be sharing the same food. They settled on Chinese, one of Saff's favorites that she missed from her years growing up in the human world.

~

Rachel sat down last with a plate of food; everyone had already reclaimed their seats in the living room. She looked down at her orange chicken and fried rice, stabbing at it with a fork. Eating with Kaylah brought up one of a thousand festering questions. "Are Ivies affected by their own poison? Like Seeders can heal themselves with their own energy?"

Kaylah finished chewing a bite, pointing her chopsticks at Rachel. "Yes. The chemicals are a little different, and you need more of it, but we're affected by our own poison."

Rachel furrowed her brow in thought. "Soren really drank poison when we were together? We shared coffee from you all the time."

Kaylah scoffed. "Not likely. Him, take one for the team? We started you on the coffee routine early, in anticipation of your bloom. That way you'd be conditioned to drinking it."

Rachel felt sick to her stomach, hearing that word again. 'Conditioned.'

"We didn't actually put the poison in until it was pertinent, when you finished your bloom and started training. He either turned down your drinks after that, or only pretended to drink." Kaylah rolled her eyes. "We soak up our poison easier—he barely would have even felt it. And ingestion is especially weak versus direct administration through leaf puncture." Kaylah frowned as Rachel continued to move around the food on her plate. "You really don't think I would have somehow snuck poison into this, do you?" Kaylah pointed her chopsticks at Eric, who'd taken a particularly large bite. "It's much more lethal to humans than Seeders, anyway. You think I'd do that to him?"

Eric swallowed his food, giving Rachel an awkward smile. "Human here. Glad to be of service as the food tester to make sure my girlfriend isn't poisoning people."

Kaylah gave him a playful scowl. "Darn. Now that you know why I've kept you around, I may have to replace you."

He stared into her eyes, stabbing his fork on her plate, stealing one of her pieces of teriyaki chicken.

Rachel grinned and took a bite of her own food. "No. Just lots of questions is all."

~

"Are Seeders sometimes immune to your poison?" Saff asked, wondering about her own ability.

"Not that I've ever heard of."

Hmm… "Speaking of poison and sharing information, how about those assassins?" Saff prompted.

With a heavy sigh, Kaylah gave information on how the Ivy assassin networks worked, how they hunted out Seeder girls in the human world. A lot of the information was quite nebulous. Traditional assassin networks usually had three to six soldiers, with a general assigned. But that could vary. Kaylah confessed their methods were far from perfect. It really *was* tough work trying to discover a Seeder network. But Seeders kept their border walls too well protected.

That was why this entire strategy had been such a breakthrough, even with so few girls kidnapped and hooked up to the War Vines. Not only could those kidnapped girls not help charge their own border walls, they could significantly amplify the power of the War Vines. It was the perfect one-two punch. Even getting those six Seeder girls in one year was something they'd been proud of. Seeders trusted so little, concealed so well, and always kept the Ivies on their toes because there wasn't just one playbook to look out for—each Seeder family did things their own way.

Saff smiled at that. Her and Devin's families had done something atypical by pairing up. Then again … that had perhaps done more harm than good, in retrospect. *Barely dodged a dart on that one.* More than three years later, she still occasionally had nightmares about her botched bloom, complete with Ivy assassins who had tried to choke the life out of her.

As they ate and chatted, Saff also pondered on the leaked information of the charms. In hindsight, the elaborate lies to their daughters afforded an extra layer of safety to Seeder family networks—they wouldn't confide in the wrong person about the purpose of the jade charms. But it didn't matter anymore. Seeders hadn't been sure if Ivies knew about them—they hadn't. And now they did. Saff filed it away as one of the first things to let their council know. This information alone could save countless lives. Certainty afforded their families a lifeboat. The girls would still need the charms, but they would need to be absolutely certain to conceal them, and only wear them when necessary, not as mementos when not in use, like Saff had.

Kaylah rounded off her explanation of their hunting tactics. Ivies rifted to a greater variety of destinations, and with relative ease, compared to Seeders. After a century, they'd been able to scope out and map out an approximate area where Seeders were likely to hide their families, based on assumed rifting locations and how far they would be willing to travel within the human world. It was like shooting fish in a barrel. Granted, it was a large barrel. Maybe more like fish in a swimming pool. But it was valuable information, knowing they'd done that work. It could help Seeders strategize better. Assuming … all this information was true…

Saff reminded herself the Ivies were expert liars. The jury was still out.

"Within those regions, it's just a lot of observation," Kaylah said.

Saff's mind wandered lovingly to Devin. "Is there anything else? I sometimes wonder if, well, it could just be a Seeder thing, but it might be a green folk thing, or maybe I'm just making it up…" She realized she was rambling. "Do you think we can sense the energy within each other?"

She sometimes still wondered if part of her falling in love with Devin in the human world had to do with their energy. There was a rightness, a pull to him. And she'd always felt it was somehow more than a coincidence that one of her attackers had zeroed in on her, and at least one of her sisters. *But maybe not.* That Ivy had tried to get close to both of them before they even began their bloom. Their powers hadn't come in yet at that point.

Kaylah twisted her lips in thought. "I've never really thought about it. Maybe? If that's a thing, maybe it also varies by the person. Like a sense of smell?"

Saff shrugged.

After thorough questioning and no hesitation from Kaylah on the topic, Saff had to admit to herself that Kaylah might be genuine.

Or a masterful liar. The sickening thing was that she knew one of those was completely true—but could they both be?

Eric lovingly rubbed Kaylah's arm after they finished eating. Dirty plates piled on the coffee table.

Saff allowed her mind to drift back to her family yet again, and how worried they must all be. Her energy was dimming, a coldness in her roots setting in. She didn't know everything, but she knew enough, and it was time to go home. "When can we leave? You said you could get us quick transportation home?"

~

Rachel noticed Eric frown; he squeezed Kaylah's hand so tight that his knuckles were white. She loved the two together, but this was bigger than them.

Eric spoke up. "You should leave first thing in the morning. We all saw how much Kaylah's display took out of her earlier."

~

Saff couldn't bear the thought of wasting any more time. Along with knowing they needed her and Rachel's help back home, Saff's anxiety was growing about root rot. Returning to the human world a second time in one year, she discovered, felt much the same as the first. Their rotting didn't seem to accelerate; perhaps they just needed to take some time to recuperate in the Green Lands between visits. Nonetheless, this was a dangerous experiment; she felt the urgency to return.

"Fine," Saff accepted with great hesitance, wary about how the combined rifting worked, and wanting Kaylah in peak condition to do it. "But I want to talk details. Tell us more about what your people have done in this Unitas. I want numbers. I want to hear a lot more so I can help with the conversations when we get back. Don't leave anything out."

Kaylah nodded. "Okay. I'll set up our return. Let's do this."

Chapter 32

KAYLAH EXCUSED HERSELF TO GO make some calls. They would need at least one more Ivy there, so Rachel and Saff both had a personal guide to take them through a rift. Rachel explained how it worked, how it felt, the pain and injury required, so Saff wouldn't be surprised. Once Kaylah returned, they covered more details—approximately where they would appear in the Neutral Woods, where they would go to gain entry, who Saff felt they would need to first seek out.

"Don't be surprised if we gain a significant escort when we approach the Outer Wall… We might even get arrested," Saff warned. "It's not like you can prove your identity. Rachel and I can try to cover with our eye glow, but if they demand to see yours, that's when things will get iffy."

Kaylah slid her phone into her pocket. "I understand. I trust you'll vouch for me and my aide. We're coming at your invitation—we're not infiltrating or attacking."

Rachel wondered who the 'aide' was that would escort them there, if she'd met them. Maybe Jon? She wished it could be Guillen, but rifting wasn't something he could do. Her heart warmed at the thought of him, and she found herself fantasizing about seeing him again, somehow working together in all of this. His knife rested heavily in her pocket, against her leg.

"Saff, do Seeders have children born without powers? I met an Ivy that doesn't have any." Rachel spotted Kaylah smirk knowingly. "How do they prove they're not an enemy, if they can't show the female eye glow, or the male hair?"

~

Saff was surprised by the turn of conversation, and to hear about Rachel knowing Ivies in such a personal way. They hadn't really talked much about those particulars in their time together.

"Yeah, I learned about that as part of our cultural lessons after I returned to the Green Lands. Of course, my education wasn't put on hold as much as yours is, with the war right now." Saff furrowed her brow, trying to remember a small tidbit of a lesson she'd once heard. "Every race has disabilities, we're not exempt."

~

Rachel cringed at that label. Guillen was perfectly able to do a lot of things others couldn't. He was determined. He was smart, and wise, and sweet, and... Taking a deep breath, she tried to push his handsome face out of her mind.

"Granted, I'm sure it's a drastically different story than the Ivies." Saff threw Kaylah a subtle look of resentment. "It's not common, but sometimes a girl randomly never blooms. Their host family and Seeder father decide whether to tell them their true nature, but I imagine most just keep living life normally as humans in the dark. It would be sad to learn about a life you could have no part in."

"Yeah, of course." Rachel mulled it over. "So, they come here and molt and then ... just stay human..." Seeder society was already lopsided when it came to gender representation, because of the poisoned lands. More girls, not returning home.

~

Saff glanced at Kaylah again, trying, somewhat unsuccessfully, not to scowl. "As for the boys, the ... defenseless babies, left to root in the Green Lands—it's not promising for them. For the same reason we girls have to leave, they don't stand much of a chance. They're essentially human—they die within our borders."

Kaylah looked down with obvious shame. Eric shyly looked down as well, gently rubbing Kaylah's arm.

~

Rachel observed all the downcast looks in the room. "I hadn't thought of that." At least Guillen had a chance at life. A limited and unfair life, but he made the most of it. Her mind wandered to the times she'd watched him tossing knives, to their conversations full of his reassurances, or his resolve to this cause. *I need to focus.* She wasn't sure why she was starting to obsess over him so much. It wasn't like she'd endlessly pined for him while she was back in Seeder lands, healing people. Maybe it was the distraction and busyness that had kept thoughts of him at bay back there. Maybe it was being in the same room with Kaylah now, or the fact that she'd called Rachel out on her feelings; it made them more real.

~

"I'm sorry for the pain my people have caused," Kaylah offered in a whisper.

Saff surprised herself, and the others in the room. "Thank you. I honestly never thought I'd hear an Ivy say that." She allowed a gentle sigh to escape as she softened. "I'm not so blinded by hate that I can't realize you didn't *personally* start this. And I *am* grateful you brought Rachel back to us."

~

Rachel's eyes teared up. The Saff she knew was generally kind, definitely kinder than she'd been so far to Kaylah. But always uptight and frustrated, always in survival mode. It was nice to hear that she cared for Rachel personally, despite her failures. And it was good to hear a hint of hope that aligned with the Unitas ideology.

Saff continued, "I remember something else my teacher said. About a small community of that type, for survivors."

Kaylah looked interested; Rachel was all ears.

"After the poisoning, there was a village that carved out a space with naturally defensible borders beyond the tainted soil. If they're strong enough for the journey and it's caught quick enough, there's a chance they can live there."

"I have to go there!" Rachel blurted, frantically looking between Saff and Kaylah. "Kaylah, I promised Guillen I'd learn about his kind in the Seeder world."

"I agree. Once he's done scouting for me, I think your research could benefit those like him in my kingdom." She smirked. "Maybe, if I got word to him of your research, he'd work even faster."

Rachel blushed, glancing at Saff out of the corner of her eye… It looked as though she'd picked up on Kaylah's teasing.

"Rachel, you…" Saff's voice trailed off. "I'd like to talk to Rachel in private. Am I right to assume we can come and go as we please?"

"Yes," Kaylah said. "As long as you don't compromise our safe house location."

Saff got up and stepped out the front door. Rachel followed, stopping at the door and turning back to Kaylah and Eric with a wink. "You two be good."

Saff waited until they were at the end of the long block to talk. "You're a lot like me, you know—impulsive. I'm not sure if you've really realized what we've done."

Rachel resented the condescension. Saff was barely older than her, but talked as if she were some wise old mentor. "Thanks. Everyone likes their flaws and mistakes being rubbed in their faces. We had to come out here to talk about that?"

Saff rolled her eyes. "Rachel, I like you. And I didn't just say it to insult you. But you're talking about some big trip to a remote village, as some kind of social research? We need you helping us back home."

"I'm not planning a vacation, Saff! I *will* be helping. You may not recognize it, but I have a unique position in all of this. I plan to make the most of it to do my part. *Every* Seeder woman can heal; I can do something more." She'd been useless before. In part, because of her naïveté; the other part she was still sorting out. Constant doubt still swirled through her mind. Her entire life—lies. But in her core, she knew who she was. And she knew this was right. Rachel had a position no other Seeder could claim. Ties, trust, having physically been in the palace and Ivy territory.

Saff huffed. "Yeah, but you talk about it like you get to make the calls. First of all, you two talk like she's your leader, like you'll follow her anywhere. We don't even have an alliance yet; this is all tenuous at best. Will you follow her if our leaders don't go along with her plans?"

Rachel stared at the sidewalk, kicking a pebble away. She hadn't asked herself that question, not in so many words. Where did her allegiances really lie? With her people, obviously. But what Kaylah wanted was in the best interests of both peoples, even if they didn't see it.

She wasn't going to tell Saff, but Rachel realized her answer would be 'yes.' She was putting her eggs in Kaylah's basket. She had bought the dream of a new world, not just going back to the way things were before Nuren's plan shook everything up.

Saff continued when Rachel gave no response. "And … you do realize that coming here could be considered treason, right?"

Rachel's eyes grew wide, just now realizing the severity of the situation.

~

"It's not like our people are going to kill us or anything crazy like that. But, Rachel, we betrayed the trust of our people, of our leaders, of…" Saff frowned, thinking of the note she'd left at home. "My own husband didn't know I was coming here for this. I'm glad you want to play a role in fixing things, but we may not get much choice in what we do after making this move. We may need to toe the line and do as we're told. You'll have to accept the possible consequences."

~

Rachel stared at the ground again, shaking her head. There had been no other way for this to happen, but Saff was right; it didn't mean they were going to get a parade in their honor, welcoming them home.

"And…" Saff continued, "I'm curious about this guy you're mentioning. An Ivy? There's something you're not telling me."

Rachel's cheeks flushed. "It's not a big deal. You're overthinking that one. He's Kaylah's cousin. He helped me escape and get back home. He's a good ally—good with weapons, and connections, and stuff."

Saff furrowed her brow. "You know, you told the council the prince kidnapped you, to get you to the Green Lands. I've always felt that story was missing some detail. Remember, I met your mom; we talked a lot."

Rachel avoided Saff's gaze, her heart sinking in shame.

"I went on a date with an Ivy once," Saff confessed. "Of course, I didn't know what he was back then. When did you first discover your boyfriend was one of their kind?"

Rachel frowned, slowly, intentionally filling and emptying her lungs. "Earlier than anyone knows," she whispered.

~

Saff had guessed that, with all the focus that had been put on Rachel by the Ivies, and on manipulating her. That was part of why she'd wanted to mentor Rachel, and had been chosen to. They'd both had traumatic experiences at Ivy hands… At Ivy *vines*. Saff knew what a lifeline her Seeder family and community had been to help her through the aftermath of the attacks. "Ivies can be convincing, can't they?"

~

"Guillen's different," Rachel blurted, shoving her hands in her pockets. "He's nothing like David. He's passionate about the cause." She fought off tears. Yeah, 'David' had pretended to be, too. But Guillen was vulnerable, and thoughtful, and caring… But that was how 'David' had bought her trust, by acting the gentleman, turning down her advances as though he were being chivalrous, by acting like he was giving up *so much* by revealing himself, when he was really just using it as a device to lull her into a false sense of security. But Guillen really *was* different. "I learned my lesson. You don't have to worry about me."

"For all our sakes, I hope you're right. Just remember where your loyalties lie, and that Ivies are fantastic at deception. Your friend back there, I'm giving her a chance, but that doesn't mean I'm sold."

Rachel scowled. "I'm a big girl. I can make my own choices. And we're just friends. I don't need your preaching!" She stopped walking, turning and heading back to the house.

Saff turned to follow her. "Forget that you've demonstrated you're a poor judge of character—you need to realize a lot of choices you're making don't affect just you!"

Clenching her teeth, Rachel fought to keep her energy in check, walking faster to get back to the house. Saff quickened her pace to keep up. Rachel yanked the screen door open and turned back to her. "You may think that you and I have similar stories, just because we've both dated an Ivy, or because we've been personally attacked by them, but don't pretend you actually know me. I'm not as stupid as you think. And you're not as special as you think you are, just because you're more powerful than most, or because you've been back home for longer than me. Just … get over yourself."

Rachel opened the front door, seething mad. Eric and Kaylah were still on the couch; she was leaning into him, wrapped up in his arms. They looked up at the Seeders, attentive, as if they'd heard some portion of the argument.

Saff entered behind her, shutting the door and glaring at Rachel. "I'm going to go lie down for a while."

Chapter 33

RACHEL STOOD AWKWARDLY BY THE safe house front door as Saff left down the hallway. She wanted to go somewhere to give the cuddling couple some privacy, but Saff was now in the Seeders' shared room. Rachel considered going back out on a walk by herself...

"Babe, I think I need some time alone with my best friend." Kaylah pressed her forehead against Eric's and they gazed into each other's eyes.

"Mmm, never enough time with you," he said, stealing a kiss.

"But I make our time worthwhile." Kaylah turned and straddled him, wrapping her arms around his neck and voraciously sucking his face.

Rachel scrunched her face in embarrassment, looking away. "I'm going outside."

As Rachel turned the doorknob, Kaylah called out, "I'll be just a minute."

Two or three minutes later, Kaylah joined her, smiling.

Rachel smirked as they began to walk. "You guys are... Well, I'd tell you to get a room, but..."

Kaylah giggled. "Sorry, but I *did* have to watch you all over my brother for two-plus years."

"Yeah…" Rachel cringed. "Thanks for the reminder."

Kaylah frowned. "Sorry." She took a deep breath, a smile reappearing on her face. "I heard you gave him some stitches."

Matching Kaylah's smile, Rachel recalled how livid Soren had been. "It's the least I could do."

"He certainly deserved it. Do you remember a while back, when he got that black eye?"

"Yeah."

Kaylah pointed to herself, beaming.

"What?"

Kaylah held up her hands. "Seriously, the ego on that guy! I was the one who talked you into asking him on a date, right? If his sole purpose in coming here was to date you, why didn't he just ask you out?" She arched an eyebrow.

Rachel shrugged.

"Ego—pure and simple. Well, I think it was partly a test to make sure I was still loyal and would follow orders, that I could convince you. But he'll take anything that strokes his ego. He wanted *you* to come to *him*."

Rachel's stomach churned. "What does that have to do with his black eye?"

"Right. Yeah. The black eye." Kaylah smiled again. "That was what? A couple of days after he revealed himself to you? He was bragging about how he'd ambushed you in the hot tub. It wasn't a heat of the moment thing at all—that was calculated. He knew what he was doing." Kaylah rolled her eyes. "I didn't realize he was going to take things that far. And once I found out… Yeah, he earned that shiner."

Rachel swallowed hard, her heart hurting. "I… I don't know if I want to hear about all the ways I've been manipulated." She looked down at the ground. A sick curiosity ate at her, needing to know every instance, every motivation, every manipulation. But the part of her hanging on by a thread knew she couldn't handle a list of her weaknesses. Not yet.

Kaylah stopped Rachel, pulling her into a hug. "I'm sorry. I'll try not to bring up the sensitive stuff when it's not pertinent, okay?"

Rachel nodded, looking up and continuing their walk. "How did you even end up with Eric? Rob married a human to get to me. But I'm kind of surprised you chose … or were even allowed … to date a human."

Kaylah pressed her lips together. "I know how it feels to be used, too. Forget they're my parents—just think about the fact that our queen and king trusted Nuren so much they allowed their only daughter, their heir, to live most of her childhood in another realm."

Rachel furrowed her brow. "I'm not following. You dated Eric to piss off your real parents?"

"No." Kaylah shook her head. "But … they sent suitors. They would have doubled as security detail if I'd have chosen to really date any of them. I couldn't always be a third wheel as your best friend. And they wanted to make sure I ended up with someone who would fit their agenda. So, when I was back home, or you were busy with Soren… I was trying to get out of an ugly dating game."

Rachel rubbed her forehead. "How is it you lived such a crazy life right under my nose?"

Kaylah blew out a long exhale. "A lot of coordination." She hooked arms with Rachel, and they crossed the street. "Remember Michael, my tutor?"

"Yeah…"

"I'm not dyslexic; he was appointed as a tutor for court business so I was properly trained in politics, culture, and manners."

Rachel just shook her head.

"Anyway, the suitors… They were all idiots. In the end, when I met Eric, I convinced my uncle it was a better cover to date a human. I promised my parents I would focus on an Ivy suitor after I returned for good. After your bloom…"

"But you're staying with Eric?"

Kaylah grinned. "I may not always be here with him physically, but a part of me is always here with him," she said wistfully.

Rachel gave her a half-smile. That had to be hard for them. "I did want to make sure… We're not delaying leaving just so…"

Kaylah gave her the stink eye.

"Okay. Just making sure…"

"Taking Seeders through a rift is not something I've done before, so it's probably for the best I regain my strength. I know I don't go all glowy like you guys do, but our energy can get drained, too."

They turned down a narrow dirt path, running parallel to a ditch. Rachel smiled at a bunny that ran out from a bush ahead of them before scurrying back. "How does that work for you guys, by the way? How do your abilities work? We imagine ours like this chamber of energy in our hearts, when we envision it."

"Hmm. That's pretty cool. I guess when we envision ours, it's in the mind. I mean, it's more like a chemical thing, right? So, I focus on what I want done, then visualize it working its way down through my veins. Through my neck, arms, then vines."

Rachel ducked under a low-hanging tree branch. "That's really cool! What all can you accomplish, if you've been working on refining the poison?"

"So far, I've gotten really good at making people pass out. Gotta have that for fighting. Numbing—there's different focus required for local results without making you go all foggy, as I'm sure you know…"

"Are you capable of doing … like, more refined medicines? Like, mind-altering stuff?" Rachel shyly asked.

Kaylah lifted an eyebrow. "Are you asking me if I can get people high? Or are you wanting to know more about what I had to do to you?"

Rachel rocked her head back and forth. "Well… I just meant, replacing happy pills, or something like that. But yeah, I guess you might be able to do a lot of good … and bad … with the right mix."

Walking silently for a moment, Kaylah pursed her lips in thought. "I don't know if I want to find out. I wouldn't want to push too far. Though, I don't *think* we can make anything that pure, otherwise it would have been exploited already. What I did to you was pretty basic poison." Kaylah sighed. "I'm just happy that, whether it's helping people or it's helping nature, we're starting to explore what we can actually do with our chemical abilities, not just 'poison.'"

"That's pretty neat. I look forward to seeing more of it."

Kaylah threw Rachel a mischievous glance. "Speaking of things we look forward to seeing more of… What about your new love interest?"

Rachel bit her lip. "It's not like that. I don't think, anyway. What did he say?" Kaylah clearly knew something had developed between them, and that knowledge had to have come straight from Guillen. Rachel's stomach fluttered at the thought he'd confided an interest in her.

"You know Guillen; he's not much of a talker. But he sure did blush when he reported how talented and smart he thought you were. I didn't even know he was *capable* of blushing."

Rachel wore a stupid grin. It wasn't like he'd talked nonstop, but he wasn't mute. They'd shared plenty of engaging conversations. She wasn't so sure she could agree with Kaylah's assessment of him not being a talker.

"It's silly to like him. We're so different—our upbringing, being on different sides of the war … all that stuff. It's not really the time to think about what I want in that way."

"Are you saying I'm selfish for being with Eric?"

"No! I wasn't saying that at all."

Kaylah nudged her arm. "It's not that different, you know. Me and Eric, you and Guillen. We have people who would say we should be apart, other priorities pulling at our attention. But love doesn't wait until life is smooth and perfect. Or at least it shouldn't have to."

Rachel wished it could be that simple. She didn't even know where Guillen was at the moment, and had no way to contact him. "I don't know how you balance all this."

"With lots of desperation, hope, and caffeine." Kaylah laughed. "But…" Her tone dropped to be more serious. "It's all worth it. The sacrifice. The time. The movement. Making things work with Eric."

"But … how is it really going to work with you guys? He lives in the human world. You're going to be a freaking queen someday; you can't exactly move here to be with him. And aren't you supposed to produce heirs or something?"

Kaylah gnawed on her bottom lip in silence for a few more paces. "We'll figure it out. I have some theories, and hope. Rach, I have to have hope. I love him, and I'm not willing to let him go. And if Guillen is what you want, you'd be lucky to have each other, and you can make it work, too."

"Well, cool your jets on that one. We barely even held hands, kind of." Rachel cleared her throat, her mind drifting back to the lake. "There was that one time I was half-naked in his arms…"

Kaylah's eyes lit up. "Come again? That's it—I need every single detail of your journey back! That's an order!"

Rachel laughed. "It wasn't like that, first of all. And secondly, I'm not sure what the relationship is between you and me. I don't know if I take orders from you."

Kaylah tilted her head, frowning. "Rach, you're still my best friend. And I can promise you, I will *always* be honest with you from now on. I don't have a reason to lie to you anymore."

Rachel nudged Kaylah's arm. "I missed you."

"I missed you too, girl. Now back to my cousin…"

Rachel chuckled. "Okay. But then I want to hear all about what he's doing to help Unitas."

***

Approaching the house on their return, Kaylah and Rachel took a small detour to the backyard.

"C'mon, two-person hammock!" Kaylah said, running to the patio and lying down.

Rachel joined her with a smile. She was beyond grateful to be back with her best friend. And to see that Kaylah was genuinely the same girl she'd known all along.

They snuggled up in the hammock, and Kaylah grabbed the edges, pulling them together. "Cocoon of love!"

Wrinkling her nose, Rachel glanced at the fabric. "Please tell me you guys haven't had sex on this thing."

Kaylah busted out laughing. "No! But you're giving me ideas." She released the edges of the hammock and wiggled to be able to make eye contact with Rachel. "He's seriously so amazing."

Rachel let out a heavy sigh. "I'm happy you guys are back together, but I really don't need to envision you and Eric in bed."

Kaylah smirked. "While I certainly have my opinions on performance in the bedroom, that's not what I meant. I just… I really appreciate the sacrifices he's willing to make." Her voice softened. "And you, too. That you're willing to give me another chance after all that's gone down."

Rachel scanned Kaylah's face. "What I don't understand is why you're doing this. If this is really you… How can that even be? Why wouldn't you be living with servants pampering you right now? Instead, you're risking your life. Why are you so different from the rest of your family?"

Kaylah met her gaze. "What makes one person or race better than another?"

After a moment of silence, Rachel realized the question hadn't been rhetorical. "Their choices and actions?"

"Hmm. Maybe your answer is better than mine. I was going to say: nothing. If I've learned anything from living so much with humans and being forced to take their history classes, it's that we're all just fools wandering around on this earth. Most of us are just doing the best we can. You. Eric. Guillen. I love the wrong people to be that entitled. And if I'm going to be known as the most disappointing crown princess my kingdom has ever had, I'm going to do everything I can to *earn* that title."

Rachel loved her for her bravery, and for her ability to throw caution to the wind. But Kaylah was making some dangerous moves here. "Are you afraid?"

Kaylah's voice softened once again. "Of course I am. How much do you think we can trust Saff? And your people? Do you think this will actually go somewhere? And it's not just a trap?"

Rachel wiggled a bit, getting a better view of the clouds as they rolled by. "They don't trust my judgment. I'm not sure. I think they'd trust her, though. I hope they do. And I don't think she's setting us up…" She glided her fingers over the teal-and-white striped fabric of the hammock. "I don't know who to trust anymore. I just… I don't know."

"Hey, I get it. But don't give up on yourself. That's the big difference between you and her, you know. You've been hurt, but you still have hope. And you forgive. Some people just get bitter."

Rachel frowned. "That's not fair. She's been through a lot. And we all handle stress differently. And… She's never had a decent experience with an Ivy. I have." Her stomach was tight, her anxiety growing. She hated being in the middle of this. Between Kaylah and Saff. Between the conflicting interests. But, in a very fulfilling way, she was also grateful to be there to hopefully bridge the gap.

They sat in silence for some time, watching the sky. A yellowjacket buzzed around uncomfortably close before heading on its way.

"I wonder how many people died because of me," Rachel whispered.

"What are you talking about? You're not to blame for any of this!"

"If I hadn't fallen for Soren's lies… Been so stupid… I know at least a couple of soldiers had to have lost their lives protecting our walls because of what my energy did for your War Vines. And how many more girls are going to fall to that same fate because your assassins know about our jade charms?"

"Look at me."

Rachel hesitantly turned her head.

Kaylah's eyebrows were raised high. "It's not your fault. It's not even your family's fault. It's *my* family's. Okay?"

Rachel gave a tiny nod. "It's true that our people got one of the girls out? Is she okay?"

"Yeah, they got one out. I'm not sure how she is. But … from what I understand … it was kind of a massacre for your people. They didn't realize how our energy barrier protects the palace. They lost the advantage they thought they had."

Rachel's heart ached. "How are we losing so badly? I mean… We can fly, and we have projectiles, and we have twenty-four flipping kids at a time… You'd think we far outnumber your people. How are we losing?"

"You're stronger in a lot of ways—I'll give you that. But our strategies and abilities do a lot to mitigate all that. Your people are split between the worlds, have more limitations, and you're too passive, untrusting, and bad at coordinating."

"Wow, tell me how you really feel." Rachel raised an eyebrow.

"Just telling it like it is. And yeah, you have a lot of kids. You outnumber us. But not as much as you think, from what I'm guessing. Twins and triplets aren't actually that rare for Ivies. And pregnancies are shorter for us than humans. Even then… Do all your Seeder teenagers come back to the Green Lands and look forward to wrestling that many dang kids?"

Rachel chuckled. "Definitely not."

"Maybe not now, because human culture has become such a big part of who you are. But back in the day … before our people split ways…" Kaylah slowly sat up and Rachel followed suit, wrapping her fingers around the rope holding up the hammock. "Your people used to far outnumber us. I don't exactly love the term, but … there's a reason my people call yours 'weeds.'"

"Because weeds are trash."

"Yes, and no. Weeds spread. They can grow out of control. They can choke out a garden. Your people are capable of building a *massive* army and obliterating my people."

"But that's not how it happens! I know I've only been over there a few weeks, but really … not a single one of these people chooses to have kids just to build up some stupid army. Like you said— they're passive. It's a hard choice to have kids at all. And it's not like we can change things… It's zero or twenty-four. We don't get a choice in that!" Rachel furrowed her brow. She hated having to defend herself like she had with Soren. This time she'd actually met other Seeders. They weren't the aggressors in all of this.

"I know," Kaylah answered softly. "I believe you. And… I don't even know what to believe, myself, about history. It's not like either of our recorded or oral histories would be impartial about what happened with the Great Division. I'm just saying… Whether it's true or not, your people have great potential. Fear. Is. Motivating. My people worry."

Rachel looked down, trying to put herself in Ivy shoes.

"Rachel."

Looking up, she met Kaylah's gaze. Kaylah's face was stone-cold sober.

"My people are as tired of this as yours are. They're frustrated. They want it to end. *For good.* This isn't the same war anymore. And it's not just about who lives on the best land anymore, either. My uncle wanted to punish your people. We're talking colonization. We're talking slavery. *Complete* population control. And *every* able-bodied male Ivy is enlisted and ready to be called up for duty. Every last one of them. I *need* your people to see my offer for what it is. I have to believe your councils would prefer to work with me, and maybe even offer some concessions before this goes further. Once my parents have taken down your borders, it's too late. We *need* Unitas to work. We need each other."

Goosebumps covered Rachel's arms as she swallowed hard. "Right. We'll make it happen."

Chapter 34

SAFF LAY IN BED, FUMING. Rachel thought Saff was conceited about her extra energy capabilities, but that wasn't true in the slightest. Yes—Saff was different. But it wasn't like she traipsed around their village expecting fanfare. With that extra power, she'd risked her life and relationships to help Rachel, to help their people. With that power, and *a lot* of extra studying and effort, she had been offered the position as a mentor. To mentor someone as ungrateful as Rachel.

Rolling onto her side, Saff angrily punched her pillow into a more comfortable blob, then shoved it back under her head.

Rachel was so … naïve. She made rash decisions that hurt other people. She was too trusting. She was selfish. She was too much … like Saff.

Maybe that was why it infuriated her so much. She remembered treating Ben just like Rachel was treating her. He had always tried to keep Saff out of trouble, and she'd never listened. She'd compromised them; she'd gotten people hurt. She was never certain what role she had played in the bloodbath at her parents' house, if she was somehow at fault for that, too. Saff had dealt with her demons and come to terms with her guilt over the last few years. This was all fresh and new for Rachel; she hadn't grown up from it all yet, at least not by Saff's estimation.

And what had Kaylah concretely done to prove she could make good on her promises? She'd killed off a patch of grass and made it grow again. That was hardly proof she could save millions of Seeder lives.

Saff couldn't help but wonder if Ben would still be alive, if just one part of the equation had been altered. If Rachel had never been kidnapped, if the Ivies had never had access to her power; the short amount of time it had pulled away Saff, Devin, and Simon, or the search parties… Could any of that have made a difference? She wasn't directly blaming Rachel for his death, though she couldn't help but wonder, amidst the sea of 'what-ifs,' if he would have still been there with her, if just one minor detail of the past had been changed.

She thought of all the time she had shared with Ben in this world, and their own. She fondly recalled their first Christmas together, before she even knew he was her real brother. Their chats as she'd sorted through major life decisions. They'd grown even closer after returning to the Green Lands—he and Heather would come over often to spend time at Saff and Devin's cottage.

And Saff had promised him she would make up for being a pain when they were in high school, when she'd almost gotten him killed. She'd promised him he'd have his wedding day. And that was a promise she could never fulfill.

Her anger, hurt, and regrets came to a head as she sobbed into her pillow. He wouldn't be coming back. Feelings of hopelessness crowded her mind. She mentally listed the names of her large family, one at a time. It was like throwing a fistful of darts and hoping none of them would stick. Who would she lose next in this war? Whether or not Rachel's mistakes truly had any effect on Ben's outcome, Kaylah's had. Her people's actions had taken Ben. She could have done something differently.

Saff gritted her teeth. She wanted to do what was right, wanted to be able to trust Kaylah like Rachel did. She hated feeling so out of control. But the logical, skeptical, careful side of her kept pulling her back from trusting Kaylah blindly. How was Saff the bad guy in all of this? If Rachel was going to just run off a cliff, shouldn't someone more grounded be there to help weigh the risks? Saff wasn't a pessimist; she was a realist.

After a good long cry, she blew her nose and picked up the cell they'd purchased at the gas station, dialing a number she had memorized a while back.

It only rang twice before being answered. "Hello?"

"Mom?"

"Melody! Is that you?"

Saff burst into tears. "Yeah, Mom. I'm just on another short visit."

"How is that? Are you okay?" Pam, her formerly-Seeder-now-human mom, asked, her voice conveying her concern.

"Yeah, it's complicated. I'm sorry I couldn't visit you and Dad this year." She sniffled, trying to keep her composure.

"Honey, we understand. We're just happy to know you're okay. Is there any chance we'll get to see you this time? You are … okay, right?"

"Yeah. There's a lot going on. I have a way home; I'm going to be okay."

Pam understood Seeder physiology; the fact that Saff had called during her visit earlier in the year, and was now back in the human world for a second time, and at this late of a season… She knew how impossible it was. And how likely lethal that made it.

"Okay…" Pam hesitantly accepted her daughter's assertion.

"I can't come visit this time either. I'm leaving in the morning. I just needed to hear your voice. And…" She started to ugly cry with all the squeaking and huffing and sniffling that comes with it.

Pam stayed silent on the phone.

Saff's voice trembled. "Mom, Ben's dead."

Pam gasped on the other end of the phone, then stayed silent. While Saff had been raised by Pam and George, Ben had only been in their home as a foster for one year, but they'd treated him like family. He and Heather had even gone to visit them briefly the previous spring.

"I just," Saff choked on her words, "thought you should know."

There was a long silence on the phone. "I'm sorry, honey. He was a good man. Your dad and I are praying for you guys every night."

"Thanks, Mom. I love you guys." Something came to Saff's mind. It seemed massively premature, but it was better to be prepared. Eric's willingness and dedication to Kaylah's cause made her think. "Has anyone approached you guys about us, about our war?"

"Um, no… We haven't talked to anyone in the network since you left, other than you kids visiting us."

"Good." Saff wiped away her tears, sitting up straight on the bed. "Can I trust you with some names and information?"

"I… Yeah. You know you can trust us with anything."

"It's a long shot. But there's a group that might be able to help us stop this war. And I may give them your phone number someday. But only if I know I can trust them, and I'm going to give you a code word so you know you can trust them, too. And… I'm going to give you the names of the other Seeder family hosts from my family and Devin's. I'd rather the information be safe with you instead of giving it to them directly. I trust your and Dad's judgment."

"Oh, honey, that sounds… Are you sure? That's a lot of sensitive information."

"I know. And you might never need it. But if things work out, it could make a world of difference. I just want you to be prepared."

"Alright, let me grab a pen and paper."

Saff listed off her siblings and Devin's, so Pam could try to track down contact information on their human host families. Discreetly, of course, especially in the case of brothers, as their hosts weren't always aware of their true Seeder identities.

Saff had no intention of just handing that information over to Unitas. But if Kaylah could prove herself, it might mean a lot of resources on the human side, if Eric and the gatekeeper they'd met upon their arrival had been right about human involvement in this conflict. No matter what they tried, Saff's people were suffering and slowly losing this war. They needed a new weapon, and this might shift the balance of power, even if Kaylah could only fulfill half of her promises.

Saff couldn't make good on her promise to Ben that he'd get his happily ever after, but she could still keep her promise to give her all, to end this.

"And unless it's Thod, Devin, or Heather, don't trust anyone without the code word, okay? Keep that information safe." Saff thought of a gorgeous flower she'd seen depicted in Seeder art, now believed to be extinct. "The code word is spelled G-u-e-n-j-a-l-i-s. It's pronounced 'gwen-yawl-iss.'"

"Okay. I'll tuck that away in the safe right now. We miss you, honey. I wish I could give you a hug."

"Thanks, Mom." Saff frowned. "I could never repay you and Dad. I'm sorry I was a pain in the butt growing up."

Pam chuckled softly. "You weren't so bad. We're proud of you. I worry about you, but I hope you're still happy with your choice to go. It sounds like you're doing great things for your people."

Saff thought about it. Did she regret her choice? If she had known this was coming, would she have chosen to stay behind and become a human? Either way, the Green Lands was her home now, and she wouldn't change that, even if she could. She would never give up Devin or any member of her family. The sacrifice was worth it.

"I am happy, and I'll be okay. We'll make it out of this stronger. And we'll be happy to see you next spring, okay? Devin says hi." There was a stab of guilt about that last part. He hadn't even known she was returning. But he would have said hi—it felt natural to say it.

"Your dad will be sad he wasn't here to chat, but I'll pass it on. We look forward to seeing you guys." Pam paused. "Honey, I don't know everything that's going on. And I know it's a hard time. I just want to remind you to consider all the options when you're making all of these important choices, okay?"

Saff smirked. Even as a married woman, her mom knew who she was. It was like her mom could read between the lines, knowing Saff's decision to come had been impulsive. "I'll do my best to make you guys proud."

"Stay safe, sweetheart. We love you."

Saff teared up again. "Love you. Bye, Mom."

***

Saff was still in bed, her emotions wearing her down. A knock on the door caused her to sit up and blow her nose. "Come in."

Rachel stood in the doorway, hesitant. Walking across the room, she gently sat on the other bed. "How are you doing?"

Saff dabbed under her eyes with a chuckle. "Not the most productive nap."

Rachel frowned. "I'm sorry about earlier. I know you just want what's best for our people. And I do, too. I'm just asking you to give me a little credit."

Pursing her lips, Saff took a deep breath.

"You met your husband when he was your protection detail, right?" Rachel asked.

"Yeah."

Rachel cocked her head to the side. "How long were you dating before you found out his identity?"

"A few months."

"I dated the prince for over two years before I found out who he was. What do you think you would have done if it had happened the other way around for you? That Devin was an Ivy, instead of a Seeder?"

Saff furrowed her brow in thought. That would have made things a heck of a lot stickier. "Well, I probably wouldn't be alive. Because he's the one that spotted my bloom in the first place."

"Yeah. Well, mine found out. And you're right; he used me and I probably would have died by his hand at the palace, eventually. But if your husband had told you what David, er, Soren, had told me… If you had shared all of that extra time between you… You don't think you might have made the same stupid mistakes as me?"

Saff looked at the wall and rolled her eyes. "Yeah, I probably would have been just as naï—" She paused. "I probably would have made poor choices."

"But you made your own mistakes, and you learned from them."

"Rachel, I'm sorry. I get what you're saying. And I'm sorry for taking my anger out on you. Everything is a bit … fresh … for me right now. And I just want what's best for you."

~

Rachel forced a half-smile. "Thank you. I don't really have a lot of people in my life I can trust, or that trust me, or care about me." She fidgeted with her hands. "Sometimes I feel like I don't have anything or anyone. Not even with my new family back home. My homecoming wasn't exactly a typical celebration."

Saff frowned. "You just have to give it time. It takes a while to acclimate and build those bonds, even if you *had* come home under normal circumstances."

Rachel nodded. "I'll work on it. I haven't given up yet."

"Good. You're a smart girl." Saff picked up her phone, offering it to Rachel. "I know we can't see your mom, and you guys have got to be dying to talk. Why don't you give her a call?"

Rachel eyed the phone with both longing and trepidation. She'd been avoiding it thus far, despite how desperately she'd wanted to hear her mom's voice. "Kaylah and Eric want to talk first. I'll call her before bed, if you're ready to join us."

"Sure."

Rachel stepped out of the room.

"Rachel?" Saff called.

"Yeah?" Rachel poked her head back in.

"I feel like there's something I should tell you."

Rachel's eyes narrowed. "Okay?"

"Duke Nuren."

Rachel frowned. She still had a hard time fully hating him. She recognized her own denial at times, having witnessed a complete one-eighty, just briefly, after years of loving him as her stepdad. "What about him?"

Saff swallowed hard. "I heard his name before, before you were even taken."

Rachel sat down on her bed again. "What?"

"My brother." Saff looked down. "The one that died. He's the one that saved my life, when the Ivy I dated attacked me."

Rachel pressed her lips together. That had to have given them a strong bond.

Saff sniffled. "Anyway, I heard that name—Nuren—in the first attack. We knew there was Ivy royalty there, but we didn't have any other problems after another fight. We killed their general and several others. We … didn't realize there was another Seeder family across town. And we wondered if maybe I had misheard the name, or if maybe we had actually killed him, or…" She fidgeted with a clean corner of her tissue. "Just, we did you and our people a disservice by not being more open about the possible threat earlier. I'm sorry."

Rachel stared at Saff, her mind running through a myriad of 'what-ifs.' But she couldn't blame Saff's family; they had been taking care of their own. That was how Seeder society worked. And trying to find Rob, with his identity so well concealed—she questioned if it would have even been possible.

Rachel's mind took a darker turn, one she'd been avoiding. She was back in that room in the palace, with Nuren—Rob, her stepdad.

She'd wondered if anyone had ever loved her; her closest relationships were all fabricated. Aside from her mom. The woman she feared talking to, the woman she'd brought so much pain upon through her misplaced trust, by her very existence. The woman who had wanted to have more kids, kids of her own, but had been lied to. Rob never could have given her more kids, but hadn't disclosed that when they'd married.

Other than Guillen and Jon, Rachel had struggled to form new relationships. Relationships were hard; they were risky. She'd never been an introvert, but she couldn't deal with the guilt and worry. And that was what this felt like. The looks and actions of her Seeder family—pity. Saff's part in this—guilt.

Rachel cleared her throat. Saff was now looking at her, waiting for a response. "I don't need your help. You don't owe me anything. I don't blame you."

~

Saff bit her lip, her heart still heavy. She admitted to herself that a lot of her actions regarding Rachel had to do with guilt and a sense of obligation. But she knew that was a dangerous line to toe in relationships. She'd navigated that all with her husband's lies under orders back when she was in high school. Even if it was a motivating factor, she would never admit as much to Rachel.

"I guess I just wanted to say… We have a lot in common. Home towns, raised as only children, dealing with rotten people and experiences. And, maybe I kind of think of you like a little sister." She grinned. "Not that you don't already have plenty of sisters."

~

Rachel smiled, thinking it over. She was at least grateful Saff had been honest with her about Nuren, that she hadn't held back. "Thanks." Her mind turned to her earlier conversation, Kaylah's eerie warning about where things were going with this war. "You ready to go talk to the others?"

Chapter 35

RACHEL WALKED INTO THE LIVING room, Saff following after her. Eric was giving Kaylah a shoulder massage. She got up from the floor and sat next to him on the couch. Rachel and Saff took their respective armchairs, both ready for more Unitas talk.

"Thanks for joining us again," Kaylah started. "I thought it would be best to discuss the human part of the equation more before we head out, since that wasn't discussed in much detail earlier."

"I'm all ears," Saff said.

"Money isn't a problem," Kaylah said. "We have some generous humans that have joined the cause." She turned to Rachel. "And Ginger and Nathan and I siphoned off a good deal of the royal investments set aside for my upkeep before I sent them away." She looked Rachel squarely in the eye. "They were never part of my uncle's plan. Their job was to keep me safe and ensure I was properly educated. They knew your identity, but never knew any plans until I brought them into mine, okay?"

Rachel nodded, grateful she'd offered another point of clarification. It helped, knowing people she liked and admired actually cared for her, and weren't part of the grand scheme.

Kaylah turned back to Saff. "Anyway… Money, humans. We do want to open up the human network to prepare for any eventuality. We have some Ivy defectors over here, and through a lot of hard work, we've gathered a few human and even a couple of former Seeder host connections, but we need more. Just to be prepared."

"Why do you need more?" Saff asked. "What are you expecting to need them for?"

Kaylah crossed her legs. "Movement, more safe houses. Ivies only ever think of humans as unknowing hosts, as simple pawns, and they mostly ignore them. They don't realize what a huge resource they really are. And, so far … our movement on this side has done really well, under the radar. But we have to be prepared for negotiations to take a while, and possibly not go the way we're wanting. I imagine the situation could get more aggressive on this side of things. Once they realize we're evacuating your girls, we may need to be prepared for extra hostility."

Kaylah bobbed her head. "I know I said we'll negotiate first. And I have hope with the research I've done, that I can sway things toward a peaceful resolution. But we need to be prepared for every eventuality. Keeping your people and borders safe, winning approval from my people."

"You're talking about them coming after the humans, too?" Saff asked.

Kaylah shrugged. "It's possible. It's not our usual method. But their tactics aren't exactly ethical; they're not above human harm."

Observing silently from her chair, Rachel mentally noted how Kaylah used her words. When she would use 'our' to show she was still an Ivy. And 'their' to disassociate herself from the brutality of the current and past regimes. It didn't sound rehearsed; she sounded genuine.

~

Saff spoke up with her usual skepticism, but tried to tone down her accusatory attitude of earlier. "So, you're asking for contacts?

Realizing that giving away those names may put them in even greater danger, if you or someone in your group betrays us?"

Kaylah slowly nodded once. "Yes. And I understand that's asking a lot."

Saff raised her eyebrows. "I'm glad you have a good grasp on that reality. *If* things pan out, I'm prepared to give you a couple dozen contacts in the human world, some of them still local. Remember that, as we move forward."

Kaylah's eyes widened in obvious shock, as though maybe she had only intended to ask for Saff's parents, or something much smaller. "I would be honored, and would make great use of that information. And I'll be able to prove my worthiness for it."

Saff suppressed a grin, even more glad she had made the call to her mom. It was an extra layer of motivation and insurance. Though her mom's words played back to her: To make sure she was looking at all of her choices. Thinking out the consequences. There was no way Saff would be giving away a single name unless she was beyond convinced this was safe.

~

Kaylah turned to Rachel. "We've moved your mom to a safe house."

Rachel's heart skipped a beat. "Really? Did they try to hurt her?"

"No. Not yet. But Soren can be vindictive." Kaylah rubbed at her neck. Eric took her hand away from her neck and kissed it.

~

Eric's attention reminded Saff of Devin, helping her through crushing PTSD as she had healed from Ivy strangulation wounds.

Kaylah snapped out of her trance. "I've arranged for her to join us at our departure point in the morning."

"Really?!" Rachel shrieked, starting to cry. "Thank you, Meg. I mean ... Kaylah!"

Kaylah gave her a reassuring smile. "Of course."

Saff was cautiously starting to warm up to Kaylah. Kaylah was competent, organized, and seemingly caring. Never traits Saff had associated with the enemy. Just like her own discovery of her people and the Green Lands, she realized it might be time to expose herself to a more neutral narrative of the Ivies.

Kaylah's eyes danced between Rachel and Saff. "I ... also need to make sure we're clear on the fact that *no one*—Seeder, Ivy, or human—can know," she paused, "that Eric and I are together."

Eric didn't make eye contact with anyone in the room, but rubbed Kaylah's arm.

"I just ... His location needs to be a secret, and I can't have anyone coming after him to get to me." She lowered her eyes. "It would not bode well for negotiations if my parents knew I was still with him. And... I have to play it safe when it comes to your council. Can you both give me your word that no one will find out?"

"Of course," Rachel said without hesitation.

Saff read Kaylah's face. Every inch of her expression and the inflection in her voice made it clear she was serious, desperate, and determined. It hadn't been wise to use his safe house for this meeting, and to show affection openly. But Saff knew how important it was to have someone you could trust and rely on, to lean on in the hard times. To have someone in your corner. For her, that was Devin. She'd missed him this week; she'd needed him while processing Ben's loss in silence. Sick to her stomach, she imagined how Devin must feel right now, after she'd deserted him.

"You can trust me." Saff smiled, meeting eyes with Eric. "We don't harm humans, especially those that want to help bring peace to green folk."

Eric gave a nod of appreciation.

"Thank you," Kaylah said.

Eric took some time to speak next, explaining the basics of how their network was setting things up and handling it all. Bank accounts, encryptions, codes. It was impressive. It was a shame they were limited to this realm, but they made good use of their resources. Unitas was even hiring hackers to combat the Ivy assassin network's efforts. To help narrow down likely Seeders and coordinate amongst

Ivy networks, Nuren had commissioned the creation of an app. Suspected Seeder behavior and spottings data were pooled and run through an algorithm.

"How long have they been that high-tech?" Saff asked, thinking back to her high school days. Nuren had lived across town, and the assassins that came after her and her family hadn't behaved normally.

Kaylah shrugged. "I don't know. It's not like I ever used the app. But I found out about it maybe two or three years ago? It could have been in beta testing for a while."

"Does the name Mel or Melody Walters mean anything to you?" Saff asked.

Kaylah raised her eyebrows. "Nope."

"She went to Franklin High four years ago."

Kaylah shook her head. "Franklin High across town from where Rachel and I grew up? The name still doesn't ring a bell."

"At least ten of your assassins were killed by a pair of Seeder families that year."

"Impressive. What's your point?"

"Melody Walters was my name before I chose the Seeder life. They came after me. They came after my family."

Kaylah looked down, pressing her lips together. "I'm beginning to see how personal this all is for you. I'm sorry."

The logic didn't add up. "But you want me to believe you didn't know a massacre happened across town, with your own people?"

Kaylah cocked her head to the side. "I want you to believe it, because it's true. I was a spy, not an assassin. I was here to … focus on," she cleared her throat, "to focus on Rachel—gathering intel from her, following orders in regards to her. But in all my 'free' time, I not only had to keep up the appearance of being a normal human teen, I had constant tutoring as the crown princess. I was too busy to associate with anyone deployed in the assassin networks."

Saff had almost started to like Kaylah, but that didn't sit right with her. "Glad to know we were beneath your notice."

Kaylah sighed. "If you're looking for a pity party, I can't offer you that."

Saff glared. "Your pity wouldn't be welcomed. Answers would be. Ten is a lot more than the three to six in a normal network you mentioned."

"I don't know how it all played out, but that sounds like backup. So, they'd obviously made you and considered you guys a threat for some reason."

"They knew my identity for a month before they attacked the second time. Why did they wait?"

"To study you? Study and experimentation were in the scope of what my uncle was doing. Or maybe they were just waiting to unravel your network. If they discover one girl, she could be the first to bloom, or the last. If they can flush out your whole network, they can take down an entire family at once."

It made Saff sick to her stomach, hearing Kaylah discuss it so coolly, so calmly. "But you don't really know. Your uncle was calling all the shots. The one *you* killed. And his secrets died with him."

Kaylah sat up straighter, folding her hands in her lap. "I can't undo the past. And I don't have any regrets about that decision. I'm sorry I can't give you the closure you're looking for, but it's not like it was all for naught. The books and scrolls he gave me access to, when he became so *proud* of me for 'stepping up' to help with his research… I don't think people have set eyes on some of those in decades, maybe centuries. He was selective about his research to benefit his strategy. I studied it *all*. There are some valuable things there that he had access to. And I did, too.

"He's gone. The reading material has been smuggled out of the palace. He can't use that information anymore. No one in the palace can."

Saff took a deep breath, crossing her legs. "I have a knack for learning new things. Especially since some of that is no doubt stolen Seeder information, I'd love access to those resources."

Kaylah gave her a soft smile. "Great. Rachel wants to help and I have a job in mind for her. Glad to hear you're on board and willing to help, too. But I'm not allowing access to those records or sharing any more information about my strategies until I'm safely speaking to your leaders. That's the deal. We get there. We talk. We negotiate with my parents. And then we'll see."

Saff rubbed her forehead. Kaylah was exhausting to work with. This whole ordeal was exhausting. The whole last year had been. "Yeah. Whatever, fine. Let's go over details of what tomorrow morning will look like."

~

The sun set as the group hashed out final details for their return. Rachel watched Eric and Kaylah, so easily and maturely conversing in each other's arms. Kaylah's hand rested on Eric's thigh as he talked and Eric's arm was slung around her, lovingly drawing a figure eight over and over on Kaylah's shoulder. Before the crap hit the fan, Rachel would have easily voted them the cutest and most compatible couple in their high school. And now, going through all the struggles and real situations they were facing, they couldn't be more perfect. She was happy for them. A little jealous, maybe, but happy.

"Well, I think we should turn in early tonight," Rachel suggested. "We're all a little drained, and the earlier we get to bed, the earlier we can get going."

"You're sure there's nothing else we need to discuss?" Saff questioned. "Especially with you, Eric? We won't so easily have this opportunity to bring human insight into this operation again."

"It's okay. Kaylah knows all of those details and procedures intimately," Eric said with confidence.

Rachel stood up, stretching. "I'm down for going to bed." She was recognizing the warning signs of root rot anyway. Not that she'd ever experienced it before, but she'd been taught about it. Her pool of energy was diminishing by the hour. Good rest and a quick exit were both what the doctor ordered.

After turning in for the night, Saff quickly fell asleep, but Rachel took a while longer. She was proud of herself for her part in these negotiations. While it had mostly been Saff and Kaylah doing the talking, Rachel had been a key piece in, well, keeping the peace. Maybe this could help make up for the shame of her previous failures, assuming it paid off.

Rachel tried to block out the thought of what she knew was happening in the other room, though she couldn't help but wish it was Guillen and her. Not exactly the full intimacy… They were nowhere near that. But just the thought of him being there in that bed, cuddling with her. Those piercing eyes, his muscular arms, his tender touch. Holding hands. Stealing a *real* kiss, not just the one she'd given him on the cheek as they'd parted ways.

She sighed, frowning. They didn't stand a chance. Distance, war, time … just everything. They had work to do, and even though she had a hint of hope to see him again with Kaylah's plans, she wasn't really sure what that would look like. But she let her mind linger on him. It was helpful to drown out thoughts of Soren and the hurt. She felt guilty, at first, for using the memory of Guillen that way, but in the end justified it. He'd earned her affection by his own merits, not just as a stand-in.

Chapter 36

GUILLEN WASN'T THE ONLY PERSON occupying Rachel's thoughts as she struggled to sleep. As an owl's hoot from the backyard pierced the silence of the night, she rehearsed in her head how things would go with her mom in the morning. It was the first time she would get to see her since the kidnapping. What exactly had her mom been told about the circumstances? Rachel would face her in shame—it was her own stupidity that had gotten her kidnapped. Her heart hurt for her mom, knowing she had to be distraught over losing her daughter. That she had been betrayed and left by another man. Rachel sulked at the irony. Like mother, like daughter—they hadn't made the best choices in men.

That had actually been a point of contention with her Seeder mom, Lyza. Lyza had insisted they'd done a *thorough* background check on 'Rob' just like they had 'David.' Rachel didn't know who to believe, and in the end, they couldn't change the past. Assigning blame wouldn't make things better.

Eventually, much later than she would have liked, Rachel found sleep. She woke in the morning to Saff stripping the other bed to be washed.

~

"Hey, you. How are you doing?" Saff asked.

Rachel groaned. "Just five more minutes? Or five more days?"

"Sorry, doesn't work that way. We've got our lives to preserve and a war to stop. Why don't you hit the shower?" Saff's anxieties were growing as she stared down the barrel of her attempt to return to the Green Lands. She was faced with the question she'd had about leaving for this trip in the first place—could she even do it? If she had failed to get through that second rift a few days ago, she would have just remained back home. If she failed to get through a second one home now… The outcome would be death.

~

Rachel grunted, pulling her comforter over her face. She didn't want to go back to a war zone, or get out of the pillowy bed so early when she'd gotten such poor sleep. But she also couldn't have any more blood on her hands, and couldn't wait to reunite with her mom. Rolling out of bed, she walked down the hall to the bathroom.

The happy couple only emerged from Eric's room once both Saff and Rachel were out in the dining room. He'd set out muffins for everyone, but didn't leave Kaylah's side to make a special breakfast. Instead of their previous aura of happiness and insatiable lust, their expressions were quieter and more downcast.

No one had to say anything. Rachel had felt just the tip of that iceberg when Guillen had left her in hiding.

~

Saff even sympathized; she missed Devin like crazy, and knew what it was like to be separated from her love for several months.

After breakfast, they hopped in Eric's car, complete with tinted windows. He held Kaylah's hand the entire way to a nearby forest. The trip went by in almost complete silence. Saff wrung her hands. This would be the first time she'd witness an Ivy rift. To Seeders, the destruction Ivies caused as a means of transportation was a repugnant and vile sin against nature. But this time, it might just save her life. She didn't have a choice.

~

Rachel bounced her knee excitedly as they pulled up to the meeting point, where another car was already waiting. She tore the door open as soon as Eric parked, running to her mom as she exited the other vehicle.

"Rachel! I'm so sorry, baby. I missed you. Are you okay?" Samantha cried.

"Yeah, Mom. I'm great." Rachel squeezed her tight. "I'm sorry for everything."

"Sweetheart, you have *nothing* to apologize for." Samantha pulled herself away, wiping away one of Rachel's tears. "I'll never forgive myself for bringing Rob into our lives and putting you in harm's way."

Rachel frowned. "Mom, he had everyone fooled. It's not like my birth dad or brothers or anyone else suspected him, either. Don't take the blame for that." Her eyes glazed over for a moment, remembering the bloody scene at her rescue. "I can guarantee you won't ever see him again, and both worlds will be better for it."

~

Kaylah and Eric smiled in unison, watching the reunion. Eric had his arms wrapped around Kaylah from behind. Saff anxiously stood there until Kaylah made the other introductions.

"Saff, these are my deployment guardians. Ginger and Nathan."

Ginger and Nathan shook hands with Saff, then gave Eric and Kaylah a hug.

~

Rachel and her mom discussed trying to find a way to pass letters to stay in touch. Being in league with Ivies that could come and go regularly gave Rachel a light at the end of the tunnel—she could stay more connected with her mom. Of course, that was only if things didn't go sideways.

Spotting Ginger and Nathan a few yards to her left, Rachel broke away from her mom and squealed, running up to hug Kaylah's parents. "It's nice to see you guys! I was really touched to hear you guys were part of the cause!"

Ginger smiled wide. "It's good to see you, too. And Unitas is important to us. Just as much as our Kaylah."

"So, you two are…" Saff started.

"We're Ivy," Ginger confirmed. "The warmth of the Green Lands is something green folk hate to live without, but once you live here on assignment for a few years, you start to appreciate the little things of the human world." She playfully swished a finger in the air. "And they don't have beaches like Cancun back there."

"So, are you guys at the safe house my mom's staying at?" Rachel asked. She was too ashamed to admit she was actually uncomfortable at the thought of it. While she loved Kaylah's parents, and they were part of Unitas, they were still Ivies, and her mom had been through a lot at Ivy hands.

"She's been with us, and it's been great getting caught up," Ginger said. "But she'll be relocated again, now that I'm coming with you."

"Okay." Rachel perked up even more. "So, you and Kaylah are our ride home?"

Ginger winked. "You got it."

"I promise we'll take good care of Samantha," Nathan reassured Rachel.

Rachel drew a deep breath and let it out. She could only do so much. She couldn't control everything. Not in her own world, let alone both of them. She'd need to learn to trust people. Out of the corner of her eye, Eric caught her attention. Once their eyes connected, he gave her a signal that he wanted to talk to her in private.

"Hey, babe, why don't you spend a minute with your parents. I've got to talk to Rachel." He kissed Kaylah's cheek and released her, looking like it took every ounce of his resolve to not stay near her.

He and Rachel moved a few feet away, and he started by talking just above a whisper. "I just wanted to ask you to, you know, watch out for her. She's entangled in a lot of dangerous stuff. I can't lose her."

Rachel smirked. "Well, I'm glad to know you care about my safety, too, Eric."

He sighed. "You know what I mean. I love her, Rach. And I can't do a single thing for her on that side. I'm counting on you to help her get through this safely. We're all counting on you."

Rachel pursed her lips. *No pressure, right?* "We'll take care of each other. I'll do everything in my power."

He smiled, grabbing her for a hug. "You're the best."

Glancing past Eric's shoulder, Rachel spotted Kaylah looking at a cell phone. Kaylah's expression dropped, heavier than Rachel had ever seen before. She handed the phone back to Nathan without even looking at him, staring at the ground with a blank face. She glanced up and met Rachel's gaze.

Kaylah's eyes shifted between Rachel and Saff, and she took a deep gulp. Kaylah gave her a tiny nod of the head, as if acknowledging that Rachel knew something was wrong, and asking her to stay silent, to trust her.

Eric released Rachel from the hug and Rachel stood still, her heart racing. Was her loyalty already going to be tested? No one postured threateningly. Other than Nathan, no one else seemed to be in on this big secret. Rachel was a split second away from reciprocating Kaylah's nod, but she couldn't. She wasn't going to walk through a rift blindly, not again. For all she knew, that look Kaylah had just flashed was one of guilt—she'd just gotten word their ambush was prepared on the other side.

"Hey, Kaylah, can we chat for a second?"

Kaylah forced a smile. "Sure, no prob."

They walked away from the group, out of hearing distance.

Rachel looked her in the eyes. "What is it?"

Kaylah frowned. "Just some bad news. It's not going to change our plans."

Rachel squinted. "You know I need more than that. I'm not going through without more than that."

"I promise. I just… Things will be better if we go right now. I'll tell you the second we get over there. I just want you to be safely back there." Kaylah's eyes showed concern.

Rachel continued to study her face, not responding.

"Rach, why would I save you and go through all of this, just to betray you? If *you* won't even trust me, then we don't stand a chance."

There it was again—trust. Rachel closed her eyes, considering the situation. She used to think she was a good judge of character. That delusion was long gone. But why *would* Kaylah have rescued her just to go through all of this? What would her end game be? The logic still fell in Kaylah's favor. If she'd wanted to hurt Rachel, she probably would have done it by now. "Fine. Let's go."

Eric rejoined Kaylah as Rachel made way. He looked lovingly, longingly into her eyes. "You stay safe."

Kaylah smiled through tears. "You, too. I love you."

"I love you, too."

They exchanged a couple of sweet kisses and a long hug. Rachel gave her mom another tight squeeze.

~

Then Saff took Rachel to the side… "What was that about, between you and Kaylah?"

"Nothing."

Saff narrowed her eyes. "Right…" Her anxiety was too high about her own problems to press further. "I … might have a problem." She lowered her voice further. "It's going to sound melodramatic, but I don't know if I can go back."

Rachel's mouth hung open. "What do you mean, can't go back?"

"I shouldn't have been able to make this trip in the first place— you knew that."

~

"I know. You said you had a theory. That panned out." Rachel whispered, "You planned a suicide mission this whole time? You've only got a couple of days before you'd die!" She couldn't imagine Saff being so reckless. Or … dead.

"I wasn't suicidal. I just … was a bit … irrational. I don't know for sure. This might be nothing. I just… In case I don't make it through…" Saff pursed her lips, unsuccessfully fighting back tears.

"Saff, you can't… And we *need* you! The council won't believe me. *Especially* now. A lot of this is riding on you. You should have at least told us earlier. Kaylah's counting on you to make the introduction."

~

"Then make this trip count. At bare minimum, get home safe and tell them about the charms so our people know to be more vigilant. Tell them everything Kaylah's told us." Saff swallowed hard, her heart breaking. "And if I'm stranded here…" She wiped away tears. "Find Devin. Tell him where you left me. Maybe he could come here in time to say goodbye."

~

Rachel's heart hurt. "Yeah. I'll do everything I can. But… I still can't believe you did this. Why do you think you might not be able to go back?"

~

Saff shrugged, at a loss for a concrete answer. She wasn't sure *anyone* had an answer about the limitations of her unique situation. "I'm not drawing from the same energy here. I genuinely don't think I have it in me to catch a breeze back. But you said you barely felt any energy drain going through *their* kind of rift? That it was different?"

"Yes."

Wiping away the rest of her tears, Saff sniffled. "Good. Like I said, I don't know. There are so many variables we don't understand. I just need you to be prepared. I guess we're about to find out."

~

"Right. I guess so." Rachel's heart was trying to escape her chest. She was dealing with too much. Eric's plea. Kaylah's cryptic secret. Saff's life or death dilemma. *No pressure.*

Kaylah approached them both with raised eyebrows. "Everything okay over here?"

"Yeah. Of course," Saff said. "I just wanted to double check… The girls you kidnapped were all unrooted, but you're sure rooted Seeders can make it through an Ivy rift? Since both of us are rooted now…"

Kaylah nodded. "Yep. Should be just fine according to our research. Otherwise, I would have warned your people in my invite to only send men. We also don't have any seasonal restrictions like you guys do."

~

That was somewhat calming for Saff. "What about fully-rooted matriarchs? Could the combined rifting work for them? That wasn't in the letter that I'm aware of."

Kaylah furrowed her brow. "No. I chose to leave out something impossible. Your people's mojo is pretty strong. I'm sorry, but I'm fairly certain we still can't help your more mature females go back and forth."

"Right. Makes sense," Saff said.

Kaylah glanced between them. "You look a bit worried. Neither of you is anywhere near old enough to be a matriarch. And I don't know how to assure you any more than I have, that I can be trusted."

Rachel shifted her gaze to Saff. "Well, it's just that Saff is—"

"Too curious for her own good," Saff said. "And shouldn't be wasting our time. Let's go."

Kaylah shared a look with Rachel. "Right. Let's go."

Moving to stand by a pair of healthy trees, Kaylah cleared her throat. "I won't be long-winded, but I feel like I should say something. This is a moment we should all be proud to be a part of. This is Unitas. This is not the cause of the Seeders, or the Ivies, or the humans. This is the cause of all of us, in unity. We're going to create something new together. To hell with the old ways—this is where we start to build a healthy future.

"Saff, which of us would you feel more comfortable taking you through?" she asked.

Saff's anxiety peaked. She never would have fathomed ever giving an Ivy a chance like this. So much could still go wrong. They could show up anywhere on the other side of that tree. Next to the palace, surrounded. Separated from Rachel. And that was if she could even make it at all. "I think I'd like you to take me through."

"Alright," Kaylah accepted. Saff joined her, holding her hand as Kaylah wrapped a vine around her wrist. Every feeling in Saff's body revolted against that vine being there. The last time one had slithered around her, it had been to take her life.

Rachel joined Ginger and followed suit.

"Guess it's you and me, kiddo," Ginger said with a warm smile.

Kaylah and Ginger each ran the end of a vine down the spine of their respective trees, causing shining rifts to open. Saff stared in wonder and terror. Her nerves were strung so tight, she feared one might snap. The other three women looked back for one last glance at the loved ones they'd be leaving behind.

~

Ginger's vines didn't cling onto Rachel as tightly as Soren's had, only as much as needed to get them both through. The pressure increased once they tried to get the mass of Rachel's body through the rift. The leaves still ended up digging in enough to cut her a little bit.

~

"This might hurt," Kaylah warned Saff.

Saff prepared for the worst; every muscle in her body tensed.

As soon as Kaylah went through, the pressure of her vine increased around Saff's wrist. Stepping into the rift, Saff winced in anticipation. And then at the pain in her wrist.

But she didn't wince at the pain in her heart—there was none.

Saff gasped on the other side, filling her lungs with the energy coursing through the Green Lands. Kaylah's vine released her and Saff fell to her knees, clutching her chest. She struggled to catch her breath, hardly believing it. Beyond grateful to just be alive. She'd made it back home.

"Are you okay?" Rachel asked, worry in her voice.

Saff stood. "Yes. Just… I am *never* doing that again!"

"That definitely sounds a lot like gratitude, and not at all an overreaction," Kaylah drawled.

Saff shook her head, realizing Kaylah probably assumed she was being a drama queen about accepting Ivy help. "That's not what I meant. Thank you. I mean it." She took a second to survey their surroundings while healing her wrist, remembering that surviving the trip back to their home realm had been only one possible risk.

But it appeared Kaylah had held up her end of the bargain so far, and there wasn't any obvious ambush waiting for them on this side. They were safe. For now.

"Right." Kaylah sighed, stepping back and stealing a glance at Rachel. "Before we get started, I need to let you know something. I just got word that one of your girls at the palace is dead."

Chapter 37

RACHEL HOPED SHE'D HEARD WRONG. "One of our girls died?" she whispered.

Kaylah frowned. "Yes. I'm sorry."

Rachel looked at Ginger, who also seemed shocked at the news.

"I … I…" Rachel struggled to breathe. As she began to cry, Ginger put an arm around her. Rachel shook her head as the tears rolled freely down her face.

~

Saff also teared up, but less from shock, more from anger. "When did it happen?" she demanded. She thought she'd cleared that hurdle, to trust Kaylah.

"I… I don't know the exact details. I just got word."

Saff's eyes glowed. "*Just* got word? This very moment? Not yesterday? Not while you were making us wait?"

Kaylah glared. "No! I just found out a few minutes ago. I haven't been stalling. As you can see," she gestured at the woods around them, "we're here, safe." She stood taller. "I'm sorry about that girl, but I still expect you to keep your end of the bargain. We still have a mission; don't forget that."

Saff was livid. "Right. Just one more of *our* kind dead." Just like Ben. He was just a number to Kaylah. They all were.

"I didn't do it, and I couldn't prevent it!" Kaylah's voice rose.

"You two need to shut it!" Ginger hissed.

Kaylah and Saff shared looks of humbled frustration. Yes, they were in the Green Lands, but they still weren't safe. They were quite literally not out of the (neutral) woods yet.

"We've got an outpost about a quarter of a mile from here," Kaylah said. "There's a map that should be helpful to get us to your borders."

"Then let's go." Saff glanced over at Rachel, who was still being consoled by Ginger.

~

Rachel dreaded another stupid cabin, but she was barely in the right state of mind to think much of it. Her heart was breaking for that girl and her family. She needed to know more.

They walked quietly for a while, alert to any danger of discovery. Soon enough, they spotted the forgotten abode, carefully checking to make sure it was clear before entering. Ginger led, then the Seeders, and Kaylah hung back, fiddling with something by the door.

~

"What was that?" Saff asked, on edge. "What you were just doing?"

"I can't endanger my people by permanently stationing them so close to your borders. We have our way of communicating," Kaylah explained.

"Well, I think I should be aware of what kind of signals you're sending, especially if we're cornered in a building, don't you think?"

Kaylah took a breath, doing a better job of trying to restore some shred of proper diplomacy. "You make a fair point. The decorative piece out there—I turned it to indicate that I've safely made it back. That means when my patrols come around, they can get word to those who would need to know. And patrols will pick up more regularly, awaiting my return or other word of developments. Hopefully good news, and soon, after we meet with your council."

Saff was pacified by her explanation, but still watched out of a dirty window to make sure they wouldn't have unexpected visitors, as did Ginger.

~

Rachel sat on a dusty old chair, staring blankly at the wall. Kaylah crouched down in front of her, holding her hands. "I'm really sorry," she whispered.

Tears still blurred Rachel's vision. "Why did you wait?" she whispered back.

Kaylah frowned. "I didn't think it was fair to your mom to hear that, or see you like this. And..." Her eyes darted to Saff. "I wanted to make sure you got back here safe, even if," she nodded in Saff's direction and lowered her voice even further, "she had lost it over there. I promise—that's all."

Rachel nodded. "Yeah." She tried not to slip back into that place, the place where she didn't care what time of day it was, as long as she was numbed well enough. Jon's words about what he'd witnessed with the first girl haunted her. Rachel didn't deserve to be the one who had been saved.

Saff broke her focus from the window regularly to look at Rachel while she recovered from the shock.

Kaylah rested her head sideways in Rachel's lap. "We'll get through this, don't forget how strong you are." She took a breath. "Sometimes it's okay, to not be okay. I'm usually good at hiding it. But I'm..." She paused. "We'll get through this."

Rachel bit the insides of her cheeks. *Right. Strength.* She puffed out a breath of air. She needed to get it together. But she first needed to know one more thing. "How did it happen?"

Kaylah picked her head back up to look into Rachel's eyes. "Exhaustion, from what I understand. I think she was one of the first to be taken there."

Rachel nodded again. She'd assumed as much with how horrifying and draining it was. They hadn't allowed nearly enough time for her to heal and recharge between sessions on the War Vines, and if the girls who had been there for months were enduring the same schedule… It sounded like death would have honestly been a welcome release.

"I…" Kaylah started. "It's more of a slight shade of grey than a silver lining, but that means the Vine attacks will be weaker for now … and maybe they'll be nicer to them, let them recover more, so it doesn't happen again."

~

Saff had been straining to overhear their conversation. She couldn't bite her tongue any longer. "Yeah, some benefit. It just means they're going to try harder to get a replacement. As for the others, that just sounds like prolonged torture to me."

"You're right." Kaylah stood, throwing one more sympathetic glance at Rachel, as if apologizing that they didn't have more time to unpack the news. "We need to figure out the next step." Kaylah walked over to an old table and crouched, sticking her head underneath. Emerging with a rolled-up piece of paper, she walked over to Saff.

They studied the map; it took Saff a minute to understand where they were. "Mmm, this is a couple villages over from ours. How far of a walk would it be if we went straight to the nearest border wall?"

"It might take a full day," Kaylah answered.

Saff continued to study the map, disappointed. She would really rather show up at her own village. But the Ivies were more active at night in the Neutral Woods, and *any* amount of time spent in them was risky, day or night. "I think we should just head to the closest point. Once we're in, we can figure it out from there."

"Alright." Kaylah rolled up the paper. "I'm letting you lead on this part." She glanced at the others in the room. "Are we about ready to go?"

~

The question and gazes were really only focused on Rachel. Closing her eyes, she took a couple more deep breaths. She could be strong. She could make a difference. She could fall apart later, but that wasn't a luxury they had right now. Opening her eyes, she stood. "Okay."

Saff pulled her attention from lookout duty again. "Remember, Rachel—you know how to defend yourself, but I have the darts. Keep that in mind; stay close."

"I'd like to remind you this is a *peaceful* delegation," Kaylah added. "But if Ginger's life or mine are in danger, we'll defend ourselves. Everyone here needs to remember to tread lightly, act cautiously. From what I last heard, my part in Unitas isn't officially being recognized by the palace. So, if we come across my people, assuming they're not yet Unitas initiated, they should still follow my orders. They could become allies."

Departing for the wall, they hoped to reach it before it got too dark. The quiet was disconcerting; they barely whispered to coordinate with each other. Saff and Kaylah took the lead, with Ginger and Rachel close behind. After walking for a couple of hours, Kaylah stopped in her tracks, holding up a hand.

Normally, the instinctive reaction would be to hide. But it had been agreed upon that they would face anyone they met—casually, as though they were patrolling the area themselves, on duty. It was a bit far-fetched, but it also depended on which scouts they ran across. If they ran across Seeders, they could show their eye glow and try to vouch for Kaylah and Ginger. Ultimately, their primary concern was just getting past Ivy patrols. Ivy women weren't deployed as soldiers, so their group would naturally be pegged as Seeders if they didn't recognize Kaylah as their princess, or as the leader of Unitas.

Soon enough, the voices grew louder—two men. The women stood in place, prepared for whatever may happen next. The men stopped, taking a defensive stance once they spotted the party. They wore uniforms—Ivy uniforms. What the women didn't know was if they were Unitas initiated. They stared at each other for only a few seconds, but it felt like hours. If the women had actually been soldiers, they'd have identified themselves right away, but they couldn't tip their hand; they were a mixed group, a rogue element. The patrolmen hesitated for some reason, to attack, or to signal or demand identification. They studied the group, seemingly surprised or confused.

"Um, our apologies, Your … Highness," one said, as they both bowed low.

The Seeders' anxiety grew. Not the side they'd hoped for.

"We just didn't…" The men continued to scrutinize the rest of the party while Kaylah stood tall with perfect posture. It was odd for Rachel to see her friend like this, so regal, demanding attention.

The other man spoke up. "Your Highness, you're alright? We're going to have to ask for identification of your party."

Kaylah furrowed her brow. "You can stand down. My mission is my own concern, and my companions are approved by me."

The men shook their heads; something was clearly wrong. "Sorry, Your Highness. But we need to see vines. Or … stunt marks?"

The very sound of that demand made Rachel clench her jaw. *You mean friggin' Nazi tattoos?* They didn't even think people like Guillen were capable of being soldiers, anyway.

Ginger stepped forward, her hands up, presenting her vines. "I don't believe the crown princess needs to explain herself to anyone. You two can be on your way."

One of the men extended his vines aggressively, standing tall. "With all due respect, that is not going to happen, until we are satisfied."

"What insubordination is this?" Kaylah demanded.

The other man took a step forward, also challenging with vines. "We have our orders, and this doesn't seem like a difficult task, Your Highness." He squinted, as if trying to understand Kaylah's reaction.

"On whose orders are you to disrespect me?" Kaylah asked.

The men gave each other a look and lunged forward, grabbing with their vines, leaf-tips blunted, at the two closest women—Saff and Ginger.

Saff revealed her blades, slashing in the air, cutting the first attempt short. The Ivy soldier scowled in recognition. Kaylah paired up with Saff, crouching low and trying to grab onto one of his ankles with her vines. He sidestepped and intercepted with a vine to thwart her attempt.

Ginger had vines wrapped around her wrists, but quickly kicked off the ground and twisted to be closer to her attacker. "Rachel!"

Rachel ran over, trying to use her Seeder blades to help with the vines. The other man's eyes widened in surprise as he thrashed about, trying to kick Rachel away while keeping Ginger in his grasp. He attempted to hold Ginger with one arm, releasing one of his vines, and focused on trying to subdue Rachel simultaneously. He lost his grip and Ginger freed one of her wrists enough to extend her own vine, wrapping it around his arm and piercing his flesh.

Rachel kept his other hand and vine occupied, understanding the strategy. Ginger closed her eyes and took a deep breath as he struggled, then quickly went limp. After he fell to the forest floor, Rachel stood by, ready for him to pop back up, but he didn't. Ginger returned her vines and she and Rachel turned their attention to the others.

Ginger swore. "Did you see where they went to?"

Saff, Kaylah, and the other Ivy were nowhere in sight.

Finding footprints heading in a different direction, they rushed to follow them, swiftly spotting the rest of their group.

Kaylah had vines around the other man, just one of his arms. Saff knelt on his other arm and wrist to pin him down, her Seeder blade extended at his throat.

~

"Get off him, Saff!" Kaylah ordered as she injected her own poison into the man.

Saff stayed there, contemplating what it would feel like. Revenge—for Ben. She was breathing hard, her Seeder eyes showing.

"GET. OFF!" Kaylah repeated as the man went limp. She swung a leg and kicked Saff off of him. "What part of *peaceful* didn't you understand!"

Saff scowled and stood, dusting herself off. "What part of 'my people will follow my orders' were you delusional about?!"

Kaylah glared at her. "They can't explain themselves if they're dead. And my people have a right to choose a better course, just as much as yours do. Don't do that again!"

"I don't take orders from an Ivy princess!"

"Saff, calm down!" Rachel interjected. "We're all fine."

Saff huffed. "So, what now?"

"They're not ... dead, right?" Rachel asked.

Ginger smirked, sparing a quick glance at the nearest soldier. "Kaylah and I have had a lot of practice refining our poison. Quick and effective, not lethal. They'll be out for a little while."

"And what are we going to do with live Ivies that aren't on your side?" Saff questioned.

"Well, we're not going to kill them!" Kaylah replied. "They'll come with us. We can get information from them, and I can try to bring them into the cause."

"Great. Are we going to *drag* them the rest of the way?" Saff asked.

"You know, sometimes, you have a special talent for being a pain in the ass, don't you?" Kaylah scowled.

Saff rubbed her forehead. Something as stupid as that insult brought fond memories of Ben. "If they stay alive for us to take them, they'll slow us down. If they stay alive and we leave them behind, that could compromise us. You understand this is war, right? Casualties are inevitable."

Kaylah glared. "Like your brother?"

Saff's eyes glowed. "You have *no* right!"

"I have *every* right! Every Seeder is a part of your family, and every Ivy is a part of mine. Misguided or not, they don't deserve to die without a fair chance!"

"Then you're weaker than I thought," Saff replied.

~

"You don't mean that!" Rachel chastised. "That's not our way."

Saff scratched her head. "Fine! Then what?"

"We'll tie them up, gag them," Kaylah said. "When they come to, we can get more information and find out why they attacked."

Saff scoffed. "I think it's fair to say your cover is blown."

"Any information is good," Kaylah said. "Once they're awake, we can make it to your borders in the dark, or find somewhere safe to camp for the night."

Rachel furrowed her brow. Why had they attacked their own princess? And if Kaylah's part in this was compromised, why hadn't they sharpened their leaf blades in the attack? Rachel decided it was worth voicing an additional concern.

"What if we come across more Ivies? Having two as prisoners won't go over so well."

Kaylah frowned. "Let's hope we don't have to cross that bridge."

Chapter 38

SAFF WATCHED IN AWE AS the Ivy women bound the men. Kaylah and Ginger wrapped vines around their wrists, arms, and legs, and gagged their mouths. Each time, they knotted the vines tightly in place before disconnecting.

"How does that work, exactly?" Rachel asked.

Kaylah checked her knots. "The vines? We usually only extend a couple of yards from each arm at a time. And it's not like we have an infinite amount. Like your powers, it can deplete us if we use a ton."

"And why couldn't you just tie them up without putting them to sleep?" Saff asked. "That would have saved us time."

"Because they're physically stronger," Kaylah drawled, obviously annoyed at Saff. "Our poison is an advantage we can offer. Our society dismisses our fighting abilities, overlooking that tool as a weapon."

Saff had understood that, in theory. But her frustration had prompted her to ask the question. They dragged the men under a weeping willow tree and gathered close.

"How long do you think for yours?" Kaylah asked Ginger.

Ginger winced. "I might have gone overboard in the excitement. A couple of hours?"

Kaylah nodded, frowning a little with disappointment. "It's okay." She smiled reassuringly. "Look at you getting some real action in. How about you do a close patrol?"

Saff couldn't bear to sit still and babysit for two whole hours; she volunteered to keep watch as well.

***

Saff and Ginger walked side by side, agreeing to patrol the area together. Saff wasn't about to let Ginger out of her sight. This whole excursion was a trust exercise, filled with unwelcome twists and turns.

"So, how do you know Rachel?" Ginger broke the ice.

"Mentor? Teacher?"

Ginger raised an eyebrow. "You can't be more than a couple of years older than her."

Saff gave a polite smile. "One of those mysterious Seeder things, I guess." She was just glad to have made it safely back home after her crazy decision to go. And just because Kaylah had shared information with them, didn't mean Saff had to divulge anything to Unitas. About her powers, about Seeders, about anything. She didn't owe them a thing.

But she was curious. "You and your husband raised Kaylah? How does that selection process work?"

Ginger raised both eyebrows this time in emphasized sarcasm. "One of those mysterious Ivy things, I guess."

Saff rolled her eyes. A silent patrol was good enough for her.

Ginger sighed. "My husband and I—the chosen human-world guardians of the heir to the throne." She shoved her hands in her pockets. "We never planned to have kids, honestly. Wasn't really a priority for us. My husband was making his way up the ranks of palace guards. A promising career." She grinned. "I admired him for his hard work. He secretly taught me a lot of moves he'd learned in training, at my request. Not that our women are *forbidden* from fighting. It's just … looked down on. No one willingly trains us. That whole 'weaker of the sexes' thing."

"I thought Ivies were matriarchal…"

Ginger glanced around. "Domestically, not as much as it used to be. Things changed after the kingdom was formed, after the Mother Vines and queen were established."

Saff considered the cultural difference. Seeder society was complicated. It was a mesh of religions and cultures brought over due to the influence of humans. And women were respected for their extra powers and place in society, but the men still did the majority of the fighting. In part, because healing could only be done by the women, so that task naturally fell to them. In part, because the men had been raised as soldiers to protect their lands and sisters. But Seeder women were never looked down on for volunteering to serve on border patrol.

"When rumors circled amongst the palace guards that an elite project was in the works, Nathan sought it out. His hard work and merit spoke for itself. His dark hair made him a believable candidate to be Kaylah's father. And, of course, we were around the right age to have a child her age." Ginger shrugged. "Bonus points went to us for being married—it was a built-in unit of two protectors who didn't have to pretend to be together."

Ginger ducked under a low-hanging branch, grinning again. "I finally got to train properly." Her face softened. "And I was surprised by how quickly Kaylah became family."

Turning to face Saff, Ginger abruptly stopped, causing Saff to halt in her tracks. Her eyes focused squarely on Saff's. "In every way that matters, she is my daughter. And she'll be my queen. If you or your people have plans to harm her, we have a problem."

Saff studied Ginger's face. She actually admired this woman. Ginger wasn't afraid to go after what she wanted, to be a soldier. And she took her charge seriously. It was intriguing to see such familial loyalty from an enemy hell-bent on destroying what mattered most to Saff, which was also family. But Saff's admiration only stretched so far. It wasn't like venomous snakes were virtuous because they didn't eat their young. Just because Ginger had developed a maternal instinct didn't mean she or Kaylah were saints. A mamma bear could still maul an innocent bystander.

Saff shook her head with a scoff. "You think *we're* the ones planning a trap? She came to *us* for help."

Ginger eyed Saff meaningfully. "Where's the 'us' you speak of? A dozen of your soldiers sent to kill her—that I expected. *One* young girl accompanying Rachel? Not much of an 'us.'"

Saff glared. "You'll have to excuse my people's hesitance. She's not exactly offering up an army of her own. She sounds more like a rebellious teen running away from mommy and daddy at the palace, than a legitimate leader capable of meeting the expectations she's setting."

Ginger shook her head. "You have to start somewhere. Every wildfire needs a spark."

Saff twisted her lips in thought. "I guess we'll soon see if she lights a beacon of hope with that spark, or if it's only a sign that she'll crash and burn."

***

Rachel and Kaylah sat next to their Ivy prisoners. The men were solidly out.

"Well, that was kinda cool, putting them out so fast like that," Rachel offered, still shaken.

Kaylah chuckled. "Yeah. Family nights for us in the human world consisted of meditation and practice poisoning each other until we learned how to get the right chemicals for different effects."

Rachel stared at her, wide-eyed. "Really?"

"Really."

Rachel shook her head. "Fair enough. My family nights, once I got my powers, involved getting beat up by my brother in training."

Kaylah beamed. "We have such healthy family relationships, don't we?"

They both laughed louder than they should have.

"I feel like there's still a lot I don't understand about your people, your anatomy," Rachel said.

Kaylah arched an eyebrow.

"I mean, like," Rachel blushed, "when our people mate, stuff happens, like an imprint kind of thing, and darts, and eyes, and stuff. What's it like for you guys?"

Kaylah grinned mischievously. "Are you trying to find out what it's like for Eric and me?"

"No!" She looked to the side, somewhat curious. "No. He's human, anyway. I just mean in general, if there's something specific that happens, Ivy to Ivy."

Kaylah waved her hand dismissively in the air. "Not really. You guys are the weird ones. With your whole imprint, root-for-life, have-a-bazillion-kids thing. I'm not aware of any exchange of powers or anything like that with us. Ivy births are different than human ones, but still not as different as your guys'."

Rachel considered Kaylah's assessment of her people. There were some crappy limitations, but some things were equally cool.

"But, uh… If you ever want to have a more detailed birds-and-the-bees talk about the interspecies thing, let me know." Kaylah winked. "And if things work out between you and Guillen, then…"

"For the love, please stop. There is practically no chance of things working out with him." Rachel wished more than anything that she could go there, to that place of hope of being with a great guy like him. But the chances were so slim they didn't even exist.

"Hey." Kaylah nudged her arm. "I'll stop teasing you. Maybe. I'll try. But you know I love you both. I'm just saying, it wouldn't be the worst thing in the world for you two to both be happy."

Rachel grinned, looking down and picking at her nails. "He is pretty great, isn't he?" She swallowed a lump in her throat, guilt washing over her that she had been the one he'd helped save, not the girl who was now dead. "Anyway." She glanced over her shoulder. "Just don't say anything around Saff. She wouldn't approve."

Kaylah rolled her eyes. "Mrs. Stiff over there clings too much to the old ways. She's going to need to change her way of thinking and join the program."

"Just give her some time."

Picking up a stick, Kaylah poked at the dirt by their feet. "I wish we all had that opportunity. To take our time to decide." She glanced at their captives.

Rachel cocked her head to the side. "It's complicated, right?"

Kaylah shrugged. "I guess you could argue that my people have had more than enough time to change things for the better."

"Better late than never?"

Kaylah gave a slight smirk. "That's one way of looking at it."

Rachel thought back to an earlier conversation at the safe house. "You really think your people would turn on you if you took the throne?" She looked over at the men. They'd attacked, knowing the princess's identity...

Pursing her lips, Kaylah drew lines in the dirt with her stick. "My family wasn't the original royal family of the Ivy Kingdom. My great-grandmother claimed the throne after having an entire line of heirs assassinated. Our people had grown tired of old policies. There had been a lot of internal fighting leading up to that."

Rachel fidgeted with her hands, not knowing how to react. Kaylah's people had such a dark past; how could they hope for the changes they dreamed of? "I think ... if anyone could do this, it's you. Look at what you've done already."

Kaylah gave her a forced smile. "Thanks." She paused. "So... Not completely teasing. But I need more dirt on Guillen. I need happy news amidst all of this crazy. When did you first get a thing for him?"

Rachel shifted on the forest floor, sifting through her memories. "I don't know. Maybe when he removed my stitches?"

Kaylah laughed. "That's the most romantic story ever."

"That's unnecessary sarcasm," Rachel defended with a frown. "He was being sweet. And I really got to look into his dreamy eyes, and…" She took a deep breath and sighed. A movement close to her caught her attention. Kaylah's guy was staring at them, looking no less than shocked.

"Well, hello, friend." Rachel smiled.

"I think it's time we find out what's going on." Kaylah pulled out a dagger and the man's eyes filled with terror. "Obey me, and you stay alive. Do you understand?" she asked.

He nodded fervently.

"You don't make any noise. And you only speak to answer my questions," she ordered, and reached over, carefully cutting loose the vines around his mouth.

"Your Highness, what—"

She gave him a stern look, brandishing the dagger.

He bowed his head, shutting up.

"Look at me. Why did you attack?"

He raised his head, his eyes moving from Kaylah to Rachel, and back to Kaylah.

Rachel flashed her glowing eyes. "Aww, I think he just realized we're friends."

Kaylah scolded Rachel with a glance. "Don't antagonize him." She addressed him again. "I asked you a question."

"Your Highness, you're … with *their* kind? *Willingly?*"

"I'm the one asking questions. Why did you attack?"

He scowled, still visibly confused at the group dynamics. "But they're weeds."

Rachel clenched her jaw.

"You'll refer to them as Seeders," Kaylah calmly corrected.

He swallowed hard. "Yes, Your Highness…"

Saff and Ginger returned.

"Thought we heard voices," Ginger said.

"Well, we're halfway there…" Saff added.

"Why did you attack?" Kaylah repeated herself.

The soldier studied the group again before wiggling to sit up straight. "I'm loyal to my kingdom and ready to die for it. Could you say the same?" He looked away, tight-lipped.

"Then the gag goes back on." Kaylah wrapped him back up, daring Saff with a glare to challenge her. The second soldier behaved in like manner after regaining consciousness.

Having been slowed down by their two captives, the mixed group of Unitas women camped out in the Neutral Woods for the night.

Kaylah tried to pump the men for information, but they wouldn't say a word. She tried to sway them to the cause, but they remained defiant and united with the kingdom for now. She told the group that she still held hope she could work with them individually, once in Seeder territory.

~

Throughout the night, the women took turns keeping watch—at least one Ivy and one Seeder up at all times. It was a rough night in the open with barely any sustenance—some still-green bananas and a few chestnuts. Everyone was ready to go at first light. Forcing the men to join them, they pushed forward.

"You're sure this is the strategy you want to take?" Saff asked. "I don't really know how it's going to be handled, showing up with four Ivies and only two of them tied up. Maybe we should have the two of you tied up, just to get through?"

Ginger straightened her posture. "We're not entering under those pretenses, or with that disadvantage."

Rachel voiced her opinion. "No, I agree. We may try to fudge things and get Kaylah and Ginger through with us as if they're Seeders, but starting off with them as prisoners is not the right way."

In the far distance, they could finally see the wall. Kaylah stopped the group to finalize their plans. She first turned to Saff. "I've been consistent in proving my intentions as a worthy ally. And you guaranteed us safe entrance into your lands. I need you to remember that."

"I'm doing my part," Saff replied, a little annoyed.

"So far, yes. But I need you to guarantee that these men won't lose their lives when we approach that wall."

"I don't know if I can do that. I can't speak for my people. To us, you and Ginger are a peaceful delegation." She pointed to the men. "They're just soldiers. Who knows how many Seeder lives they've taken!"

Kaylah frowned, looking at the men. One seemed more proud, defiant. The other, more scared at the talk and prospect of being dragged into enemy territory. "You two should be grateful for these Seeders, that they've spared your lives so far. I hope you'll come around."

Kaylah went back to addressing the women. "Whatever happens, I'm going in there and holding my head high. What we want is worth it, and I've sworn an oath to see this through. Ginger is here, risking her life. She's pledged herself to the cause. I need to know what you two really want out of this. Your people are going to ask you, and I need to know where you stand."

~

Saff and Rachel looked at each other. Rachel had already made her decision, but she hadn't voiced it out loud. She was wary to see Saff's reaction. "I stand with my people. And because I want what's best for them, I'm pledging myself to Unitas."

~

Hearing Rachel say it was like a punch to the gut for Saff, like Rachel was a traitor to their people. She knew it wasn't that simple. Unitas was about peace, but it wasn't a Seeder movement—not yet. It was headed by an Ivy, run by Ivies and humans. And things hadn't exactly gone smoothly thus far.

Saff frowned, avoiding eye contact while they all stared, waiting for an answer. The goals they talked about, the morals they preached—she agreed with them. But she kept telling herself she wasn't ready to drink the Kool-Aid just yet.

"I don't know what you want me to say. I betrayed my people's trust to parley. I promised you safe entrance. I'm an ambassador, not an initiated member of your cause."

Kaylah frowned. "I understand. But I hope that changes. Just ask yourself why you wouldn't want to join, why you wouldn't want to be numbered as one of us? We don't want to just end this war; we want to end *the* war. All of it. Why wouldn't you want that? Why would you want to go back to shadow wars and being hunted in the human world, just as long as the current surge of attacks calms down?"

Kaylah's eyes narrowed ever so slightly. "Is your hate so strong? Because if that's the case, you're not much better than our prisoners here. Ask yourself why you wouldn't want the same kind of relationship with Ivies that you have with humans. When you can answer those questions for yourself, that's when you can really give me an answer. And hopefully, you can convey that to your people. We need to convince your people of our goals just as much as we do mine." She locked eyes with Saff. "You seem like a person who will do the right thing."

Saff rolled her eyes. "Let's go."

As they moved closer to the Outer Wall, the women gained a better view of the damage being done by the War Vines. Each vine emerging from the woods was as thick as an arm. They converged, bundling and forming a mass that burrowed into the thicket.

The Seeder energy sustaining the wall's protective barrier was generally not something perceptible to the naked eye, but a bright light shone around the penetrating War Vines in the struggle to keep the wall from entirely failing.

Seeders usually caught a breeze over the wall, but today they would be aiming for one of the sporadic stone doors built into the base for transportation and passage of the wounded or dead.

Saff gazed at the wall, sick at the sight of her home under attack. Her energy surged within her. She'd already given so much of herself, sacrificed so much, to try and keep her people safe. Her heart ached as she imagined Ben standing nearby. He'd been stationed at a section of the Outer Wall just like this when he'd died.

~

Rachel glanced at the War Vines with a frown. This was just one of many places on the Seeder borders that had been fighting such an attack. An attack only made possible by kidnapped girls like herself, by subjecting them to unimaginable torture. She allowed a couple of tears to escape, her mind again turning to the girl who had died. She wouldn't even be afforded a proper Seeder burial in their lands.

The group stopped at the edge of the tree line, pausing to take in the awful sight, hesitant to walk into the clearing where they'd be discovered. Kaylah stood with bunched eyebrows, her eyes focused on the War Vines.

"Is everything okay?" Rachel asked.

Kaylah kept her attention on the War Vines. "Something's different."

"What do you mean?"

"Um… I… I'm not quite sure yet. Let's get going." Kaylah's tone was eerie, disconcerting.

"Wait," Saff said. "Do you hear that?"

Chapter 39

THEY ALL STOOD ON EDGE, listening. A persistent murmur filtered through the trees, slowly growing louder.

A horn sounded in the distance, and Saff's heart dropped. "Crap."

~

"What?" Rachel looked around, unable to tell which direction the growing murmurs were coming from. But the horn had come from the wall. Not the Outer Wall—it was too faint for that. It had to have come from the Inner Wall, the wall three times as tall, tall enough to get a great view of the Neutral Woods.

"An attack," Saff answered. "We need to get going."

They pushed their captives forward as a closer horn sounded—one from the Outer Wall. Every inch of the Outer Wall had a Seeder soldier at the top now, poised and ready to fly down and meet the enemy head-on. The door they needed to get the Ivies through was right next to the weakened thicket, where the War Vines were, where the Ivy soldiers would be aiming for.

The Unitas party picked up their speed.

"This would be faster without these soldiers…" Saff said, shoving one forward.

Kaylah grunted, looking over her shoulder.

"What if they attack us, thinking we're part of the fight?" Rachel's heart was racing. She glanced behind them. The rustling of trees was more distinct now.

A ways to their right, the first Ivies emerged from the trees. A dozen or more Seeder soldiers took off from the wall.

Saff urged her captive forward again, and he resisted. "That door can take *several* minutes to open. It has multiple locks in place and we still need to negotiate our way in. They're not prepared for incoming wounded if this is just getting started."

Kaylah joined in, pushing one of the soldiers forward.

More soldiers continued to march forward from the woods behind them, rapidly closing in. More Seeders launched from the wall to intercept.

"We need to be *running*," Saff stressed. "These two are dead weight, Kaylah!"

Kaylah's focus was squarely on the War Vines as she pressed forward. "I… I just… I don't get it."

"Don't get what?" Ginger glanced around them. Dozens, maybe even hundreds of Ivies were emerging from the woods. The sky buzzed with an equal deployment of Seeders to meet the enemy. "They're right. We need to go faster."

Rachel was panicking. She *wasn't* a soldier. "Kaylah. They're not worth it if they won't cooperate."

Kaylah stopped in her tracks, her gaze dancing between the War Vines and the approaching soldiers. Her fists were balled, her expression calculating.

"You said something was different. Why are you hesitating?" Rachel asked between quick breaths.

Kaylah whipped out her dagger, facing the soldier who had been the least cooperative. She sliced through the vines that covered his mouth, narrowing her eyes. "Is my mother dead?"

The man clamped his mouth shut, glancing at his fellow troops from the corner of his eye.

Kaylah plunged the dagger into his upper arm, twisting. He groaned.

"Is. She. Dead?"

"Yes," he mumbled between clenched teeth.

"Then your life belongs to me." She yanked out the dagger and moved it to his throat. "Who do you follow?"

He stared defiantly. "No queen of mine would align herself with weeds."

"Wrong answer." She slashed his throat and pushed him over.

Rachel gasped, going pale at all the blood.

~

Saff's stomach lurched.

The sounds of battle drowned out any remaining noises the soldier made as he bled out. Kaylah cut the vine from the second soldier's mouth.

"I follow you! My life is yours!"

She proceeded to slice off the other vines around his hands and arms, allowing better movement. "Come on!" Kaylah yelled.

Saff glanced behind them. Ivy soldiers were pressing in toward the wall, a few breaking free from fallen Seeders. Seeder soldiers kept coming over the wall.

Recent battle tactics at sections of weakened wall had required a lot more hand-to-hand combat than usual—this was likely to get ugly. She considered whether she ought to let the others move on, and help in the battle with her darts, but they were cutting it too close.

That door. She knew what she needed to do. "Keep running! I'll get the door open!"

Pushing energy to her legs, Saff strengthened her muscles. She bolted forward and kicked off the ground, shifting energy to her core and hands, balancing on the wind. The whistle of air in her ears helped drown out the surrounding chaos of death. Her flight announced she was an incoming friendly.

With all available concentration, she sensed the wind, tugging at it, aiming for her mark as quickly as possible. Swooping low, she launched the energy back to her legs. Dropping down, she landed with extra momentum and barely kept herself from face-planting. A half dozen guards stood by the door.

"I need it open!"

They stared at her, confused. No wounded were being dragged in. "Excuse me?" one asked.

Saff looked behind her. The other four were in a dead sprint. She and Rachel were the only ones who could fly over that wall. She pointed at them, turning back to the guard who'd spoken. "Those four will lead us to the Ivy princess. They need in."

"What?" The man's eyes grew large.

"Yes. Three of them are Ivy. They need to meet with the council. They need in. *Now!*"

The guards exchanged glances. "You're sure?"

"Absolutely. I'd stake my life on it."

He looked up, sending a signal to someone watching from high up on the wall. "This better not be a mistake."

Saff caught her breath. *I hope not.*

She paced, a ball of nervous energy and adrenaline. Her mind danced, deciding if she should join in the battle or maybe even find wounded to heal. But she needed to make sure their group got in. She needed to make sure they hadn't just risked everything for nothing. She needed to make sure Rachel made it back safely.

And she needed answers.

Her heart was still pounding as the group got closer. "They're opening it?"

"Yes. It takes a while. How do you know they can locate the princess?"

Saff swallowed hard. "I'll tell that to the council."

"What village are you from?"

"South Fortinda."

The guards stood firm at their station as more Seeders launched from the top to intercept approaching Ivies. Rachel was in the back of the approaching group, her eyes lit up to full glow.

The group finally reached the wall, panting heavily and clutching their sides. The guards stood defensively, facing the three Ivies.

Kaylah pulled out her dagger, pointing it at the male Ivy. "I have more questions for you."

"Whoa! No way we're letting any of you in with a weapon," a guard protested.

Kaylah chucked the dagger into the battlefield, then pointed at the Ivy again, her hand still covered in blood. "Why did you attack and clam up in the first place?!"

"He was my superior! I had to follow orders."

"The hell he was your superior." She pointed to the soldiers in battle. "I outrank them all put together. *Especially* now."

The man searched Kaylah's face, panicked. "We had orders! We thought you were here against your will. And then when we saw you were working *with* them…"

The large stone door opened behind them.

"Get inside!" a guard ordered. "We need to close this back up."

The Unitas members entered with one of the female guards, and the door closed with a thud behind them. The guard bolted it shut and pushed them forward. Lined with giant stones, the corridor was only lit by quartz-and-jade lightkeepers hung on the walls. After a couple more doors, they emerged on the other side.

While grateful to be alive and safe, it killed Saff that her own people were dying just on the other side of this wall. "How did you know she was dead?"

Kaylah frowned. "As we approached, I just knew."

Saff ground her teeth. "How? That means you're in charge, right? You can stop this!"

The guard explained to other posted soldiers that they'd need extra guards and to fetch members of the council. Letting in Ivies was *definitely* not standard procedure.

Kaylah shook her head at Saff. "I can't explain it. I could sense the change in the Vine's allegiance. That would only happen if…"

"Then that means you're the queen now?" Rachel asked. "You can stop this Vine?" Her eyes shot to the War Vine that had punched through the Outer Wall and was snaking its way to the Inner Wall.

"What?!" the guard said. "You told us they knew how to *find* the princess. This is her?"

Saff pursed her lips. She'd kinda hoped to keep that one under wraps until they met with the council.

~

"Yes," Kaylah said. She glanced at Rachel. "I don't actually get the title until my coronation. And I can't stop the Vines from here. They have to be retrained at the roots, at the *palace*."

Saff gestured at the wall. "Then stop your troops. They should still recognize your authority. A lot of soldiers out there are going to die. Your family and my family, right?"

Kaylah nervously bit her lip, then turned back to the male Ivy. "You had orders, explain."

He surveyed the group, shrinking from all the eyes on him. "We were told you were kidnapped by the Seeders."

Kaylah's eyes narrowed. "Did my father issue your orders?"

He squinted, shaking his head in obvious confusion. "No. He's dead, too."

Kaylah's shoulders fell. "When and how did they die?"

He glared at all the Seeders around them. "Ask your friends. It happened when they attacked the palace."

"That's a lie!" the guard shouted.

In no time flat, it turned into a screaming match full of pointed fingers.

"Wait!" Kaylah yelled over them. "If they're both dead, who lied about me being kidnapped and issued the orders?"

"His Highness, Prince Soren."

Rachel's chest tightened.

Kaylah covered her face with her hands.

~

Saff was still a bit sketchy on what it all meant. "So … what now?"

Kaylah sighed. "My brother knows good and well that I wasn't kidnapped. And I never imagined the prick had it in him to do it, but he killed my parents and is pinning it on your people to fan the flames. It's another way to pit my people against yours, if they think you're the aggressor, instead of outing me as a traitor."

Saff was beyond tired of Ivy games and drama. "Then maybe you should set the record straight with the soldiers out there killing each other and go home to claim your throne."

Kaylah rolled her eyes. "Have you ever witnessed an Ivy retreat, Saff? Or even a solo scout doing their job? It takes a *single* soldier and a *single* tree out there for one to slip out, rift to a human-world outpost, and send for reinforcements. The moment they realize I'm in your custody—you're not going to see hundreds out there, you're going to see *thousands*. All dutifully here to 'rescue' me from my captors and not stopping to listen to someone they assume is under duress." She arched her eyebrows. "And if Soren had it in him to kill my parents and issue bogus orders, you'd better believe he's prepared a warm homecoming that includes me being a puppet for him."

Saff huffed, turning to the guard. "How long until we can see the council?"

The guard shrugged.

"Fine. I guess we'll wait to see what they say."

"How about we all calm down and take a seat," the guard said. Shortly after, other guards brought restraining straps for the Ivy wrists to bind their hands and vines.

Kaylah held up her wrists without hesitation. "I've come here to prove myself and propose a peaceful solution. We have no problems complying."

After they were tied up, all sitting on the ground, Ginger leaned against Kaylah. "We'll be okay. It'll be alright."

Kaylah stared straight forward, nodding.

~

After a few minutes of silence, Rachel glanced at Kaylah with a frown—she looked to be in shock. "I'm sorry about your parents," Rachel offered in a whisper. "I guess negotiations are out the window…"

"It probably had to happen, anyway," she whispered back. "I doubt she would have willingly given up control of the Vines or accepted half of my plans. We've lived with different moral compasses for a long time now."

"But it's still not all bad news, right?" Rachel said. "Sounds like Soren was pretty stupid killing your mom. Doesn't he need a queen to control the War Vines? If he's lost some of his control on the attack…"

"Does that mean you're asking for asylum?" Saff tacked on.

Kaylah shook her head, visibly frustrated. "It means we have work to do. He might have shot himself in the foot, in a way. But he's not a complete idiot. With three girls gone, those War Vines are still primed for new kidnapped Seeders, even without my cooperation. And he trained under Duke Nuren for years." She lowered her voice, her expression somber. "I didn't see this coming. Maybe I should have. But he was the golden child, not me. He was the favorite; my parents were actually proud of him. And now… I'm not really sure what he's capable of. I… I don't know that we're talking about my kingdom's goal being colonization and slavery, anymore. Soren would make offhand comments now and then… I don't think he'd stop there. It would be easier to wipe your people out altogether so you'd never be a threat again."

Rachel was sick to her stomach. The thought of ever having cared for him was revolting, painful. "I know he's a bit … unhinged and cruel, but you really think he'd go that far?"

Kaylah frowned. "You know firsthand how manipulative he can be. And he has no qualms with taking what he wants and hurting people."

Rachel looked down, visions of her torture back at the palace running through her mind.

"Rach, he's done worse. I'm not trying to minimize what you went through, but honestly—I think part of him genuinely liked you. I'm just saying, we shouldn't underestimate him."

~

Saff tilted her head to the side. "Guess you should have taken him out, too, when you were rescuing Rachel."

Kaylah glared. "I told you—that was a precision extraction. And he wasn't even at the palace that day."

"So, the plan remains the same?" Saff said. "Negotiate with him, and if it doesn't work, take our armies and claim your throne?"

Kaylah shook her head. "My parents might have been capable of some type of negotiations. Not him. He doesn't feel any sense of obligation to me. Or apparently any of our family or traditions…" Kaylah sighed. "And yes, I still need your armies."

Saff sat up straighter, trying to sort out Kaylah's logic. "He trained under your uncle, just like you. You need our armies while our armies are already fighting … and losing. Remind me why we just risked everything to bring you here."

Kaylah's jaw clenched. "We might be tit for tat on strategy, though I still think I got the better education. And I told you—my research on our powers has a lot of potential to boost things for your people. We both studied under our uncle, but he was the one chumming around with the assassins. I was the one involved in the research. Our playbooks are bound to be different. It means we need to figure out his game. And we will. It also means your people still need me. We need each other. We need Unitas."

Chapter 40

AFTER AN ETERNITY OF WAITING, a handful of Seeder soldiers arrived to escort the group to the Inner Wall. The full Unitas party stood up.

"How many council members were gathered?" the Outer Wall guard asked.

"Two."

She shook her head. "We'll need a full council now—this one is the princess." She pointed to Kaylah.

The new guard's eyes widened. "Okay."

Saff was desperate to contact her family. "Can a messenger be sent to South Fortinda to let them know we're okay? Our families … didn't know we were doing this." She and Rachel shared a guilty glance.

The head guard eyed them with disapproval. "Sure… Who do we contact?"

"I'm Saffrona Murialsdotter; my father is Thod. This is Rachel Lyzasdotter; her father, Garrett, is still human-world deployed. We're both near the long lane of the western glen."

"Okay. We'll send someone once we're past the Inner Wall."

Saff blew out a breath of relief. Her stomach was still in knots, not knowing if her family members were all safe, but at least they could stop worrying about her.

Once guided past the Inner Wall, they gained a much more significant escort, additional council members were summoned, and a messenger was sent to Saff and Rachel's homes.

After more waiting, the Ivies were placed under heavy guard as Saff and Rachel went into the council alone to present their pleas. They talked about why they went to the human world without council permission, what they'd witnessed, and what was being proposed. They weren't exactly being offered a parade for a hero's return.

But the intel Kaylah had provided about Ivy assassins was being acted upon immediately. They took a short recess to discuss a course of action. Saff and Rachel were invited outside, where they were greeted by family.

Saff fought tears at the sight of Thod, her Seeder father. Thod had to be a mix of emotions—glad his daughter was back safe, angry she'd defied the council, and still mourning the loss of a son.

~

Rachel's anxiety grew at seeing her Seeder mom, Lyza. Lyza frowned, shaking her head.

Rachel gave Lyza a shy hug, and Saff took a strong squeeze from Thod.

~

"Please tell me everyone's okay," Saff pleaded. She needed to know she hadn't lost anyone else she loved during her absence, especially Devin.

Thod's intimidating features and deep voice conveyed no fondness. "Everyone's fine, Saffrona. Physically."

That hurt. She knew she'd have a lot to make up for. But she could breathe, knowing she wasn't looking at another burial in the immediate future.

"How did you even do it?" Thod asked.

Saff fidgeted with her hands. "I, uh… I'm not completely sure."

"*Why* did you do it?" he asked.

She swallowed hard. "That's a longer answer."

He glanced around. "Let's take a walk."

Saff followed after him. "I'm sorry I left the way I did."

Thod didn't respond.

Saff tried again to justify abandoning her family and betraying their leaders' orders. "This wasn't just an impulsive mistake. I've seen what Kaylah can do, and this can legitimately help us."

The lack of response stung.

But Thod finally spoke up. "Not impulsive? Not childish? It was important for you to leave that exact day? Right before your brother's burial? One day would have made a difference?"

She stared at her feet in shame. Of course it had been impulsive. The lectures she'd given Rachel were now falling on her own head.

Saff gathered the courage to defend the decision that she still wasn't sold on herself, remembering Rachel's words back at the safe house. "If this war ends one day earlier, that means one less day of lives lost."

Thod shook his head with a sigh. "We're all relieved to hear you're back home safe. That includes Devin."

She was viciously homesick at hearing his name. What she wouldn't do to be home in Devin's arms at that moment.

~

Rachel and Lyza followed Saff and Thod's example, taking a short stroll in the vicinity.

"How are you doing?" Lyza asked.

"I'm fine." Rachel didn't know what else to say. She'd already struggled to get close to her new Seeder family. Only a couple of her sisters had ever attended school with her. And she'd distanced herself from everyone because of her shame about the kidnapping.

What message was this sending to them now? She hadn't chosen this world, this family. It had been forced on her. And the first chance she got, she ran away from home. That wasn't why she'd done it, but she couldn't help but wonder if that was what they were all thinking.

"Well, we're glad you're safe," Lyza responded.

"And the rest of the family's okay?"

Lyza nodded.

"Good." Rachel wasn't sure if she should mention anything, but she figured she might as well throw it in there. "My mom… Um, I mean, Samantha… She's safe. I think she'll be okay."

Lyza bit her lip, nodding again. "Good."

They continued to walk in silence. There was hurt in Lyza's eyes whenever Rachel would slip and name Samantha as her default mom. Lyza had given Rachel life, had waited for her to come home safely, and was hurt that she'd allowed her childhood friend and 'cousin' to raise her daughter, only to have Samantha misplace that trust and hurt their whole family, their entire nation. Not that Lyza spoke so openly about it, but she wasn't that great at hiding her feelings, and Rachel could read between the lines of their conversations.

It hurt. Rachel loved Samantha. Samantha had made mistakes, so Rachel couldn't fault Lyza. But she loved them both, in different ways. And now she was a point of contention between the two; two women who used to be best friends and could now never really reconcile, being trapped in their own worlds. In a way, it reminded Rachel of being caught between Kaylah and Saff at the safe house. It made her sick.

***

Rachel was grateful when they eventually recalled the girls and brought Kaylah in to the council meeting. Ginger and the soldier remained in custody elsewhere. Kaylah reiterated her strategies, her plans to help. The council didn't jump at the ideas she shared, but they seemed open enough to hear her out. Their main objection to accepting her invitation to negotiate had been about it being a trap. But since the damage had been done and she'd walked willingly into their custody, they knew they'd be fools to not hear her out now.

After talking into the wee hours of the morning, they were to adjourn for sleep, and then deliberate the next day.

Before the regional war council leader called the meeting to a close, he turned again to Rachel and Saff. "Neither of you had position or permission to act in any official capacity," he censured. "Consequences will be discussed. For now, you're free to return to your village, with supervision. The princess will remain here in detention until such time as we deliberate her proposals, and decide what her fate will be, and that of the other Ivies in our custody."

"Your Honor." Rachel spoke up. "We went into this knowing we held no position or permission to do what we did. And we apologize for the offense that may have given our people." She wrung her hands nervously. "But it doesn't require position or permission for someone, anyone, to do the right thing. And that's what we're doing. And I'm here to see it through. I'll be staying with the princess, even if that means I have to be detained as a prisoner."

She glanced at Kaylah, thinking of her promise to Eric back in the human world, to keep Kaylah safe, and fearing what may happen to her friend if she was left alone, should the Seeders decide to go another route other than accepting the Unitas movement.

Kaylah's tired eyes showed a glimmer of gratitude at the gesture.

"You have no right to demand entrance to our meetings, or frankly, to demand *anything*. But if you would like to stay in this village under close guard, we'll allow it for now," he replied. "We may have further questions for you."

~

The attention of the group focused on Saff, as if to see if she would request the same. She hadn't taken the same oath as Rachel. She wanted nothing more than to be back home with her family, healing, helping, visiting the graveyard Ben now rested in. The council had it under control now, right? She'd done her job. She'd taken Rachel to meet up with Kaylah. She'd gotten them safely through the Outer Wall.

But, thinking of Thod—her dad, who she loved and admired—Saff's mind replayed his accusations of her actions being childish, impulsive. She considered Kaylah's speech as they had approached the Seeder borders, asking Saff if her hatred mattered more than ultimate peace. Kaylah *had* also proven herself when it mattered most, out on that battlefield. Saff's human mom's reminder to consider all of the options sounded in her ears. Last of all, she had to ask herself what Ben would have wanted her to do.

Putting aside her yearning to immediately return home, Saff sighed. "I request to stay as well."

Chapter 41

WHILE THEY WERE GRANTED THE opportunity to stay, Rachel and Saff were kept separate from Kaylah and the others, despite Rachel's wishes. They were given a room to share for the night. It was basic, but comfortable. Near the border walls, it used to be family housing, but was now used as barracks. A guard was stationed at their door.

Rachel woke from a nightmare, sweating and disoriented. Saff sat on her own bed, chin on her knees.

"You have a lot of nightmares, don't you?"

Rachel sat up, pulling her covers up. "Yeah. Most nights. Sometimes more than once a night." This one had been about Soren and his sadistic perversion. "Have I been waking you up?"

Saff shrugged. "Not a big deal."

Rachel frowned. "Sorry."

"You have nothing to be sorry about. I sometimes get them, too. But I know I haven't been through as much as you. I'm sorry you've had to go through all that."

"Thanks," Rachel whispered, rubbing her face as if she could rub away the haunting visions still dancing in her head. "It's like, even when you try to talk it through with someone, and things start to make sense, you start to feel better … and then you have a bad day. And it all floods back in. And you question everything. And start all over again. And then the nightmares come, and it's hard to function the whole day when you start off that way."

Saff frowned. "There's no timeline for healing, you know. You just work at it one day at a time." She fiddled with the lace trim of the nightgown she'd been lent. "Some days you dissect it, to rework things for better understanding. Some days, you do your best to bury the feelings, just to get through, or just to allow yourself uninterrupted joy. I don't know if that's wrong, but I think it's okay."

Rachel stared at Saff. It was nice, the friendship they were beginning to build. Shared trauma and risk could do that. It wasn't just her family that Rachel had struggled to connect with since coming 'home.' Rachel hadn't made *any* real friends. No one could relate to the sheer horror she'd been through. Saff obviously still struggled to understand Rachel's mindset, but her mentorship and friendship helped Rachel feel a little less like an island.

Looking down, Rachel tried to shake another recent nightmare from her mind that had just popped up. The vision that haunted her most was that of Duke Nuren—Rob, her stepfather. His lifeless body after revealing himself as the author of this surge in the war. Prince Soren's betrayal was on a different level, and while he was more perverted and unhinged, and the current threat, Nuren had held a different role in her life. Seeing him dispatched so suddenly as she was rescued had given her no time to properly reconcile those feelings. Yes, she was glad he was dead. But she also wanted him to not be the person that he was, in that one hour, compared to the father figure she had known for an entire decade.

"Thanks for staying," Rachel said, forcing herself to focus on the here and now.

"Yeah, well… I think it was the right thing to do. But I hope we don't have to stay long."

"What do you want to do, if they actually let us choose? Whether or not they accept Kaylah's proposals?"

~

Saff considered it for a moment, smoothing out the comforter around her. "Honestly, I just want to go home. And have family nights, and take care of my garden, and go on walks with my husband, and take a *really* long nap." She scrunched her face. "But nothing is going to be that simple."

"It can be, if we work for it."

Shaking her head, Saff let out a long sigh. "You really think this could work, don't you?"

"I do. I think Kaylah has it in her."

Saff reflected on Kaylah's actions since she'd met her. Kaylah was the first Ivy Saff had met that gave her pause, that made her consider things differently. And when it had mattered most, Kaylah had made the hard call out there by taking the life of her own soldier. Saff had to set aside her pain from Ben's death at Ivy hands, and her own trauma from being personally attacked by the Ivy assassin network. She had to focus on the big picture.

"If they don't accept Unitas, I imagine I'll go home and go back to fighting, healing, and training, until we can stop this. And the fact that she's here, that they can't activate any more War Vines to torture our girls and use their energy—that gives me a sliver of hope. And any of my free time will be used trying to repair things with Devin and my family.

"And if we *do* accept Unitas… I don't know. I still want to go home, but I'm open to other tasks that I'm asked to do. I'm willing to do my part." She shifted on her bed, fighting a frown. "I just hope Devin can support me in whatever choices are made."

~

"You guys are a really cute couple," Rachel offered. Saff smiled in return. "Do you think you guys will decide to have a clutch?" Perhaps that was too personal of a question. "Sorry, you don't have to answer that."

"No, it's okay. Kids… Yeah… That's kind of a huge decision for us Seeders, isn't it?"

"Just a tiny one." Rachel chuckled.

"I don't know about you, but I didn't grow up dreaming of having twenty-four kids at once… Granted, not having a traditional human pregnancy *does* sound appealing if you go the Seeder route. But yeah, we've talked about it. It'll be a few years before we're able to make that choice." Saff twisted her wedding ring. "If things turn out the way Kaylah wants—in a heartbeat. Most of my sisters already know they don't want a clutch of their own, but they'd make great aunts. Growing up as an only child, I always pictured myself having a large family.

"If things go back to normal—that's a lot harder. It's hard to imagine going through what Murial did. But I'd consider it. If this war keeps up like this… I just don't even want to think about it."

Rachel sat up straighter, leaning against the wall. "Yeah. Well, I think we should keep our goal in mind. Plan on a new normal."

Saff pointed at her, smiling. "I don't know about you. You're more of a dreamer than I am. But maybe that's not all bad." She winked. "What about you? Positions and kids?"

"Kids…" Rachel blew out a puff of air. "Well, that one is really up in the air, isn't it? I don't have any romantic interests, no mate to talk with about it." Her mind wandered to Guillen. If somehow, in some way, in some world, they actually worked out—they wouldn't be able to have kids. Seeders, Ivies, and humans didn't have a biocompatibility. "I guess back when I was human, I imagined maybe I'd have one or two. Even if I loved someone like you love Devin, I don't think I could commit to the Seeder way of family life, not in that way. It's just not for me.

"And positions… I don't know. I don't have those family ties dragging me back to our village. I want to make sure Kaylah's okay, and that we have success. And I want to travel, and learn more about our histories and cultures."

Saff slid back down in bed, lying on her side to view Rachel. "I think that—despite our differences, and no matter what others decide—neither of us are the type to just sit here and do nothing."

Rachel smiled.

***

They didn't have a wake-up call the next morning. When Saff opened the door to check for an update, the guard told her they would have to stay put until they were summoned.

"We should at least be allowed to help. Do some healing or go to the temple," Saff insisted.

He said they'd discuss it at the change of guard, and a few hours later, they were greeted with an escort. They allowed them to make an energy deposit at the local temple well, then returned them to their room. To their relief, the guard reported that the skirmish outside had subsided, and upon further questioning, he shared his opinion that the way it had been done appeared to be in line with normal Ivy tactics. It sounded as though the troops hadn't known about or noticed Kaylah's presence there.

Hours passed before they were finally summoned back to a council meeting. Kaylah again joined them.

"Saff. Rachel. You will both be returning home." The council leader held up his hand before they could protest. "We'll consider your willingness to help with Unitas, and your unique skills, as we move forward with consideration of the princess's recommendations."

~

That gave Rachel hope. This sounded good… But she hadn't just gone through this nightmare to be cut out of things, and to leave Kaylah hanging. "I want to stay."

He raised an eyebrow. "I understand. And I just made it clear that you will be going."

Anger grew inside her, her heart racing, as she tried to figure out where to go from here. "No one believed me. No one trusted me.

Not in my village, not in *any* of the council meetings I've been summoned to. But she's here, because of me. And I'm going to see this through."

Gingerly resting his hands on the table, the council leader sat back in his chair. "You're right. Princess Kaylah is here because of you. After you *lied* about not knowing how to find her. You'll have to forgive us for our hesitation." He glanced at Kaylah. "Trust isn't something easily won, and strong-arming doesn't change this council's decisions, either."

Rachel was fuming. They were all treating her like she was incompetent, like she was brainwashed. But she saw it clearer than anyone. "I don't care what you say. I'm—"

"Rachel," Kaylah interrupted, making eye contact with her. "Go home."

Exchanging a glance with Kaylah, Rachel decided to stay quiet.

"You can choose to go home and be with those you love, contributing to society; or you can stay here, in detainment, being kept from your family, friends, all knowledge of what happens in these deliberations, and any useful contribution to the war effort. Which will it be?" the council leader asked.

Rachel clenched her jaw, shooting another look at Kaylah.

"Go," Kaylah mouthed.

Clamping her mouth shut until she could control her anger enough to not tell them off further, Rachel finally spoke up. "I'll go."

"Wise choice." He continued, "For now, your parents will escort you back and your village leaders will assign you duties."

~

"Yes, sir," Saff said. She was thrilled to go home, and also to hear they were giving Kaylah a chance. There were a lot of details she wasn't privy to, but it looked promising.

~

Rachel stayed silent as they were dismissed. Before Saff and Rachel left, they were each given a supervised opportunity to talk with Kaylah.

Rachel frowned. "So, what's next? That's bullshit in there, what they're doing to me. You know that."

Kaylah sighed, putting her hands on Rachel's arms. "You're not doing yourself any favors by fighting back right now. They don't need your approval. And right now, they just see you and I together and imagine I'm controlling you. I don't blame them."

Rachel rolled her eyes. "I'd still rather be helping in *some* way with you."

"One step at a time." Kaylah gave her a gentle smile. "They'll listen and observe as I try to show how my plans can work. I think we'll be okay. This new development just means a different timeframe and order than I'd planned, but we can do it.

"Make amends with your family. Serve with your whole heart. Once they trust me, they'll trust you. And the *moment* they'll let me put you into action, you'll be ready and we'll really get things rolling."

Rachel frowned again, deflated.

"You're so cute with your little temperamental green eyes." Kaylah grinned, pinching Rachel's cheek. "Lit up like an adorable lightning bug."

Rachel crossed her arms. "A bug?"

"Now that I think about it, those bugs glow from their butts, right? And probably not because of emotions. So, never mind." Kaylah flashed pouty lips. "Not a glow-butt bug. Just my favorite Seeder."

Rachel shook her head, chuckling. She loved how Kaylah knew how to build her up and calm her down. "You're sure you can handle this? Please tell me you're not going to head back in there and call the council 'glow-butt bugs.'"

Kaylah wore a toothy grin. "Dang it! That was going to be my first order of business." She winked. "C'mon. I've got this. I know you haven't seen this side of me, but I was tutored in diplomacy. I'll be okay." She bit her lip. "Granted, my people aren't so great at diplomacy… We're kinda more 'you have—me want—me take.'" She rubbed her hands together. "But I feel like I can read a room.

Call me crazy, but I think the next appropriate step in negotiations is … interpretive dance?"

Rachel choked back a laugh, not wanting to give Kaylah the satisfaction of another one. "We're so screwed."

Kaylah gave her a kind smile. "Keep your chin up. We've got this. The millisecond I can manage it, you'll be by my side again." She looked away for a moment, as if calculating her next sentence. "One thing you *can* do, while you're back there, is some research for me. I don't know where your people keep all your old texts, but anything on the history of your village would be helpful."

"Okay, I'll ask. But ours isn't one of the oldest villages," Rachel confessed. She wasn't well-educated on their culture yet, but she still knew some tidbits.

"At the very least, I need you to find out whatever you can about how your village was named."

Rachel furrowed her brow. "South Fortinda? What does the naming have to do with anything?"

Kaylah pursed her lips. "Trust me. It means something. It's important. I have a feeling the name behind *each* of your villages will be an important piece of the puzzle."

They gave each other one last hug before Saff had a word with Kaylah.

~

"Don't disappoint me," Saff warned.

"I have no intention of that. Thank you for holding up your end of the bargain," Kaylah said with a handshake.

Saff and Rachel walked toward their parents, leaving Kaylah and the council behind.

"You were conveniently silent in there," Rachel chastised.

"You threw enough of a fit for the both of us," Saff mumbled.

"Really? What was the point of all of this?" Rachel scowled. "Right, you didn't *officially* commit to Unitas. Wouldn't want to actually have conviction."

Saff stopped abruptly, a few yards before meeting their parents. "Don't you dare!" Her eyes filled with tears as her fists clenched. "I just risked my life to take you. To bring her here. I walked out on my husband. I missed my brother's burial. Don't you *dare* judge me for wanting to be back home with the people I love!" Tears trickled down her cheeks, her ears warm with anger. "And I want to help, too. If the council approves of her plans and they ask for my help— I'll be there. I want to do my part. But right now, *my* part is back home."

Rachel swallowed hard. "Sorry. Let's go home. Do you want a hug?"

Saff wiped up her tears. "No. I just want to go."

They met Thod and Lyza, who weren't blind to their confrontation and Saff's distress, but tastefully skirted around it while discussing their plans to return to their home village. Seeders could fly with relative ease in the Green Lands, but they didn't do it all the time, considering the necessity and conservation of energy. This time, they'd fly home, crossing the distance to their village to get back significantly faster.

With a short sprint, Thod and Saff lifted into the air. Saff didn't know how to feel. Beyond relieved her family was okay. Beyond terrified about how her husband and family would react to her betrayal. Beyond worried that the war pressed on, despite the risks she'd just taken. She grasped at a ray of hope—the council was working with Kaylah, or at least considering it.

~

Rachel took off, still wobbly from a lack of practice. Lyza followed after her, catching up and gliding by her side. Out of the corner of her eye, Rachel could see over the border walls—where the skirmish they'd narrowly escaped had taken place. The land below her was beautiful, the lanes crowded. She knew she should appreciate all of that. But going 'home' to be with 'family' felt like a punishment, rather than a victory. She wanted to be helping Kaylah. She wanted to keep Kaylah safe. Every day, every hour, that she waited to hear word from her, would be one filled with worry. Giving Rachel a little hope and forcing a small smile on her face was one of the last things Kaylah had mentioned—that their timeframe and the order of things were going to have to shift. She'd also hinted that Rachel might see Guillen sooner than originally planned.

***

Kaylah was permitted to watch as they took off. She crossed her arms as Saff lifted into the sky. While Saff was a bundle of energy and sass, Kaylah was grateful she'd made this possible. Observing Rachel catch a breeze brought a smile to Kaylah's face; this was the first time she'd gotten to witness her friend flying.

Kaylah sighed, feeling the weight of the realm on her shoulders. Eric was back in the human world. Her parents were … dead. Her brother had cut her off from her own kingdom, forcing her to redraft her approach on the fly. And she had to win the Seeders over. She had to fix things for them and her people. She had to claim her throne.

"Alright, please follow me, ma'am," a guard said as the four Seeder bodies shrank in the distant sky.

Kaylah's eyes lingered longer for one last look as she took a cleansing breath. "Right. Let's get to work."

Order Book 3 Now!

Leading Princess Kaylah to Seeder borders was only Rachel and Saff's first step in stopping a never-ending war. The Ivy queen and king's assassination leaves Prince Soren in sole control of their troops and resources.

Banding together, the Unitas group sets out to discover forgotten secrets to their pasts and powers. They work to discover how to cure the poisoned Seeder lands, as well as how to best infiltrate the Ivy palace, all while recruiting and training in secret.

Going undercover behind enemy lines, Rachel's forced to face the trauma and betrayals in her past. Saff has to face the family she abandoned, come to terms with news about her unique power-wielding capacity and future, and learn to trust allies of the nation that has already taken too much from her family and people.

Tensions rise at the Unitas camp and safe houses, threatening their unity movement. Amidst kidnappings and mysterious disappearances, Unitas is forced to dig deep and take unexpected measures to bring the battle to Soren with hopes of a win.

*For bonus scenes between books 2 & 3, grab a copy of Seeder Stories!

More by J. Houser

THE SEEDER WARS TRILOGY

THE HEIR'S DUOLOGY

Also available in the

Seeder Wars world!

Magic in the Match is a series of standalone Adult Fairy Tale Sweet Romances.

Magic in the Match

Fairy Tale Romances

A selection of premium book journals. They each accommodate entries for 250 books and have individual aesthetic touches.

For more information, go to JHouserWrites.com!

Don't forget to leave a review!

On Amazon, Goodreads, StoryGraph and/or anywhere else this book can be found.

This goes a long way to support authors!

Don't forget to sign up for J. Houser's newsletter for publishing news, promotions, and bonus content!

JHouserWrites.com

Also, connect with the author here:

On YouTube, TikTok, Facebook, Instagram, and Twitter under:

JHouserWrites